BECOMING JESSE

Celebrating the Everyday Magic of Childhood

Patsie McCandless

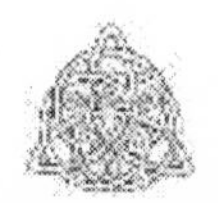

Light On Publications

Printed in the United States of America by Light On Publications
August 2018

Composition and Editing by Polished Print - Stacey Kucharik.
Cover formatting by WorkingType.com.au - Luke Harris.
Cover and interior images by Patricia S McCandless.

Library of Congress Control Number: 2018954212
Publisher's Cataloging-in-Publication data

Names: McCandless, Patricia S., author.
Title: Becoming Jesse : celebrating the every day magic of childhood / Patsie McCandless.
Description: Philadelphia, PA : Light On Publications, 2018.
Identifiers: ISBN 9781732506602 (pbk.) | 9781732506619 (ebook) | LCCN 2018954212
Subjects: LCSH Grandmothers--Fiction. | New York (N.Y.)--History--1951- --Fiction. | Neighborhoods--Fiction. | Grandparent and child--Fiction. | FICTION / General | FICTION / Visionary & Metaphysical | FICTION / Magical Realism | FICTION / Family Life / General | FICTION / Friendship
Classification: LCC PS3613.C26545 B43 2018 | DCC 813.6--dc23

Becoming Jesse is dedicated to my love-adores,
especially, my husband Tom.

ACKNOWLEDGEMENTS

My husband, Tom, for his love and his patience and belief in me and my stories.

The inspirations of all our Baby Grands: our grandchildren – the music of our lives.
Our children: Scott who offered his Light thoughts; and Kate, who listened and counseled through all Jesse's iterations, and read it aloud to her boys, making me believe all over again.

All those I taught - in sailing class and school - who, as it turns out, were some of my best teachers.

My generous readers, who took the deep dive into my original manuscript, swam through to the end, and came up bubbling their encouragement and critiques: Gay Wasik-Zegel, Mary Cullen, Dot Sved, Krista Whipple, Ria Revenaugh, Sue Maden, Sue Nicholson.

Those who read my First Pages and offered appraisals and support: Bill Garth, Ludmilla Bochillo, Kate Farrell, Silvia Joseph, Paulette & Jim Smith, Sue Pfiel, Giovanna Arrellano, Aidée Mercado and her family (Teresa, Pamela, Heidi; and her Grands, Anthony, Arianna, Leanna, Gianina, and Hugo) and Jake Schomp.

My editor, Stacey Kucharik of Polished Print.com, who helped me articulate my vision and turn my manuscript into a novel with her superb, thorough, insightful and delightful professionalism.

Luke Harris of WorkingType.com.au, who patiently and beautifully put all the cover details in place.

Steve and Bill Harrison, of Quantum Leap (Bradley Communications Corporation), leading me to 'move onward and upward', helping me to realize my dream-book with the help of their coaches, especially Martha Bullen and Geoffrey Berwind.

TABLE OF CONTENTS

Prologue ~ Light On!

The stars are glitterering. Aye.

You. Your wishes. Making them all glitter.

You. Shining back at the stars. Wishing.

Oh, the world cannot do without the glittering stars. Just as the world cannot do without you. Together you are the brightest, the shiniest of everything in the Universe.

Back when I walked the earth, I was called Old Barret, storyteller to the *Lucht Siúl* (Loook See-ul), the 'walking people' of Ireland, the Irish gypsy Travellers. And aren't we all travelers, in this world and beyond?

My walking days are over, but I can still run out the yarn, even from here in the Great Illuminations. The Great Illuminations of pure joy, pure love, pure knowing. What some call Heaven. Or the Universe. The Hereafter, Nirvana, or Paradise. Many names. Same thing. Same Light.

It's life. It's Light. In you. Becoming. Moment by moment. Kind of like watching grass grow. Can't see it happening, till one day you look, and there's the green, playing in the sunlight.

It's in you, just as it's in a six-year old boy named Jesse Seamus O'Neil. He lives with his love-adore grandmother Dearie. She was a particular favorite of mine, born into our gypsy caravan, knowing she was the stuff of stars, and not forgetting.

Dearie's twenty-year old son, Conor, is Jesse's uncle. They all live together in New York City, on the top floor of a brownstone apartment building, which just happens to be owned by Mac MacCarthy and his wife Bridget. Mac was my esteemed old storyteller-apprentice.

Now, Jesse. He's a shiner. Has been since he was born…an orphan. He's six now, and he's got his shadow wonderings. Life secrets. Swirling around his mother. And her mother. Jesse calls her his *disappeared grandmother*. No one knows a thing about her. She's a big puzzle. And little Jesse, he loves a puzzle. That's a fact.

But, I'm going down the waterfall afore the river. At the moment you're still outside. Not to worry. I'll show you round, so's you can find your way.

Midtown New York City, between Fifth and Sixth Avenues is a neat-n-tidy grid pattern in the early 1950s. Easy to see a tall oak tree growing there. Aye, Mac calls it the Tree of Life, rising over the courtyard, between Mac and Bridget's apartment house and their business next door: Bridget's Laundry. Mac likes to say, "The mighty oak thrives and reminds us all to thrive."

Back out on the sidewalk, you're greeted by the impressive brownstone apartment building with its bowed-window tower, soaring to the rooftop, and its front steps bookended with greeneries. Climb up. Come in.

It's a pleasant lobby, don't you think? Filled with light. There in the corner stands a wood-and-glass telephone booth, and beside that are the open mailboxes. At the side is a door leading to the courtyard stoop, where metal crates await the milk deliveries.

And there is the staircase, fanning out into the lobby. Now, stand right here at the first step and look up. See how it makes a splendid spiral. Like the Universe. Coiling up to the top floor. Kinda makes your soul spin!

But here now, let your shoes touch the dark-stained oak treads. You feel that? A slight dip, like a shallow saucer, left behind from countless footfalls. At each landing you see scuff-scrapes swinging round the newel post; and up and down those stairs you hear the echo of voices: the melting pot of neighbors, with the lingering accents of their old countries, who came to America with not much more than hope in their pockets.

I grant you, it's unusual to have families of different nationalities living together under one roof, but this is not any usual apartment house.

That's all because of the two fairlights I told you about: Mac on the first floor and Dearie on the top floor, who have invited the dear ones from their old criss-crossing gypsy travels to share this shining place of refuge.

So. It's New Year's Eve 1952, becoming 1953. A new year, beginning again, like the old Roman god, Janus, looking back in the glow of memories, looking forward in the luminosity of dreams. Aye.

I'll pop in from time to time to lead y' along. But for now, let's turn the page and go inside.

Part One

Birthday Revelations

Look into the eyes of those

who love life.

There you will find

The Light of the

Universe.

Chapter One

New Year Birthday

"Cracker Jacks!" Jesse jumped on his bed, showing off for Billy Maguire. "Tonight's my birthday!" He popped down on his bottom and snapped back up, still jumping, with his curly, straw-thatch hair flying high.

"Watch out, birthday boy!" Billy Maguire's older, scarecrow body jumped on the other bed. "You're not five anymore. Six changes everything!"

Jumping higher and higher, Jesse gasped, "Change-change-change! Ready or not, here I come!"

"C-r-a-c-k-er Jacks," Billy laughed. "You're gonna crack the ceiling, Jesse!"

Jesse grinned back and jumped higher. But a deep drumbeat thrummed in the hallway, and their heads swiveled to see Jesse's grandmother, Dearie, thumping her bodhran drum: *Da-da-rrrum. Da-da rrrum. Da-da-rrrumy-Rummy-Rummy Teedle-dum.*

"Alrighty then. Hold your Cracker Jacks, you two," Dearie chuckled, setting her bodhran on the dresser. "I'm glad you're sleeping over, Billy, but it's time for bed. Come along. In you go."

Jesse snapped down and snatched his little stuffed rabbit, Velvet, gushing, "It's almost my birthday, Dearie! When the fireworks go off. It's so *thrill-digging*!"

Jesse loved saying Dearie's made-up words. It felt like a game between the two of them.

"*Thrill-digging*!" Dearie smiled and *gandered* his clock, "Yes. You will become six years old at the stroke of midnight, New Year's Eve." She folded back the covers, "When you are fast asleep."

Looking at Billy, she said, "You too, Billy Maguire. You may be older, but you need a good night's sleep for our birthday outing tomorrow."

The two boys punched at their pillows awaiting Dearie's bedtime story. Their black cat, Gypsy, bounced in to join them, and bestowed her trademark 'wink': the tip of her tail and her right ear crooked a salute. It was so fast, it looked like she winked. No one was ever quite sure of it, but it was her little salutation when she entered a gathering.

Jesse beamed, "It's Gypsy's birthday, too. We have the same birthday."

Billy grinned, "Yeah, and you're both orphans."

Jesse's small face was rosy with color, brightening the turquoise in his eyes; his mouth was open just so, as if taking in new thoughts, new ideas.

"I don't think I can be an orphan," he *quizzled*, "because I've got Dearie and Conor. And they told me about my other disappeared grandmother, too. Wherever she is. She's a mystery."

"A grandmother and an uncle don't count," Billy said, unaware of his bluntness, "Ya gotta have parents, or else you're an orphan."

"Well," Dearie added, "perhaps Gypsy is a faerie cat—like a black malkin—sent to watch over Jesse."

Gypsy winked again.

"That'd be right," Billy shook his head with a laugh, "Gypsy follows you everywhere."

The boys and Gypsy stopped and looked expectantly at Dearie. Awaiting her story, Jesse made a request. "Dearie, let's not read *King Arthur* tonight. Tell about when I was bored."

Billy guffawed, "Bored?"

"When you were *born*?" Dearie smiled, sitting on the edge of the chair. "When you became my grandson! My *Baby Grand*!"

I told you Dearie's a fairlight, but she's had her share of life jolts. Tonight, she felt a slight *shiveral* as she recalled the leaping joy and the deep sorrow of Jesse's birth. Her hand went to her pocket, feeling for her old smooth white stone: the stone that I, Old Barret, had given to her, oh, rivers and streams and stories ago. She touched its memory, feeling its rising warmth, and she closed her eyes. I let my voice waft through her:

"When you live in the past, you are walking backward through life. So, you cannot go back. But you must choose to go forward."

She breathed. Smiled. Feeling again the flow of her Light energies.

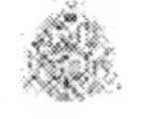

"When you were born." Dearie put down the *King Arthur* book and stood up, seeing the photographs sitting on Jesse's bureau. Family photos framed in love. Smiling, she poked about the room, straightening this and that as she observed, "Like tonight, it was New Year's Eve."

A sock hadn't made it into the hamper and she put it on her hand like a puppet, smiling and talking to Jesse in a low, squeaky voice: "Do you know your birthdate?"

"The first day of January," Jesse answered the sock.

"Yes, and what year?"

His eyes rounded and their turquoise flecks seemed to glow. "Every year."

Billy *giggleburst* and Dearie chuckled. "The year was becoming 1947." She tossed the sock into the hamper and turned around, using her beautiful, silvery Dearie-voice. "It was a night of great celebration. And great sorrow. When your mother, Jane, died, and went to the Great Illuminations, where your father—my son James—was waiting for her."

"Um, Dearie," Jesse twisted the long ears of his stuffed rabbit, "not the sad part." His eyes twinkled, "tell a fun story."

"Oh *diggety-boo*!" Dearie's chin went up and she laughed. Then, hanging Jesse's robe on the old loom standing in the corner, she settled back in the chair. "A fun story. Well. I can tell Billy's story, when he first met Jane."

"My mother!" Jesse blurted.

"Does that suit?" Dearie grinned.

Billy hooted, "Oh yeah! Angel Jane!"

"My *favorish*." Jesse chimed, using a Dearie-fun word.

"All righty then."

Dearie breathed out a chuckle, "Billy Maguire? His daddy liked to say Billy was born just a whisker shy of notorious. And when Billy met Jane, he did not disappoint." Dearie smiled.

"Now, Billy's Daddy, Liam Maguire, and Jesse's father, James O'Neil, were best friends. So when James brought home his beautiful wife, Jane, I invited all the Maguires up to meet her.

"Billy was four-years-old, and instantly smitten with Jane. He stood in his Sunday best clothes, with his dark red hair curling over his dark blue eyes. Stood there, staring at Jane and twisting his little hands together, with his mouth agog. He didn't say a word; just stood with love-love-love in his shining eyes.

"Jane wore her golden hair in a thick braid that circled her head splendidly, and it did look very much like a halo. When Billy finally spoke, he said one word: 'Angel.'

"Jane smiled and self-consciously turned her wedding band around her finger. There was a tinge of secret sadness about Jane, for she had left her mother back on their farm. Somewhere. We think it was Port Haven, our favorite old summer place up the coast. But we don't know for sure. Jane never spoke of her mother, or her farm. Even to this day we know nothing of Jane's mother, Jessica."

Jesse added, "Jessica's my disappeared grandmother. I don't know why she doesn't want to know me. She's a big mystery secret."

"Well," Dearie pulled her lips together, "Jane looked utterly charming, and Billy climbed up to snuggle on her lap, resting against her heart. His nimbly little fingers tickled Jane's tummy, and she giggled softly. With that, Billy suddenly pulled away, found his tongue, and exclaimed, out of the blue, 'You have a baby inside you.'

"Jane gasped, 'Oh, I don't think so.' She blushed to the sun and back.

"But Billy was right: Jane was expecting a baby! It was so exciting. Even the children here in the apartments were thrilled, for Jesse would be their new baby. They already loved him. From then on, Billy greeted Jane with, 'Hello Angel!'

"This went on for weeks. Then another Sunday rolled along and Billy's family was again visiting."

Dearie stood up to act out Billy's part. "Billy stared at Jane. Then he told Jane directly: 'Angel, sit down—here—and open your mouth.'

"Jane was highly skeptical, as well she should be with Billy, but she followed his instructions. And Billy! He stood up, and yelled. Down her throat, 'Hello in there, baby!'

"We all gasped, but Billy's eyes popped. And he shouted, 'I saw him! Standing on tip-toes! I saw him! He waved at me!'

"My James scooped Billy into his arms, laughing heartily. 'So it's a boy in there, is it?'

"'Oh yeah! He's real cute!' Billy grinned, and turned to Jane, asking, 'Angel? When's he coming out to play?'"

Jesse and Billy laughed like the dish running away with the spoon, as

Dearie plopped back in the chair, sighing, "The end!"

Abruptly, Jesse sat up. "Billy? Did you see my disappeared grandmother in there? Inside Jane?"

Billy shook his head and his mouth *grimmeled*, "I knew you were in there with Jane. There was lots of shiny lights. All sparkly. But that's all I remember." His laughter puffed again, "You waved at me!"

More *giggle-snickens* erupted.

Straightaway, Dearie's twenty-year-old son, Conor, popped into the room, "Great Lakes! What's all this jocularity?" He teased about their laughter. "I thought Jesse and Billy would be sound asleep by now."

He leaned his lanky body against the doorframe with his dark hair waving over blue eyes that danced in merriment. Dearie thought he looked utterly handsome, especially in his crisp white shirt framed by his short black tuxedo jacket and bowtie, which he wore when he was a waiter. He looked like he belonged in a movie. A romantic movie.

Jesse's head snapped-up, "But. I didn't get my lullaby."

Billy hopped back to his bed as Dearie flurried, "That's because *someone* asked for a special story."

Jesse forced a giggle and Billy spurt a loud, "Hah!"

"*Hiss-and-leer*, you two," Dearie said in fun, using a spoonerism that cleverly changed the beginning of the words.

Jesse translated, "*Hiss-and-leer*," he giggled, "that's *Listen here!*"

"Yes," Dearie grinned, "Blue ribbon, you. Now, you boys are fine. So fine. But it's time you were asleep. Billy, you know your parents and Grams are at my *Lady Bird Theater* celebrating New Year's Eve, which is where I will be. Conor is working tonight at Rockefeller Center." She stood with a puff of laughter, "Now I shall go make myself look *gahslahzerous*!"

"Gah-slah-zer-ous?" Billy dubiously repeated, while Jesse crowed, "Oh, I love that word *gahslahzerous*!" He laughed. "*Gahslahzerous*!"

"What is it?" Billy asked.

"It's not a thing," Conor answered, "it's an attitude. A glamorous attitude."

Dearie's eyebrows arched over her dark eyelashes, fringing her deep blue eyes. Her long, thick white hair framed her high, broad cheekbones, now dimpling into her beaming smile. Her smile that always felt like a blessing.

"I may be a grandmother, but I can still be a glamour girl! Of sorts!" She reminded them, "Now, Siobhan will be your babysitter tonight."

Billy groaned, "Not my sister."

But Jesse buzzed, "Maybe Siobhan will tell us another story. Maybe about Amanda."

Billy changed his tune, "Amanda Wynne! I saw a poster for her new movie. It's called *Dancing*. She's the greatest!"

"Sorry boys," Dearie ruffled Billy's hair. "By the time Siobhan arrives, you will be fast asleep,"—she brushed Jesse's cheek with a kiss—"in your deep *wispy slips*."

As she left the room, Jesse looked to his uncle, "Conor? Will you story-tell us?"

Conor's head swagged back and forth.

"Well then...will you sing?"

"Fret not, birthday boy, I'll do the lullaby honors."

Billy noted, "Conor, you look gah-gah-slahz..."

Chuckling and tugging his lapels, Conor said, "Tonight I'm a waiter at the *gahslahzerous* Rainbow Room New Year's Eve party, and Aislinn will be working there, too."

"I really like Aislinn," Jesse beamed.

"Me, too," Billy chimed.

"Me, too," Conor nodded. "Do you know, *Aislinn* means *dream*?"

A crooked little grin met Conor's chin, "Pretty dreamy, isn't she?"

Jesse gushed over the lovey-doveys, and Conor made a show of straightening his bowtie, "Now, your lullaby."

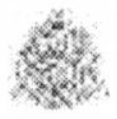

Conor was only fourteen the night Jesse was born and Jane died. He had been overwhelmed, first with joy, but, too soon, with grief. Holding infant Jesse, not knowing what to do, he had stood at their parlor window, watching the last flits of New Year's Eve fireworks. Then one tiny baby hand curled up and wound itself around Conor's finger. It was a Great Illuminations moment, and Conor felt his heart thump in a precious, ethereal connection. And in the dark quiets, he sang to the baby. A Christmas lullaby: "Silent Night".

He sang it then. And no matter the time of year since, he was obliged to sing it again.

"Silent Night" was Conor's come-what-may lullaby for Jesse. And it worked. His pure, rich voice gently sang, and Jesse drifted into his deep wispy slips. Conor quietly turned out the light and whispered, "Goodnight."

Billy Maguire slid something under his pillow and whispered back, "G'night Conor."

⁂

A dull, quivering ring woke Billy. It was his alarm clock, which was muffled under his pillow. Jesse dimly heard it click off and Billy's whisper, "Jesse. Wake up, Jess."

"Whaaat?"

"Shhh. We don't want Siobhan to hear us." He smiled with his eyelids hitching to his eyebrows, "I've got a birthday present for you, Jess," Billy whispered. "You know how Dearie says you always get fireworks for your birthday? Well, this year you're gonna actually see 'em." He slid off the bed and stood over Jesse. "Come on. I'm taking you up to the rooftop."

Jesse barely whispered. "But, Billy. Our coats?"

Billy grinned and knelt on the floor, sliding out coats, hats, scarves, and shoes from under the bed.

"Golly," Jesse murmured.

"I thought of everything," Billy crowed quietly. "Come on, birthday boy. Let's go see your fireworks!"

Silently, the boys dressed in their winter woolies as a muffled *boom* sounded from far off, lighting their eyes with a keen hankering. Jesse tucked Velvet in his pocket and tiptoed down the hallway after Billy. He saw Siobhan standing down at the parlor window, but he followed his feet out to the entry.

Billy noiselessly opened the hallway door to the rooftop, pushing Jesse into the cold dark and squeezing in after him.

"Don't you be a feardy cat in the dark, Jesse," Billy murmured as he fumbled with a flashlight. He finally got it on and jiggled its light up to the landing where the stairway took a turn to the last three steps.

Jesse breathed, "I'm not a feardy cat. We're on a secret exhibition."

Billy couldn't help setting Jesse right: "Expedition."

"Oh," Jesse shrugged, "ex-pe-di-shun."

Up they climbed, following the glowing circle to the top door and out to the cold rooftop, where Jesse's eyes filled with the city lights and dark silhouettes. "Billy! This is so *thrill-digging*!"

"Yeah!" Billy surveyed the rooftop. A genuine rumble went off in the distance, and thrill bumps teased into their shoulders. "Let's get on top of your daddy's long table so we can see over the roof."

Billy knelt on the long tabletop, peering north. "There's the Times Square Ball–ready to drop at midnight." His eyes scanned the western scape and he pointed, "Over there are the docks for daddy's tugboat."

Jesse saw lights there, reflecting on the water. "I wonder… if that's Port Haven over there."

"I don't think so, Jess. Port Haven is away-away." Billy turned south, and pointed again, "Say, there's the Empire State Building."

Jesse hooted, "The skyscraper buildings!"

Billy turned again to the east, "Yeah, there's Rockefeller Center. And the Chrysler building. This is a great view."

Jesse was delighted. "It is a great view. I'm glad James built this table. It's just right."

"Your dad was all right, Jesse. I'm glad my dad and your dad were best friends."

"Liam and James," Jesse cheered, "best friends. Just like you and me, Billy."

Billy shrugged. It wasn't like he and Jesse were best friends. Jesse was a might too young, though he seemed older, on account he was one tall glass of water—like his daddy. But Jesse was more like, well, a little brother. A real special brother. Billy had to admit, Jesse was something else. Jesse could make Billy feel star-bright even when he was in one of his *feisty-dregs*. Billy and Jesse were humming together even before Jesse was born. Fact is, Billy loved Jesse and Jesse loved Billy.

In that moment, a far-off light lit up the clouds in the south and the boys wheeled around to gaze at the swirling sky. A good, rolling rumble followed the light, and Jesse gasped, "It's almost time!"

Another far-off light, and another boooom had Billy swaggering, "That's gotta be fireworks down in Jersey." He pointed knowingly. "Their clocks must be set ahead of ours."

A cold breeze feathered their cheeks, but instantly turned to a keen gust. Startled, the boys laughed as a closer cloud lit up in bright whites. In the quick following rumble, Jesse laughed again. "These are going to be the best fireworks ever!" They both grinned with the thrill of it.

And that was the moment when their world turned upside down. All at once, from the flashing clouds, a shuddering storm blasted them. Cold air gusts shrieked like a banshee. Pushed them over like piffling little dust puffs. Desperately, they clutched at the edges of the quaking table as the wind stifled their useless cries. In the next blink, a thick lightning bolt struck a building down south in the Battery, followed by a sizzling, white lightning branch snapping into the black sky. The boys helplessly goggled each other as another walloping lightning bolt cracked with ear-splitting thunder, and the howling wind battered the rooftop.

Chapter Two

Illuminations

Siobhan had heard the thunder rumblings and gone to check on the boys. "Billy? Jesse? Where are you?" But no one answered.

She looked everywhere, checked every floor, flying down to the landings with her long dark red hair lifting like a cape, and her clear blue-green eyes searching the nooks and crannies in the hallways. No Jesse. No Billy.

Desperate, she ran out and around the corner to the *Lady Bird Theater.* Flinging open the front lobby door, she was surprised to find Dearie.

"Siobhan!" Dearie exclaimed, turning from the circle of guests, "What's happened?"

Siobhan's thin arms tried unsuccessfully to close the door from the wind. "I…can't find Jesse and Billy."

"Well," Dearie said sensibly, "we know they're not lost, they're somewhere." She pictured Jesse. Bouncing on his bed. What had he been chirping-on about?

It's almost my birthday, Dearie. The fireworks will go off and it will be my birthday!

"Fireworks. Yes! The roof," she blurted. "Did you look on the roof?"

A far-off light suddenly lit up the clouds in the south and a good rumble followed, keeping time with Siobhan's shaking head. "No."

"Go find Liam and Teresa."

A wild wind rose up, whirling Siobhan into the theater to find her parents, while Dearie raced against it. Up to the apartment roof. To find the boys.

The ferocious wind walloped Jesse from his scalp to his toenails, and the cracking thunder ricocheted through his eardrums. The table shuddered relentlessly, and Jesse's arms and legs flailed while Billy clawed through the windblast trying to reach him.... He *twiddly-switched* on the flashlight and saw the yellow circle dart along the wall, seeking the doorway to the stairs.

"Jesse!" he yelled, "Jesse, get inside!"

The black sky filled with another jagged white shaft, and Jesse gaped at it, covering his ears as it screeched through the electric air. "Bil-leee!" he screamed.

Billy forcibly rolled into Jesse, pushing him off the table, shouting, "Get to the door, Jesse!" He heard him land on the flooring, and lifted the flashlight to show Jesse the way, bellowing, "Get to the door!"

On the rooftop floor, with his eyes screwed up tight, Jesse saw bright Lights swirling behind his eyelids. Beautiful Lights. In radiating circles of spinning, sparkling colors. He felt himself floating in the Lights. He felt a calm. Even with the wild storm breathing down his neck. Calm. Deep inside.

Jesse hesitated for just a second, then ran like a streak to the door and ducked inside. Safe. He stopped on the top step, looking back for Billy.

But suddenly it was raining. Pouring. Jesse was looking through a wall of rain, the blasting wind sweeping it across the rooftop. He saw Billy's rain-blurry silhouette leap from the table and land at the far side of the flat roof.

Billy picked himself up, running through the rain as if slashing through a dark curtain. But halfway across, he slipped. He slid. Like a rocket, he shot through the doorway. His head and shoulders bounced down the steps, barreled down to the landing, and tumbled on top of Jesse.

On the dark landing, ever so slowly, Jesse pulled himself out from under Billy. Feeling stunned, and a little bruised, he sat for a moment, then shook his head. He was fine.

He pushed at Billy's soggy coat, but Billy didn't move. "Billy?" He bent to Billy's ear. "Billy. Wake up now."

In the deep dark, Jesse was alive with sparkling sensations. Inside him. He sat, gently cradling Billy's head in his lap, soaking in these glittering energies.

The rooftop quieted. The lightning flashes paled. The raging storm moved away, leaving behind a soft patter of rain on the roof. Jesse took Velvet from his pocket, rubbing his fingers on its soft fabric.

Jane's old rabbit, Velvet, he thought, and he whispered, "Jane. My mother. Jane." Gently he put the worn little rabbit to his cheek, and he thought of Jane's mother: *Jessica. Mystery-us. Disappeared. Jessica.* Yet...Jesse felt her. Now.

He whispered, "Jane. Jessica." He felt a deep love, and he sighed, letting Velvet caress his cheek, and then Billy's cheek.

"Billy?" Jesse said tenderly, "I love you, Billy. And you love me." He copied Dearie's words, "Billy, we are fine, so fine...."

In that moment, he felt his heart thump. "Jane?" he whispered, taking a breath. "Jane!" And strangely he smelled...*chocolate?*

Time stood still. In a beautiful Light. Jesse saw it. Felt it. He knew it. Love. Love-Light. Filling him. Fillling Billy. His heart throbbed with it.

Jesse touched Billy's cheek and Billy's eyes opened. Eyes shining with the beautiful Light. Billy murmured one word, "Angel...."

Jesse gaspered as a rising bubble of Lights filled his eyes, "Jane! And James! And Lights! So many Lights! People! In Lights!"

He recalled Dearie's *Lady Bird Theater* the night they turned on the Mirror Ball and lights glitter-sparkled everywhere.

A beautiful smile crossed Billy's face and he closed his eyes. Jesse, too, closed his eyes and sat for endless moments in his bubble of love-Lights.

He didn't think further, because the door at the bottom of the stairs opened. In the next moment, he felt a soft padding of cat feet at his arm. "Gypsy," he whispered, as she jumped into his arms. He felt the Light again. In her eyes. Her glowing cat eyes.

Then. A sweet voice calling: "Jesse…? Jesse…?"

"Dearie…." He smiled.

But a dull click sounded somewhere, and a garish light bulb cast a harsh scowling light. Jesse was vaguely aware of strange shadows climbing the walls. A jumble of noises stomping the stairs. Voices shouting. Crying.

But Jesse gave his ears to the sound of the rain falling lightly—like pins dropping out of Dearie's sewing box. And the following kettle drum of distant thunder, rolling over them all.

⁂

With Gypsy tucked under his arm, Jesse quietly insisted to the Maguires, "I'm fine. We're both fine. Billy's with Jane."

But Billy's mother and grandmother, Teresa and Grams Maguire, did not listen to him at all.

Grams screamed to Siobhan, "Go back to the theater and fetch Doc Hennessey."

Teresa's arms darted forward and she anxiously peeled Billy off Jesse, settling him flat on the landing. But that left Jesse teetering on the steps.

Billy's father, Liam Maguire, caught Jesse in his arms, and Gypsy flopped to the floor. In Liam's arms, Jesse heard bells chiming, and thought, *the bells of the New Year. My birthday bells.* His eyes looked over Liam's shoulder, up the stairwell. Through the open door he saw that the rain had turned to snow. Falling gently. Like the soft dandelion seeds he liked to blow in autumn; they looked like tiny parachutes, drifting in slow motion.

But Teresa was crying, "Billy! Wake up, Billy!"

Liam handed Jesse to Dearie and moved forward bending over Billy.

Silently, slowly, Jesse slipped from Dearie's warm embrace and took her hand. Together they turned the corner, going back to his bed with Gypsy at their heels.

A cup-of-calm was Gypsy, curling into Jesse's bedcovers. He pet the cat, contritely looking at Dearie from his pillows. "Dearie," his quiet voice belied the tremors his body had so recently experienced. "I'm sorry Billy and I went up to the roof. I knew…" his newly-six-year-old self struggled to find the words, "…we shouldn't do it."

"I'm glad you do know that. You learned a lesson. A rather frightening lesson. But I am glad you are safe. And sound." She smiled, "So fine."

Gypsy sat on Jesse's chest, staring into his eyes and Jesse sat up, remembering: "I saw the most beautiful Lights…and I knew I was safe. And Dearie, I saw Jane. I did. And, I smelled chocolate."

"Chocolate?" Dearie repeated. "Really?" She grinned. "Jane loved dark, rich chocolate. She rarely had it, but she always savored it." She smiled at Jesse, "I'm glad you smelled Jane's love for you, wrapped in chocolate."

Jesse snuggled back into his pillow. "The stairwell was dark, but the Light went on behind my eyes, and I saw James and Jane in glittery Lights. Sailing. And other Light-people were there. Lots of Light-people. Some I didn't know. They were sparkling on the water. Like the Mirror Ball in your theater."

"Jesse, the love-Lights know just where to find you." Dearie put her hand to his cheek, "All is well..."

Jesse finished the saying they liked to share, "...and so it is." He touched Velvet. "I said that to Billy: All is well. Even though we shouldn't have gone up there."

"Good. Blue ribbon, you." She leaned back on her elbow. "Just one thing, Jesse. You know how important your words are. Try not to use that word 'should.' 'Should' is full of bossy judging. You're using it on yourself and Billy. You don't need a 'should' to guide you."

"But I knew I sh - - - -. I knew.... What do I say?"

"If you hear yourself using 'should', don't say it at all. Turn your thoughts. Think of those gorgeous Lights. 'Should' is not lit up with those Lights, is it? Let the Lights guide you. Try something like, 'Isn't it great that we're safe. I love feeling Jane and James loving me.'"

Jesse smiled, "I do! Even though I don't have an alive mother and father, I'm glad I got to feel James and Jane with me tonight."

"And, you went sailing with them," Dearie smiled encouragingly, helping Jesse to turn his thoughts. "Your darling father loved to sail. As a teenager he worked in Port Haven; woodworking lessons with Uncle Conn, working at the big lumberyard at T.J. O'Farrell's, and later, during the war, he was stationed at the Construction Battalion nearby. But all on his own, he rebuilt an old Catboat, and he loved to sail the bay in Port Haven, the beautiful island we visited every summer, when we stayed with Aunt Clare and Uncle Conn."

"Uncle Conn was Grandfather Galen's brother," Jesse said confidently.

"Yes," Dearie answered and caught her gold locket in her fingers. The locket Galen had given her so long ago.

Dearie's husband, Galen, had died at the very end of World War II. He was gone to the Great Illuminations. But Dearie knew he was always here. Always. Dearie kept her Light on for him.

Jesse leaned forward fingering Dearie's locket, "It says, 'To my Dearie Lady Bird'. That's what Grandfather Galen called you, his *Lady Bird.*" He clicked it open to see the picture. "There's my Daddy James with Conor, and there's Galen. I saw his Light, too." He clicked the locket shut. "And…I felt Jessica, my disappeared grandmother. Jessica was calling…*Jane*…and *Papa*…and another man…*Dan-yell.* She loves them. And they love her…wherever she is. I don't think she's in the Great Illuminations." He looked at Dearie, "Is Grandmother Jessica on Port Haven Island?"

"We think so, Jesse. But we don't really know. We don't have her last name or her address. We have written to the Town Hall there, but they couldn't give us any information."

Jesse's eyes opened wide, "She's so mystery-us."

Dearie stood, picking up Jesse's winter clothing. She draped everything on the old loom and reached to touch the colorful yarns. "So many weavings," she murmured. "Growing together, tangling the roots of our magic." She looked at Jesse and smiled, touching the loom. "Mac, my dearest, oldest friend…this loom was Mac's clever idea, to fold up so that my Mam could fit it into our old Vardo wagon when we traveled. Then my brilliant old friend Elliot designed it. And my Da built it. I made my first scarf on it. My first present to Galen. You can just feel all our energies, spooling and weaving with our Light-threads. Even before we strung up the yarn on the loom, our energies were woven together. They still are."

"You mean we're like the yarn. And we weave together?"

Dearie grinned, "Yes, we hum and weave together. We are the warp and woof. Weaving our own fabric in our own life."

Jesse slumped into his pillows, "We just need the disappeared grandmother's yarn."

"Yes," Dearie smiled. "And one day, who knows what beautiful fabric we shall weave. So fine." She bent over him and kissed his cheek. "Light on, Jesse. My brillish birthday boy."

⁂

The morning sun woke Jesse with gold in its mouth, spilling over the coverlet, trailing to the door. He *kafluffled* into his clothes and followed the gold to Dearie and Conor, who were sitting in its glorious pool at the breakfast table.

Jesse's head turned to the Victrola, hearing his favorite Mozart record, *Eine kleine Nachtmusik*. When Jane was pregnant with Jesse, she played it most mornings. It seemed Jesse was born knowing it. Dearie played it often, and he delighted in unconsciously conducting, waving his arms and fingers with every note.

Dearie's kitchen clock had no numerals; it always read NOW for every hour. Even so, Jesse looked up and said, "It's almost nine o'clock!"

Twiddling a sigh, Dearie murmured, "Old Barret used to call the NOW 'the one eye, winking in eternity.'"

"Whaaat?" Jesse blurted, and Dearie smiled.

"Hmmm. Well, the clock is just right for NOW. No *Lady Bird Theater* to dash off to. Just a leisurely morning. We'll make your birthday pancakes next."

Conor opened the ice box and groaned, "Uh-oh. No pancakes. B-e-e-e-cause, there's no milk."

Jesse went to the front door, "We can get milk from the Maguires, and I can check on Billy."

Conor offered, "I'll go with you, Jess."

Little Gypsy sashayed along behind Jesse and Conor and they looked down, laughing, "Look at Gypsy! I bet she thinks we're going to the Romanos for her olive treat."

"Oh, Gypsy," Jesse smiled, "no Romanos, no olives."

Gypsy padded along anyway. But at the next floor she stopped. Grams Maguire was leaving her apartment. The little cat hissed, and pffted back up the steps.

You couldn't miss Grams, even in a crowd, because of her spotlight of shiny white hair. She wore it straight. Down to her chin. And fastened it back with a black bobby pin at each side. Without those bobby pins, her hair swished back and forth like curtains in the wind, brushing at the cauliflower wrinkles in her face.

It was pretty factual that Grams was eccentric, and she liked herself that way. Mac had once told Jesse that Grams Maguire was a tiny little lady with a great big personality.

Jesse had replied, "I think Grams is filled with colors."

"Yep," Mac had chuckled. "That's about right, Jesse."

But Conor thought, *You never know what Grams will do next. She's as mad as a box of frogs!*

He and Jesse stood still, watching Grams lock her apartment door. Oddly, she then knocked on the door, standing back expectantly.

"Who's there?" she demanded in her lingering Irish accent. No reply. She knocked again. "Answer me!"

She waited, wondering if it was her long dead husband. "Is it you there, Willem?"

All of a sudden she cried, "Oh! I remember." She knocked her own noggin, "I knocked for good luck."

In relief, she turned, but startled mightily at Conor and Jesse, "Glory be to heaven and fifteen saints! I nearly had a canary!" Her startle turned to a sneer, "Well! If it ain't the bad-luck-boys!"

Conor puffed, "Happy New Year to you, too, Grams."

"I'm not your grandmother, sonny," she gibed. But she peered at him, "Am I?"

Conor stifled a chuckle, while Jesse gushed, "It is a Happy New Year's Day! It's my birthday!"

Grams rolled her eyes…*and*…clicked her false teeth out in front of her lips.

"Hunh?" Conor jumped back. But Jesse laughed, "You are hil-l-a-i-r-y-u-s!" He looked up at her with his merry turquoise-flecked eyes.

Grams clicked her teeth back and pointed her finger, "Aye Jesse O'Neil, you're a bewitcher for sure. Those eyes of yourn. Long ago, I fell in love with eyes like that." She sighed dramatically. "My first crush."

Jesse grabbed her hand and pecked a little kiss, "Ohhh," Grams raptured, "a kiss!"

Jesse reached to give her another, but Grams giggled, "No, no! Once is enough!"

Conor smiled at Jesse's magic, quoting Thomas Mallory, "*Enough is as good as a feast.*"

"What?" Grams poked Conor, "I'm not a *beast!* Don't be callin' me a beast!"

Jesse giggled, "Conor said f-f-feast!"

Everyone knew that Grams was deaf-as-a-doorstop when she wanted to be. Billy liked to say, "She's got real 'hearwaxers.'"

"No matter to me," Grams was saying, "I'm off to the MacCarthy's to see Bridget." She scribbled toward the stairs, but turned, pointing her gnarly finger at them, putting on the drama, "Ach! You got the cloak of the banshee about-cha." Her head stuck forward, and she hissed, "Don't you two be following me with your bad luck!"

Jesse smiled, "We need milk for my birthday pancakes." He turned toward the Maguires' door and waved, "Happy New Year to you and happy birthday to me!"

But Grams stepped back to stop him. "Oh no. Don't you be after my Billy. Doc says he's gotta rest."

Jesse smiled, "I'll just peek in."

"No." Grams said stridently. "No. You keep away from Billy. You're always gettin' him into one tangle or another. Nothin' but trouble."

Jesse's mouth opened, but Conor put his hand on Jesse's shoulder, and his other hand made his gesture that meant *enough*.

As Grams jittered down to Bridget MacCarthy's first floor apartment, Jesse and Conor heard the Maguire's door unlock. Siobhan put her head out.

"Sorry, Jesse. Grams is right. You can't come in. Billy's resting."

"But, what about my birthday outing? Billy's supposed to go."

"I'm so sorry, Jesse." Her eyebrows shrugged and the door closed.

Vexed, Jesse backed up and plopped on the step. "I know Billy is okay. I know it."

The doorknob turned again and the door opened wide.

"Liam!" Jesse's frown turned upside-down as Liam sat down on the steps.

Jesse respectfully called most of the grown-ups by Mister or Missus. But Liam insisted, "Jesse, you call me Liam. That's what your daddy called me."

So for Jesse it was Liam. Always.

A smile emerged from Liam's broad, jolly face, framed in his rusty-colored beard. His great, strong arms and his great, strong heart nuzzled at Jesse and he said, "Well me boyo, this too shall pass."

Jesse pulled his head back, "This too? What does that mean?"

"It means Billy and you are pals. Always will be. You ain't seen your last adventure. But right now, Billy's Ma is worried 'bout him. Don't press her. Can't get milk if the cow ain't ready."

"Oh," Conor blurted, "we came looking for milk."

"Then milk you'll get." Liam chuckled and stood up, lifting Jesse in a spinning hug.

"Ohhh…!" Jesse laughed, feeling like he was flying.

But here was Grams, trotting up the steps, shaking her finger. "Jesus, Mary, and Joseph! I told you two villains not to bother us Maguires."

Liam stopped her, "Ma, they just need milk."

Jesse brightly reminded, "For my birthday pancakes…?"

Grams opened the door, "Well. Wait out here. I'll get it for you."

Aromas of toast and honey-tea met Grams in the kitchen. Teresa gestured, "For Billy."

She pulled open the cupboard doors, and her dark, bobbed hair swung back to her ears, showing off her darling face. Teresa was so young looking, people often thought she and her daughter, Siobhan, were sisters. Even as tired as Teresa felt this morning, she couldn't hide her adorable looks.

Sourly, Grams talked at Teresa: "Dearie—the 'Queen of Perfect'—forgot to order extra milk." She launched into a rant, enjoying every word. "Don't know why Dearie keeps Jesse. She can't care for a little tyke at her age. She's past sixty. Now Conor's got his acting studio and college." She opened the icebox, pulling out the milk bottle. "Ave Maria! I can't keep up with Conor. All the jobs he scrapes up, and that girlfriend of his, Miss *AshyLinn*."

Sloshing the milk into the bottle, she sloshed a few more thoughts around the kitchen as Teresa buttered toast and poured boiling water.

Grams rambled, "It's past time their lot took Jesse to that other

Grandmother—wherever on earth she is. Hah. And orchidaceous Dearie should go, too!"

Teresa picked up the tray and raised an eyebrow at Grams, "Orchid–da-shus? I don't know where you get this stuff!"

She disappeared, leaving Grams huffing, "It's a real word! Hoity-toity flower she thinks she is!" She talked to the walls while she looked for the cardboard top for the milk bottle. "Hmmm," she hummed quietly. Wickedly. "Maybe I put in half vinegar? Real sour milk for a real sour New Year's Day." Her eyes glinted. "Oh yes. That'll tip Dearie's crown. They'll never forget these pancakes. Hah!"

Grams returned to the hallway with a small bottle of milk. "Here you are," she smiled tepidly, "For your birthday pancakes. Savor every bite."

Jesse playfully hugged Grams' legs, looking up at her, "Thanks Grams, you're the best." And he ran up the steps.

Chapter Three

Humming

"Dearie!" Jesse surged into their apartment, setting the bottle of milk on the kitchen counter, "I smell your Christmas Sin-Man rolls! And I hear my song!"

With spatula in hand, Dearie spun around, laughing, "I beg your pardon! My *cinnamon* rolls are not a sin–for any man! They're just sinfully delicious!" She guffawed at her herself, adding, "I just put on Nat King Cole's "Nature Boy" song for your birthday!"

Conor grabbed Jesse and waltzed him around the kitchen, extravagantly overacting and loudly singing Jesse's song with the record:

'The greatest thing you'll ever learn, is just to love and be loved in return.'

Ending the song with a flourish, Conor and Jesse bowed to each other and their invisible audience.

Dearie "Bravo-ed" and waved the spatula. "You two are a pair of *Quatchkopfs*! But you are *my Quatchkopfs*!" Smiling, she turned back to the stove, "We have plenty of leftovers, so I started breakfast with a new menu."

Grinning, Conor took Dearie's spatula. "I shall do the honors with the eggs, madam."

"Here's the milk!" Jesse galloped. But he tipped it over. "Oh no!" he squawked, as the milk slopped onto the floor.

Dearie reached for a cloth. "Easily cleaned," she said as Gypsy dashed toward the milk. But the cat only sneezed, and padded away.

Dearie puzzled, "A cat spurning milk?"

Conor turned the eggs, frowning, *Grams.*

A yoke burst and a yellow stream slid into the pan. Conor felt that old seeping poison, *Grams Maguire. But,* he chided himself, *Jesse so loves the Maguires. He doesn't know Grams' taradiddles.*

Conor's inner voice spoke, *You mean her lies.*

But he dismissed it. *Jesse loves. He really is a little love-adore. He just hums his love.* Conor decided to stick with that feeling. *No use aggravating the bear.*

After breakfast Jesse opened his gifts.

"A music box!" he marveled. Turning the tiny handle, he recognized "Twinkle Twinkle Little Star" and he said impishly, "I can sing this for my disappeared grandmother, how I wonder *where* you are!"

Giggle-snickens bounced around the table as Jesse opened his second present.

"Oh good, another Beatrix Potter book: *Squirrel Nutkin.*"

Dearie smiled, "You've been reading Beatrix's books since you were three. Squirrel Nutkin is a naughty little thing, but I think you'll like his riddles."

Jesse flipped the pages and saw the picture of Squirrel Nutkin under Owl's huge talons with the caption: '*This looks like the end of the story; but it isn't.*'

"Oh...a mystery!" Jesse *jim-jammed*, closing the book. "I'll solve it later."

Conor gestured toward the last present and Jesse burbled, "This must be my puzzle! I wonder what James made for me this year."

Jesse's father, James, had created many puzzles when he worked with his Uncle Conn, a master woodcrafter. After Uncle Conn and Aunt Clare died, Dearie collected James's jigsaws, bestowing one each year on Jesse's birthday.

Jesse laid out the puzzle pieces, and in no time, fit it all together. "Look, this way it's birds. And upside down they're fish! This is clever," Jesse smiled, "Thanks, James."

Conor noted, "James wasn't the only one who made puzzles. Jane did, too. Her favorites were the seven shapes in the Chinese Tangrams."

Jesse remarked, "In school, Missus K said Jane visited the class and showed how the shapes make all kinds of pictures. Did you know everything is made of shapes? I see shapes everywhere. I see shapes in everything."

Conor looked at Jesse's birds and fish. "I don't see it. At all."

Jesse demonstrated: "It goes like this." He took it apart and put it back together right before Conor's eyes. But Conor only shook his head.

Dearie declared, "Well Jesse, now for your surprise birthday outing." She went to the closet. "I'll get our coats. You put away your puzzle in the lumber room."

Jesse picked up his puzzle, bubbling, "I love that name, lumber room. Like that Saki story called *The Lumber Room*. You know"—he shook the puzzle box—"about the boy who goes exploring in the attic—but it's called the lumber room." Distractedly, Jesse put the puzzle box on top of his head, continuing, "And he pretends that his bossy aunt is the *devil*, so he can't possibly help her get out of the well." Jesse cackled. "He's so imagining-clever."

Dearie reached into the closet for their coats. She was thinking of her old friend, the writer, *Saki*: H.H. Munro. His clever short stories. His unique sense of humor. *Dear old H.* She thought of the war. *World War I. When H. was killed.* Her lips pursed. *Death,* she mused. *Well it takes us all.* She made a slight shake of her head and looked at Jesse thoughtfully, *Oh, to raise children who will make the world magic again.*

She puffed and put her chin up, gathering the scarves and hats. Smiling, she said, "I think, Jesse, that you are just as clever and imagining as Saki's Lumber Room boy. You're *brillish.* For certain."

Jesse was trying to walk with the box on top of his head, but it slipped off. He caught it *brillishly*, and skipped off to their very own lumber room.

This room was the once-upon-a-time bedroom of Jane and James. Putting his puzzle on a bookshelf, Jesse saw other puzzles and baby books, and toys in a basket on the floor. He touched the wooden rings made by his father.

The sun poked in, pointing to a slant-top desk with three long drawers below. On top were a small lamp, a wooden box, and a framed photograph.

Jesse picked up the photo: *James and Jane. They look so happy.* He smiled. They were smiling back at him. Jesse felt a curious flutter. Like love. Fluttering. James and Jane. Their smiles seemed to get bigger, and Jesse beamed back at them.

He reached for the small wooden box with different colors of wood, set in stripes around the sides. *Strange*, he thought, *no opening. Maybe it's not a box.* He set it back on the desk. The desk that his father had built. He pulled out the sliders that supported the top when it was open, but the top itself did not budge.

The sun melted away and the room filled with shadows.

The desk is locked, Jesse quavered. *I wonder. Why is it locked? What's in there? Where is the key?*

"Dearie," Jesse *quizzeled*, "where is the key for the desk? In the lumber room?"

"We don't know," she said, handing him his coat. "Your father loved to have clever hiding places for things. We think he, and Jane, too, hid it someplace."

"Ohhh. A puzzle." Jesse smiled, "Maybe I can find it."

He buttoned his coat and tucked Velvet into his pocket, startling, "Gosh, look what I found!" He pulled out a penny.

Dearie smiled, "That's a nice surprise, Jesse. Light on."

"My surprises already started," he chuckled.

"Just keep humming what you like," she added, "and you'll get surprises galore. For now, let's begin your outing."

Conor went to the door. "I'll go down and get the stroller."

"I'm not a baby!" Jesse yelled after him, "I don't need a stroller!"

Pivoting back, Conor said, "You're right, you're not a baby, Jesse. You're too tall and too heavy to carry. So, stroller it is."

Jesse stopped. He stared at the wall of framed photographs. At the top was the spectacular rooftop of the Chrysler Building; on the bottom was a photo of a very surprised, laughing baby Jesse.

"Jesse?" Dearie called.

"I'm looking at my surprise."

She walked towards him saying, "Both photographs were taken by Galen's famous photographer friend, Margaret Bourke-White." Dearie chuckled, "What a time you had with Margaret! She came to visit after…after the second World War...after Galen was gone." She cleared her head, and let a snicker pop out of her mouth. "Oh, curious you! Push-pulling at Margaret's tri-pod. It crashed down around you! But you just laughed, and Margaret snapped that picture! *Brillish*!"

Dearie swiped at the photo glass with her hanky. "You have that look on your face that always reminds me of my old friend, Elliot."

"That boy," Jesse declared, "who used to meet up with you, wherever you were gypsy-ing."

"Right Jesse," she said, tying his wool scarf, "wherever we were, Elliot appeared, out of the blue!"

Jesse skipped to the door ahead of Dearie. At the Maguire's landing, Grams stood at her door with her fingers fretting at her gold Claddagh necklace.

"Hi, Grams," Jesse gleamed.

She could barely wait to ask, "Did you like your pancakes?"

Jesse's chin went down. "Oh, I spilled all your milk. It was a n'accident. I'm sorry, Grams."

She rolled her eyes and said acidly, "You're good at losing things. Your grandfather, your father, your mother, your milk, your pancakes." Her hands went up in the air. "Your disappeared grandmother's lost, too. What's next to lose, eh?"

Jesse didn't answer, for Teresa Maguire nudged past Grams, saying, "I'm going to church." But when she saw Jesse she knelt to give him a tender hug.

Jesse smiled, "Can I see Billy now?"

"No, I'm sorry Jesse, Billy's sleeping. He's worn thin."

Jesse went down the stairs with Teresa as she added, "Billy isn't talkin' 'bout last night."

"He probably just wants to stay with Jane. We saw Jane."

Teresa was skeptical. "That just makes me worry about Billy even more."

"Ohhh no!" Jesse cautioned. "Not *worry*."

"It's my job to worry. That's what mothers do."

Jesse wagged his head, "No." He looked into Teresa's face. "Dearie says mothers *love* their children."

"Well, of course," Teresa rustled, "worrying shows how much I love Billy."

"No," Jesse said sensibly. "Dearie says love and worry are two ut-ter-ly different streams of energy. No match. Worry is a black cloud. Love is a shiny Light."

Teresa's shoulders sagged. "So now I can't worry?"

"It won't help." Jesse's head wagged and he added, "At all."

"Well, I'm goin' t' church to light a candle for Billy."

Jesse hopped down the last step, "That's great! A love-Light! Oh, Billy will be back in no time!"

Teresa smiled at Jesse and touched his cheek, "Love." That's all she said, and went out the door.

Dearie pattered down the steps, reaching for Jesse's hand, "Come along my little hummer-bug! We're off!" She spun about in her bright red wool cape and they went outside where the slight dusting of snow *tinteled* the air and rosied Jesse's cheeks.

Conor offered, "Wanna get in the nice warm stroller, Jess?"

"No thank you. Velvet can ride." He stuffed Jane's rabbit under the wool coverlet that Dearie's Mam had loomed for her long ago. "I'll push."

But Jesse didn't push the stroller. He took off his mittens, and bent down. "Look I found another penny! I like finding these pennies!"

"Lucky you," Conor crowed.

"Dearie says it's not luck. The penny was waiting for me."

Dearie added, "Old Barret used to say that a found penny means someone is thinking of you."

"You mean, like from the Great Illuminations?" Jesse looked at the penny.

"Could be," Dearie replied, "here or there, it's nice to know someone is thinking of you, Jesse."

He put it in his pocket. "Now I have two pennies." Skipping ahead, he stopped again, hooting, "Look! Another penny!"

Putting it in his pocket, he pointed and shouted, "Oh, good g'ory! There's another penny!"

"Good *glory!*" Dearie laughed.

"Good glory!" Jesse found penny after penny after penny, all the way up the avenue. A treasure hunt of pennies. "This is like a trail. I wonder where it leads. Maybe it will take me to my disappeared grandmother." He looked up, "Dearie, is this my surprise?"

"It is a surprise. But no, my *brillish* boy, your surprise is waiting in Central Park." Dearie turned to cross the street, putting out her hand, "Come along."

But Jesse did not take her hand.

"Jesse?" Dearie and Conor whirled back, "Jesse?"

He was picking up another penny and singing, "I'm rich. I'm rich!"

Leaning on a stone building, a tattered-looking old woman watched Jesse. Her overcoat dragged on the ground and her old knit hat barely hid her scraggles of escaping hair. Jesse saw her gazing at him, and he gazed back quizically.

"Hello," he said, looking up at her with his eyes wide and glowing. "Are you…?"

The woman cut him off as she joggled Jesse by the shoulders. "I heerd y'. Y' lil sparker. Y're rich. Give an old lady some o' your loot."

Conor and Dearie darted forward, but Jesse opened his hand, offering his three copper coins.

The woman blurted, "That's it? That's all you got?" She coughed,

"I don't need any Abe Lincolns! Gimme some Thomas Jeffersons, or FDRs. Better yet, gimme George Washingtons!"

Conor started forward again, but Dearie stopped him. Jesse was looking into the woman's face saying, "I think they're magic...so I thought you were.... Well, I've only got Abe Lincoln pennies. You can have them."

The woman stared at the pennies. She stared at Jesse. Her voice softened, "Nah. They're yourn. You keep 'em." She turned, but rounded back to Jesse, "Bless you boy. Y' lil sparker." Down the alley she scuttered and disappeared into a basement door.

Jesse put his pennies in his pocket, looking at Dearie and Conor with wondering eyes. "I thought maybe that lady was my disappeared grandmother. But I guess not."

Dearie closed her eyes for a moment. *All is well.* Taking Jesse's hand, she gave it a kiss, "My Baby Grand."

Together they crossed the street and the first thing Jesse saw was...another penny.

"Somebody is really, really thinking of me!" Jesse crowed. "I hope it is my disappeared grandmother. "

Dearie smiled, "You're humming to beat the band!"

Sooner-later they entered Central Park. And there, the amazing penny trail, and Jesse, stopped.

"Um," Jesse quieted, "I think I'd like a ride. Please."

Conor chuckled, "Well, climb a'board, Mr. Toad! We'll take a wild ride!"

Jesse laughed, "Like *The Wind in the Willows*?"

"Blue ribbon, you!" Dearie smiled, covering Jesse and Velvet with the warm blanket. "But this ride is more like going into another world, especially into the woods of the Central Park Ramble."

Jesse was soon drowsy, and his eyes closed before he could see the zoo entrance, or the statue of Hans Christian Andersen with the little duckling, or the lake for the model sailboats. He was sound asleep.

Crossing to Belvedere Castle, Dearie declared, "Oh bunky-dinks! We've made it to the castle, and Mr. Love-adore is fast asleep."

Conor bent over the stroller. Jesse's eyes were shut and his mouth was open. "He looks like a puppet. Look, I can make him talk." He moved Jesse's chin up and down, saying: 'I'm not a baby! I don't need a stroller!'

It really looked like Jesse was talking, and Dearie and Conor guffawed. Jesse didn't wake, and Conor moved his chin again: 'Where's my disappeared grandmother?'

Dearie started to laugh again, but stopped.

Conor said, "Okay, not so funny. Jesse seems to be looking for her everywhere he goes."

"Jesse is searching now," Dearie acknowledged. "He's curious. I see him watching the other children with their mothers and fathers, wondering about Jane and James. And his Grandmother Jessica."

Conor muttered, "You mean his disappeared grandmother."

Dearie nodded. "Jesse truly hums with love. Overflows with love. He's looking for places to put it...like Jessica. He knows about spooling out his weaving threads. He believes. And I believe he'll puzzle her out. Just like he found all those pennies." Dearie smiled, "Jesse's a little *love-adore*. He can't help it." She lowered her voice. "But right now, I'd say he's deep, deep in his *wispy slips*."

Chapter Four

A Quest

Little Belvedere Castle seemed a true sentinel sitting atop Vista Rock, overlooking Turtle Pond and the Great Lawn.

Dearie brightened, "Let's stroller Jesse downhill. When he wakes, the first thing he'll see is the castle, rising out of the quarry rocks."

Conor stroller-ed down the hill, but the path became bumpy. Pitted. Potholed. Abruptly, the hill became much steeper than Conor counted on. The stroller took off!

"Whoaaa. Aaghhh. Oh no!" he cried out. The stroller tipped dangerously. "Oh no! It's keeling over!" Conor tried to balance it back on four wheels, but it popped off another rock and hurtled on like a non-stop rollercoaster.

Jesse was now wide-awake, hooting, "C-c-c-racker Jacks!"

"Hang on, Jess!" Conor yelled, forcefully steering down to the safe grasses of the Great Lawn. "Whoa! Whoa!" Slowly, he turned the stroller to face the Castle. "Whew!"

All at once, Jesse sounded like Grams Maguire, exclaiming with all his might, "Glory be to Heaven and fifteen saints!" He stood up in the stroller, "Oh! Oh! This is *fabulush*! *Thrill-digging*! Oh Dearie! Conor! This is the best surprise I could ever wish! A castle! A real castle!"

Jesse's heart boggled as he climbed out of the stroller. "It's Camelot! King Arthur's Castle! How did we get here?"

Dearie pointed at the castle, lifting her red cape like a flag, "It does feel like Camelot, Jesse." She let him *wonderlush* before saying, "But actually, we're still in Central Park. James and Jane liked to come up here, pretending they were the king and queen of their very own castle."

"I'd love to live here, in Jane and James' castle," Jesse gushed. "But. It's really King Arthur's castle."

"Sorry to say," Dearie informed him, "it's not King Arthur's Castle. It's not really a castle. It's a decorative structure, a 'folly', though it's called *Belvedere Castle*, Italian for *'beautiful view'*."

"*Bedivere*? Like Sir Bedivere the knight?"

"No, Jesse."

"You know!" Jesse *chatter-babbled*, "*Bedivere* gives *Exkalber* – the magic sword of King Arthur – back to the Lady of the Lake."

"No." Conor explained, "No Excalibur and no Bedivere. It's *Bel-*vedere."

"Oh." Jesse stopped.

Dearie proposed, "Would you like to go inside?"

Jesse's head went up with his eyelids. "Can we?"

Oohs, Ohhs, and *Ahhs* filled Belvedere Castle. Jesse couldn't get enough of the details: the corner tower and the lookout over the parapet walls, the stone canopied porch, arched windows, and especially, the green dragon in the top window.

Jesse was disappointed not to find King Arthur's Round Table, but they investigated the exhibit rooms with the Weather Bureau instruments (wind speed and rain gauges). Dearie said they had been operating there since 1912 "...the year Mac came to America by surviving the sinking of the *Titanic*."

Jesse studied the glass cases with the stuffed animals. "Look at the owl!" He aimed his finger, "like it's flying in the night."

"Yes, owls are nocturnal," Conor offered.

"I know owls are not turtles," Jesse answered.

Conor opened his mouth, but in his surprise, nothing came out.

Winkwhile, Jesse observed the other animals. "There's a stuffed possum! With its skeleton right beside it."

"Speaking of stuffed," Conor teased, "Time for our picnic. How 'bout on the bench under the castle portico?"

Jesse munched away, but his eyes were all over the castle crannies. "I love this castle. It's just like King Arthur." He copied an expression Mac liked to use, "It's grand!"

"Well, Jesse," Dearie tempted, "every castle must have its king." She crooked her finger to follow.

They safely walked down and around the far end of the castle pond, and Conor and Dearie heard Jesse gasp. "Oh, glory be to Cracker Jacks!"

There was the king. The magnificent king. Riding a colossal steed. His mighty arms raised high above his head. Each hand holding a sword. Slicing through the sky.

All this danced into Jesse's eyes, even when he scrunched them closed. He felt a spark, shimmering within, exploding into: *A quest! I will go to Port Haven Island. I will seek and find my disappeared grandmother!*

He opened his eyes and breathed, "My quest! I have a quest now, just like the *Knights of the Round Table*! I shall go to Port Haven Island to find my disappeared grandmother. My quest! Like King Arthur!"

"Actually, this is King Jagiello," Conor remarked, "a Polish King…"

"He's King Arthur! And the castle is Camelot!"

And that was that.

Jesse reveled in castle and king all the way home, riding in the stroller. He *blabber-gabbed* to Velvet, "I love Camelot! Merlin! And King Arthur! And his mighty sword *Ex-cal-i-bur*; the quests of the *shiver-roll-us* Knights of the Round Table: Sir Kay, Sir *Grain*, and Sir *Lance-a-lot*; ugh, the dreadly Invisible Knight, Sir Garlon; oh, and the *mystery-us* Lady of the

Lake."

Jesse looked up at Dearie and Conor, exclaiming, "I love you! I love my birthday outing! I have a quest now!" He looked at Conor, "I can use the weather instruments at Belvedere Castle to help me find her."

Conor started to object, but a policeman was standing at the corner, and Jesse began to chatter at him.

"I'm on a quest to find my grandmother. She maybe is on Port Haven Island, but no one knows for sure. Can you help me find her?"

The policeman smiled and pulled at his sleeves. "Well, we'd have to do a search for a missing person."

Jesse blurted, "She is a missing person. Can you search her?"

The policeman smiled.

"Her name is Jessica."

The traffic began to clear and Conor rolled the stroller back and forth, with the policeman saying, "I'll see what can be done. What is your name, young man?"

"Jesse. Jesse Seamus O'Neil. You can tell Sergeant Hannity about the missing search. He's the officer on our block."

The policeman tipped his hat, "I'll do that, Jesse Seamus O'Neil."

Jesse settled back into his seat and grinned. "That was great." He looked at Dearie, "That's what you mean about all weaving together. That policeman must have been waiting to weave with me. This is so great. My quest is really started."

Drawing close to the apartments, they saw a new family in the courtyard. The father was playing a game with his two sons, who looked about Jesse's age.

"Those boys must be twins," Jesse said, looking at their dark, curly hair and their smiles. "They're just the same."

Dearie observed, "I wonder if that's the new family, come to live here."

Jesse laughed. "Did you see that? The man put something on top of his head and rubbed it in—then he knocked it out of his ear. He's a magician!"

The man gave a little salute over his cheerful eyes. "Hello!" he called with a French inflection, "My name is Etienne Bonheur. Most call me Teppo."

"Oh, yes! We have been expecting you," Dearie beamed. "You will be managing Bridget's Laundry. Welcome!"

Teppo embraced his wife and boys. "These are our twin boys, Jean and Paul. And you know of my wife, Jeneva, from your long ago time with her family."

Dearie turned to Jeneva, "Yes, I knew your dear family in France, during World War I with my Mam and Da."

"Oh yes," Jeneva replied happily, also with a French accent, "I have enjoyed my family's stories about you—and your horses—many times over."

Dearie introduced Conor and Jesse. But Jesse was watching the boys, taking turns rubbing a quarter into the top of each other's head, and trying, unsuccessfully, to make it come out the ear.

Jesse looked at Mr. Bonheur, "Mr. Teppo, sir, could you show us your coin trick, please?"

"But of course," he answered, taking the quarter from Jean–or was it Paul? No matter. He deftly rubbed the quarter into his head-top and easily knocked it out of his ear.

"A-m-a-a-a-zing!" Jesse *gaspered.*

Everyone grinned, and Conor took the opportunity to say, "I hope you'll find this apartment to your liking."

"Yes," Teppo beamed, "We live in so small a place, I have to go outside to change my mind!"

Their laughter was interrupted by a honking taxicab.

"Ah," Jeneva smiled, "we must be off."

"*Bon chance!*" Teppo waved.

The O'Neil's waved farewell, calling, "See you soon."

Inside the apartment lobby, Conor chuckled, "That was a pretty good trick. Mr. Bonheur made the quarter look like it disappeared into his head. But it was really in his hand the whole time. He made us think it was in a different place."

Jesse echoed, "The disappeared quarter! In the place we didn't look."

An unexpected quiver went up Jesse's spine. Slowly, he repeated, "Disappeared. The place we didn't look." His head went up. He looked at Conor. "It really was in a different place the whole time. Maybe...that's the disappeared grandmother. Maybe she's not really where we think she is. In Port Haven."

As Conor and Dearie put away the stroller, Jesse took the apartment key and ran all the way up the stairs.

On the way, he did not notice that Velvet had fallen out of his pocket. And he did not notice that Grams Maguire had picked it up.

Chapter Five

Light on!

Jesse was bursting with—he didn't know what—but he had something bursting inside him. Entering the lumber room, he felt it popping up like a hiccup. He turned on the light switch, and it lit up the little lamp on the desktop, shining on James and Jane. Jesse's dream stared back at him, and he stood, waiting. Curious. Wondering.

Now, I have to tell you, revelations are tricky things. Ideas can float to the surface like a popping cork. Some would never give it a second look, or a second thought; while one who's Light is on just happens to see the very thing that's been looked for all along.

Jesse actually hiccupped, blurting a laugh that strangled another hiccup. He was feeling like a *Quatchkopt*. But he lingered. *Hiccup*. The little light flickered and for just a second it was very bright. He *shiveraled*, staring at it. Slowly he moved toward the light and stood in front of the desk. He felt his heart thump as he gazed at the three long drawers under the slant-top. Now he surely felt like a *Quatchkopt*, for he had not tried to open these drawers at all. *Hiccup*. He pulled the handles of the top drawer. It opened.

The smell of cedar drifted out. Jesse breathed it in as his hands felt the old quilted coverlet that belonged to James and Jane. But there was nothing else in there.

He closed that and opened the middle drawer. This time he smelled something else. Lavender. Like the lavender behind Mac's garden. Inside were his old baby clothes and baby blankets. But nothing else.

Jesse knelt down and opened the last drawer. Scrap books and photograph folders. He had seen these before. The pictures were all of himself. Photos Conor had taken with Galen's old camera. Dearie had been saving these for him since he was born. He lifted the scrapbooks one at a time. One for each year. With the last one, a cardboard folder fell forward. This was something he had not seen. He pulled it out and opened it.

At the top of the paper was one word: *Island*. Below that, neatly inked printing flowed down the page with watercolor drawings of flying seagulls and high, puffy clouds, a lighthouse with a little black peak, sitting on a rocky shore, a sail boat, and two different kinds of boats. At the bottom was written the name Jane Danielle.

"Jane Danielle." Jesse whispered. "Jane…? Dan-yell? This is Jane's," he said out loud. "This is her island."

Ah, how the Light seeks. The Light reveals, in more and more Light.

Jesse stood up with the island poem and put it under the light. Carefully, he read it. He didn't know every word, but his imagination let loose, filling in with pictures of rocks and waves and docks and birds, sails and sunsets and starry nights.

Here be the island,
yours and mine,
Earth's child,
enchanted for all Time.
Her heart beats on in ancient rocks
that keep their watch o'er ocean lines.

She's resolute, of plucky stock,
a refuge for the harbor docks
where canvas sails
may tack and fly
with silver shadow
seabirds flocks.

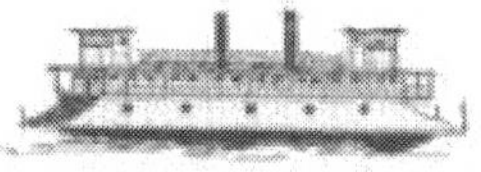

Such charms she lends in every sigh,
her calloused beauty chaps the sky;
as, come what may, the winded Four
blow salt sray rosing lullabies.

Here be the island's sunset lore,
Here her starry nights that pour
their deep sea dreams upon her shore.

In reveries she waits for me...
... is waiting still,
and always
will.

Jane Danielle

Jesse's eyes stopped. He breathed. He stared at the words. *The words.* He traced them with his finger. *The words are in shapes. The words make a pattern. Puzzle pieces of words. Jane's shapes.*

He had to find Dearie.

"Dearie…?" he called walking down the hallway. "Dearie?"

"Jesse, I'm in the kitchen," she called back.

"I found something. I think I found Jessica."

Dearie wiped her hands on her apron and looked at Jesse. "What do you have there?" She moved next to him. "Oh. My. This belonged to your mother Jane. She wrote it and painted the pictures."

"I know. I think this is her island. Do you see it? In the words?"

"Do you want me to read it to you, Jesse? It's a lovely poem."

"No. Yes. I mean…look. See the shapes? The words make a shape."

"What? Do they? Let me see."

Jesse pointed, with his little fingers outlining the shapes he could see so clearly. "See…? It's the shape of the island…."

Dearie gasped. "Oh. Oh, Jesse! I see it. I do! The words make a map! You are right! It's a map of Jane's Island! And it's not Port Haven! It's…it's Elizabethtown!"

What is real, you ask. The things you can touch?

More often it's the things you can't. Like jumping for joy.

Their apartment jumped with joy and thrilled with excitement. Dearie hugged Jesse, "Oh, Light on! You are my *brillish* boy!" Jesse beamed up at Dearie, and she *gaspered*, "Why! You! You have the very look of my old friend, Elliot. My! You are full of surprises!"

Conor appeared then, asking, "What's all this hullabaloo?"

"Conor! Conor!" Jesse ran to him. "We found Jessica!"

"What?" Conor stopped cold.

"We found Jessica! She's in Elizabethtown! Not Port Haven!"

Dearie rushed to her bedroom office and returned with her stationery box and a copy of her last letter to the Port Haven Town Hall. She had written to them countless times asking for information about Jessica and her farm. Now she sat down at the kitchen table while Jesse and Conor watched her every written word. She copied most of the letter, but this time, it was to Elizabethtown. After she read it out loud, Conor addressed the envelope, Jesse licked the stamp, and all three of them fairly flew down the steps to post it at the corner mailbox.

Dearie offered another spoonerism for Jesse. "I'll let you *mend the sail*, Jesse."

Jesse translated without missing a step: "Ok, I'll *send the mail*."

Conor laughed, "You're getting too good at these spoonerisms, Jesse!" He gave him a boost to pop their letter into the mail slot. And they dashed back inside the warm apartments.

Jesse *widdly-skiddled* ahead of Conor and Dearie to find Mac and Bridget. When Bridget opened the door, Jesse saw her light blue eyes, magnified like marbles, through her clear eyeglasses that seemed to float on her face. Her hands went to her wrinkled cheeks as she greeted him with fun surprise.

"Oh, here's the birthday boy!"

Jesse liked her welcome hug, and he exclaimed, "Mrs. Mac! You and Mac have to come upstairs with me! You have to hear what we did! And what we found!"

Mac stood up and yanked his wool vest down, smiling, with his long teeth shining like ivory piano keys. "Howdy do, Jesse. Here we are. And here we come."

Dearie stopped to ask for milk and she and Bridget went to the kitchen. But Mac was dragged up the stairs to the tune of Jesse's non-stop

Island and Arthurian enthusiasms.

Mac and Bridget gladly settled on the comfy sofa with her plumpness nestled into his bony shoulder. Their silver hair seemed to shine with their eyes as they listened and watched Jesse showing off his map discovery and the details of his special day.

"My, Jesse," Bridget complimented, "You are one clever boy."

Mac grinned and finally said, "By japers, Jesse! You have more words in y' than a library."

"I remembered King Arthur. The quests." Jesse spun on, "I'm going to go on a quest to find my disappeared grandmother. I hope Jessica's not *horrifull*—like Sir Garlon, the Invisible Knight."

Bridget said, "It may be that Jessica has a mystery hanging about her, but I'll bet you a doughnut hole she's a Lady of Light. Like Jane."

Jesse hugged her. "Then, I am going on a quest. I'll find her Light for sure!"

"You'll find her a lot easier," Mac added, "if you stop calling her 'disappeared'. Think on the words you use, Jesse. You don't want her to be disappeared."

"Ohhh," Jesse stopped. "Oh. Well, I'll call her Jessica. Lady Jessica? Yes. That sounds like a quest. I'll call her Lady Jessica from now on."

Mac's head went up and down, "Done and done, Jesse."

"Mac," Dearie came into the room beaming, "do you remember, on the train, traveling out of Russia? The old Chinese gentleman?"

Bridget hummed, "I remember that story: the Chinese gentleman, who taught you one hundred thousand miracles."

"Precisely," Dearie beamed. "He told us: 'Find in each day, one hundred thousand miracles.'" Dearie looked at Jesse. "I'm finding such miracles! I thought I knew how to dance with life. But this is a whole new dance."

Mac leaned forward, "Yep. I recall, the Chinaman told us a bunch of wisdom, like: 'There is not one simple note in a symphony that makes it so. There is not one step in a dance. There is not one moment in a child. It is in the flow. Therein lies the magic.'"

Dearie nodded in agreement, "Yes! It's all so much…."

"More," Mac finished. "Life is more. The Baby Grands are teaching us, 'cuz they still know their Light. It's all about the Light—keeping your Light on—as bright as the stars—every time y' choose joy."

"And appreciation, too," Bridget said and patted Jesse's knees, saying wistfully,"I'm still learning. To choose feeling good instead of bad. Life is meant to be glee. And miracles. Just like the Baby Grands."

Jesse spoke up again, "I'd like a miracle."

Conor poked in, "A miracle quest?"

"No," Jesse said sincerely. "I want a miracle to have Jane and James here. Not dead. Then I'd have a real mother and father. And we could go on a quest to visit the disappeared, I mean, the Lady Jessica. They'd know where she is."

A silence *gushered* into the room until Mac said, "It doesn't matter who is here or who is not here, Jesse. It's all up to you. You'll always have a quest. It's your life journey. It's how you go. And more important, it's how you grow."

Conor brought in the tea tray and Dearie set out the mugs and plates.

Jesse asked Mac another question, "I wonder if King Arthur's Avalon is like the Great Illuminations? Oh, and I want to know, what is the mystery-us Disappearing Black Gang Sheen?"

"What?" Mac piqued, "Who told you about Blackgang Chine?

"Grams Maguire told me," Jesse answered Mac. "She says my other Grandmother isn't in the *Great Illuminations*. She says I'll never find her 'cause she's *traptured* in the disappearing Black Gang Sheen. Do you know it, Mac?"

Mac nodded.

"Tell me the story!"

"Ready for some magic, are you?" Mac grinned. "Well, fact is, Grams left out an important word: village. It's known as the disappearing *village* of Blackgang Chine."

Jesse *quiver-quavered*, "Spooky! Grams says, 'it's like a dark, dark room.'"

"Not spooky," Mac twitched. "It's a real place. You see, back when we were still traveling with our gypsy caravan, Dearie was just a little lass. And she met a beautiful, talented lady, who called herself Mrs. Alberta Campbell. It turned out, she was really Queen Victoria's daughter, the Princess Louisa. But she didn't like all the royal folderol, so she had us call her plain old Berta. She was dead on."

"She was dead?" Jesse gulped.

Dearie tittered, "Dead on means she was so fine."

"Anyway," Mac snickered, "Berta and Dearie became fast friends, even though there was a big age difference. Berta could have been Dearie's grandmother, and accordingly, she thought Dearie was the cream of the buttery!"

"What's a buttery?" Jesse interrupted.

Bridget smiled, "It's an old fashioned word for a pantry."

"Anyway," Mac rustled, "that's how we got invited to Queen Victoria's home on the Isle of Wight in England. It was Christmas, 1897."

"That's sooo oldy-the-hill," Jesse giggled with wide eyes.

Mac smiled, "I was twelve and Dearie was seven."

Bridget added, "Queen Victoria invited them to present their Christmas Revels to her whole Royal family at Osborne House."

Dearie smiled, "While we were there, we got to *whirly-wander* all over the island."

"I'd like to take an adventure like that! But..." Jesse's hands went up, "what is the *disappearing* part?"

"Well. A *chine* is a cliff or a ravine," Mac explained, "It's made of muddy black rock that sometimes gets so wet that it turns into a landslide. It's been known to take a house or two with it. They just disappear."

"Danger-us...."

"Well, the village is still there, and a fairgrounds, too. It sits along the *gang*, which means a path or walking way. Oh, we had a *cracker pet* day there."

Jesse looked at Dearie for a translation.

"*Cracker* means spectacular," she smiled, "*pet* means unseasonably warm."

Mac continued, "The fairgrounds were closed up when we visited. Our old friend Elliot was there doin' research with his father, and he showed us a cave. Filled with bats!"

Jesse giggled, "Maybe they were playing baseball! Get it? Bats!"

Dearie muffled a laugh, "Oh Jesse, my *Quatchkopf*."

But Mac tittered with a grin, "It was a grand day."

"But why did Grams say my other grandmother is there?" Jesse puzzled.

Conor spoke, "It's the *disappearing* part. No matter how we've tried, we can't find your other grandmother." He shrugged, "It's as if Jessica's disappeared."

"Oh," Jesse reckoned, "the Disappearing Grandmother. Like the Lady of the Lake." His voice went spooky, "She goes down under the water. You see her hand, and then, she disappears." He looked at them, "I'm not sure how I'm going to find my disappeared, I mean. Lady Jessica. Maybe I'll ask everyone I know about Jane and Jessica."

Mac leaned back, "You just keep your Light on Jesse. You'll find her. Even in the dark."

Chapter Six

Jesse's Song

Jesse jumped. "Someone's at the door!" He ran to open it.

"Happy Birthday, Jesse!" It was the three Schuyler girls, the only little girls in the apartments. Their family was from the Netherlands, and they were affectionately called the 'Dutchies'.

Jesse looked at them, standing in their crisply-ironed dresses, with their pale, golden hair shimmering over their clear, blue-gray eyes. Annika started to speak, but Jesse interrupted her. "Do you girls remember Jane?"

They looked at Jesse. They looked at each other. Annika, nine years old, held out a plate of cookies. "We made these for your birthday, Jesse."

Marijke, who was eight, pushed the plate into Jesse's hands, "Unh-huh, see, oatmeal with raisins and walnuts."

Elke, who was only a month older than Jesse, said, "We hope you like them, Jesse."

Jesse was surprised to receive such a gift. A whole plate of his favorite cookies. All for him.

Maybe not.

Dearie spoke up, "Just in time for tea."

Jesse shrugged and added the cookies to the low tea table as he and the Schuyler girls sat on the floor around it. Annika picked up Dearie's metal mug with the glass jar inside. "I like this design," She traced the trinity knot pattern of three intertwining circles.

Mac said, "That's the *Triquetra*, the unending, weaving circles of the universe. Eternal. Connected. Dearie's Da had the tinker make these mugs with that trinity knot design. But that was *yonks* and *yonks* ago."

Jesse leaned toward the girls and said, "*Yonks* means a real long time ago."

The girls nodded, but Marijke's brain was scanning something else.

"*Trichinosis*," she blurted "A disease you get from eating bad pig."

Dearie squelched a smile, knowing that Marijke often blurted out medical words she learned from her father's work in his drugstore. "You mean that the *Triquetra* reminds you of the word *Trichinosis*."

Marijke looked gratefully at Dearie, but changed directions, saying to Jesse, "Mama told us Jane was very beautiful, like a princess from a storybook."

Elke added, "Mama always said Jane looked like Cinderella. When she went to the ball. Not when she was in rags."

Annika came up with her two cents, "Once I asked Mama how old Jane was. She didn't say, but she said Jane told her that *her* mama, Jessica, was real young-like."

"Ohh," Jesse murmured, "so Lady Jessica's not *oldy-the-hill*. That's good."

Dearie sashayed to the Victrola to put on the Nat King Cole record, *The Nature Boy*.

Jesse smiled, "That's my song!"

"What do you mean, your song?" Annika frowned.

Marijke asked, "How can it belong to you?"

Mac smiled, taking a cookie, "I remember this story. It's a good-un."

"Is it a long story?" Annika asked.

Mac laughed through the cookie crumbs, and Bridget said, "He's

Irish. He has no idea how to make a long story short."

The grownups chuckled, and the Dutchies pleaded, "Tell us the story!"

Mac nodded. "Well, you just said the four words that ask for magic: *Tell me a story.*" Mac smiled, "And there are four more magic words to begin the story: *Once upon a time....*"

"Ohhh..." the girls sighed, with magic already filling their eyes.

"So," Mac began. "Here it is...and here it goes.

"Once upon a time, there was a wondrous music composer named Antonin Dvořák. This song comes from his music *yonks* and *yonks* back. We met him after his magnificent concert in Vienna where he conducted his New World Symphony, full of dancing jigs and haunted yearnings.

"Now, I didn't know Dvorak from a Jabberwock..."

"Oh! I love the Jabberwocky!" Jesse perked. "In *Alice in Wonderland. Callooh-Callay!*"

The girls laughed, but Conor smirked, looking under his eyebrows, "Jesse, let Mac tell the story."

And Jesse yielded, "Oh, okay."

Dearie winked and whispered to Jesse, "I love the Jabberwocky, too."

"So, in Vienna, with Dvořák," Mac continued. "Dearie was only eight, but she played violin with Dvořák's conservatory students, and Dvorak himself. One of the pieces was the "Dumka" from his piano-violin quintet."

Dearie interrupted, "It is a trilling, thrilling melody. It brought me and Galen O'Neil together. Quite romantic. Back in 1916, onboard a transport ship in World War I. The war, not so romantic. Dvořák, mmm."

Mac muffled his agreement, but Conor looked under his eyebrows at Dearie.

"Oh," Dearie realized, "back to the story. Mac?"

Mac rubbed his knees.

"Well, that's pretty much it. Jesse's song is part of the spooling, weaving energies. You see, the notes flowed through Time—as music always does—from Dvořák to Dearie; then to Galen and Dearie. Then the notes went rippling through Life, until they were written with new notes, as *The Nature Boy* song: the notes are similar in the *Dumka* and the *Nature Boy*. Well, that was just the moment when Jane was expecting baby Jesse. Then Jesse was born, and the song was recorded by Nat King Cole. Dearie changed a few of the words to fill 'em with Light. So it was—it is—Jesse's Song."

Jesse crowed, "And on my quest, I am going to *travel very far, very far, over land and sea*...and I will find the Lady Jessica."

Dearie put on the song again. Mac got up, holding out his hand to Bridget, and they waltzed around the parlor, while Dearie and Conor sang in harmony. Jesse tootled his penny whistle, and the girls bounced up, dancing in a circle, swaying and twirling round and round.

There was a boy, a beautiful enchanted boy
They say he Travelled very far, very far, over land and sea
Bright of eye, and never shy, and very wise was he.

And then one day, one magic day, he passed my way
And while we spoke of many things, fools and kings,
This he said to me:

Jesse sang with them:

The greatest thing you'll ever learn
Is just to love and be loved in return.

The story and the song ended and the tea tray was empty. Dearie glanced at her 'NOW' clock and announced, "Time, Mr. Birthday Boy! Off to your snuggery!" She looked at the girls, and laughed lightly, "And as for you darling girls, your time is up. Go home and tell your mother she wants you!"

The Schuyler girls looked perplexed, but they departed with many 'Thanks,' filling the air.

Jesse waved, saying, "Thanks for your cookies. And thanks for telling me about Jane. *Eye ball!*

Excitedly, Marijke turned back, "Eyeball? Like dry eye? Or sty eye?"

Jesse laughed. "No, Dr. Marijke, *eyeball.* It's a spoonerism!"

"A what?" Annika perked.

"A spoonerism game Dearie and I play. We switch the beginning of the words. *Eye ball* really means, *Bye, all!*"

Elke Ohhh-ed and clapped her hands delightedly. All the way down the stairs the girls giggled and waved, "Eye ball! Eye ball!"

Jesse turned around, "Mac? Bridget? Will you put me to bed and story-tell me?"

They smiled, and Bridget answered, "That's an easy yes."

In the quiet of the kitchen, Conor and Dearie cleaned up the dishes while Gypsy the cat took turns *twirly-purring* around their legs. Conor chuckled, "That Jesse! You never know what's in that head of his!"

Dearie snickered, "Jesse's quest has me remembering that Jane wanted to call him Jesse James."

"Like the outlaw, Jesse James?" Conor baffled.

"Precisely." Dearie elaborated, "Jesse for her mother, Jessica. And James for James. I told her that would never do. Jesse James! So I told her, Seamus means James in Irish and *voila*! Jesse Seamus."

"Blue ribbon, you!" Conor smiled, copying her expression.

Dearie rambled, "Jane said, maybe Jessica would let her come home with her baby if he was named after her."

"What?" Conor bewildered, soaping the dish.

Gypsy prowled away, as Dearie swallowed, ruefully replying, "Well, you know Jane married James without her mother's approval. But, actually, it was a bit worse." Dearie stopped and touched Conor's arm. "You're going to rub the blue paint off that dish if you don't stop."

Conor stared at the suds, "After all this time, and all our attempts to get to Jessica. What else is in this mystery?"

Dearie explained, "This is about all Jane's letters that she wrote to her mother. They were all returned to Jane. Her mother never opened them."

"How wretched for Jane!"

Dearie nodded, putting the dishes in the cupboard. "I wish I knew where Jane hid the letters. They'd at least give us Jessica's name and address."

Conor murmured, "Maybe she threw them away."

"May be. Nevertheless, you may as well know, Jessica's last words to Jane were severe: 'If you marry that boy, do not ever come back. Ever.'"

"Oh. Great Wall of China!" Conor closed his eyes. "What a monster!"

"*Rule of Tongue.* No name-calling." Dearie's eyebrows arched decidedly, "We don't know Jessica's reasons."

"Hmm, you're right. Jane obviously loved her. If only we could find Jessica."

Dearie sat with both elbows on the table and her chin on her hands, "That's *Lady* Jessica. And I...have a thought."

The kitchen light seemed to glow brighter and Conor sighed with relief. "Good. A Dearie thought."

"I propose—as Jesse said—a quest. We go to Elizabethtown. To find Jane's mother. You. Me. Jesse."

"When?"

"How about tomorrow?

"Tomorrow! Really?" Conor was astonished. "I don't know. It's a long, tough trip. It'll take two days. And once we get there, we have nothing to go on. No information. Jane was so secretive. Even after all these years we know nothing of Jessica."

"Right," Dearie agreed, "even on the marriage registry, Jane used the last name, Daniel."

Conor shook his head, "That was obviously fake. So even if Jessica is in Elizabethtown, we still have no last name. No address."

Dearie went on, "No. All my Port Haven letters, telegrams, newspaper queries; they garnered absolutely no information. But I feel Jesse has started a new ball rolling. Something's in the air. Let's get up to Elizabethtown and try to find her in person."

Conor perked up, "Hey, maybe we can go to the lumberyard at T.J. O'Farrel's. I know it's in Port Haven, but I'm pretty sure that's where James first met Jane. Maybe somebody there could give us a clue."

Dearie put her hands together on the table, "That sounds like a good start. I say we get up there, investigate her whereabouts, and show up on her doorstep. Bewitch her with Jesse. Her Baby Grand!"

"He's not a baby anymore," Conor murmured, "Six years. Too long. For gosh-all-sakes. Jessica doesn't even know Jane is dead."

"We have to start somewhere. And we have the time right now, which will not soon be the case."

Conor nodded, "Right. Once your theater starts up, Dearie, and I start my classes and lessons and jobs, our schedules will be full-up." He sat down across from Dearie. "Okay. But we'll need money for train and bus fare and a hotel." He looked at Dearie, "Golly, are there hotels in Elizabethtown? Because we don't have a free place to stay since Aunt Claire and Uncle Conn died."

Dearie nodded, "We'll find out. As for money, I still have some set aside from the sale of Conn and Claire's house. Money may be tight"—she smiled—"but the show always goes on."

"Okay, I won't argue." Conor teased. "I know your hummings and weavings, and what you can conjure out of absolutely nothing." He laughed, "I'm on board. This is exciting. We'll take the train tomorrow."

Mac came into the kitchen looking tuckered. "Bridget and I are headin' home. But sorry to say, Jesse's still awake. Velvet's missing."

A hunt for Jesse's stuffed bunny ensued. Even Gypsy scoured the apartment. Finally, Conor snapped his fingers, "The stroller. I'll go down and check."

Jesse stood on his bed with his eyes closed and his arms raised above his head, like the statue of the King in Central Park.

"Ah, my little King," Dearie quiped, "You're on the right track. Light on. Highest and best thoughts." She handed him her stone.

He warmed it in his hands and smiled. "When I hold your stone I hear my song in my head…*the greatest thing…*"

Dearie's eyes twinkled back at him. "Old Barret gave me that stone." She sat on the bed and Jesse sat down with her. "Old Barret…" she sighed. "I can hear him telling me, 'the earth has had its turn with this stone. It is filled with the sun, the wind and the rain…cold and heat. And me. Now it is your turn to fill it with your wondrous energies.'"

"I feel it, Dearie."

"You know, Jesse," she assured him, "nothing is ever lost. It's somewhere. Just waiting to be found."

"Like Jane's map! And my disappeared, I mean Lady Jessica. She's somewhere. Maybe waiting to be found, too."

"Like your pennies."

"Thirty-nine pennies!" Jesse beamed. "Mac and Bridget and I counted. By ones, by tens, and my favorite, by twos: two, four, six, eight, ten—start all over again!"

Dearie smiled, "Jesse, you revel in numbers. They're like your puzzles and games and riddles." She sat back on her elbow, "You have a magic in you, Jesse. It's real. Your real magic is your Light. To be the Light. No matter what life tosses your way. Be the Light. Spooling and weaving happy-joy-fun-laughing and loving."

Jesse looked into Dearie's eyes. "I like the way you say that...and your eyes go all shiney."

Dearie's eyes twinkled. "That, my darling Jesse, is the Light of out human-to-human connections. It tells us: Yes! Be here. Be now. Be present."

"With me!"

Dearie leaned forward, touching her nose to Jesse's. "Yes, with you." She leaned back a bit, adding, "Whoever you're with! My Mam and Da always told me, 'Our Inner Light lets us use our ancient Imprints.' That means the deep impressions all human beings have." She let a little burst of smiling breath escape her lips and her eyes flickered.

"What...?" Jesse spurted out. "Why are you smiling like that?

Dearie tittered, "Oh I was thinking of our walk through Central Park, back in the Spring, when we came upon the little ducklings marching along behind their mother."

Jesse smiled, "You mean they learned to march like that from their mama duck?"

"Precisely! That's the imprinting...that goes way back to the dawn of human beings: First, whenever a baby is born, we look into our baby's eyes...and...our baby looks back! Through the windows of the soul! Second, we touch...together, and a thrill of pure knowing goes through us both. Third, we embrace, in our full, electric, human connection!'

Jesse's shoulders twitched in a little *shiveral.* "Your eyes just got extra shiney!"

"Indeed," Dearie titled her head, "You see, Jesse, we carry these imprints with us throughout our lifetime, in the beautiful bond of parent and child."

"Or"—Jesse nodded—"grandmother. You and me."

Dearie embraced Jesse and they both smiled and sighed. A silence flurried into the room and Jesse picked up his birthday music box, turning the handle. "Twinkle Little Star" plinked along with Jesse and Dearie's smiles. As the last note hummed in their ears, a familiar voice interrupted.

"Triumph!"

It was Conor standing in the doorway. He flashed a big grin, and with a grand flourish, he produced Velvet right under Jesse's nose.

"Velvet!" Jesse squealed, hugging his bunny, kissing its tattered little black nose. "You got found. Maybe you can help me find Lady Jessica."

"More like Gypsy can help you," Conor explained. "Gypsy's the one that found Velvet. She kept pawing at the Maguire's door, so I knocked there.

Grams said, 'No, they hadn't seen Velvet,' but Liam looked in their catch-all-basket and pulled your Velvet out of the blue."

"Ohhh," Jesse drowsed, "Thank you, Gypsy. I'll thank Grams and Liam tomorrow." His head melted into his pillow.

Relieved, Conor turned out Jesse's lamp and left the room, but Dearie stood for a moment at Jesse's window, wondering about lost things. *The lost grandmother, Jessica.* She smiled, *soon to be found.*

She could see her breath fogging the windowpane and she hummed to herself, *hmmm, winter....* Her Mam's voice floated through her memories in an old song, and she swayed with the melody as snatches of lyrics found their way into her musings:

'Winter–you with your cold weather. Short days, long nights.... You. And I. Together. Let us find the heart that melts the frost, the soul that lights the stars.'

Find the heart...Jessica, she reflected. *Soon. Tomorrow!* Looking up through the window pane, she searched for the stars. But peering through the glass, she did not find the stars. She couldn't believe her eyes! Large, feathery crystals of snow were wafting through the dark air.

Oh no.

Part Two

Winter

A snow fall,
much like your life,
is made up
of billions upon billions
of glitters.

Chapter Seven

Glistenings

All night the snow conspired with the darks and partnered with the wind, blowing into whirls of thick, white banks. By early morning it was still a whiteout.

Jesse padded to the kitchen, marveling, "Dearie, Conor, it's snowing!"

Conor declared, "Yup. It's a blizzard, for sure. The radio says we're getting a huge dump of snow. Everything's shut down all over the coast."

"I smell chocolate," Jesse said. It reminded him of Jane.

Dearie was stirring a pot on the stove. "Snow and hot chocolate go together," she smiled. "Jesse you go wash up and dress while it cools off."

She turned to Conor and sighed, "Well, that's that. No Elizabethtown today."

"No travel all week. Man-o-man." He put down his book. "Dearie, this is crazy. Think of all our canceled trips to Port Haven."

"Hmmm," Dearie blew on the hot chocolate, "When Jane was first pregnant with Jesse, we wanted to go with her and James, but she was too sick to make the trip. Then James…died. Then Jane." She stopped. Took a deep breath. "Hmmm. And after Jesse was born, another trip was kiboshed when you got pneumonia and ended up in hospital."

Conor frowned, "Seriously Dearie, sometimes I think Grams Maguire is right: Mother Nature conspires against us and we are cursed. These last six years we've canceled trips because of freezing rain, then the incredible flood, and that hurricane of a Nor' Easter. Now this blizzard. It's a curse."

Dearie shrugged, "I wouldn't go that far. It reminds me of my weaving loom. We've got our long, stable *warp* threads out, now we're looking for Jessica's horizontal *woof* threads, weaving under and over ours."

Conor joked, "*Warp* and *woof*. Hah! Trouble is, there's no barking from Jessica's side."

Dearie slid her gold locket back and forth on its chain. "Nothing we can do right now."

Conor murmured, "No. But it's crazy."

When the blizzard blew itself out, a world of white beckoned. Snow swirled through the courtyard in high, crested drifts. It disappeared the steps, and turned the street into a deep river of white. The lamplights looked like white scarecrows and the fire hydrant like a curious little snowman peeking out of a pure white blanket.

Dearie brought out a set of large, round, wooden trays and showed Jesse the handgrips on the sides.

"These will make great slides for the snow banks!"

Jesse didn't know what she meant but it sounded like fun. On the way downstairs, he stopped at the Maguires, and to his surprise, Billy answered the door.

"Billy!" Jesse exclaimed, hugging him.

Billy saw familiar sparks squirting out of Jesse's turquoise-flecked eyes. "Jesse," Billy whispered, "I saw Angel Jane...."

"I know! Me, too! Wasn't it the greatest?" Jesse hopped, "Wanna go sledding with us? Dearie says we'll have a *brillish* time of it!"

Liam came to the door. "Sledding? Count me in!"

Billy grinned, "Well, me too!"

They opened the lobby side door and Conor helped Jesse sit on a tray, cheering, "Hold on, Jess!"

A shriek of surprise blared out of Jesse as he whizzed down the white hill and across the courtyard, with Billy right behind him, yelling, "Holy mackeral fanny!" Then Liam gave it a try, letting loose with a long "Whoo-hoo!" and sliding so fast he had to jump off before he ran into Bridget's Laundry.

Laughter filled the air and Gypsy couldn't resist, popping out the door. But she instantly sank into the snow up to her chin. *Meooow!* She yowled like a little banshee. Jesse plowed back through the snow to save her, and she scuttled inside to watch from the window.

Jesse and Billy slid down again and again, and their squeals brought out the other children: Joey Romano, who was Billy's age, and his little brother Mikey, older than Jesse by a few months, but smaller than Jesse by a few inches. Also, the Gorecki boys, Andros, nine, and Danek, seven, came out; their father, Seph Gorecki, came out too, bellowing 'Hallooo' in his deep voice. He was a mountain of a man, and his boys liked to tell Jesse that their name, Gorecki, meant mountain in Polish.

They all took turns with Dearie's trays, whizzing down the ramps of snow. Soon Siobhan and the little Dutchies came out to join in: the snow rides and snowmen, snow angels, and snowballs, rolling in the white stuff till their cheeks were wet and rosey.

Dearie looked at Jesse and took out her hanky. "Jesse," she laughed a spoonerism, "*Know your blows.*"

He stopped in his snow tracks and grinned. "I get it, *Blow your nose!*"

As he swiped away, he heard Sergeant Hannity's "Hello!" and Jesse turned to slump through the snow towards him.

"Sergeant Hannity! I met a policeman at Central Park and he told me you can do a search for a missing person."

"Yes, I found a note in my box about your search for your grandmother." He pulled his scarf down, "Now Jesse, we work in New York City. Far as I know, your grandmother is from way up, along the New England coast. We can't do much about that. Your best clues are in what you already know about your grandmother." Sergeant Hannity saw Jesse's face go down at the mouth, and he encouraged, "Put your clues together, Jesse."

"Well, I already found out, she lives on an island called Elizabethtown...."

"That's what I'm talking about. Each thing you know or find out is another clue. It's just like all the single snowflakes that make up all this snow."

He bent down and took a handful of snow, throwing it into the air with the sparkling flecks showering Jesse.

Jesse laughed with his eyes hopping from one glittering snow crystal to another to another. "Snow clues," he cried.

"That's the spirit, Jesse." Sergeant Hannity waved and tromped away.

Jesse and Billy noticed the big snowdrift at Mac's garden and there Liam helped carve out an open snow fort. Jesse liked lying inside, looking up at the snow-laden branches of the oak tree swaying above him.

Liam poked in his head, "Whatcha thinkin', me boyo?"

"Oh, Liam," Jesse sat up, "Did you know Jessica? Jane's mother?"

Leaning against the snow wall, Liam puffed, "Nope. Never met 'er. Jane wasn't from here. James met her in a busy little port city, up north along the coast, called Port Haven."

"Yes, but I found out she's really from another island, called Elizabethtown."

"Elizabethtown?" Liam was surprised. "That's an island across the bay from Port Haven. Elizabethtown's a beautiful place, but it's not got much to say for itself. Just military forts, fishermen, and farmers."

Liam's cheeks rose up in a smile that looked like a snowman, as he recollected, "The summer when James first met Jane, I knew he was up-in-the-clouds in love. They hit it off the minute they met at the Port Haven Yacht Club. Turned out, they both loved to sail. By autumn, James was making all sorts of alibis to get back to Port Haven, like he had a special wood-crafting project with his uncle Conn. But really, he just wanted to see Jane again."

"And did he?"

"O' course. James'd meet Jane at the yacht club, hoist the sails on his catboat, and off they'd go." Liam stared off, "I never thought Jane'd be from Elizabethtown. All she told us was she lived on a farm with her ma."

"So, how did she learn to sail on a farm?

Liam chuckled, "Those two islands, Port Haven and Elizabethtown, have a perfect little bay in between them. Plenty of opportunity for sailing."

All at once, Liam ducked. "Uh-oh! Incoming! Snowballs!"

The blizzard switched off the city but good, shutting down the trolleys, buses, and trains. It nixed all work and plans for most of the week. The apartment street was closed to traffic, and all the families came out to clear the snow from the sidewalks.

But digging out the city roadways was slow, slow work. Like a snail riding a turtle. Then, since there was nowhere to put all the snow, huge hills of it were piled up at the avenue corners.

⁂

One morning, Joey Romano came speeding into the courtyard, yelling, "Come on! Bring your saucers! Wait till you see what's down at the avenue!"

It was a mountain of snow. Their eyes went up. And up. Staring at the icy white behemoth.

"Good gravy on toast!" Billy gushed.

"It's past the second floor of our grocery!" Joey hooted.

Jesse ohhhed, "C-rack-er Jacks!"

Holding up his saucer, Andros shouted, "Let's go!"

But the traffic light changed, and a rush of cars sped up the avenue, skimming the edge of the snow mountain.

"Whoa! Too dangerous!" Billy shouted, "We can't slide here!"

"Rats!" Joey blurted. "Rats, rats, rats!"

Jesse knew Billy was worried: the speeding traffic on the other side made him nervous and he kept saying, "Watch it. Stay back."

Jesse said nothing. His face felt the sun. He saw sunlight spreading through the glistening mountain of snow. Warm. Bright. He remembered the Lights from New Year's Eve, thinking—*I can see my Lights! Even in the daytime!*

He knew, inside, he was safe. And he knew there was a mountain of fun waiting in the Light.

"Look," Jesse pointed, "we can slide on the other side just fine!"

"Yeah!" Mikey Romano shouted.

"Let's go!" Andros shouted again. The Gorecki boys had new snow saucers from their hardware store: *Flexible Flyers.* They couldn't wait to spin down that mountain of snow.

"Come on, Danek, we'll be trail blazers!"

The boys kicked in footholds as they went up and up. At the top they stomped out a rough platform…and…they zoomed…whizzed… zipped! *Blisterquick*! Down, down, down! Like saucer-rockets at a carnival! Their whoops and shrieks sent the others climbing up, and streaking down, hurtling, one after another.

The Dutchies appeared with their trays, ready for the snow ride, but Joey stood in their way. "No girls. It's too steep. You'll never make it up. And it's too fast going down."

Annika and Marijke started to argue, but Elke turned and scrambled up like a little goat. The two older sisters closed their mouths and opened their arms, calling, "Wait for us, Elke!" Up they climbed, and down they streaked, screaming with glee, "S-s-s-u-u-u-p-e-r! Super-super-duper!"

It was!

Jesse couldn't believe how fast it was. "This is grand!" he crowed, and he couldn't help thinking: *Like my quest! I'll slide! All the way to Elizabethtown!*

For the best ride of all, Andros and Danek let the others try out their metal *Flexible Flyer* saucers, and over and over, they rocketed down.

Crowded together at the top, their trays and saucers bounced off each other. Marijke yelled down at Annika, lying on the snow at the bottom, "Here I come! Get out of the way!"

Annika rolled over, "Come and get me, Marijke!" She teased, "Sister-itis!"

Marijke yelled back, medically, "That's *cystitis!*"

Elke pointed, "Look at Annika! She's lying in her winter bed with sheets of ice and blankets of snow!"

Andros traded goofs with the Dutchies: "The snow is so ice-y! It's s-kid stuff," And he flew off the mountain.

Joey joined in, hopping up and down, yelling, "My feet are so cold. I'm BRRRfooted!"

Kneeling, waiting his turn, Jesse was mesmerized by the sun in the glistening snow. The light inside the crystals. Shining. It reminded him of something...something he had seen... some-where.

Behind Jesse, Mikey Romano sat on Danek's saucer. He was raring to go, making engine-revving noises and shifting his weight back and forth. Jesse turned and, unexpectedly, he saw the saucer go into a slow slide. Backward! Down. To the traffic rush!

"Help!" Mikey screeched.

Jesse stretched, grabbing at the saucer handle. "Hold on, Mikey!"

Mikey grabbed Jesse's arm, but the saucer kept sliding.

"H-e-l-p!" Mikey wailed.

All at once Jesse slid off, too, tumbling on top of Mikey. The saucer slipped out from under them, skidding down on its own, bumping over the chunky ice. Straight down to the speeding traffic.

Clinging to each other, the boys slid helplessly after the saucer. Jesse had a sense of flying, and he shut his eyes, feeling the rushing sensation.

Bright Lights swirled behind Jesse's eyelids. Glistening Lights. Inside him. Even with the inescapable slip-sliding, Jesse felt a calm. Deep and quiet.

From below, there was a thwack-whack of crushing metal. A taxi had run-over the saucer, spitting it under the wheels of the following cars, till it looked like a mutilated trashcan cover.

But Jesse felt himself stop. Stop…in mid-slide. He opened his eyes, still holding Mikey. They were stopped on a shelf of snow. Safe. Above the avenue.

The other children were screaming. Mikey was whimpering. But when Jesse opened his eyes, he saw—at the edge of his cheek—sun-glistening beads of snow. He softly smiled, whispering, "We're safe."

Next thing, Mr. Romano lifted his little boy off the snow shelf, and Jesse felt Mr. Gorecki scoop him up. Jesse's head was on Mr. Gorecki's shoulder and he closed his eyes, watching his beautiful Lights softening. Slowly softening.

The children had to get off the ice mountain and glumly followed

Mr. Romano and Mr. Gorecki back to the apartments. Mr. Gorecki brought Jesse to Mac and Bridget. As he put him down inside, Jesse squeezed his hand, and his turquoise eyes sparked with his smiling, "Thank you."

Mr. Gorecki pulled his lips together, trying to maintain a serious outlook in the face of Jesse's irresistible charm. He shook his finger and wagged his head, "No more sliding into traffic." Even so, Jesse saw the twinkle in his eyes before he turned away.

Bridget went to make tea, and Jesse turned to Mac, trying to explain, "Mac? On the snow mountain, I saw…sparking light. I knew, I just knew, it was my real magic. And I knew I was safe. I remembered. When we went to the Met Art Museum and we walked through all the old dark art, and then we came out to the rooms of light art, especially Money's Haystack picture in the snowy, beautiful light."

"Money?" Mac puzzled, but straightaway he understood: "Oh, Haystacks!" Mac chuckled, "So y' mean the great artist, Monet. Claude Monet. His winter Haystacks."

"Yes, Mo-nay. I…"

"Well Jesse, just like the artist, Monet, painting his pictures filled with Light, you chose your loving, joyful, glistening thoughts, and y' created your joyful, glistening world. Y'r safe and free. Blue ribbon, you."

Billy knocked at the door, and smiled when he saw Jesse, "I don't know how you do it Jesse! You're fine!"

"I am fine! And I have an idea!" He stood up, "Let's get out the shovels and make a new platform on the mountain."

"Wha-a-a-t? Nooo Jesse. That's impossible," Billy nixed. He reckoned it was both forbidden and too dangerous. "Jesse, we can't go near that thing."

Jesse beamed, "*Impossible* only means: *I–M–possible*! Get it? *I am possible!* The shelf where Mikey and I landed gave me an idea." He took

Mac's crossword puzzle pencil and drew a triangle, with a chunk out of the top. "See? We make a new platform, with a safe wall behind it. Safe on our street side."

Billy looked at Jesse's drawing. He stared. He pulled back. "Good gravy! Jesse, I think this'll really work!" He sat down, "But, the grownups don't want us back there."

"Well, let's go build it and invite them all back to play!"

Billy looked skeptical. He looked at Mac. "Mac, if you give the okay, I say okay."

Mac chuckled and stood up. "Let's see what-cha got, an' we'll see which way the cat jumps."

The late morning sun had softened the snow and made their job, as Jesse crowed, "*Easy-please-y*!"

Billy declared that Jesse deserved the first ride down the snow mountain, and Jesse proclaimed, *a la* the Dutchies, "S-s-s-u-u-u-p-e-r! Super-super-duper!"

The big surprise was Mac giving it a try! "W-h-o-o-o-H-o-o-o!" Jesse jumped up and down watching him. "Mac!" he shouted, "This is a *cracker pet* day!"

And that was only the beginning. The apartment Misters were returning for lunch and were astounded. Mr. Gorecki had a new snow saucer with him, and when he saw Mac slide down, he stopped. And climbed up! Everyone laughed to see such a mountain of a man, sitting on a saucer, on top of the mountain of snow. And oh! He sped down like Superman! Flying! Booming his deep cheer up and down the street.

All the Misters tried it. Jesse never heard them laughing so. Everyone was laughing. What's more, after lunch, everybody came out! The children, fathers and mothers! It was a mountain of pure whiz-bang-zip-zooming fun!

That night the Romanos invited Jesse to supper. Mikey told him, "Mama's making spaghetti! *Delicioso*!"

Jesse helped Joey and Mikey set the table while Mrs. Romano stood at the stove, her apron wrapped about her, stirring the pasta sauce. Jesse saw her thick curly black hair, pulled back with her hair combs, and he heard her gold bangle bracelets softly jangle as she returned the pot lid.

He smiled and breathed in, "Mmmm, it does smell dee-lish-ee-o-so! Yum!"

Mr. Romano came in and took a breath, too. His dark wavy hair fell over his dark, shining eyes, eyes that sparkled when he looked at his wife. He took her hand and kissed it.

She tittered, "Oh, Alberto!"

He grinned and kissed her wrist…kissed, kissed, kissed, up, up, up her arm, saying, "Mi Bernadetta, mi deliciosa, mi yum!"

He winked at Jesse, and smiled as Jesse blurted a laugh. Joey and Mikey rolled their eyes.

Mrs. Romano laughed too, "Alberto! You didn't finish…"

Mr. Romano leaned in and kissed her neck, turned her chin and kissed her gently on the lips.

"Ohhh!" Jesse stood still. Then he clapped. He clapped with all his might. "Ohhh!"

With such an audience, Mr. Romano took his wife in his arms as if he was finishing a dance, and he dipped her to the floor. Mrs. Romano giggled and sang, "Oh, Solo Mio!" The two of them drew upright, and Jesse was agog as they danced around the table swaying and twirling and singing her song.

My. My. It was a supper to savor…to relish…to remember. *Delicioso*!

The snow stayed in the city a good long time. But as the days turned into weeks, the sun and wind and rain eventually had their way, and the courtyard bricks once again showed themselves in the bare, cold days of winter.

Chapter Eight

Love Stories

Winter-chapped lips and cheeks looked for relief, and Jesse was sent to the Schuyler's Drugstore to buy a jar of Vaseline. When he walked in, he saw two older girls sitting at the soda fountain counter, sipping and laughing and playing a rhyming game. Jesse stood in the far aisle listening to their banter.

"My mother and your mother were saying good-bye…"

Jesse's head wagged with their patter as he heard the girls go on.

"My mother told your mother a great big fat lie." The other girl finished, "My mother punched your mother right in the eye!" They laughed all the more.

But Jesse was startled. *Dearie would talk to them about those words. They need her Rule of Tongue.*

He took the jar of Vaseline to the counter and paid for it as the girls went out the door still laughing. Taking his change, Jesse looked at Wit Schuyler and asked, "Mr. Schuyler, do you know any stories about Jane or her mother, Jessica?"

Wit smiled at Jesse, "A story. No." But he stopped and stared into a memory. "Though, I do have my own story about a beautiful young lady I met long ago. Her name was Jessica. I've never forgotten her."

"Maybe it's my Lady Jessica?" Jesse hoped.

"I doubt it. We met in Philadelphia. I was studying pharmaceuticals and working in a drugstore right off a city park called Rittenhouse Square." Mr. Schuyler went into a deep reverie. "I could see the flowering white dogwoods when she opened the door, and it was as if one of those blossoms—

dressed in white and pink—had floated in to the shop. She was a breath of sweet, innocent beauty. She handed me her script for quinine and I asked for identification."

Wit Schuyler winked, and Jesse smiled. He was beginning to understand the *wink* as a little bit of a secret. Sharing a secret. He wasn't sure what it was, but he liked it.

Mr. Schuyler smirked at Jesse, "I didn't need identification. I just wanted to know who she was...my talking flower!

"'Oh,' she told me, 'I need this for my father. We actually have the same name, but I am called Jessica.'

"As we spoke, I found out she lived on Delancey Street, and her father had returned home from Africa, and needed the quinine for an experiment he was conducting with fish. I was fascinated, especially since the beautiful young Jessica seemed to know what she was talking about."

"So what happened?"

"Well...the wicked witch appeared! Her grandmother walked in, stern and commanding. She seized Jessica by the elbows and set her aside." Mr. Schuyler's voice became imperious: "'I shall take care of this business, Jessica. We must be off to Port Haven this afternoon.'"

"Port Haven!" Jesse almost jumped out of his cap.

Wit Schuyler nodded, "Yes, Port Haven. Many Philadelphians go there for the summer." He shrugged and finished, "Jessica never said another word, though she did look back at me and smile. But she was whisked away by the witch." Wit sighed. "I looked for her every day. I hoped to see her again. But it was not to be."

Jesse breathed, "I'd like it if my dissapp—my Lady Jessica—was like your Jessica."

"Well, she was a dream. Life is funny. When I went back to the Netherlands, I think I carried that love-struck fancy with me. Because, the first girl I met was my Katelijne, and we fell in love at first sight. And here we are, in this loving place, still loving, and multiplying our love with our three girls."

Jesse *grimmeled*, thinking, *I like the love. Like Mr. and Mrs. Romano.* He looked at Mr. Schuyler and said, "That's a good love-story."

Love and hope often take pleasure in each other, and Mr. Schuyler's love story made Jesse hope for a Grandmother Jessica of his own love.

Taking the change from Jesse, Dearie told him to put the Vaseline on his face.

"E-a-a-ac-h-h! It's all slimey! Sticky!"

Dearie laughed, "Maybe not quite so much, Jesse!" She helped him wipe it off and he went off to the lumber room. He wanted to be near Jane and James...and Jessica.

The day was lit with grays—the kind of sky that hunkers down and hovers, saying, 'Think-think-think.' Jesse poked around, doing just that.

The key to that desk is in that box, he thought to himself. *I know it. And the box is like Excalibur in the stone. I am the one to open it. I am!*

Someone knocked at their apartment door. Jesse heard Siobhan say,

"Special Delivery! I found this letter stuffed into the junk mailbox downstairs. It's addressed to you. From Elizabethtown."

Jesse's eyes conjured a letter looking like a blossoming white-and-pink flower. But he came out of the lumber room to see Conor take a dirty, wrinkled envelope, fussing, "We've been waiting for this letter! What magician got it mixed up in the junk mail?"

Conor knew. Their mailman, Mr. Paul, didn't do it. He was very particular. It was Grams. Up to her tricks hiding the mail.

Siobhan left, and Jesse held his breath, watching Conor open the letter and read it aloud.

Jesse was surprised. Disappointed surprised. It was as if the gray light had all-at-once seeped into the apartment. Into Jesse.

"Ohhh!" he groused, "We finally get a letter from Elizabethtown but it's for nothing."

Indeed, the town clerk was sorry to say:

...without a last name, there is no way to trace a Jessica or Jane registered in the Town Hall records.

Dearie calmed: "So, Elizabethtown—or Jessica—is not ready yet."

But Conor growled under his breath, "No luck. Ever!"

Jesse vented, too, "I am being patience. But it's not working! Can't we just go to Elizabethtown and find Lady Jessica by ourselves?"

Dearie tried to smooth things over: "Well, we can't go..." Though she recalled how she had so spontaneously planned to go, just a month ago; but now she could not free-up her theater schedule. And Conor was in the same boat with his timetable. And there was still no way to find Jessica.

But Jesse only heard, 'we can't go...', and his eyes flashed, while his tongue lashed, "Why not? You used to go all the time."

"We can't possibly..."

"That's a great big fat lie! We can go. You don't want to! We'll never go!"

"Jesse," she said very quietly, "we will talk about this when you are calm and respectful." She left the room.

Jesse huffed to the lumber room. Flopping on the carpet, pounding the floor, Jesse felt a good old *feisty-dreg* boiling inside. *My mother and your mother* bounced between his ears and he thought, *I could punch somebody! Right in the eye! Right now! I solved Jane's puzzle! I found Elizabethtown.*

I can find Jessica. I just have to go there. I.... His heart beat in his head. Pounded. *I...eagh....*

He stopped. He looked at the little box on top of the desk and he slowly simmered, *Hmpf! That box. That desk. Puzzles...puzzles....*

He stood up and grabbed the box, fingering its edges, across the stripes of different colored wood. White. Black. Red. He held it up to the light. There was no top. Or bottom. He dropped it on the carpet.

His head pounded. He felt upside down. He stared out the window and a big hot tear rolled down his cheek.

"Eagh...." He brushed it away, but his fingers stuck to his cheek. He rubbed his sticky cheeks, but more tears spurted over the Vaseline. His head hurt. He took a deep breath. A sob escaped and he let out a gush of hot air.

Slowly, he went to the door and tottered down to Dearie's bedroom door, snuffling, "Dearie...?"

She looked up, "Jesse...?"

His face looked like an apple pie, scrunched and shine-y and oozing. "Dearie..." his voice cracked and his mouth opened, but no sound came out. Dearie held out her arms and Jesse fell into her embrace, bawling like a small donkey. Between his gasps he muffled, "Oh Dearie... I'm s-s-s-o-r-r-y."

As he quieted, he pulled back and looked into Dearie's eyes, "I really, really am sorry. I was... mean. And nasty. And it feels horrible. I don't know why...I...Conor was..."

"This is not about Conor. This is about you, Jesse. Remember? No one can make you mad. You chose to be mad. It happened very fast. But it was all you."

Jesse nodded. "It was...me...oh, Dearie...."

Dearie spoke quietly, "It's good that you know, Jesse. We all get mad when things don't work out. But mad doesn't help anything. Mad unplugs your energy. Your Light."

"Is that why I can't see straight?"

Dearie muffled a little laugh. "Yes. But even with your eyes closed, I think you know that trying to find Jessica is a challenging search with so little to go on. In the *winkwhile*, Jesse, you are collecting the best clues." She touched his cheek and smiled, "They're practically sticking to you!" They both smiled, and she said, "I am sure, when the time is right, everything will fall into place."

"I get it," he sighed, "it's like the box and the desk in the lumber room. They're not ready yet. Or I'm not ready yet."

⁂

School started again in the building next door to Dearie's theater. It was originally the house for the minister of the church. The church was now Dearie's *Lady Bird Theater*. The house was now the Montessori School.

Mac told Jesse, "We knew Maria Montessori. She died last year in the Netherlands, but Dearie first met her in 1899. Berta—the princess Louisa—wanted Dearie to attend a women's congress in London, and Maria was there. Plus, Dearie was there when Queen Victoria granted Maria an audience.

"That Maria!" Mac enthused, "She was a glittering star. Brilliant. And what she built, why it's just astonishing. And now we have one of her schools right here."

"You mean she built my school?" Jesse *quizzeled*.

Mac laughed, "Hah! Well, in a way she did. Not the building, but Maria built a new way of teaching children. She saw children in a way most people had forgotten; shining with Light, like starlight that each and every baby is born with. Maria polished her little star children so they'd know how to keep their Light on and shine-shine-shine better than ever."

Dearie smiled, "Maria liked to say that the play of childhood is the greatest teacher." Clapping her hands in appreciation, she added, "Like Princess Louisa, Maria was much older than I. But we hummed together from our first moments, and many times thereafter. We met again…in Spain and the Netherlands. In Rome, we even met the aides to Mahatma Gandhi when he visited her school there. Gandhi was a great leader from India, a peacemaker; Gandhi and Maria, weaving the Lights of peace."

Jesse remarked, "In school we learn about being peacemakers."

He was happy to go to Maria's school, and now that Jean and Paul Bonheur joined the class, it was better than ever. They were always ready for fun.

Jesse loved his teachers, especially Mrs. Katelijne Schuyler, the Dutchies' mother. They all called her Missus K. Jesse thought she was the best teacher in the world. She had clever puzzles and she played piano and taught the best songs. Jesse loved school: sitting on his own little rug, playing with the number tasks or the wooden map puzzles; exercising and playing free; or playing with clay.

Jesse thought back to Parent's Day. He remembered being very quiet, watching the other children with their mothers and fathers. He had gone to the clay table and slowly rolled and stretched clay figures. Tall clay figures. James and Jane. He gave them big happy grins and he smiled back at them.

What he remembered most was that Missus K had noticed, "Why Jesse!" she smiled, "you have James and Jane with you!"

And Jesse loved her more than ever. He was smiling at her when he saw Dearie and Conor walk in the door. How he leapt out of his chair and hugged them with all his heart.

Now, Missus K was also helping him make a little book, *Dearie's Dictionary,* with all of Dearie's favorite words. Jesse loved to read on his own; and he liked to read out loud when the other children asked him.

Jesse couldn't wait to get back to school. He knew Missus K would help him make a new booklet, *Island Quest*, to gather details of Elizabethtown, and to make his own Elizabethtown map. He wanted to discover as much as he could about the island. He was sure that Elizabethtown must be where Lady Jessica lived.

Jesse's quest was waiting. Yes. Waiting. But it was not alone. Jesse had other dreams that he carried in his heart. Things wished for, and unexpected.

A sharp whistle floated in from the winter street. Jesse got out of Mac's chair and stood at the front bay-window. "That's Billy."

Mac nodded, "He's whistling at the newspaper delivery truck."

Jesse turned back to Mac, "Yep. Billy is the Boss of the Block. He makes money and saves it in the bank. For his family. To make ends meet, and for the rainy day. I have to go now. I'm Billy's quiet helper."
Jesse wanted to add, *I wish I could be Billy's real partner. Maybe. Someday.*

Billy was hauling his newspaper bundles down to the corner when Jesse came out the front door. Grams Maguire was sitting there, proudly watching her grandson. Jesse sat down next to her, calling to Billy, "I'm going to get a wagon, Billy. Then it'll be *easy-please-y* to move all your papers to your corner."

"You do that, Jesse." Billy trailed off down to his corner.

Pulling her Claddagh charm on her necklace, Grams scoffed at Jesse. "You ain't never gonna see no wagon. Any more than y'll ever see that disappeared Grandmaw of yourn."

Billy had told Jesse, "Grams is sometimes tetchy by afternoon, cuz she works for a slave driver down at the fish markets."

Jesse patiently looked at Grams and said, "I don't say *disappeared* anymore. I call her the Lady Jessica."

"Hmpf. You and all your 'J' names. Y're cursed. The J's are dead: Jane and James. Or disappeared like Jessica. Y'd best watch y'r step, Mister J is for Jesse."

"There's no such thing as a curse," Jesse laughed, "That's just make believe, to make people afraid." Jesse looked at Grams. "I'm not afraid. I'm on my quest. Like the cour-age-us Knights of the Round Table. I know my quest will come true. Someday. You just have to believe."

"Believe," she repeated bitterly. "Y're astray in the head. Och! I can't listen to such nonsense." She got up and went inside.

Jesse stayed on the front stoop. Watching. He thought Billy was the cat's potato. The Boss of the Block in everything he did. The way he rolled the papers and folded them just so. And Billy was really good at yelling out the news. He could hear him, already yelling out the headlines for the day:

"Ted Williams crash-lands his jet! Get yer news here!'"

Jesse knew not to interrupt Billy when he was working. Billy would hold up his hand and say, "Nunh-unh Jesse. Not now." But, at the end, Billy allowed Jesse to help count the coins, saying, "Jesse, you always count right-on-the money. You take to figuring like a pancake to syrup!"

Jesse wanted to be Billy's newsboy partner. But Billy liked being the boss.

Truth to tell, Billy didn't know what to do with Jesse, who was so smart and clever it was hard to believe, 'specially cuz he was so young. Still, it seemed to Billy that, when Jesse was there, his newspapers sold fast and easy. He'd say to his dad, "That Jesse, he's got the touch."

One afternoon, Billy came out of Bridget's Laundry with a big grin on his face.

"Hi, Jesse," he called, "wait till y' hear this! Jean and Paul's dad, Mr. Bonheur, just offered me an after-school job sweeping the floors in the laundry!"

"Is that good?" Jesse asked.

"It's real good!" Billy exclaimed with dollar signs filling his eyes.

"But what about your newspapers?"

"Yeah. I gotta figure that out." He sobered, "I'd be late gettin' my papers set up. Lose my customers for sure."

"I could help," Jesse offered. "Set up the papers and even sell them, till you got back. It's right next door." Billy looked skeptical and Jesse prodded, "You always say you started when you were six-years-old."

Billy slowly shook his head, "Yeah, daddy set things up with the older newsboys."

"I'd have to ask Dearie," Jesse said, "but she lets me go to the Romano's grocery and Goreki's Hardware and the Schuyler's Drugstore by myself. I would take real good care of your newspaper corner, Billy."

Billy rolled the idea around. "I don't have to start in the laundry till next week." He looked at Jesse, "We could try it out."

"Really?"

"How 'bout tomorrow?"

"Golleee yes!" Jesse grinned.

Billy grinned back, "If I can work both jobs that'd be swell." He slung his arm over Jesse's shoulder, "Partner!"

Jesse's smile fire-worked across his face. One big, huge dream, come true!

⁂

On his first newsboy day, Jesse was almost jumping out of his pants, and it wasn't from the frosty cold. He was just plain thrilled. The delivery truck dropped off the newspaper bundles, and Jesse hopped in a little circle, noticing that Grams was watching.

Jesse beamed at her, "My dream came true, Grams! And next, I think Lady Jessica will come true."

"Oh you, Jesse O'Neil! You think everything's just gonna come your way. You think yer disappeared Grandmaw's gonna pop up outta thin air. Well, life is full of disappointments. And hard work. Yer gonna get a taste of it today. You'll see."

Just then Billy waved the truck away and swaggered to Jesse, "Okay, Jess, let's go."

Picking up a bundle, Billy hauled it down to his station near the corner.

Jesse reached for a bundle. "Uhnnh!" He pulled. *Uh-oh. Way too heavy.*

He heard Grams shriek and clap her hands. "I knew it. You can't keep up with my Billy."

Jesse straightened up. He stood still for a moment, then turned on his heel and walked into Mr. Schuyler's Drugstore. In just a minute, he walked out with a handful of brown-paper-bags. He rolled a newspaper. Put it in a bag. With ten papers in the bag, he walked to Billy, proudly handing them over.

Billy grinned at him, "Pretty smart, Jesse O'Neil. Pretty darn smart."

Grams shook her head and went inside.

Jesse earned a penny for each newspaper he sold. He attracted a good little crowd playing his penny-whistle, but he wasn't selling the newspapers.

Sooner-later, Billy told him, "Listen Jesse, ya gotta sell these dailys like hot-cakes flippin' off a griddle! You gotta get to your customers in the nick of time!"

Jesse quizzled, "What's a nick?"

"Just follow my words," Billy exasperated, "Learn from the Big Boss!"

Then Jesse mimicked Billy to a T, as he raised his voice, shouting over the traffic. "Read all about it! Jonas Salk inventing polio vaccine! Get the latest news!"

Billy couldn't believe Jesse's take-charge voice, projecting all over the corner. "Where'd that come from?"

Jesse felt someone tap his shoulder. "Sergeant Hannity!"

"You're doing great work, Jesse. I'll take a paper."

Jesse smiled, "Mac says to call it *play* instead of *work*, then it goes much better for me."

"Mac, he's got something there. Play does sound much better." Hannity smiled and paid Jesse.

"Gosh, you're my very first customer!"

Hannity patted his shoulder, "And I won't be your last."

He was right. Pennies filled Jesse's pockets, and he told Dearie, "My dream came true. It's so much fun to be a newsboy. Billy teaches me all the perpendiculars. And I sell all my papers!"

"So you're *thrill-digging* all the *particulars*!"

Jesse was quiet.

"Are you?" Dearie asked.

"Well…" Jesse balked, "Billy's the Boss. Sooo…."

"Sooo…?" Dearie questioned.

"So sometimes he's, um, kinda gruff-and-rough."

"Ah, Jesse," Dearie gentled. "There is something wonderful–something still and calm–that can always save you from a rough-and-gruff."

"Whatever that is, that's what I need! Like when the papers don't sell fast. I get real worried 'cause Billy's gonna get mad." Jesse's face worried, "When Billy gets mad he's extra gruff-and-rough."

Dearie exhaled, "Jesse, you really only have two feelings: bad or good. When you choose the bad you don't like the taste, but you keep chewing on it."

"Yeaghhh..."

"So, stop chewing on it. All it does is spark the bad in Billy. That's how energy works. You are electricity. And you're plugged into something you don't want. Worrying-so, being anxious, you're humming the bad. Billy feels it, and he hums back the bad."

"But...?"

"You want to hum, and feel, and think the *good.* Remember Old Barret's lesson?

You create your hum—your energy stream—in the way you feel. The universe always says 'Yes' to what you're humming. Good or bad. So it all depends on you. You choose your hum. Good or bad. You choose."

"So," Jesse puzzled, "I guess I chose getting to be a newsboy with Billy?"

"No guessing about it. Your *good* thoughts did that. And your *bad* thoughts? They have the same energy to create. That's what you're doing with Billy. Thinking bad, *you* create more *bad.*"

"*I...I* cre-make *bad*? That is not pleasant."

"No," Dearie stifled a laugh, "It is not pleasant to *create* bad. But it's true. So... Light on!" Dearie stood and turned around on one foot, "Pivot! Leave your bad thoughts, and get into your best *bliss-t* thoughts. The best! Why waste any of *you* on the worst?"

Jesse remembered how he had turned on his heel down on the sidewalk. He stood up and spun on his foot. "Pivot! To the *bliss-t*!" He laughed, "I like it! Pivot!" He turned again, "Hey! I can pivot to Jessica's *bliss-t*, too. All my good thoughts about Jessica. No matter how Grams teases about her."

"Yes, Jesse. It works for everyone. But let's stick with Billy. Start right now, *before* you see Billy. Have a little list of Billy-Bests. Practice-practice-practice it in your mind: 'Fun with Billy-Bests'."

Jesse smiled and rambled, "I love Billy. He's my best friend. He shares things with me. Even Liam. He loves Liam. And he loves Grams. And she loves him. He works real hard. And he's so much fun! His stories and jokes. Billy *is* the best!"

"Yes," Dearie beamed, "humor and fun lift the corners of your mouth as they lift the corners of your heart." Her mouth grimeled and she reminded him, "So, if Billy still gets gruff-and-rough, then you can stop, and do your 'T-H-I-N-K'."

"I remember now," his head went up and down. "I do all the letters for the word:

T = Take a deep breath
H = Hold myself high
I = Imagine the best
N = Now
K = Know that ALL IS Well ~ *And So It Is!*"

But Dearie wasn't finished, "Here is something you can add to that. Begin your deep breath with *ujjayi* breath"

"Ooo-jah-yee breath?"

"Ancient Sanskrit, meaning: *Victorious Breath.* Sometimes called *Ocean Breath,* because it sounds like ocean waves rushing on the shore. Watch...."

Dearie sat up straight, closing her eyes and her mouth. She breathed in through her nose, along the roof of her mouth, and out again, making a soft whooshing sound.

Jesse was surprised, "It sounds like Mrs. Gorecki's new steam iron!"

"Yes! Shhhoooshh."

Jesse closed his eyes and breathed. After a few tries, his eyes flew open and he exclaimed, "I did it! Did you hear it?"

"Yes!" Dearie clapped. "And did you feel it? The stillness? The calm?"

"I felt…quiet."

"Now you're ready for T-H-I-N-K!"

Chapter Nine

Treasure Islands

"What a wonderful word is 'thriving'!" Dearie enthused to Conor. "Jesse is awakening and flourishing and thriving."

"He sure is. I saw his notebook for his Elizabethtown *Island Quest*. He's like a little explorer!"

Jesse's *Island Quest* was, indeed, thriving. Names and details appeared like magic as he collected more and more information. Missus K brought in historic maps, and Jesse identified the islands in the bay. He was excited to find the old Indian names:

"The bay is called Tanagasuq Bay after the Indian tribe that had lived there, Kecaniduq is Port Haven, and Nocanituq is Elizabethtown." He rolled the names around his tongue.

Also, Mr. Schuyler found a set of old postcards in the drugstore, and one of them was a photograph looking at Elizabethtown over Tanagasuq Bay. It was winter, and the bay was frozen over with horses and sled carriages crossing over the ice.

"Golly," Jesse considered, "I'll have to brave the ice to get to Elizabethtown. Like Dearie's stories of Shackelton's danger-us journey at the South Pole. Well, Shackelton did it. I can do it, too."

Missus K said, "Actually, the Bay doesn't freeze like that anymore."

Jesse shrugged, and she handed him a magnifying glass to study the photo. He felt like quite the detective, gathering his clues, one by one.

Jesse showed Missus K, "Look, I found a boat with black smokestacks just like the one Jane drew on her Island map. See it says *Governor Keane* on it. It's parked at the shore."

Missus K gentled, "Boats don't park, Jesse. That boat is a ferry, and it is 'docked' in the harbor."

"Oh, docked," he corrected himself. "But look here," he pointed to the island skyline. "No trees."

"No," she noted. "Only rooftops and chimneys."

"But see," he pointed. "Up on the hill, in the middle of the island, I think it's a ferris wheel, like the picture Mikey Romano brought to class from Coney Island."

Missus K smiled, "I believe it's a windmill, Jesse." She reached for an encyclopedia, "Believe me, I know windmills. But let's look it up."

Sure enough, there was a picture of a building much like the one on Elizabethtown. Jesse read out loud, "*Windmill: a building with sails that turn in the wind, which ro...tate stone wheels on the inside; used to grind gr...rain into fl...our.* Golly. That's how they get their flour? We just go to the Romano's grocery store."

Missus K smiled. "Jesse, this is a very old photograph. Perhaps they have more modern conveniences on the island today."

Jesse swayed his head back and forth, "I really have to go there to see."

"For now," Missus K encouraged, "perhaps you can draw the windmill on your map."

Elizabethtown's island began to take on a floating, *Neverland* feeling for Jesse, as Dearie had been reading *Peter Pan* at bedtime. In the afternoon, before his newspapers duties, he was hoping to get in another chapter, and he appeared at Dearie's door, though without Velvet. She was not to be misplaced again, and was relegated to Jesse's bed pillow.

"Dearie...?"

"Jesse, I am writing a letter now. To my old friend in Port Haven,

Carly." She looked up, "There's a chance she may know of a connection to Jane and Jessica. Carly works in the Port Haven Hospital. Who knows? The people with whom she could be connected?"

"Oh. That's a good idea." Jesse leaned on the doorframe, "Sergeant Hannity said to collect as many clues as we can." He turned, "Well, I'll go down to Mac's."

Mac had been watching over Jesse most afternoons since the day he was born. Back then, Bridget was still running Bridget's Laundry business next door, so as Jesse grew, he and Mac filled their time together, reading and puzzling and playing games.

Jesse liked Mac's jigsaw puzzles and checkers and cards, but his favorite time with Mac wasn't a game. It was reading. Jesse and Mac sat in the wide wingback chair, with a book on Mac's lap so that Jesse could see the pictures. He liked the warm, soft wool of Mac's vest, and the smell of pipe tobacco in his pocket, though he only smoked it outside. Most of all, Jesse liked the sound of Mac's voice, luring him into a story.

Today, Jesse wondered what book Mac would choose. They had read the *Boy's King Arthur*, and before that it was *Robin Hood.* Jesse could read those tales over and over again.

But at the moment, something else captured Jesse's eyes. Something Mac used for a bookend. Jesse had thought it was an old rock, but now he saw that it was a large oval shell with a shiny inside that looked like a coil, spiraling from the middle. He pointed, "Mac, what is that?"

"*Yonks* ago, when I was still a Traveller ..."

Jesse interrupted, "Traveller–with two ll's for being an Irish gypsy."

Mac looked at Jesse, amazed at his memory, but he continued his story. "I found this half-chambered nautilus on a beach in western Ireland." He handed it to Jesse. "The nautilus has been on Earth for millions of years. It lives in the Indian Ocean, so some sailor must have left it on the sands of

Ireland."

Jesse ran his fingers over it. "I like the smooth inside with these curvy little rooms."

"That shiny-smooth is mother-of-pearl, and those little rooms are chambers." Mac held it up. "The soft animal inside is long gone, but when it was living in there it grew from a little chamber to a bigger chamber; and the empty chambers helped keep it floating."

Jesse stared, "It's beautiful."

"Yep. Like the sacred geometry of the universe: the perfect spiral building block curling through so many things in all the universe."

"Like our spiral staircase?"

Mac nodded, looking into Jesse's eyes. "And the spiral's in just about everything in my garden."

"Like that snake I found coiled up in your watering can!"

Mac ruffled, "I was thinkin' more of sunflowers and cauliflower and kale. And, also, the top cap of the little acorns from the Tree of Life."

"I'm going to look for those spirals."

Mac smiled, "You do that, Jesse. You look for it, and you'll find it. That's how everything works. Especially the spirals of energy."

"What do you mean?"

"I like to think the spiral shows how we are connected to everything in the universe and here on Earth. The ancient people of Egypt knew that the spiral is a never-ending coil that grows and grows, upward and onward. Like our life journey."

"I'm going on a journey. I'm still going to find my grandmother, Lady Jessica. "

"Ah, your quest."

"Yes. Maybe, if I don't get too dizzy, I'll go in a spiral."

Mac chuckled, "Well Jesse, whether you know it or not, most

journeys end up that way. A spiral."

"The spiral," Jesse repeated. "It makes me picture the nautilus. I like it."

"Good. Now off with y' to your newspapers. Next time you visit, I have a special something else to share."

Nothing like expectation to raise enthusiasms, and the next afternoon, Jesse eagerly arrived at Mac's and watched him reach for a special book from his shelf.

"If you're planning a trip to an island, Jesse, you'd be wise to know this story. I think you're ready for my all-time favorite, *Treasure Island*. From the great *imaginator*, Robert Louis Stevenson."

"I know him. I have his book *A Child's Garden of Verses*." Jesse recited, "'I have a little shadow that goes in and out with me…'"

Mac chuckled the next line, "'And what can be the use of him…'"

They finished together, "'Is more than I can see….'"

Jesse laughed, but Mac seemed to float away, describing his favorite author. "Stevenson was a great *imaginator*, though he was terrible sickly, as a child and a grownup. Trouble breathin' with coughin' and fevers. Spent a lot of time in bed. Maybe that's what made him a writer. He imagined."

Mac stopped and looked at Jesse. "Y' know, Stevenson had a quest, something like yourn for your Lady Jessica. Stevenson and his Fanny Osbourne were in love, but life kept gettin' in their way, keepin' them apart. They were separated for years."

"Really?

"Yep. He traveled across the Atlantic Ocean and across America lookin' to find her. His money ran out and he was penniless and sick. Almost died. But Fanny finally found him in a miner's camp in Napa Valley, California. There, her deep love nursed him back to health, and they married. He and Fanny had fifteen full years of marriage."

"His quest," Jesse breathed in a sigh of hope. "He did it. But...I'm not going to marry Lady Jessica."

"No," Mac smiled. "You won't be marrying your grandmother. But one more thing about Robert Louis Stevenson: it was after he found Fanny that he wrote his greatest works, creating characters and stories that are, to this day, unforgettable. Love. It's a great inspiration."

Mac thumped the book, "Here it is and here it goes. Just take a *gander* at the cover illustration: the treacherous pirates, daring you to open the book."

"Mac," Jesse thrummed, "This picture in *Treasure Island* is like the ones of *Robin Hood* and *King Arthur*. I love those pictures and the wash-bucket stories!"

"You mean swash-buckling stories," Mac *tiddly-winked*. "But, you've a good eye, Jesse. The illustrations in this *Treasure Island* are by N.C. Wyeth. Same as your *King Arthur* and *Robin Hood*."

"Well, he does the pictures just right."

Mac smiled, "I'm sure Mr. Wyeth would have appreciated your words. Let's gander these other pictures."

That pretty much did it.

Picture after picture, Jesse was beguiled. "Look at the ship! And the treasure chest!" he enthused, "Brave young Jim Hawkins! He's just a boy. Like me."

Jesse sat in timeless moments staring at the pictures of the fierce characters, especially the way Mac scraggled their pirate words:

Avast ye! (Stop!)–Hornswaggle (Cheat)–the Black Spot (the mark of death)–Shiver-me-timbers! (Gosh-n-golly!)–Flash his Cutlass (pull out his knife blade).

"Golly, it's like the *Jabberwock*." Jesse enthused, "You know. *Alice in Wonderland:* 'One two! One two! And through and through. His vorpal sword went snicker-snack!'"

"Good one, Jesse." Mac laughed.

Jesse didn't know which was better, Mr. Wyeth's pictures or Mr. Stevenson's words under each picture:

The feared pirate Captain Flint:

"'Heard of Captain Flint!' cried the squire. "Heard of him, you say! He was the bloodthirstiest buccaneer that sailed. Black-beard was a child to Flint."

Israel Hands:

"For thirty years, I've sailed the seas and seen good and bad, better and worse, fair weather and foul, provisions running out, knives going, and what not."

Mac saved *Long John Silver* for the last, saying, "Here you have one of the cleverest, most charming of all the pirates: Long John Silver," he laughed, "Or 'Barbeque' as Robert Louis Stevenson nicknamed him."

"Barbeque?" Jesse's face quizzeled, "Like cooking outdoors?"

Mac nodded, "Silver was the ship's cook, so it fit."

Jesse giggled, "Barbeque."

"And there's more," Mac said. "You see, Stevenson and James Barrie..."

Jesse interrupted, "James Barrie! He wrote *Peter Pan!*"

"Yep," Mac smiled. "Stevenson and Barrie were friends who never met, but corresponded by letter from wherever they traveled. Barrie loved *Treasure Island* so much that he put Long John Silver into *Peter Pan.*"

"Really?" Jesse was impressed. "*Treasure Island* is in *Peter Pan*?"

"Yep. Barrie wrote that Long John Silver—Barbeque—was deathly afraid of Captain Hook. Those two crewed for the fearsome Blackbeared himself. But Barbeque never trusted the dastardly, villainous James Hook."

Jesse could see it all in the pictures. He could see it in his imagination. But best of all he could feel it.

Jesse was filled with the pirates of *Peter Pan*, and most assuredly, the pirates of *Treasure Island*. At dinner, he announced, "Dearie, I want to go to the library with Mac tomorrow. He's reading *Treasure Island* to me, and I want my own book." He took a spoonful of tomato soup and blew on it.

"That sounds like a good plan, Jesse," she answered.

"It is a good plan. It's my quest."

Jesse recounted both Robert Louis Stevenson's quest to find Fanny, and the successes of his own quest.

"Liam told me Jane sailed with James from the Port Haven Yacht Club. And she and Lady Jessica lived on a farm. And Mac is reading me *Treasure Island* because Jessica lives on an island. And Mac showed me his Nautilus shell and told me about the spiral journey, and it can go wherever you want. So I'm going to take it to find Jessica."

Dearie smiled, "What an excellent plan, Jesse. Light on."

But Conor was stewing. He had caught Grams red-handed, mixing up the envelopes in the mailboxes. So far, the mail always was delivered by someone in the apartments. Still, Conor was vexed, and he needled Jesse.

"Okay you little *Quatchkopt*, just how do you plan on finding your Lady Jessica, with no last name and no address?"

Jesse wasn't bothered in the least. "It's part of the spiral. All connected. That's why I want to take the spiral path."

"Well my *brillish* Baby Grand," Dearie puffed, "no one could argue with that." She passed him the bread and continued. "When you're at the Fifth Avenue Library tomorrow take a good look at the lions out on the front steps. They can teach you something about your journey."

"Lions? The white-stone lions?" Jesse wondered.

"Yes. The one is called Patience, and you will need that for you're journey. The other lion is called Fortitude."

"Fort Dude?" Jesse guffawed, "That sounds ridiculous!"

Dearie coughed on her soup, and Conor chuckled in spite of himself, saying, "Jesse, the word is For-ti-tude. It means to have courage in the face of challenge."

"Ohhh. Patience and Fortitude. Okay, I'll do that on my journey."

Dearie nodded, "You know Jesse, sometimes a journey is difficult when it does not have to be. There may be clues to the mystery of Jessica that are right under your nose."

"You mean I can smell them?"

Dearie giggled, "Well maybe you can. But it really means to look at all the possibilities. The universe is always showing you details that fill in around your dreams. Like the library lions giving you patience and fortitude.

"There are many examples of things you would never know or think to consider. Like the special library books buried in the vaults under Bryant Park."

Jesse's eyes brightened, "I remember the library photograph you showed me of the huge, old New York City Reservoir that used to be at Bryant Park. It looked like a castle."

Dearie added, "Yes. Who would ever guess there was once a high-walled reservoir on that land or, who would guess that today so many books are right under the grasses of Bryant Park?"

Conor made a sour face and Dearie flicked her eyebrows at him. But Jesse wasn't giving any attention to Conor. "I'm just like Jim Hawkins: making plans for my quest."

Jesse felt his quest thriving as he left for Mac's the next morning.

They were to have tea together before walking to the library. But Conor was still stewing about Jessica. "You know, Dearie, I think this hunt for Jessica is complicated. I think Jesse is really searching for James and Jane. He wants his mom and dad. And I don't think it's good for him to keep getting kiboshed. We have to go find Jessica. She could be dead for all we know! We have to go back to Port Haven…to Elizabethtown. Talk to the people there. Face to face."

"Conor, of course you're right. But you know we can't go now. The *Lady Bird* is at full throttle. My director for *Mousetrap* is superb. But he thinks just because I knew Agatha Christie once upon a time, I have all the angles on putting her show together. He relies on me for every little detail." She sat with her tea mug. "And you are in full overload yourself, Conor. Your college classes, the Actor's Studio, your lessons with Joe Pilates, not to mention the jobs you take on."

Conor tried again, "Well, what about your friend from the Port Haven Hospital? Carly? The one you traveled with when you went to see Pa in Nova Scotia, during the war?"

Dearie sipped her tea, "I already tried that. I didn't say, because I didn't want to discourage you. But my letter to Carly was returned. Evidently, she doesn't live there anymore."

A low moan came out of Conor's throat. "We are cursed, Dearie. Cursed. We're like a serial movie show: always *to be continued.*" He stood up. "The someday…that never comes."

Returning home from the library, Jesse was on cloud nine, with his copy of *Treasure Island,* plus a Beatrix Potter and Winnie the Pooh book. He saw Grams Maguire going into her apartment and he crowed, "Look! I have brand new books!"

Grams peered at Jesse, "New looks? You look the same to me." And she closed the door.

Jesse shrugged and ran up the steps.

Conor was in the parlor practicing his lines for the stage play *Harvey*. Jesse walked in but stopped.

"Aislinn!"

"Hello, Jesse. I was hoping I'd see you." Her dark ponytail swung back and forth, and her dark eyelashes brightened her sparkling dark eyes.

Dearie was always talking about how everyone and everything is connected. Some more than others. Jesse was glad to be connected with Aislinn. She was a breath of fresh and cheery.

She gave Jesse a quick hug, saying, "I hear you're on a quest."

Jesse lit up, "I am."

Conor interrupted, "Jesse, we have work to do. Aislinn is helping me practice my *Harvey-pooka* lines."

Aislinn continued to talk to Jesse:. "Conor is working with the Director, Bobby Lewis, at the Actor's Studio and hopes this will impress him."

"Well," Conor said defensively, "it is for the lead part of Elwood P. Dowd." He explained, "In the play, Elwood's best friend is *Harvey*, a six-foot tall *invisible* rabbit! It's a *pooka*!"

"*Pooka*?" Jesse laughed, "*Pooka Bazooka!* Bubblegum!"

"No," Aislinn giggled.

Jesse tried again: "Like the *Hokey-Pokey* dance?"

Aislinn laughed, "No, a *pooka* is a mischievous faerie-folk, from Celtic mythology. *Harvey-pooka* is fond of unusual human-folk, like Conor's character, Elwood P. Dowd."

Conor pulled out the *Harvey* scripts, "Let's get started."

Jesse pointed, "I'll go read over there in the big chair." Gypsy draped herself over the chair's arm and Jesse snuggled in with the illustrations of

Treasure Island. But when the acting began, Jesse's eyes and ears went straight back to Conor and Aislinn.

They were practicing the scene in which Elwood explains that *Harvey*—the six-foot invisible rabbit—has the power to stop time:

"'Did I tell you he could stop clocks? Well, you've heard the expression, "His face would stop a clock"? Well, Harvey can look at your clock and stop it. And you can go anywhere you like—with anyone you like—and stay as long as you like.'"

Jesse thought, *I'd like to stop time. I'd go on my quest…to Elizabethtown…with anyone I like…and stay for as long as I like.*

Conor stopped acting and took Aislinn's hand.

"Aislinn," he said, "let's stop time, you and I. We can dance the night away at the Winter Gala. If you'll let me escort you? Please say yes."

Aislinn laughed. She blushed. "Well. Yes!" she answered.

And then, Conor kissed her.

Gypsy hopped down and bounced to Conor's legs, twirling in and out.

Jesse clapped, "Do it again!"

Conor's head swiveled and Jesse saw his face. He looked like he'd love to kiss Aislinn again: his big smile, and his dusky eyes, with sparks in the centers, jumping up and down.

That's how Jesse felt. Like jumping up and down. Like time really did stop. And danced The Hokey-Pokey! In sparking, *glint-a-ling* love-Lights.

⁂

Dearie always tried to be home for teatime, and when she arrived, she invited Aislinn to stay. Jesse lit up again with the chance to talk with her.

"I'm investing-gating Jane and Jessica." Jesse began, "Did you know Jane?"

"You are investigating! Well, yes," Aislinn smiled, "That's how I met Conor. Jane was my Latin tutor. I'd never have mastered *veni, vidi, vici* without Jane," she laughed lightly. "Jane was brilliant."

"I couldn't agree more," Dearie noted, "Jane was always coming up with bright, thoughtful little gems."

Conor chuckled, "Dearie called them Jane's 'gemmy' ideas."

"Jane. Brilliant and beautiful!" Aislinn smiled, "She reminded me of Amanda Wynne."

"I love Amanda!" Jesse gushed.

"Amanda and Jesse have a *diggety-boo* history together," Dearie explained.

Conor added, "Jesse had a special connection with Amanda. It's partly how she went on to become a famous Hollywood actress."

Aislinn's eyes snapped. "Well! Do tell."

So began a Dearie story.

"Right after Jesse was born, I still had to run my *Lady Bird Theater*. But, what to do with Baby Grand Jesse?"

Aislinn interrupted, "I love the way you call him your Baby Grand."

"Yes," Dearie smiled at Jesse. "The music of our lives in our precious Baby Grand." She laughed, "Well, when Jesse was born, I kept him in our theater costume shop. In the bottom drawer of a bureau. There he cooed and sang, slept and ate—and pooped."

"Oh, Dearie!" A *giggle-snicken* puffed through Jesse's mouth.

"Back then I had written a musical called *Is It You?*"

"I love that song," Aislinn beamed.

Dearie smiled, "Thank you. So, I hired a young actress from Georgia, Amanda Wynne, of the honey-dripping drawl." Dearie exaggerated Amanda's sugary speech, "'Hellooo-ooo.' Amanda whirled into the Costume Rooms, 'I am Amanda Wynne.'

"A Light seemed to glow all around Amanda: in her golden hair, her eyes, her smile; as if she had brought the morning sun along with her."

Jesse gurgled, "Light on!"

"Yes!" Dearie patted his knee. "Amanda drawled, 'Here I am, ready for your pins and needles.'

"But she stopped, and *squintled* at the bureau drawer.

"'Well Tweedle-Dee and me!' she exclaimed, 'A baby! In a drawer? Why! The most beautiful baby I ever laid eyes on. Oh, do let me hold the little creature.'

"She swept Jesse out, lifting him to the ceiling. And Jesse let loose his long, adorable baby laugh, 'Aaahhhrrrooo!'

"Amanda laughed. Jesse laughed. Amanda sang. Jesse sang."

Conor interrupted. "Actually, Jesse had been laughing and singing since he was born. Remember Jesse's first laugh?"

Dearie gurgled, "Oh! A laugh to behold! Utterly contagious! Ohhh...."

Jesse beamed, "That's when you called me your *brillish* boy."

"So right," Dearie put on her old Irish: "and *brillish* boy you be. Full o' fancy and faerie flecks y' are."

Jesse sniffed. "Then?"

"Then. Amanda spied Jesse's little stuffed rabbit, Velvet, still in the drawer.

'And what is this lil darlin' doin' in there? Why, she wants to come out and play.'

"And play they did. At every break, Amanda, Jesse, and Velvet, singing, dancing, storytelling.

Conor was only fifteen then, and how he gabbled about Amanda: 'She reminds me of Jane,' he'd say, 'She even looks a little like Jane.'"

Jesse sat up, "That's what Aislinn said. Sometimes I think I feel Jane's Light inside me and inside Amanda. Like it's the same Light. And Lady Jessica, too."

"My, Jesse," Dearie touched his cheek, "that is wonder full!"

"But, the story, Dearie!" Jesse laughed.

"Well! Amanda rehearsed all her *Is it You?* songs with Jesse. And Jesse cooed right along. Then opening night, *Is It You?* began as a full house success. The audience applauded, laughed, and tapped their feet in all the right places.

"Between acts, I went to the stage to repair a costume, bringing Jesse along, depositing him in his baby swaddle box in the wings. There, Amanda found him, and blissfully snatched him away. "Next came the second act. That's when it dawned on me: *Oh! Dim-wittles! I'm over here in this wing! Baby Jesse's over there. Alone!*

"The stage catwalk was yet to be built. I couldn't cross the stage unnoticed. And just then, the curtain opened."

Jesse giggled, "Oh, Dearie."

"Well! You can just imagine what happened!" Dearie exclaimed, "Amanda had an echo from the stage wings! 'Aaahhhrrrooo!'"

Jesse laughed, "That was ME! Aaahhhrrrooo!"

Dearie continued, "The song was poignant, but the audience was erupting in laughter. My guest director was beside himself—though he was standing right next to me! *Winkwhile*, Amanda sang, and Jesse 'Ahhhrrrooo-ed!'"

Jesse squealed and bounced on the couch.

"Uproariously, inappropriately, the crowd hooted with laughter. The director reached to close the curtain. But. Clever Amanda whirled into the wings, fetching Jesse on stage!

"The audience went wild with applause. And, Jesse and Amanda sang in duet:

♫ *The Why or How - the Here and Now leave their clues*
('Ooooooooo')
The Gift of Chance - a second glance - Is it you?

"With Jesse's soft, tender 'Ahhh-rooooo...,' the audience was *splendishly* enchanted. Charmed. Oh, they were still laughing, but sweetly so, especially the way Amanda held Jesse so endearingly. With the last line, she raised Jesse above her head, and his long baby laugh 'Aaahhhrrrooo-ed' once more.

"The audience leapt to its feet in applause! The clapping went on and on!" Dearie clapped, "Amanda and Jesse! The *brillish* hit of the show!"

"Ahhh," Dearie breezed, "The End!"

Jesse 'Aaahhhrrroooed' a *finale* and they all laughed like diddle dumplings.

Winter. You know how Old Man Winter goes. The cold days slip by, dressed in warm winter woolies, under snug blankets of low grey skies, and the early dark nights shut everyone indoors. It is a season of lamplights, reading and playing games; and at bedtime, casting an eye out the window to the glittering stars that spiral through the deep, endless universe, guiding your deep, endless journey.

Part Three

Spring

*The magic
is not to be found
in a wand
or a potion.
The magic is in you.*

Chapter Ten

Jots & Tittles

Before you could say crocus and daffodils, spring poked her lovely head into the courtyard. Mac looked out his side window.

"Ya see that, Jesse? How the Tree of Life spreads her green fancies? The birds in her branches know. They're singing their little hearts out, telling us: Winter has released us, and Spring is well come."

Jesse smiled, "Spring is well come. I like it."

The weather was perfection. Early Saturday afternoon a tinker's wagon rolled by and the ladies of the apartment brought boxes of Good Will items for him; the children surrounded the wagon, goggling the horse as well as the hanging pots and pans and utensils.

Mrs. Romano had a set of knives she wanted the tinker to sharpen, and the children were agog at the pedal, that moved the belt, that spun the sharpening stone, that spewed bright orange and white sparks off the blades. It was like miniature fireworks!

After that, the old tinker pulled out boxes of old toys, and Billy found a big bag of marbles to buy.

All the children stayed outdoors to play. Siobhan came out, too, sitting on the stoop with her pencil and sketchpad, drawing all the goings-on. Jesse liked the way she put all sorts of little drawings on one page. Like Mac's little picket fence around his garden, a robin's nest fallen out of the Tree of Life, a box of graham crackers that Mrs. Gorecki had brought down to share, and Jesse's bowl of milk he brought for dunking.

The rope swing hung from the oak tree, and Joey Romano swung into action. "Whoooo! I'm Tarzan! Aaaeeehhh!"

Billy's bag of marbles included the long string to make a marble circle, and most of the boys were down on one knee popping their thumbs and squinting at the glass cats-eye marbles.

The Dutchies sang a catchy little clapping song:

"Oh-my-oh playmate, come out and play with me,

Bring out your dollies three, Climb up my apple tree…"

Jesse usually played, too, but today he was in Mac's garden, helping to turn the soil. Mac stood, with his pipe in his teeth, leaning on his shovel, surveying his patch. "This is looking fine, Jesse. Just that corner there and we'll be all set to plant."

Jesse knelt in the corner, turning over the dirt with Mac's hand trowel. "Look at this Mac. It's a caterpillar. Look at him go!"

Mac took a gander. "Yep. A butterfly in the making. As the garden grows, we'll have to keep an eye out for the cocoon it'll spin to become a butterfly." He shook his head, "Y'know, this garden can teach you every jot and tittle about life."

"Jot and tittle," Jesse exclaimed, "That sounds like tiddly-winks!"

Mac chuckled and explained, "Jot and tittle means every tiny detail. 'Jot' comes from the Greek, iota, with i being the tiniest letter in the Greek alphabet; and believe it or not, 'tittle' is even tinier. It's the tiny dot atop the letter 'i'." Mac set his spade back into the dirt, saying, "That's what life is made of: jots and tittles."

Jesse watched the little caterpillar critter wander off. "Go on, you little jot. You're too big to be a tittle." When he went back to digging, the metal trowel hit something hard. Jesse kept at it, ready to pull up a rock, but what he found surprised him.

"Look at this! It's a little knife." He brushed it off and spit on it, rubbing it with his flannel shirttail. "Mac, an old jackknife. It's orange." He turned it over. "And there's a butterfly on this side." Jesse opened the blades. "Oh, the little blade is broken."

Mac looked at it. "Still, you can use that as a screw driver, need be. The bigger blade looks fine."

"I can use the big blade to slice through the string on Billy's newspapers. This is a *wallopper* of a surprise!"

Mac grinned, "I hope y' mean *whopper*!"

Cheerily sharing in the Saturday sunshine, the grownups appeared, one-by-one and two-by-two. Gypsy, the cat, followed the Maguires out the door, sitting on the stoop next to Liam, giving her trademark hello wink. Then she flipped over, and stretched out on her back, with her head hanging over the step.

Annika Schuyler laughed. "I'd like a cat like that."

Gypsy gazed at her, as if saying *Thank you.*

Liam chuckled, "Gypsy magic!" And he sang out a popular song, though he changed one word: "How much is that *kitty* in the window?"

Grams played with her gold Claddagh necklace, singing out a long, "Mee-owww."

The kids looked up, tickled pink, and sang along: "The one with the waggily tail."

Gypsy flipped her tail and everyone laughed.

Mr. Romano knew all the words to the song, and he sang it loudly, looking somewhat comical.

"Och, Joseph Romano!" Grams crowed, "Those Elvis Presley eyes. Those shaggy eyebrows. The likes of a handsome man singing the daylights out of a giddy-kiddy song!"

No one minded Grams' words. Everyone enjoyed the singing. Best of all, it inspired a courtyard songfest, harmonizing in songs that accompanied the children's games and play.

Jesse and the Bonheur twins had found a box of curtain rods, and they hooted, "Hey, look at the back of these rods. Let's make a track for the marbles!"

They built curtain-rod tracks from the stoop down to the street, like a mini marble rollercoaster. But first they had to get Gypsy off the rods. She walked across the suspended curtain rods like a perfect acrobat. They all laughed, but rolling the marbles was much more fun. At first, Jesse pretended he was building a miniature highway system to Elizabethtown. But he was soon lost in the game of it.

With marbles and singing, the children gathered, sitting on their parents' laps, or draping around shoulders. Dearie brought down her instruments and soon Jesse tootled his penny whistle, Dearie fiddled and Teppo Bonheur played Dearie's bodhran, till their music echoed down and around the block.

Within minutes, Conor turned the corner and strode into the courtyard. He brought along friends from the Actor's Studio, including Bobby Lewis. In his mid-forties, Bobby was an actor, director and a founding member of the Actor's Studio. This songfest was right up his alley.

Conor hugged Jesse with a, "Howdeedoo!"

And Jesse grinned up at him, "Conor, this is so much fun! Everybody has their Lights on!" Jesse straightaway sniffed at Conor's sleeve, "I smell Aislinn," he smiled and breathed-in. "Nice smell…I like that you love her."

"So glad you approve," Conor smiled, and they joined the fun and song.

Glow Little Glow Worm, glimmer, glimmer…

Baby Face, you've got the cutest little baby face…

You, You, You, I'm in love with you, you, you...

When "Oh Susannah" came up, Jesse sang loudly, "*So I'm goin' t'*

Alabama, with a bandaid on my knee!"

Everyone laughed at the idea of turning the song's 'banjo' into 'bandaid'. But the next song had them swaying, clapping, and singing along. Some acted out "Walkin' My Baby Back Home", and they danced, twirling to the "Tennessee Waltz". Al Romano started the chorus of "Jumbalaya", and the children rambunctiously swung each other around the courtyard while Gypsy winked at everyone.

As the sun dropped behind the city buildings, Bobby Lewis begged, "Just one more." Dearie obligingly fiddled the notes for "Dear Hearts and Gentle People" as the actors strolled away, still singing.

Jesse felt the song. And he felt...*Jessica! And that man...that man, Dan-yell, who loves her. Singing. Loving.*

It is no wonder so many love songs are written. Love and song just go together.

Jesse looked up at the apartment windows and saw the window boxes blooming in a riot of spring flowers. He and Dearie were heading to the *Lady Bird Theater* for his piano lessons. But when they sat down at the piano, Bobby Lewis showed up. Ever since the sing-along in the courtyard, the O'Neils had been seeing more and more of Bobby.

When Jesse heard that Bobby had been in Hollywood films with famous actors like Katherine Hepburn and Charlie Chaplin, he crowed, "I love Charlie Chaplin! He is so funny-fun! But...why didn't you stay in Hollywood and play with Charlie Chaplin?"

Bobby's shoulders went up, "Well, I was too short and round for Hollywood! So I returned to New York, to be the Director of the musical, *Brigadoon."*

Dearie's eyebrows snapped in admiration, "Yes, the enchanting—and highly successful—*Brigadoon!*"

Bobby grinned. Their feelings were mutual. Conor truly appreciated his direction in the Actor's Studio, and Dearie enjoyed discussing theater productions with him. Jesse liked going to see the *Peter Pan* movie with him, especially afterward, when Bobby came to dinner.

Bobby had grinned at Jesse, "*Peter Pan* is my all time favorite. The pixie dust, the flying...." He winked, "The 'Ohhhs' and 'Uh-Ohs'. I want *Neverland* to never ever end."

"Me too!" Jesse exclaimed, trying to wink back in agreement with Bobby. Jesse wanted to crow like Peter Pan. "It's like my quest! I want to fly to Elizabethtown and sprinkle pixie dust all over the island. And I'll find Lady Jessica. And sprinkle the pixie dust on her. And we'll fly together!"

Dearie grinned, "The truth is, we all want to live in *Neverland*. In the magic. We all hear Peter. Calling us. Into all the cheeky fun. The magical adventure."

Conor smiled, "Peter Pan is a pure magic *imaginator* for sure."

"*Peter Pan*'s author, James Barrie, was the true imaginator." Dearie blurted and laughed, "Ohhh, James Barrie! What a caution. He was always surprising me. Do you know, James Barrie could waggle his ears and eyebrows at the same time?"

"R-e-a-l-l-y?" Jesse *quizzled.*

Dearie laughed, "Yes! Hilarious!"

Jesse asked seriously, "Can you do it? Waggle your ears?"

"Of course. When I saw Barrie do that, I had to try it. So I practiced-and-practiced. And one day I got the hang of it."

Dearie pulled her hair back to give it a try. All of a sudden, her ears moved back and forth like...like... Oh, Jesse didn't know what! He had never seen anything so clever.

Conor and Bobby dissolved into laughter, and Jesse, too, giggled in astonishment. Holding on to his own ears, he begged, "Oh! Do it again!"

"Enough!" Dearie cried. "I haven't done that in years. I don't want to wear them out! I'll teach you to do it one day, and you can carry on the tradition."

Jesse exclaimed, "I want this magic to last forever!" He stopped and held his ears. "A-N-D… I want to learn how to waggle my ears!"

Bobby laughed, "You never know how that could come in handy one day!"

⁂

Now, when the famous Bobby walked into Dearie's theater practice room, she was surprised.

"*Diggety-boo!* The celebrated Bobby Lewis! How does the director of *Brigadoon* fame have time for our little theater?"

"Not only time. Inclination. I've been itching to rub theater elbows with you, oh *Lady Bird.* You and your crazy optimism make for a regular dream factory." With a sly twinkle he said, "And now I have a dream proposal to match your dream theater. Think of a timeless story. A story written by one of the Greats. In 1843, over one hundred years ago, this Christmas."

Jesse asked, "Is this a riddle?"

Dearie smiled, "I know the answer! *A Christmas Carol.*"

"Right," laughed Bobby, "Dearie, let's have your *Lady Bird* produce Charles Dickens' masterpiece! This Christmas!"

"Charles Dickens," Dearie snickered, "or, as Roald Dahl says, 'Dahl's Chickens!'"

"Funny!" Jesse tittered.

Dearie sighed, "Funny. But Dickens' Christmas play is gloomy."

"Dearie! *A Christmas Carol* changed the world for the good!" Bobby insisted, "And isn't that what our theater art does? Helps people to see mankind, and themselves, in a brand new way? It gives people a new compass to imagine how things could be. And it's all connected. Everything. And the connections keep reaching out, touching, and making more connections.

"Why, *A Christmas Carol* helped to launch new Child Labor Laws, Poverty Laws. Did you know the Queen of Norway sent gifts to the crippled-children's home of London, signed, *with Tiny Tim's Love!* As if Tiny Tim himself sent the gifts."

Bobby scuffed his hands together, "Then the upper class got into the act, raising oodles of money for the poor by reading it aloud in public. A weasley old factory owner named Mr. Fairbanks heard it and gave his workers the day off and sent them each a turkey! And in the First World War..."

"Yes, I know," Dearie murmured, "it was read aloud in the trenches. By Captain Corbitt-Smith." She remembered, "In the First World War, my Mam and Da and I moved up and down behind the trench lines in our vardo wagon, supplying the hospitals in France."

Bobby looked at her with wonder, "I'm trying to imagine the life you've led, Dearie. Social chaos, the Industrial Revolution, two world wars, the Spanish Flu pandemic, the Great Depression...."

"Well," Dearie sighed, "I wasn't the only one living through all of that."

"But you've come through it, with your...magic...intact." Bobby said, with high regard.

"Hmmm..." Dearie mused modestly, "So very many people created magic even in that chaos: writers, composers, artists, dancers. The magic is always flowing if we tap into it."

"You're in it, Dearie." Bobby smiled, "You *are* the magic! And you're giving it to Conor. And Jesse. And your theater. Your audience.

You are a gift, Dearie."

Jesse popped his eyes at Dearie, "Maybe we can tie a ribbon around you."

Dearie laughed, "Oh, wouldn't I look like the cow jumping over the moon!"

They laughed and Bobby went back to imploring.

"Dearie, just hear my ideas!" Bobby winked, "And then—say yes!"

Dearie laughed, "Go on…."

"We can write merry lines and happy songs! Dances! All through the audience, all over the stage streets and shops. And for Fezziwig's party!"

"Fezziwig!" Jesse burst in, "What a name!"

Chuckling, Dearie admitted, "Charles Dickens was famous for his intriguing names."

Jesse got that. "Like Tanagasuq Bay and Kecaniduq and Nocanituc."

Bobby looked at Jesse like he was speaking Greek, but he continued, "Dearie, I promise, this *Christmas Carol* will be fun! And, nobody does community theater like you, Dearie. I've seen you in action: the joy, the fun! The cast will include your wonderful apartment people. Mac can be Scrooge, and you and Conor and Jesse can be the Ghosts of Christmas."

"Ghosts!" Dearie stopped him, "you see, gloomy."

"Okay, we'll call them Spirits! Uplifting! Flying Spirits! On new fly-wires!"

Jesse popped off his seat, "Can I fly?"

In the end, with Bobby's irresistible prodding, Dearie decided to say, "Yes. *Lady Bird Theater* will present a rollicking Charles Dickens' *Christmas Carol*—emphasis on *rollicking*!"

She and Bobby worked hand-in-glove; and most everyone in the apartments agreed to the casting. Bridget volunteered to take over the costumes; and engineering designs were begun for new fly-wires in the *Lady Bird,* all over the stage and way out to the back of the theater.

Then Bobby told Jesse, "You shall be the little Spirit of Christmas Past. And, YOU shall fly. Like Peter Pan!"

Jesse leapt out of his chair, and Dearie laughed, "Jesse, you look like Gypsy after she's eaten her olive treat. The only thing you didn't do was purr!"

Chapter Eleven

Sliding Doors

"It's none too soon to begin planning the *Christmas Carol* costumes," Dearie explained to Bridget and Jesse on the way to the *Lady Bird Theater*.

"But," Bridget noted, "it's only April, and we don't put on the play till November and December."

"True, but because of the amateur cast, I want 'Pre-Costuming' for every rehearsal: light costumes to help the actors feel their characters more keenly."

"Oh," Jesse said, "Like Jemima Puddleducks!"

Bridget was lost.

"You know, from Beatrix Potter." Jesse beamed, "The mother duck who took all Tom Kitten's clothes and walked around in them, *pit-pat-waddle-pat*. Did you know Dearie met the real Jemima Puddleduck when she and Galen visited Beatrix Potter?"

"Ah yes," Bridget grinned, "I remember Dearie's stories about Beatrix Potter."

Dearie nodded and smiled, "All right Jesse, we'll call it Puddle-Ducking. Blue ribbon, you."

Dearie was thankful for Bridget's help because she was familiar with organizing clothing from her long years in her laundry business, and she could operate the revolving clothes rack that hung from the ceiling.

Dearie left a folder of costume notes for the large cast of characters, and she left Jesse to help Bridget sort and hang the Puddle-Duck practice costumes.

He liked the way the rack went round, snaking from the ceiling, down toward the floor. They could see all the costumes and Bridget could stop it when she came to the right one.

Bridget went to the storage closet in the adjacent room and slid open the wide doors.

Jesse followed her and stared, "What a smart door. It just slides open to a secret room." He blathered on, "We have a secret box in our lumber room. No top, no bottom, no lid."

"Oh, like the riddle," Bridget said, "*A box with no hinge, no key, no lid. Yet a golden globe inside is hid.*"

"What is it?" Jesse asked.

But Bridget teased, "You'll figure it out. One day you'll just know." She began rearranging the long, shallow cardboard boxes filled with the costumes they needed to sort through. She slid one box over, pushing the next one back, and sliding out the box she was after.

Jesse was amazed. "You did that so fast. Easy. Like a game."

"It's just like a game. Didn't Mac ever show you his Chinese puzzle?"

"No," Jesse shook his head while Bridget rearranged the boxes and slid out another one.

"It's a square, with one little red tile and the rest white tiles. There is only one tile space empty, and you have to slide the tiles, one by one, to get the red tile smack-dab in the middle." She put the box on the table. "I'll show you when we're finished here."

They busily switched costumes on and off the rack, labeling and putting them back in their proper boxes. But, by-and-by Bridget looked at her watch, "Time to put everything back into the closet."

Jesse watched her, sliding things back and forth, making room for the boxes once again. "One more and we're done," Bridget announced.

Jesse sang to her. "Did you ever see the boxes, slide this way and that way...."

Bridget chuckled and said, "That's the key, Jesse."

Jesse stopped cold. "Slide," he whispered. "The key. Slide. The box!" His eyebrows popped and his feet followed. "Bridget!" he shouted.

"I'm right here Jesse, no need to shout."

"Bridget! I have to go home. Right now!" He grabbed her hand, gave it a kiss and was out the door.

Jesse was bubbling like a teakettle as he ran all the way up to their apartment and slipped his key in the door. Nobody home. No matter. He ran into the lumber room and picked up the box. Wiping his sweaty hands on his pants, he took the box to the windowsill. Slowly, he pushed on the different colored stripes of wood. One at a time. "Press. Push. Slide," he said under his breath.

Red. No.

Black. No.

White. Y-e-s! Like sliding his crayons out of the box, the white line of wood slid out of its groove.

"Ohhh," Jesse gulped and his eyes flickered. "Ohhh!"

He turned the box and saw the white-slide sticking out of the end. He pushed a bit more and the whole piece fell out. It was in the shape of a wide, flat key.

"Now what?" He held it in his hand. "Well...it's a key. Maybe..." He put the key in the long open side and gently pushed. Something moved! He pushed more, then looked on the opposite side of the box. He stopped breathing. A little drawer of white, red, and black stripes was coming out of that side.

He pushed again, the drawer fell out, and a little metal key fell on the floor.

His ears rang with it. His heart sang with it. He picked up the key, staring with his mouth agape. But he came to his senses, closed his mouth, and took the key to the desk.

"A perfect fit!"

He turned the key. *Click.*

Excitedly, he pulled out the desk sliders, reaching to lower the top.

It's opening!

Inside…was…a leather folder. That's all. Jesse opened it and found a photo strip. He remembered the photo booth pictures that Joey and Mikey Romano had taken at the arcade in Coney Island. This was the same, with three pictures, all of Jane and James.

Jesse couldn't help smiling. In the top photo Jane and James were crossing their eyes. In the middle one they were laughing. And in the bottom, they were giving each other a little kiss. Jesse stared at each one. He liked them.

He decided he'd best put the key back in the puzzle box, and he twittered at himself, enjoying each step of the task. Then he reached to put the photo strip back in the folder, but he dropped it on the floor. That's when he noticed something else. "Oh, there's writing on the back: *James Galen O'Neil & Jane Danielle Roberts ~ 1946.*

"Jane Danielle Roberts! Her whole name! With her last name! Jane's last name is Roberts!"

Jesse was as high as a kite when he found Dearie in her theater office with Bobby Lewis. Neither of them understood what he was trying to tell them.

Finally, Dearie insisted, "Jesse, slow down."

Ever so slowly, he said, "I. Opened. The. Desk."

"Desk?" Dearie said curiously. But then she *gaspered*, "Desk! Jane and James' desk?"

Jesse's head moved up and down.

Dearie looked at Bobby, but she said: "Conor! I've got to find Conor."

"This sounds sensational," Bobby grinned. "Conor's working on the sets. I'll get Conor. You get the details."

The three O'Neils rushed into the lumber room, gathering around the open desk. Simultaneously, six hands reached out for the leather folder. Dearie laughed, "All righty then! Let's have some decorum here!"

Conor handed it to Dearie. When she saw the pictures, she blurted a laugh and gave it to Conor. He laughed, too.

Jesse said, "I told you you'd like them!" But when he looked at Dearie she had tears in her eyes. He hugged her legs.

"I'm all right, Jesse. It's just...."

"They're so funny!" Jesse crowed. "And...fun!"

"Yes! Very, very fun!" Dearie laughed, hugging Jesse.

But Conor was serious. "Roberts," he breathed, "A last name! Oh, let this be the missing piece."

Dearie pointed, "But what about these two drawers? One on each side of the little door in the middle. What's in these?"

Conor opened one drawer and found a square glass jar. "Oh, I remember this. Jane's shells and sea glass from Elizabethtown."

Jesse gazed at the beautiful soft colors in the jar, but he couldn't resist pulling out the other little drawer, and he handed it to Dearie.

"Hmm...there's only a thimble." But she laughed at herself, "only a *thimble*! That's what James Barrie called a *kiss*!"

"Yes! I remember! Jesse's eyes widened. "In *Peter Pan,* Wendy tells Peter she's going to give him a kiss, and he, doesn't know what a kiss is! So he holds his hand out."

"Right," Dearie smiled and finished the story, "So as not to embarrass him, she hands him a thimble. And Peter calls the thimble his kiss."

Jesse smiled, "Jane left me a kiss!"

Dearie smiled back as she pulled out needles, thread, and a ball of fine, colored yarns. "Jane's embroidery yarns," she noted. "Jane told me she used to cross-stitch words and pictures in thread."

Jesse took the ball in his hands and a funny feeling tingled his fingers.

"The loom," he thrummed. "Remember, Dearie? The weavings?" He smiled and held up the yarn ball. "Jessica…?"

Conor was trying to open the little door in the middle. "Aeghhh. Jesse where's the key to open the desk?"

The sun was setting and Dearie turned on the light, chirping, "Light on," as Jesse took the box, opened its secret compartments again, and dropped the key in Conor's hand.

"Honestly, Jesse," Dearie crowed. "How you unravel puzzles!"

Conor looked at the key and looked at Jesse's glinting turquoise eyes. "I'll never know how that brain of yours figures out something so puzzling."

Dearie laughed, "Children just know. Everything. They're all born knowing they are the stuff of stars."

Conor only shook his head and turned to the desk to try the key, "Nope. This key is not even close. Too big for this little door."

Dearie said, "Well, James hid that key somewhere."

She took the folder and smiled, "In the *winkwhile*, I am going to write to Elizabethtown with our new information. They asked for a last name. And now we have it: *Jessica Roberts*."

Jesse took to carrying Jane's thimble in his pocket with his orange jack-knife. He liked slipping the little metal cap onto his finger to feel Jane's kiss.

The sea glass and shells he brought to school to show the class, and they all learned the names of the shells: the deep blue mussel, fan-shaped scallop, purple-lined clam, gnarly oyster, and the yellow jingle shell (which Jesse thought looked like a toenail). But his favorite was the tiny conch shell, a perfect spiral—like a winding road leading to Elizabethtown.

Every day Jesse checked the mail, looking forward to an answer for his quest. Even so, he was diverted with scatterings of neighborhood amusements, surprises, and more clues.

Chapter Twelve

The Maguires

On a hot Saturday afternoon, Billy and the neighborhood boys tramped into the Maguire's kitchen for a drink. Teresa was ironing in the corner and Grams sat at the window working a crossword puzzle. She pursed her lips together because she didn't have her false teeth in her mouth.

Siobhan walked in with Gypsy following her. "I'll pour the lemonade, Mommy, then finish the ironing."

Teresa looked relieved, "Thanks, Siobhan. I'll just finish this shirt. Oh, but the lemonade's not sweetened yet." Teresa pointed to the new sack of sugar.

Siobhan opened the drawer. "Where are the scissors?"

"I can cut that," Jesse perked. Taking out his orange butterfly knife, he confidently sliced through the top of the paper sack.

Grams' eyebrows knit together, and her mouth *murmeled*, "Let me see that knife." She grabbed it, turning it over in her fingers. "I remember seeing this. Where did I see this?"

Billy answered, "Jesse found it in Mac's garden."

Grams looked at Jesse, "Hmm. Maybe it belonged to Jane. Jane. She didn't have much of nothin' when she first come. Looked like a church-mouse-gypsy. Dressed from Dearie's costume shop."

Teresa winked at Jesse, and he smiled agreeably, realizing that Grams was teasing.

But Grams added, "That Jane. She had some kind of dark secret: always posting letters and checking the mailbox. Letters, letters, letters."

"Did you hide *her* letters?" Jesse wondered out loud.

"Me-e-e? Bosh!" Not answering, she blurted a laugh, "Hah! Secrets! Easy to let the cat outta the bag, but y' can't get it back in so easy."

Teresa rolled her eyes. Jesse shrugged his shoulders and wondered at the same time.

Meanwhile, Siobhan was ready to pour the lemonade. Jesse saw her face and he knew she had a trick she wanted to play. He felt a spark, just like when he opened the little key-box. He thought, *Siobhan is like Dearie. She has magic.*

Siobhan elaborately wiped the table with a soaking-wet sponge. Their kitchen table was tipsy, and Siobhan knew that a very wet lemonade glass would slide right down the wet, tilted table. She put down one wet glass, pointing at it, commanding: "*Limonada! Mo-vi-air!*"

Gypsy sat up in Jesse's lap and pawed the air, as—all by itself—the glass obediently slid down the table!

Grams shrieked. Billy's eyes almost exploded, and he and his pals ran *sca-reeeaming* out of the kitchen.

But not Jesse. "Golly, Siobhan! How'd you learn to do that?"

"Oh no," she laughed. "A magician never tells her secrets."

"But Siobhan, you could use your magic to find the missing key to our desk!"

Siobhan chuckled, "Oh Jesse, you make me sound like Houdini! It was a trick." She produced her spoonerisms: "*And my zips are lipped*! It's my *micky tragic!*"

With the thimble on his pointer finger, Jesse raised his hand in a solemn vow, "You can count on me to keep your secret. I'm *ready as a sock.*"

Siobhan burst out laughing. "Jesse, I should have known Dearie would teach you to use spoonerisms. That was a pretty good one. Not perfect, but pretty good!"

Billy returned. Alone. He glugged a normal glass of lemonade, set down the glass, and looked at Grams, who was once again, deep in her crossword puzzle. Then he motioned to Jesse and mouthed, "C'mere."

Jesse wondered what Billy had in mind, especially when he brought Jesse to Grams' bedroom door, saying, "Wait till you see this."

He led Jesse to Grams' bed, pointing to a glass of water on her bedside table. Jesse looked.

"What is that?" Slowly he realized, it was Grams' false teeth. Floating. Grinning. In the glass of water. Both boys stared, until Jesse whispered,

"It's like the Chess Eye—I mean, the Cheshire Cat."

"Whaaat?"

"You know, in *Alice in Wonderland.* The cat disappears, but its smile stays. Floating. Did Grams disappear?"

"No."

All at once, a knock-knock clacked on the door.

"Grams!" Billy *gaspered*, grabbed Jesse, and tried to push past Grams.

But she snatched hold of Jesse, sneering with a teasing smile, "Remember your curse, Jesse with a J."

She pushed him off, and he and Billy high-tailed it out of there, returning to the kitchen. They tried to look innocent, but their flushed faces said otherwise.

Siobhan asked, "What have you two been up to?" She turned over the shirt collar to iron it flat. "You know what Mommy says: 'When Irish eyes are smiling they're usually up to something.'"

Jesse turned to Siobhan and gave her a Cheshire Cat smile. She knew right away and laughed. "So you've been sneaking around Grams' bedroom." She shook her head, but looked at Jesse again, "You reminded me of Jane when you smiled like that. Your eyes got so big."

Jesse gave Siobhan his full attention. "Jane? Did Jane have big eyes?" he asked.

"Oh yeah, the biggest, bluest eyes. Beautiful," Billy rhapsodized. "With pieces of turquoise like yours."

"But Jane's eyes were quieter than yours." Siobhan smiled.

"What else?"

Billy spoke up again, "Jane was real smart. She knew everything. She taught me how to count by 10s and 5s and 2s—like a game." He smiled like he was the champion of numbers.

"What else?"

"Well, nothing else." Siobhan answered. "Jane wasn't much of a talker. She was a good questioner; she said she wanted to know all about me. Can you imagine?" Siobhan hung the shirt on the hook with the others. "Because of Jane, I started believing in my impossible dreams."

"What dreams?"

Siobhan turned around, "Aren't you the little interrogator?" She smiled at Jesse. "My dream is that I will graduate high school. Mommy and Grams wanted me to drop out and get a job, like them, working all morning at the fish market. But then Mac arranged a job for me after school."

"Yeah," Billy said, "taking care of that family with the deaf mother."

Jesse remembered, "That's where you learned the sign language you taught me when I was little." He tapped his fingers together in the sign for 'more' and Siobhan smiled.

"Yes, it's a wonderful, well-educated family."

Siobhan went into her room and returned with a little card. "See. Jane wrote this out for me:

If you are not willing to learn, no one can help you.

If you are determined to learn, no one can stop you.

"So, I am determined to finish my schooling,"—Siobhan took a breath—"no matter how hard it is."

Jesse looked at Siobhan and declared in his small but stouthearted voice, "And I am determined to find my Grandmother Jessica, no matter how hard it is."

They both smiled at each other. Determinedly.

Siobhan looked at her watch. "It's time to get down to the docks. Daddy's tug will be coming in."

Billy jumped up, but looked at Jesse. "Hey, Jess, come with us!"

The threesome asked Dearie's permission and, together, walked down their street. At every avenue, Billy held Jesse back, making sure the traffic was clear. Even so, Billy told him, "This is the easiest walk in the world. We call it 'Tugboat Street'. You just stay on this street all the way across town till you get to the docks."

Jesse *shiveraled*, "This is an *avenger*."

"Adventure, Jesse. Yes." Siobhan chuckled.

"Ad-venture." Jesse corrected himself. "I knew that."

As they walked, Siobhan challenged, "How about trying this tongue twister: 'Irish wristwatch'."

"Iris wish wash." Jesse blurted with a laugh. He tried it again. Slowly. "Irich wrish wash. Ohhh. I can't say it!"

Billy gave it a try, "Iris –witch-wash."

Laughing, they passed a big warehouse along the street, and came out to a crisp breeze at the open harbor where the docks poked into the Hudson River.

"Look," Siobhan pointed, "There's Daddy's boat."

Billy exclaimed, "Daddy's *Harbor Lady!*"

The red-and-green-painted tugboat neared the docks, and there was

Liam. He was standing at the pilothouse door, waving his arms over his head and shouting through an enormous megaphone.

"Hallo-o-o, Siobhan! Hallo-o-o, Billy! Who's the little critter with you?"

Jesse waved with both arms, yelling. "It's ME! It's JESSE!"

First Mate, Steve, set up the little wooden gangplank and Billy saluted Liam, saying, "Permission to come aboard, Captain?"

Liam had his gold watch open in his hand as he saluted Billy, saying, "Time of arrival noted." He clicked his watch shut, his voice boomed, "Welcome aboard!" – and he embraced Billy and Siobhan in one big bear hug.

Jesse stepped on the gray deck, and Liam picked him up, swinging him in a flying circle. Then the three Maguires gave Jesse a tour of the old boat.

Inside the pilothouse, Jesse pointed and asked about this and that, and which and how. Liam laughed, "Jesse, me boyo, you got more questions than a parrot."

Jesse tittered, "Like Captain Flint, Long John Silver's parrot in *Treasure Island*. All he says is, 'Pieces of eight, pieces of eight!'"

Liam set Jesse high on the stool in front of the great wooden wheel. Siobhan showed him how to honk the foghorn, and Billy turned the running lights on and off. Liam spoke into the 'funnel' down to the engine room, "Halooo...."

Jesse peered into the funnel...and almost jumped off the stool when a deep 'Halooo' came back up at him.

Then Billy slid open a door, "This is Daddy's Captain's Quarters."

It was a small area with only the light of the porthole windows, one on each side. Jesse's eyes had to adjust to the dusky shadows. Billy pointed, "On this wall is Dad's sleeping bunk. See, with the drawers below."

On the opposite wall, Siobhan showed off a tall slanted table with long skinny drawers for the large maritime charts.

Jesse loved being on Liam's tugboat. He loved the click of Liam's beguiling gold watch. He loved the tangy smell of salt in the water, on the deck, and in the lines of the huge coiled ropes drying in the sun. He loved the safe feeling of holding hands with Billy and Siobhan as he continued to tour the boat's fantail and engine room. Jesse *love-adored* Billy and Siobhan and Liam. And this boat.

Jesse and the Maguires strolled back to the apartments, happy to find Mac in the lobby. He was looking up the steps, with a light in his eyes, and *Treasure Island* in his hands. Jesse ran to him, and found a lovely scent in the air. A fragrance he knew…from somewhere.

But he wrapped his arms around Mac's long legs, exclaiming, "Mac! We went on Liam's tugboat! It was a *cracker pet* day!"

Mac laughed, and Liam shook hands with Mac, smiling at his book. "*Treasure Island,*" he remarked, "The best pirate book ever."

Mac scraggled his voice, quoting, "'…the toughest old salts imaginable—not pretty to look at, but fellows, by their faces, of the most indomitable spirit.'"

Liam applauded, and Jesse looked up at both Mac and Liam with pure delight.

Just then the side door opened, and Jesse noticed that the lovely scent disappeared, like a pillow thrown over his face. A man wearing a uniform walked in, with Grams on his arm. Jesse was surprised that Grams looked, well, flirty—in a cauliflower sort of way. She brought the man forward.

"Mac, this is the young man I told you about."

The man didn't look that young to Jesse. His face had a little stubble showing. His sandy hair was longish, tucked behind his ears, but snipped across his forehead like he had cut it himself. Mostly, Jesse noticed his eyes. Empty. Nothing behind them. In them.

The man shook hands with Mac, "My name is Tim Braedon." He shook hands with Liam, too, and the three young ones stepped forward to be introduced. Jesse was startled at Tim Braedon's handshake. Like seaweed in a bucket of water swishing across his palm. Jesse *quiver-quavered* as he stepped back.

Tim Braedon turned to Mac with a crooked smile, "By coincidence, Maude here tells me you might have a room to rent to an old war veteran."

Grams blushed at being called Maude. It had been a dark age since anyone—any man—had called her Maude.

But Jesse felt a strange fog in his brain. He knew there was no such thing as coincidence.

Mac looked at the man with the same inkling, "Braedon, you say?" He looked at Grams, "Don't usually rent to anyone off the street."

"Why, Mac," Maude oozed, "Mr. Braedon, Tim, is a war hero. Doesn't he cut a handsome figure in his uniform? He works at the Army Recruiting Office."

There was a long, empty pause, till Mac said, "I'll see what I can do."

Tim Braedon turned to Grams, "Maude, may I walk you to your door?"

Grams blushed to kingdom come, "Oh, an old thing like me."

"Now, now," Tim dripped, "the older the violin, the sweeter the tune."

"Ohhh," she *pshawed* and slapped the air.

Liam said, "I'll walk my mother home, thank you."

Tim Braedon gave a short, awkward salute and walked away,

whistling under his breath.

Jesse got a strange feeling. He couldn't describe it, but it was like watching an oil spill, moving across the floor, slick and oozing out the door.

Mac saw Jesse watching Tim Braedon and he added another *Treasure Island* quote: "'You're a lad you are,' Jim, 'but you're as smart as paint.'"

Jesse hugged him, and Mac chuckled, "Oh, you're not Jim. You're Jesse."

Liam sat down on the steps to take off his work boots, and Jesse moved in between Liam's legs for a good hug, "Thanks for the visit on your *Harbor Lady* tugboat." Then he kissed Liam's forehead, pulled back, and rubbed-in the kiss, saying, "I want to rub in my kiss so you can have it whenever you want."

Liam laughed, "Thanks, Jess. Ain't nothin' like lovin'." In one swoosh, he stood and picked up Jesse, twirled him around in a short flight, and set him on the step. Then he took out his gold watch and clicked it open. Nodding at it, he clicked it shut, pointing up the stairs. "Home's callin'. Billy. Siobhan. Let's go!" He waved his hand at them, "You, too, Ma."

Chapter Thirteen

Pirates

Mac, too, pointed up the stairs. "There's a big surprise waitin' for you up there, Jesse. Best get on up."

Jesse shot up the stairway. He could hear his song, "The Nature Boy" coming from their apartment, and he sang it as he hopped up, stair-by-stair: '*...spoke of many things, fools and kings....*' He dashed through the door, to find:

"Amanda! I knew I smelled you!"

"Oh my darlin', Jesse!" she hugged him, showering him with her sugar-sweet accent. "Why, look at you. You're a bean pole."

Jesse laughed, "You look *gahslazerous*!" But he abruptly blurted, "Amanda, did you know my mother, Jane?"

Amanda stopped. Her eyes turned tender. "Why no, I did not have that pleasure."

Jesse explained, slipping Jane's thimble on his finger, "Jane had a secret. I don't know why she kept her mother a secret."

Amanda told him, "My momma has a secret. She never ever talks about it, but I see her holding her heart—and her eyes are filled with far away." Jesse saw Amanda's eyes go far away, but she came back, touching his shoulder, "You see, I never met your mother. I only met you after...."

Jesse finished, "After Jane went to the Great Illuminations."

"Yes. And I have known you all these six years. And look how you've grown! Don't you just remind me of a young Jim Hawkins."

"Jim Hawkins! My *favorish*!"

"Your *favorish*. Well then, I think you are in for a surprise."

Dearie smiled, "I told Amanda you're enjoying *Treasure Island*."

"So-o-o…I went through the studio costume shop jus' t' see what I could see. She opened the box, "A-a-a-nd. I brought you… *Treasure Island!*" She reached into the box and pulled out….

"A green parrot!" Jesse squealed, "It's Long John Silver's parrot, name of Captain Flint! It looks so real!"

"And a red parrot?" Amanda laughed: "let him squawk,'*pieces of eight, pieces of eight!*'"

Jesse crowed back, "*Avast ye! I remember him as if it were yesterday….*"

Amanda macawed, "Let's parlay!"

Dearie pulled out a black eye-patch and a telescope, swaggering, "I'll parlay! I'm a pirate! That I be! See me peg-leg under me knee!"

She stomped round the table, waving the telescope and chasing after the two parrots, who turned to tickle her.

"Aye! Stop!" she laughed. "Ye cockamamie magpies! You'll tickle me peg-leg right off me breeches! Stop! Stop!"

Jesse stood back from Dearie. "Stop? *Shiver-me-timbers*, Dearie! You don't say stop if you're a pirate! You have to say: '*Avast! Savvy? Avast!*'"

"I *savvy!*" Dearie laughed, "*Avast! Avast!*"

Amanda twirled, "Oh, I love to be here with you!"

Conor poked in, "Jumbalaya! This sounds like fun!"

Amanda laughed, and sang out the popular song:

♫ *Jambalaya and a-crawfish pie and fillet gumbo…*

Jesse clapped as Conor twirled Amanda around, singing and dancing.

♫ *'Cause tonight I'm gonna see my ma cher amio*

Pick guitar, fill fruit jar and be gay-oh
Son of a gun we'll have big fun on the bayou

Conor gave Amanda a hug and she exclaimed, "Take a seat, *shugah beet*!"

"*Shugah beet*!" Jesse repeated, grinning.

Conor shrugged a laugh, "I wish I could stay and play, but my busy schedule won't permit it. I'm off."

Life had changed for Conor. He didn't see much of anyone anymore, particularly Aislinn, since she was in college in Boston. Jesse noticed lots of letters back and forth. But Conor spent all his time studying, or at the Actor's Studio, or working the jobs he found, in or out of theaters.

"Conor," Amanda drawled at him, "Remember, it's not about how busy you are. The bee is applauded, but the mosquito gets smacked!"

Swatting her hand, Conor laughed a farewell.

Jesse pawed through the box, "*Blimey*! More pirate costumes."

Dearie marveled, "A treasure trove for Halloween."

Jesse threw on a three cornered hat and a long coat, "We'll be pirates," he exulted. "Weigh anchor and hoist the mizzen! This is the greatest Ca-juma ever!"

"Ca-juma?" Amanda and Dearie said together.

Jesse explained, "It's really the Good Humor ice cream truck. But one day Billy was yelling Good Humor so fast, we all thought he was saying 'Ca-juma'. So now we call the ice cream truck Ca-juma, and everything fun is a Ca-juma."

Ca-jumas poured out of Amanda's costume box and Jesse shared them with all the children. He taught them the pirate lingo from *Treasure*

Island, so that they raucously greeted each other with '*Ahoy Matey!*', '*Avast ye!*', and '*Shiver me Timbers!*'

Soon Mac was reading the "greatest pirate story ever" to a roomful of spellbound *kidlins.*

They gave each other real pirate names and played all over the apartments, especially in the hallways and stairwell. Every landing became the deck of a ship and they yelled to each other in whatever words *Treasure Island* gave up to their tongues.

"*Who goes?*"

"*Keep your head down!*"

"*Pieces of eight! Pieces of eight!*"

"*Drop anchor!*"

"*At 'em- all hands! All hands!*"

"*Out lads out and fight 'em in the open!*"

"*Use your cutlasses!*"

"*I'll have that treasure if I search a year!*"

They swashed and buckled with their wooden blades as their costume breach-coats swept behind them like capes. At the smallest victory, they tossed their three cornered hats into the air, and ran to the railing to watch them swirl down, down, down to the lobby, which was the rolling, roaring sea itself. It was grand.

Siobhan didn't play, but she liked to sketch their pictures. They called her *Lady Savvy.* And one day, they followed her…into the *dungeon.*

The very word—dungeon—gave the young pirates the *jim-jams.* Though in truth, they all knew it was just the basement rooms. Siobhan had gone down to fetch cleaning supplies for her mother, and once she saw all the little pirates, she jumped ship.

"No time for pirate play!" She laughed and left them to it.

Jesse—*Mister Blimey*—ballyhooed. "These wire store-closets are perfect for the yardarms of our pirate ship!"

But behind them, Jesse heard an odd, whisper-whistling. He twitched. It was Tim Braedon, poking around the storage units.

Grams liked all the attentions from Tim Braedon. She acted like he was her personal discovery. Like some matinee movie idol. She had badgered Mac and Bridget until they agreed to let Tim rent the apartment on the first floor.

Jesse had been on the landing when he heard Bridget poking fun at Grams, calling Tim, "your new beau." But then Jesse heard Mac caution, "There's something about Tim Braedon that gives me pause. But"—he shrugged—"he'll be right behind our apartment, so I can keep an eye on him."

Now, Jesse and the pirates were face-to-face with Tim Braedon.

"Hi, kids!" He sounded too friendly. "I see you're up to no good pirating!"

They stood still looking at him, with his stringy fingers thrumming on his pant leg. Jesse replied, "This is our dungeon."

"Oh," Tim lifted his long, pale fingers to his chin, pretending to be scared. "I don't want to trespass in your dungeon." And he left.

The little pirates got right to their fun, climbing the yardarms and brandishing their wooden blades, 'arrg-ing' at one another at the top of their lungs, until a shrill screech was heard above it all.

"Help! Help! I can't climb down!"

Elke—*Miss Aye-Aye*—was shrieking, her little legs thrashing the air.

"She's *traptured*!" Jesse—*Mister Blimey*—exclaimed.

Andros—*Pirate Jolly*—yelled, "Rescue *Miss Aye-Aye*!"

Danek—*Pirate Roger*—yelled, too, "All hands ahoy! Mac's—I mean *Old Salt's*—closet has a ladder!"

Jesse saw them head for two wide panels set in the wall. Mikey—*Pirate Dubloon*—slid one panel aside, and inside was a little room.

A curious sensation shivered Jesse's scalp. Something about sliding doors. *Oh,* he dismissed the thought, *they're like the Costume Rooms.*

The pirates pulled out the ladder and valiantly rescued *Miss Aye-Aye.*

But when she was safe, they all scuttled back to *Old Salt's* closet to investigate. Something was in there that they had not seen before.

They slid open the other door and stared. Marijke—*Lady Doc*—pushed her way forward. She knew just what it was. "Oh, it's daddy's old ice-cream freezer chest from the drugstore. He got a new one for the store."

"Did you say…ice-cream?" Paul—*Pirate Hearty*—tempted.

In a split second, all the pirates exclaimed, "*Treasure!*"

They hauled out the big cardboard cylinders of ice-cream and opened them on the workbench.

"Jumbalaya!" Jesse—*Mister Blimey*—crowed, "It's real!"

"Oh," said Elke—*Miss Aye-Aye*—"we need spoons."

They all scrambled upstairs, promising they'd wait to dig in until every Pirate returned.

One by one they returned. And waited. Spoons at-the-ready. But Jesse—*Mister Blimey*—didn't return. Finally, Annika—*Lady Commander*—proclaimed, "Well, let's take a Pirate Oath."

"Oh, right," exclaimed Jean—*Pirate Ahoy*—"we can s-w-e-a-r!"

The boys *gaspered* at the thought of swearing. But *Lady Commander* dramatically raised her eyebrows, and her chin and her voice: "Yes, an *oath.*"

Billy—*Captain Cutlass*—loudly repeated, "An oath!"

Annika raised the drama: "An oath! To save plenty for *Mister Blimey.*" She pointed at them with her spoon, "Swear!"

With true *gravitas*, a chorus of "I swear" resounded and pilfer-looting spoons flashed through the air!

"Try the chocolate, it's the best."

"The strawberry has real strawberries in it."

"Yeah but they're frozen, cold."

"Vanilla's my favorite."

Finally, amid the digging-licking-slurping, they heard Jesse's footsteps.

"Come on, *Mister Blimey!*" Andros—*Pirate Jolly*—yelled to him, "It's the greatest!"

"*Mister Blimey!*" laughed Danek—*Pirate Roger*—"It's better than the Ca-juma Ice Cream truck!"

"Bring your spoon and dig in!" Billy—*Captain Cutlass*—invited.

But *Mister Blimey* did not have a spoon. And he was not alone.

A well-known voice spoke. "I hear-tell there's treasure down here in the dungeon."

It was Dearie.

Shamefaced, the Pirates confessed to their parents, and most especially to Mr. Wit Schuyler.

He had installed a new freezer chest in his drugstore, and the old one was his gift for the families to use for extra freezer storage, since the apartment iceboxes only had enough freezer space to make a tray of ice cubes.

The Schuylers had planned an ice cream social to welcome Tim Braedon. After finding barely a dent in the ice cream, they decided to forgive the pirates and carry on. In the courtyard, not the dungeon.

Liam MacGuire was home from his latest tugboat trip, and he came down with his arms about Billy and Siobhan. Grams and Teresa were not with them. Grams had lost her gold Claddagh charm necklace, and she enlisted Teresa's help in turning their apartment upside down to find it.

Nevertheless, Liam was in fine fettle. When he saw Jesse, he picked him up and flew him around.

"So...*Captain Blimey,* is it?" Liam laughed holding Jesse.

"Oh no," Jesse chiggled, "Billy's the Captain. *Captain Cutlass.* I'm *Mister Blimey.*"

"Well, *Mister Blimey*, I hear tell you didn't get any ice cream this afternoon." He wheeled him round again, setting him down. But Jesse wasn't thinking of ice cream.

"Liam?" he pulled at Liam's shirt cuff, "Does your tugboat *Harbor Lady* go up to Elizabethtown?"

"Oh, yeah. Sometimes. It's a far, long haul. But, yeah, my old tug can make that trip. I've taken her up that way more than once. But, as I said, it's a long haul, me boyo."

Jesse didn't say anything. But surprisingly, Tim Braedon poked into the conversation. "My dad worked on a farm on Elizabethtown."

Jesse nearly had a canary. *Elizabethtown!* "Did you ever go there? To Elizabethtown?"

"Yeah, once. I was just a kid, during the Depression and my dad was working any job he could find. The farm job didn't last long. But I remember the island, and him telling me stories about the farm."

"What stories?"

Tim wanted to go talk to the grown-ups and he answered vaguely, "Oh, nothing much. Just chickens and cows. Farm stuff." He moved away to talk to the other grown-ups.

Winkwhile, Wit Schuyler had scooped ice-cream cones for all the grown-ups. The little pirates stood about, mutely, ogling him. A generous smile crossed Mr. Schuyler's face, and he called out, "Next...! Ice cream! For all reformed pirates!" Magnanimously, he served the *pilfer-looting* pirates their own ice cream cones.

Jesse licked his cone and said to Billy, "Let's all cheer Mr. Schuyler. Like the pirates do, you know, salute their champion. Um, well, maybe that's the Knights of the Round Table. Oh, I've got it all mixed up."

"It's still a good idea, Jess." And Billy cried, "Three cheers for Mr. Schuyler!"

The pirates weren't sure if their cheers were for Mr. Schuyler or the ice cream, but they stopped licking long enough to shout, "Hurray! Hurray! Hurray! For Mr. Schuyler!"

Abruptly, Mr. Schuyler jumped up on the stoop. In a grave pirate's voice, he commanded, "Avast, me mateys!" And he *arrg-ed* above the grown-up laughter, "We have to parlay here."

"Jumbalaya!" Jesse grinned, "He sounds like a real pirate!"

Andros gaped. "He's great!"

Dearie thought the same. *Impressive, Wit Schuylar.*

Mr. Schuyler's voice rang out in his amazing pirate lingo, "From this day forward, Mac has decreed: the dungeon will be off limits to all pirates. The door will not be locked. You will be on your honor not to trespass." He looked at them all, "Savvy?"

They murmured, "We savvy."

He finished, "Alas. No little pirates allowed!"

Annika's chocolate mouth frowned and she sighed, "Well. I guess we won't be needing *Ahoys* and *Avasts* anymore."

⁂

The next day, Mr. Paul, their mailman, finally delivered the long-awaited letter. He waved it in the air and announced, "For you, Master Jesse!"

"Elizabethtown!" Jesse's anticipation puffed up like a balloon!

But it burst in his face.

"We are sorry to inform you that there is no farm on Elizabethtown registered under the name of Roberts. Also, for your information, there is no birth record for the name Jessica or Jane Roberts."

Conor was disgusted.

Jesse sat in silence. He felt his stomach knot. He took a breath… then he said with determination, "I need to go there. To Elizabethtown. I know I can find Jessica. Just like I found Jane's map. And the key in the box. I can find Jessica!"

Dearie felt the sting in Jesse's words, recalling his bawling disappointment last time. But she aimed at helping him pivot, appealing to his highest and best.

"That's it, Jesse. You are so good at creating your wishes-come-true. From finding pennies to collecting all kinds of details about Jane. From making a new map for Elizabethtown to becoming Billy's newsboy partner. You are a blue ribbon creator."

"I know I am," Jesse said insistently, "But, finding Jessica is taking so long."

She joked, "Remember the library lions, Patience and *Fort Dude*!"

"Hah!" Jesse blurted a laugh. "Fort Dude!" He sat up straight and exhaled, "I have to remember my quest. With patience and fortitude. I can do that." He stood up, "I have to go take care of my newspapers." He swung back to Dearie, "But I still want to go to Elizabethtown to find her."

Part Four

Summer

At the first burst of laughter,
Time stopped
and
surged with promise.

Chapter Fourteen

Two to Tango

In the glories of a June weekend, the apartment families were having their first outdoor potluck summer picnic. This was special because the famous actress, Patricia Neal and her fiancé, Roald Dahl, were invited. Patricia Neal was one of Conor's favorite actresses in the Actor's Studio. Her fiancé, Roald Dahl, was a favorite of Dearie's.

"Long ago, Galen and I ran into Roald Dahl, literally, when he was a little boy attending the Cathedral Boarding School for boys in Wales, a part of England."

"Was Roald an orphan?"

"No," Dearie replied, "Though his father had died. His mother sent him there, knowing it was what his father had wished."

"So, he didn't live with his mother? On purpose?" Jesse asked incredulously.

"No, he didn't."

"I wouldn't like to be sent away. When I go to Elizabethtown, I'll take you with me."

Dearie put her hand over Jesse's, "Thank you, Jesse. And I will go with you."

Jesse lifted her hand and kissed it. He looked in her eyes and said, "I'm glad I live with you, Dearie. I love you."

"And I love you, Jesse." She paused, looking into his eyes.

"What?" Jesse asked.

"Oh, it's just that you have that look. At first I see my James in you, but it always turns into my old friend."

"Elliot?"

Dearie nodded. "Well, let me finish my story.

"It was long back, in 1924, when Galen had an assignment to photograph the famous Cathedral School Boy's Choir. I remember arriving to a sudden dash of white shirt and dark hair flying out of the Headmaster's office. I went after him and found him in the hedgerows. Little eight-year-old Roald, his face a muddle of dirt and tears. I crawled in and sat with him, and we hit it off instantly, like a lost river looking for its wellspring.

"Over the years, we've stayed in touch. And now I am only too happy to have him in New York City. You never know what to expect when Roald is around."

Roald and Patricia arrived, and the families gathered for their potluck picnic. Bridget put out a bowl of hard boiled eggs, and the Bonheur twins pick up one each, skillfully tossing them back and forth…till one hit the ground.

Jean laughed, "Good! Now I can eat it!"

Jesse watched as he peeled away the shell. All at once, he knew the answer to Bridget's riddle: *A box with no hinge, no key, no lid. Yet a golden globe inside is hid.* "It's an egg!" He ran to Bridget to tell her, and rollicked from one to another sharing the riddle.

Mrs. Romano clapped her hands at Jesse's cleverness, and he heard her gold bangle bracelets jingling together. Gypsy appeared like magic, and Mrs. Romano chuckled, feeding her a few of her favorite olives. Gypsy purred like a Cadillac.

Meanwhile, Mr. Romano set out a big tray of cold meats and cheeses from their grocery store. Tim Braedon was attacking it like there was no tomorrow, and Billy was watching, looking like he had a lemon stuck in his mouth.

Billy had been down in the dumps. Summer was Liam's busiest season, so he was gone more than ever. Since school was out, Billy had taken on another job at Teresa and Grams' fish market. He collected the fish scraps to sell for bait down at the docks. It was hot, stinky work, but he made good money; especially on top of sweeping Bridget's Laundry, and his newspaper job.

Jesse stood with Billy, trying to send him good Lights by singing his song inside his head...*just to love and be loved in return.* Jesse's hum felt really good. But Billy wasn't in receiving mode. He was saying disgustedly, "Look at Tim Braedon. He didn't even bring nothin' to share."

Tim was gulping down another huge bite of sausage and he wiped his hands on the corner of the tablecloth.

Billy grunted, "Aegh! I hate that!"

Jesse's eyes grew large. That word. *Hate.* That was a big one for Dearie's Rule of Tongue—her word lessons to help turn your Lights on and keep them on.

Old Barret had taught her, 'Precious our words. May we use them so.'

And Dearie had taught Jesse, "Remember your Light. Hum with your Light. Hate doesn't hum with you Light. Hate is a very powerful word. Even if you say it lightly. 'Hate' runs deep into your body. It's like a thorn in your back and you can't reach it to take it out. Hate doesn't give anybody or anything a chance. And it only gathers more thorns. But most of all, you don't want such a word on your tongue."

Jesse had said, "Well, I heard Joey Romano say it to Mikey, 'cause Mikey was really bothering him."

"Hmm. Did Mikey stop?"

"No. They called each other names. Mrs. Romano finally came out and took Mikey with her."

"You see? Joey began hating Mikey, and Mikey gave it right back. Joey only got more of the hate he was putting out there."

"Sooo... so..."

Dearie looked under her eyebrows at Jesse, "You're wondering, what to do instead? Well, just like anything you don't like, you pivot. Talk about what you *do* like. What you *do* want. Be sure the words on your tongue taste delicious."

"Like...?"

"Like, Joey could make an offer. 'Mikey, I'm playing marbles with the boys. You can be my marble banker if you want.' Dearie waited. "Hear the difference?"

"Ohhh....Yes."

Dearie tilted her head and Jesse knew she had one thing more to add. "Jesse," she began quietly, "I'm recalling something more of the Rule of Tongue from ancient teachings that Old Barret collected on his travels. It goes like this:

Before you speak, let your words pass through three REMARK-able Gates:

Is it kind? - Is it true? - Is it necessary?

Jesse repeated, "Kind. True. Necessary."

"Yes, K – T – N."

"Sounds like kitten!"

"Kitten! Blue-Ribbon, you!" Dearie gestured. "It's all the same, isn't it! Highest and Best, *Bliss-t*, Rule of Tongue, Remark-able Gates. When you hear words that don't fit into the Bliss-t, simply give it no attention, no energy. Don't hum with it. You just hum the good stuff, Jesse!" Dearie laughed. "Nobody has to hear you! Hum inside of you. It's all good!"

Now when Jesse heard Billy say that H-word, his hum stopped. He felt it. Like a thorn.

He looked at Billy, who was tossing acorns against the building, like the icemaker in Mr. Schuyler's Drugstore. Just spitting them out whether the wall wanted them or not.

Jesse turned back. He saw Tim Braedon push through the groups of neighbors and plant himself in front of the famous Patricia Neal.

"I've seen all your films!" Tim spouted. "Best actress in Hollywood!"

Patricia drolled dismisively, "I don't think Amanda Wynne would agree with that." And she turned away to greet the Gorecki family.

"Hah!" Billy said to the acorns, "I like that Patricia Neal."

Jesse was relieved that he didn't say the H-word again.

When Jesse looked at Roald Dahl he was surprised. Roald had a glow. Jesse could see it and he moved toward him as if pulled by a spool of Light.

"Mr. Dahl..."

"No, no, Jesse O'Neil, you must call me Roald." He laughed, "Nothing else will do."

"Roald, did you ever know my mother, Jane? Or her mother, Jessica? They were from Elizabethtown."

"No, I never had the pleasure of meeting them. Now as for Elizabethtown, never been there. But I do know for a fact that it had several substantial coastal forts. One had a superb radar station. Kept the airplanes safe. And that interested me, since I was a pilot in the war."

"Oh. Do you know anything else about Elizabethtown?"

"Let me think. Why, yes. From Port Haven, you have to take a ferry there."

"Really? A ferry boat?"

"Yes. I believe it's named for a Governor."

"Governor Keane!" Jesse blurted.

"Yes, that's it."

That was the end of Jesse's interview, because the other children spied Roald, and hung about him like Monday's laundry. He didn't disappoint. He pulled Annika Schuyler up from the stoop, blindfolding her with a dark napkin. Everyone laughed when he turned her about and introduced her as, *Her-Royal-Blindness.*

Then Roald spun her about again and walked her around the courtyard. Next, he said, "Ahhh, here we are on the island of Elizabethtown."

Jesse's ears piqued and Roald winked at him, but continued with Annika.

"Nothing like a walk in the country. "Uh-oh," he challenged, "we must cut across this cow field. There's no way around it. Mind your step. Around the cow poop, if you please. Ooops, over this way. Oh no, now that way."

Annika began mincey-toe-ing through the imaginary field, trying, in her plucky way, to avoid cow plops, that were becoming less imaginary and more real with her every blind step. Everyone burst into *giggle-snickens.*

"Oh no! Cow plops everywhere!" With that, Roald tripped Annika, and...pushed her hand into a bowl of warm mustard!

"Aaeegghh!" Annika shrieked, "Cow-poop!"

The children laughed so hard they were holding their stomachs.

Joey Romano roared, "That's hysterical!"

Marijka exclaimed, "She really thinks it's cow poop!"

Roald bowed and displayed his big grin. Then he took off Annika's blindfold, cleaned off her hand, and twirled her around in a dance. "This, is a tango!" He strutted a bit and dipped Annika theatrically. She squealed as he declared, "The Unexpected Tango!"

Grams exclaimed, "The tango! I love to dance the tango!" She got up and, like a little cat, prowled behind the tables, one arm up, one arm extended, gliding in short little steps, her toes pointing and flicking, her head snapping this way and that.

Mr. Romano stood and held out his hand to dance with her, but she dismissed him, "Get away with yer hairy eyebrows!"

A blurt of laughter erupted from the crowd, and Jesse squealed, "Hairy eyebrows!" His laugh sounded like Elmer Fudd. Highly contagious. Everyone laughed and laughed, and Jesse gasped, "Hil-lair-ee-us!"

When the laughter died down, Mac stood and everyone looked expectantly for a story. Instead, he gave a little blessing. "Here it is and here it goes. This is like a Thanksgiving gathering." He looked around the tables. "We are so thankful for this sublime day, this delectable food, and all of you glorious people here to share it."

"Here, here!" - "Thanks Giving!" - "Thank you!" circled the tables.

Then the lovely Patricia stood up and announced:

"We have something else unexpected to share: Roald and I are to be married on Thursday, July 2! At Trinity Church in lower Manhattan."

Everyone clapped like crazy. The women blew kisses and the men tossed napkins into the air. And Roald took Patricia in his arms and danced an Unexpected Tango all around the courtyard.

⁂

Though summer was in full swing, a frigid fog pawed at the city in shivery gusts. Jesse watched the misty greys spritzing the window. "This fog is really thick," he noted, "like the clouds fell down."

Dearie smirked at that and joined him at the window, "This reminds me of the summer fog that would roll into Port Haven over Tanagasuq Bay. Suddenly, you couldn't see a thing."

Jesse brightened, "Missus K gave me another map of Tanagasuq Bay. There are little islands there, even between Port Haven and Elizabethtown."

"Yes, that's right, Jesse. And in the fog, the islands just disappear."

"Disappear. Like Lady Jessica." He turned to Dearie, "Sometimes I think my quest is just a dream."

"Just a dream?" Dearie eyeballed him. "Just a dream?" she *gaspered*. "Jesse your quest *is* a dream. It's your dream. Your special dream." She looked out the window into the swirling mists. "Jesse, when you believe in your dream, your dream begins to belong to the universe...and...your soul knows its path. That's when your dream bubbles up like a firefly and comes looking for you. That's when you invite it in. To your party. Your dream is like your guest. Treat it with love and fun. Let it know how precious it is. And it cannot resist you! Feel it, like it's here right now."

Jesse smiled, "You help me feel it, Dearie."

"Remember, Jesse, it's all you." She smiled, and rubbed her arms, "My! This fog is a cold one. We need something to warm our cockles. Summer or not, I'm cooking up my favorite stew."

Chopping and stirring, she offered, "Why don't we invite the Maguires? And Mac and Bridget, too. I think I have enough stew to feed an army!"

Jesse heard their visitors thump up the stairs and he was cheerfully surprised to see Liam. The fog had closed the river traffic, sending Liam home, and Billy flying high.

Jesse went to the Victrola and played Debussey's sporty "Golliwog's

Cakewalk" saying to Billy, "Come on! Let's set the table with the *Golliwog*."

Billy laughed, and strutted to the music, "Swell!"

Everything felt swell. At the table Mac was in rare form, bright with ideas that captivated everyone.

"Tell us a story from *yonks* and *yonks* ago," Jesse begged, "Tell from the very beginning." He expected Mac to say his familiar, *Here it is and here it goes*. But he didn't.

"The beginning." Mac grinned, "Well, Jesse, there is no beginning."

"No beginning?" Jesse flustered. "Everything has a beginning!"

"Ohhh?" Mac took off his gold wedding band and held it up to Jesse. "Where is the beginning of this ring?"

Jesse touched it. He *squintled*, "I don't see a beginning."

Liam understood and furthered the question, "And where is the beginning of wind? Or water? Or fire?"

"Fire is easy," Billy blurted, "cuz you strike a match and get fire."

"And where does the flame come from?" Mac challenged, "And when the match burns out, where does the flame go?"

Siobhan said, "That's fascinating, Mac. I never thought of that."

Mac's fingers made a roof that he tucked under his chin. "It's the eternal beginnings."

Bridget slyly smiled. "And let us not forget chickens and eggs!"

Conor looked at Jesse's quizzical face and laughed out loud. "You know how it goes, Jess. What came first? The chicken or the egg?"

"Oh. I was thinking of the Lady Jessica. I wonder if she has chickens and eggs."

Liam was laughing. "Well, I think it had to be the chicken that came first. I mean, can you see God sitting on an egg?"

Everyone laughed, but Jesse felt baffled. "Where is the beginning? I don't know."

"Well then"— Mac smiled—"we'll not call it the beginning. We'll call it what Old Barret called it: *Time before Time*."

Jesse reflected, "Like *Once Upon a Time*?"

"That'll do, Jesse," Mac nodded and launched into a story about the first King of Ireland, Brian Baru, and an amazing cat called Egypt.

At the end Liam gushed, "A warrior cat! Streaking down hill, leading the king's army into battle!"

"Glorious!" Grams agreed, though her exaggeration of the word made everyone chuckle–as it it sounded more like "glare-ee-us".

Siobhan remarked, "I didn't know people thought cats came from Egypt." She turned to Dearie, "So that's why you give your cats names from Egypt. Like Pharaoh and Cleopatra and Gypsy." Her face puzzled. "Wait, is Gypsy a name from Egypt?"

Dearie answered, "The word Gypsy comes from Egyptian. People thought gypsies were exotic, and Egypt seemed like an exotic place."

"Were you?" Teresa enthused, "Exotic?"

Dearie laughed, "We were plain as plain could be. It was the Gypsies from Europe who were exotic."

Mac added, "Yep. The Romanof Gypsies had extravagant everything: clothes, music, vardo traveling wagons."

Dearie said, "But we Irish Travellers had a very special, very particular leader in Old Barret."

Mac leaned forward, "Ours was a small caravan, led by Old Barret, who insisted we Travellers possess a sterling reputation. He invited only upright peoples, with excellent skills to share with one another; and also, share with the farms and monasteries that often took us in."

Dearie nodded in agreement, "My Da was an expert woodworker and stone builder; Mam was a master weaver. And so we joined their roving ranks. They—we—were the *Lucht Siúil*, or the walking people.

Mac rumbled on, "Old Barret was our leader, from east Wexford County, a Traveller for fifty-plus years, ever since the Potato Famine in 1845 left his parents dead and forced him off their farm. So he travelled, exploring the Isles, Europe, Africa, and Asia. He was our expert on survival, our teacher, and our storyteller, raising our spirits, to seek and find highest and *bliss-t* in all the earth, and all the universe."

Dearie *memory-smiled*, "He taught young Mac as his apprentice-storyteller. And he taught me every musical instrument that came our way."

"What a wonderful way to grow up," Siobhan said.

"Sounds like these apartments to me," Teresa Maguire remarked, "Sounds a lot like what we've got right here."

The rest of dinner was a riot. Billy, the *rough-n-gruff*, was so fun and funny, loaded with jokes and riddles, one after another. He kept everyone in stitches.

"Okay, Jesse," Billy riddled, "If two's company and three's a crowd, what are four and five?"

"A gang?"

"Nunh-unh! Four and five are…nine!"

Amid the groans, Grams surprisingly chirped, "How 'bout a leprechaun joke…"

"Leprechaun?" Jesse bewildered, "Marijke says that's a disease where your skin falls off!"

"Eeewww!" Billy laughed. "Marijke's wrong on that one."

Siobhan explained, "Marijke was talking about a disease called leprosy. But a leprechaun is a mischievous little sprite."

"Anyway," Grams huffed, "the leprechaun's riddle asks: what's at the end of a rainbow?" She paused and answered herself: "The letter *W*!" She shrieked, startling the table into hilarious laughter.

But Teresa stopped laughing, "That reminds me, Liam's lost his gold watch."

"Well, Dearie always says it's not lost," Jesse remarked, "It's somewhere."

"I just hope I didn't lose it overboard," Liam said, "it belonged to my father."

Grams added, "I still haven't found my gold Claddagh charm neither."

Billy ignored them, smiling about the rainbow. "If I found a pot of gold at the end of the rainbow, I'd take it all to the bank."

Conor teased, "What if there is no bank where you find the rainbow?"

"There's always banks."

Teresa chimed in, "Not in Elizabethtown."

That galvanized Jesse. "No banks in Elizabethtown? How do you know that?"

"Oh..." Liam answered, "I was in a tremendous storm way up the coast and took refuge in the harbor there. Afterwards, I had practically no fuel, and no money. I tried to find a bank, but there was none on Elizabethtown. I had to chug across the bay to Port Haven."

"No bank in Elizabethtown," Jesse said. "I wonder if there are stores there."

Chapter Fifteen

Heat Spell

The cold fog was sent packing only to be replaced by a summer heat wave that knocked the shoes and socks off everyone. Grams said it was 'dreadly'.

It was so hot that the mothers got together and brought the children to a matinee show of old films. Jesse was invited to join Missus K and the Dutchies. The theater was filled with noisy children, but also welcome cool air.

Jesse thought the features were "hil-ar-ious!" From *Bugs Bunny* cartoons: "ehhh – what's up doc?", to *The Little Rascals*: Buckwheat, Spanky, Alfalfa, and Darla; and especially the crazy antics of Charlie Chaplin in *Circus*.

"Oh, Charlie Chaplin! His face!" Jesse laughed to Dearie, "He had monkeys climbing all over him on the high tightrope, and then he got locked in the lion's cage! Hil-ar-ious!"

Dearie laughed, "Hilarious! Your new favorite word!

Jesse grinned, "It was a hilarious—and a cool—afternoon!"

But the cool didn't last, because the heat didn't go away. In the sweltering early morning, Jesse felt his sheets sticking to him and his feet sticking to the wood floor. In the bathroom, he splashed cold water on his face, and for good measure, put his whole head into the sink, letting the cool water run over his hair and drip in his ears. Toweling off, he saw the reflections of the red morning sun, seeming to warn, "Get ready for a blister hot day."

Out in the parlor, Conor was not in the best of moods. It didn't help that Aislinn was spending the summer in Boston, working at her college. Jesse knew nothing about that. His Mozart record played and he blithely conducted.

But Conor gruffed: "Not 'Eine kleine Nachtmusik' again." Exaggerating his 'enough' sign with his hand, he pointed, "That's one record that needs breaking."

Jesse protectively held the Mozart record cover, but he saw Conor, sitting with his head in his hands. "Conor…?"

"Sorry little man, I'm just"—he tried to laugh—"in a *feisty-dreg*." He shook his head, "About everything." Thinking Jesse would understand, he added, "Like not being able to find Lady Jessica."

Jesse interrupted, "I'm still on my quest. I'm still gathering lots of information. Did you know we'll have to take a ferry boat? From Port Haven to Elizabethtown."

"Yes," Conor wagged his head, "I did know that answer. I wish I had the answers to all my problems."

Jesse picked up an orange crayon and opened his coloring pad. He drew a big circle with *sad-mad* eyes and mouth. Next to it, he drew a big circle with *happy–fun* eyes and mouth. Underneath he wrote: "You choose."

That was all. Two faces. One happy, one not. He went back to his Mozart.

"I choose…." Conor chuckled quietly and *wonder-gazed* at Jesse. *Hmmpf,* he thought, *six-year old wisdom.*

⁂

The afternoon was *dreadly* hot, and *dreadly* news spread through the apartments: Liam's tug was due back three days ago, but there was no boat and no message. Dearie was with Teresa and Grams when a Captain from the Coast Guard visited.

"There's been no sign of the vessel. But we've alerted all marine travel to be on the lookout." He stood up, "And we always have hope. Hope for the best."

Billy. Now he was more on edge—more *techy*—and more sullen than ever.

Sitting at the kitchen table, Jesse felt at a loss. "Dearie, I love Liam. And I love Billy. But it's a big puzzle. I can't solve Liam missing, or missing Liam."

He groaned. He knew it was really all about Billy. Billy was miserable. The fish stank to high heavens; the laundry sweeping was sweaty, sticky, dusty; and on top of that, he had little time left for the newspapers. But this. This was the hardest: not knowing anything about Liam. Where was he? What happened to the tug? Billy didn't like the fearful answers that poured in, darkening his thoughts.

Dearie interrupted Jesse's broodings, "There are ways you can help, Jesse. You can be kind and keep your Light on."

"Oh! My Light…I forgot. Well…maybe I can help Billy feel light if I take extra good care of the newspapers for him."

Dearie leaned across the table, "Now that, my little man, is a good plan."

⁂

The sidewalk was like a griddle-hot frying pan. But Billy's newspapers were there waiting for Jesse. It was a relief to get inside the cool-darks of the drugstore with the high ceiling fans.

"Hello there, Jesse," Mr. Schuyler greeted, standing in his window display above Jesse. He was swatting the air around him: "I've got a Beelzeh-bug in here."

Jesse stopped, "A Bee-el-zeh-BUG?"

Mr. Schuylar chuckled, "That's what I call this *devil* of a fly." He looked down at Jesse, "Is it still a scorcher out there?"

"Golly-gee-willakers. It's an oven."

Mr. Schuyler chuckled, "In winter, you say, 'It's a freezer chest'."

"Well for winter," Jesse reflected, "more clothes keep me warm. But for summer, I can't take off enough clothes to be cool."

"Hmpf. Abe Lincoln once said: 'It's so hot I'd like to take off my skin and sit in my bones.'"

"Hah," Jesse barked, "Sit in my bones. Good one."

Jesse took the brown bags and went back outside to roll and pack the papers. But the hot-humids seeped into everything, turning the paper bags soft, wet, and ripping like soggy jelly sandwiches. Useless. Jesse stared at the papers.

"I gotta get you down to the corner."

He rolled each paper and took a small pile to the corner. Back and forth he walked, dripping till his shirt was soaked and his hands were covered in ink. Every time he swiped at the sweat, his face got blacker.

Jimineeeez! I'm dripping like a coffee pot. I need...ohhh...! He thought of, *Jim Hawkins and the pirates of Treasure Island!*

Looking like a raccoon, Jesse went back to the drugstore, stopping to read the sign at the door: Pharmacy, Soda Fountain & Sundries.

When he opened the door, Mr. Schuyler smiled. Grinned. Laughed. "Jesse you are one black, inky mess."

"I know," he puffed. "Mr. Schuyler, do you have bandanas in your sundries?"

"Bananas? Banana sundaes?"

"No. Ban-*dan*-as... in your *sun*-drees."

"Oh. Yes." he chuckled, "right over there."

"I'd like two bandanas, please. Red ones. To wear right away."

"First, let's go to the sink to wash your face."

With the fresh, splashing pool of water Jesse sighed, "Ohhh, this is great. Cold and wet. I could swim in this."

He all-at-once thought of Elizabethtown. *I wonder if I'll go swimming there. I wonder if there's a beach? I'd jump in the water and stay there all day.*

Mr. Shchuyler was talking, "Jesse? Let's wet your bandanas. You'll stay cooler in the heat."

Together they rolled the wet bandanas, tying one round his neck and one round his forehead.

"Swell! I feel cooler already!"

Jesse touched the wet bandana at his neck. "Hey…maybe this would help keep Billy cool." He bought two blue-bandanas for Billy, and exultantly left the drugstore.

Mr. Schuyler returned to the window display, arranging beach balls, pails, and shovels in a bright red wagon. Jesse stared at the display. He sensed a sudden *zing* of *shiverals.*

"A wagon!" he breathed, walking to the corner, "I forgot. I said I'd get a wagon for the papers!" He touched the window with his finger, "Oh, I have a new dream! Bubbling up! Like a firefly! And it came looking for me. Like my quest." He grinned, "A dream wagon! I'm gonna start saving-up!"

Jesse grinned and another idea popped in. He unrolled a newspaper, folded it into a fan, and fanned the air, calling-out, "Get your cool news here! Fan the heat away with the evening news!"

By the time a red-faced, sweaty Billy showed up, Jesse had sold almost every paper. His money apron was heavy with coins…for his dream wagon.

But when Billy saw the papers almost gone his hands balled into fists and he yelled, "Nothing left for *me!* Might as well give up. Give it all up!" He turned sullen. Silent. Jesse could see tears in his eyes. He passed the money apron to Billy, who jerked it out of his hands, dumping the coins into his tin box.

Quietly, Jesse offered the blue bandanas to Billy. "These really help keep the sweat away. I got you two blue ones."

Billy swiped at his eyes and looked at Jesse. He actually had not noticed the red bandanas Jesse was wearing. A big breath gushed out of him and he laughed.

"Oh, Jesse. You are…I don't know what you are." Jesse saw Billy's face change. The deep line between his eyebrows disappeared; his hands relaxed and he touched Jesse's shoulder. "Cool, Jesse," he chuckled, "Cool."

Jesse was on the way up the stairs and he met Mrs. Romano coming down. She was looking for something.

"Can I help you, Mrs. Romano?"

She held her wrist. "Oh, Jesse. I lost one of my bracelets. I'm retracing my steps to find it.

Jesse nodded, "Well, nothing's ever lost. It's somewhere." A smile pulled his lips. It felt good to have so many bubbling good ideas. *Oh,* he thought of another, *before Dearie and Conor get home, I want to show Jane's shells and sea glass to Mac and Bridget.*

Walking to the desk, he pulled on the sliders. The left slider glided out as usual, but the right one was stuck. He yanked on the knob. It twisted in his hand.

"Oh no. Now it's come loose." He knelt down to tighten it back, but turned it the wrong way. The knob loosened even further.

"Oh, Great Lakes," he said at first, but then, "Hey, look! The knob is like a big wooden screw."

Unexpectedly, the knob fell into his hand. He chuckled, turning it slowly in his fingers. "Well, I'll screw it right back in." He reached to the slider and looked in the hole, ready to insert the knob back where it belonged. But. "What is that?"

Jesse knew instantly.

He reached in and pulled out…a key! *The* key!

"Light on!" He laughed, talking to it, "I found you! This is the greatest! I found you!"

His fingers hummed as he inserted the key into the little door, he heard the *click*…took a breath…and opened it.

"Now what's this?" He pulled out a stack of envelopes bound with a green ribbon. Another stack was behind that, with a purple ribbon. Jesse read the address:

Mrs. Jessica Roberts ~ 100 North Star Road ~ Elizabethtown

Jessica's address!

Jesse didn't quite know what to do. He thought he might fall on the floor. Or leap to the ceiling. Or open the window and yell to the sky. But he didn't do any of these things. He stood. Very still. He was looking at the framed photo of James and Jane. They were still smiling at him.

He smiled back and talked to them. "I know you showed this to me." He took a deep breath, "I know you wanted me to find this."

With the sunlight in his eyes, he jigged a little hop and skip.

There was much, much more than shells and sea glass to show Mac and Bridget. And by evening, the O'Neil apartment hooted and danced.

Together, with grand decorum, they composed a letter to Jessica. Jesse kept asking Dearie to add this or that.

"Tell her I am learning all about the island and Tanagasuq Bay."

"Oh, tell her Jane and James helped me find the key."

"One more thing, tell her I'm on a quest to find her."

Jesse read the words as Dearie wrote, then he asked, "Can I sign my name?"

"Of course," Dearie grinned. He signed, picked up the letter and kissed it.

Conor addressed the envelope, Jesse put on the stamp. Dearie tucked in the sheaf, "In go our dreams and wishes!"

"And kisses!" Jesse hopped as Dearie licked the envelope, Conor licked the stamp, and all three O'Neils flew down to pop it in the mailbox, and hug in ecstatic celebration.

⁂

The glaring summer heat was relentless. Jesse noticed that the more people talked about it, the worse they felt. He decided not to think about it as he slowly wound his way up to their apartment. Dearie had drawn the heavy curtains and was sitting with a fan blowing on her. Well. It was supposed to be blowing on her, but Gypsy had planted herself directly in front of the flowing air; her cat eyes were shut tight and her fur was blown back, like she was in a wind tunnel.

Jesse *giggle-burst*. "Oh, Gypsy! You look like a faerie cat! Flying, but sitting still!"

Wiping her brow, Dearie smirked and looked at her kitchen clock. "Gypsy knows how to be in the NOW."

Gypsy didn't move, and Jesse gushed to Dearie for the umpteenth time, "Well, I'm still flying about the key! And our letter! And now I have two dreams! One for Jessica...and one for a wagon!"

"*Fab-you-lush,* Jesse! Light on! That's how dreams work: you keep bubbling Jesse. Be *brillish* together with the Universe, and let the Universe deliver."

"Oh I hope, I HOPE it all comes true!" Jesse gushed again.

Dearie stood up and looked at him, "Watch your words, Jesse. Hope is good. A nice place to start. But real genuine *belief* in your dream is best. No doubts. Just *believe* it's here already. You'll *see* it when you *believe* it!"

"Oh, like a game. I like that," Jesse smiled, "I believe, and like the key—they show up!" He looked at Dearie, "Is that the game?"

"That's it, Jesse." Dearie poured them ice water, "Happy-up your day! Go through your days in your *brillish*, happy dream place and see what happens. And you'll feel so good in the bargain."

⁂

The *dreadly* heatwave persisted. People were *dreadly* fearful, talking about polio cases reported every day. Conor read the newspaper story of the families in Queens, New York, demanding the *gamma globulin* polio vaccine for their children.

"Everyone's worried it's going to be another summer like last year," Conor said.

"Why?" Jesse asked, "what happened last year?"

"Last year set records for the most polio cases in the city's history," Conor shook his head, "Polio's a huge worry."

Jesse knew polio was serious, but he remembered Dearie's words from Old Barret, "*The world is bent on parading life's miseries. You have to constantly choose your best thoughts. Bad thoughts and bad words are only going to bring on more of the bad. Choose the bliss-t!*"

Jesse did not march to the parade of miseries. He remembered, *Pivot:* spinning on his foot, and spinning his thoughts.

He said nothing to Conor, but pivoted to the window. The Tree of Life stood outside, oblivious to the weather or wearies of the world. Jesse closed his eyes, enjoying his beautiful Lights. Liam came in to Jesse's thoughts and he smiled…on purpose.

Dearie had said: "That's the Light! The Light you want for yourself. And the Light to send to people who really need it."

Jesse wanted to send his Light to Liam, and he recalled Dearie clinking her glass to his, saying, "That Light! It's the energy to really help others through the darks. Stick with your happy *brillish* Lights."

Chapter Sixteen

Sparklers

Mac had the windows open, and Jesse heard Sergeant Hannity talking to someone: Tim Braedon. Jesse watched him back away from Sergeant Hannity and almost fall into the bushes, and he giggled. But Tim quickly pulled himself out of the greenery, and oozed away down the street.

Jesse and Mac and Gypsy went out to the front stoop looking for cooler air. Jesse was still infused with his happy dreams. He didn't seem to mind the heat at all.

Mac looked at him and smiled, "That's a good place to be."

"Conor says there's a lot of bad going on," Jesse mused, "Liam missing. Polio."

Mac sighed, "There's good. And there's bad. Something of everything here on earth. It's all about what *you* do with it. The bad'll teach you to want the good." With his hands on his knees he said, "It's the opposites, all leanin' on each other:

Good and Bad teach each other.
Difficult and Easy support each other.
Long and Short define each other.
High and Low depend on each other.
Before and After follow each other.
Who can tell how one will guide the other? Only you.

"Yep," Mac slowly nodded, "Bad or good, you create your world, Jesse. You. Each thought, word, deed. It all becomes. And you become. Like your dreams."

Jesse looked at Mac, "I like becoming my dreams."

Mac patted Jesse's knee, "Just don't push your dreams, Jesse. Let them unfold. Become. All in good time."

Gypsy was peering into the thick greenery at the side of the steps and Jesse looked over the stoop. Something glimmered back at him. "Golly," he pointed. "Look! I think it's Mrs. Romano's gold bracelet!"

Gypsy leapt into the bushes, and Jesse ran down the steps to find her pawing at the gold bangle like catnip. Jesse reached into the bushes and pulled them both out.

Mac laughed, "Well! From now on, that Gypsy is going to get all the olives she ever wants!"

⁂

Five steaming hot days passed—and still no Liam—the Maguires were having a hard time keeping their hopes up. Jesse said nothing, but he remembered what Dearie had told him about ratcheting up *hope* into *believing*. So he did it, in his mind. Believing. *Liam is fine. All is well. And so it is.*

Finally, as all things do, the heat wave passed, when a dandy of a storm blew into the city. It rained cats and dogs and the dreadly hot air evaporated. A crisp breeze tickled everyone's fancy and, by the afternoon, everyone enjoyed the welcome contrast of clear, fresh air. Jesse saw that Billy was still in his dark miseries, but he kept pivoting to send him his good thoughts filled with his bliss-t Lights.

After selling the newspapers, Jesse was in Mac's garden, supposedly picking green beans for Dearie, but he was practicing waggling his ears.

"Yes! That felt like a waggle," he surprised himself.

Dearie appeared and snickered, "Oh Mr. Waggles, am I going to get any beans today?"

Jesse guffawed, and Dearie helped him pluck the rest of the beans, putting them into the newspaper catchall. Dearie noticed a picture and read the headline,"Perseid Star Showers Tonight." Jesse asked, "Is it going to rain stars?"

She chuckled, "Almost. We call them shooting stars, but actually they are meteors, huge rocks in outer space; but in earth's atmosphere they burn up in a streak of light."

"Oh. Shooting stars. But what's Pers-sid?"

"Per-see-id," Dearie corrected as they walked upstairs. "In Greek mythology, Perseus was the son of Zeus, and a great hero; one of his feats was to save Queen Cassiopeia's daughter, Andromeda, from a sea monster called Cetus. These are the names of some of the best-known stars in the heavens. The constellation Perseus is where most of the shooting stars can be seen at this time of year."

"But Dearie, there are so many stars, how do I find Per-see-us?"

"We find the Big Dipper—*easy please-y*. Then go across to the 'W' of Cassiopeia, and down to Perseus. But there are so many meteors flashing, it will be easy to see them."

Conor met them in the kitchen and Jesse invited him to join their shooting-star gazing.

"I wish I could," Conor shook his head, "but I've got class tonight. We're reading Agatha Christie's play, *Witness for the Prosecution*. Bobby Lewis will direct it."

Dearie smiled, "Agatha and Bobby. A great combination." She lightly touched Conor's shoulder, "But I wish you could be under the stars with us, Conor. You could use some fresh energies. After class, go out to the stars and feel the fresh energies in the fresh air all around you." She took his hand, "Give it a go. Feel the fresh."

Jesse got busy making a SHOOTING STAR poster to invite

everyone to the rooftop. In the lobby, trying to hang it on the message board, Grams appeared and grabbed it from him.

"Shooting stars, hunh. I remember wishing on a shooting star once. A lot of good it did me."

She gave it back, and Jesse tacked it up, then walked up the steps with her.

"Liam," she mumbled, "he's still gone. Lost at sea."

Jesse nodded, "I miss Liam. Out on the sea. But I dream he is safe. And he'll be back any day." He looked at Grams and wondered, "What was your wish, Grams? Once?"

She sighed and said, "It was a dream. I dreamed the love of my young life would fall in love with me, and we'd run away together and live happily ever after."

"So it came true!" Jesse smiled.

"Hardly." Grams puffed. "I met Willem Maguire when I was working in the fish markets up in…up north. Willem Maguire. I couldn't miss him. A great chuck roast of a man, with that red hair of his flagging me down. I married him to get away from the fish." She chuckled glumly, "But the stars played a mean trick on me, cuz I been working in the fish markets of New York ever since."

"That's hard work!" Jesse nodded.

"What? I'm not a jerk," Grams teased. But her smile drifted away as she shoved her hands deep into her pockets. "Fish work," she muttered. "Always in my hands."

She suddenly gushed, "Hah! Work! My mother before me always said, 'Just give me strong coffee and make my Mondays short.'" But she added, "Aegh!! No matter what, work drags on and on. Never ending." She sighed as they rounded the newel post to the landing. "Willem died at sea. And Liam and I were left alone. So we had to just keep on keepin' on."

At the mention of Liam again, Jesse heard the gloom in Grams' voice and he beamed, "But it all came out just right!" He blurted, "Liam and Teresa and Siobhan and Billy and you—you're my favorites."

Grams looked at Jesse. She stared into his turquoise eyes. Her own eyes seemed to get very wet. But she only shook her head and let herself into her apartment.

Twilight dusted the heavens as neighbors greeted one another and spread their blankets on the rooftop. Mr. Gorecki's deep voice marveled, "Now, the deep purple falls."

Everyone smiled, but Marijke said, "*Old Purple*. That's a skin rash. And your skin bleeds from it."

Katelijne *gaspered* and pulled Marijke into a hug, "Let's watch the sky turn into night, shall we?"

Slowly, like a beautiful lady, the sky slipped into her black velvet dress and showed off her glittering necklace of stars.

Jesse brought his music box, wanting to play it for Billy. But Billy turned away.

Billy was having a good old wallow. His heart was sick over Liam, and he was as filled with anger as yearning…and worry, too. Jesse tried to talk to him about not worrying; about just sending Liam his love Lights, but Billy was having none of it. He didn't want Jesse or Jesse's sparks near him neither. And he hardly looked at the sky.

But everyone else stared at the swath of Milky Way stars, looking like a glorious ribbon of Lights.

Jesse saw Grams and he asked, "Are you ready?"

Grams looked at Jesse, and back at the stars. With a hint of her old cantankerous voice, she said, "I got my wishes, all right. One for Liam and one for my old hankerin'."

"Light on!" Jesse beamed. He took out his music box, plinking "Twinkle, Twinkle" into the summer night. The tiny notes danced into ears and twirled through hearts; and when it was finished, everyone clapped.

Delighted, Jesse skipped back to Dearie. As she hugged him he noticed the top of the Chrysler building.

"Oh," he realized, "That's the photo in our hallway."

"By the famous Margaret Bourke-White." Dearie reminded him, "A stunning photo from the stunning, dare-devil Margaret!"

"A *first-er*!" Jesse remembered.

"*First-er*?" Dearie quizzled.

"You said she was the first famous woman photo-grafer."

"Right! First to photograph inside steel mills and diamond mines; and as a war correspondent, she got into Russia and photographed Stalin; in India she snapped Gandhi. Margaret survived being torpedoed by German submarines, straffed by German air fighters, bombed in Russia, and stranded in the freezing Arctic!"

Jesse was flabbergasted, "But no matter what, Margaret dared-the-devil and snapped her picture!"

Dearie nodded in agreement. But she was immediately distracted, helping everyone find Perseus. Next thing you know, Paul Bonheur shouted, "Look there's one!"

"Oh! I saw it!" Annika jumped, "It was so fast!"

"Lightning fast!" agreed Andros Gorecki.

His brother's arm darted in front of his face, "There's another!"

"Golly-gee-willakers!" Jesse hooted, thinking of the sparks that flew off the knives the old Tinker sharpened. "They're so bright! And so fast!"

"They're like firework sparklers!" Jean Bonheur crowed.

"Too fast," Billy said in a sour voice, "Can't make a wish on any of those,"

But Jeneva Bonheur hummed, "There is nothing like looking up to the stars. So hopeful. So inspiring."

"Yes," Dearie added, "This is a perfect night for making a wish and letting it in." She looked over to where Billy sat in his glumps.

Jesse blithely agreed, "I want to let in my dream wagon. And, my Jessica quest." Silently he thought, *And Liam comes home safe.*

Dearie put her hand on his shoulder, "Every time you make a wish, it invites life's energies to come in and play with you. To dance inside you. It's fun. That is what your quest is really all about. It's not finishing your quest. It's about the fun of *being* on your quest."

Jesse looked up to the sky sparklers. "Dearie," he murmured, "I like my quest. I'm thinking.... I wonder, if maybe Jessica is watching the shooting stars tonight." He was still thinking of Liam, too, but he didn't want to aggravate Billy. So he kept that in his heart.

"That is a lovely thought, Jesse. After all, we're under the same night sky, with the same sparkling stars."

Dreams that night were filled with sparkling stars. Those sparkles lasted right into the morning, ushering in a brand new day. A day of *coolifying* airs, filled with breezy, carefree greetings.

Chapter Seventeen

Bliss-t

In the refreshing, crisp afternoon air, Jesse hummed down to the newspapers. He waggled his ears and laughed, talking cheerily to himself:

*I love my dream. I love my dream wagon bubbling-up, like my Jessica quest. Dearie said, like a firefly! Maybe like a shooting star!*Billy was at the corner, ignoring everything, so Jesse focused on rolling the papers, and feeling fun *quiver-quavers.* With the heat gone, Jesse felt new. As if the world had opened a new door.

Sitting in the perfect sunlight, he vaguely heard the old Tinker's wagon horsing down the street. Curious, he looked up. The high cluttered wagon pulled up right in front of him. Stopped. The old Tinker tottered to the back of his wagon, opened the double doors and pulled out…a *wagon!*

A bolt of shivers *zippity-pippt* through Jesse. *My dream wagon!*

The Tinker said not a word. Just left it and tottered back to his seat. He clucked to his horse and drove away.

Jesse stood stone still. He stared. Finally, he yelled at the back of the clattering wagon, "THANK YOU!" He saw a hand wave back at him, but that was it.

Wit Schuyler came out of the drugstore behind Jesse. "I saw that, Jesse!" His head wagged, "Knock me over with a feather, you got your dream come true!" Smiling, he held a brass key. "You can keep your wagon in my storage shed. I'll get an extra key made for you."

Jesse gushed like a geyser, "Oh, Mr. Schuyler! My dream! It's here! Right here!"

Inspecting the wagon, he thought: *It's an old wooden wagon. Not bright, shiny-new red. But it's got sidebars and a long handle.* He looked under the wagon bed, *Yep! It's got all four wheels!*

He *thrillishly* loaded the newspapers into his new-old wagon and rolled toward Billy.

Y' see how it goes. Dreams really do come true.

But, y' may as well know, even with a change in the weather, there was no change in Billy. He was *dreadly*. Truth to say, he didn't like feeling so cantankerous. But he kept chewin' on his worries, especially about his daddy. The worries just got bigger and blacker, spilling over on everything. And everyone.

Billy knew he felt ornery. But he didn't want to talk about it. *I'm workin' like a dog everyday. But nothin's workin' for ME,* his thoughts grumbled. *And every day, Jesse sells more and more papers. Jesse's takin' over my corner. Pretty soon there'll be nothin' left for me.*

Billy felt his chest tighten. *If only Daddy were here...* His thoughts swirled in a tornado of blacks, and he unleashed them on Jesse.

"You're late!" Billy growled.

But Jesse beamed, "I told you I'd have a wagon!"

"You and your stupid magic," Billy jeered.

"It is magic. Real magic. It's me. And the Universe. *Brillish* together."

"I don't wanna hear it. You sound like a quack. You and your stupid Universe."

"Dearie says..."

"Don't say it. You're melting my head off with your useless Universe."

"But..."

Jesse impulsively protested—insisted.

Billy impulsively ranted—raged, actually.

And *blisterquick*, a *foolrashy* squabble eruptured.

Jesse forgot all about Billy's Bests. He forgot all about T-H-I-N-K. He forgot...about breathing. Humming.

With one more fuming, exasperated *wisky-dooly*—

Billy shoved Jesse!

Jesse shoved Billy!

Billy SHOVED Jesse—and Jesse went f-l-y-ing!

Billy felt like his arms were spring loaded. He couldn't believe he made Jesse fly through the air like that. He felt completely discombobulated. Frozen to the spot. Even when he heard Jesse's head hit the wagon. Billy didn't move.

Jesse's eyebrow looked like the raw edge of a slightly open sardine can, with the inside oil running down his face. Except it was blood. Leaking into his eye. Swelling like a dark blue balloon.

Blustering, Jesse rushed into the apartments, looking for Mac and Bridget. But he hadn't seen them all week. It was someone else who took care of Jesse. Grams Maguire.

Grams was just hanging up the hall phone. When she saw Jesse, she pulled out her long handkerchief, holding it over his eye.

"Hmpf," she muttered, "Many a time a man's mouth broke his nose. Looks like you got it but good, Jesse."

Even in his upset, Jesse noticed that Grams had a notepaper with Conor's name on it. But she threw it in the wastebasket. Jesse stared at her. She stopped. She looked at Jesse's one turquoise eye. She turned to the basket, fished it out, and muttered, "Here, you can deliver this. Come on."

Jesse stuffed the note into his pocket, and, trying not to sob, he followed Grams up to her kitchen. He climbed onto the kitchen counter while Grams fussed with a steeped-teabag for his bruised and bleeding black eye. She wasn't her old cantankerous self, she was more…sad. And Jesse thought again of Liam. How he loved Liam. How he loved all the Maguires…especially Billy.

"Grams," Jesse mewled miserably. "I love Billy…but I…ohhh"—his breath stuttered—"… I forgot all my lessons…."

"Lessons?"

"My T-H-I-N-K, and my Billy-Bests. And my hum. And my breathing. I forgot."

"Well nothin' y' can do…."

"I knew my happy-hum didn't match Billy's ornery-hum."

"Oh," Grams understood that. "You arguing north. Billy arguing south. That's life."

Jesse *moogled*, "I just wanted to make Billy feel happy, like me." He looked at Grams with one eye, and sighed. "But Dearie told me, I can't *make* someone be happy. I can't *give* my happy-hum to anyone. And, no-one can *take* my happy-hum away from me. Unless, I let them take it. I…I lost."

Grams suddenly laughed, "You have the black eye to prove it!"

"No. I lost my happy-hum. I gave it away. To Billy. I let Billy take it away from me." Jesse moaned, "I chose the *turribles*."

Grams piqued, "Y' mean you're looking to forgive…?"

"Not forgiving. It's like Dearie says, there's nothing to forgive." He wiped a dribble off his cheek, "I didn't have to be right. Love is better than right. I love Billy. I didn't need to show-off. But I did."

Grams looked bewildered.

Jesse sighed, "Dearie says, love loves. No matter what." Jesse removed the teabag and looked at it. "Like my song: *the greatest thing you'll ever learn...*"

"The greatest thing...?"

He whisper-breathed his song for her, "*Is just to love, and be loved in return.*"

Jesse looked at Grams. Her eyes. Her eyes were filled with...something. Many things. Dismay. Darkness. Misery. Melancholy.

There was a knock on the door and Grams trembled. She shook herself and yelled in her harsh, familiar voice, "It's open. Let yourself in."

Mac walked in, looking long in the face, saying to Grams, "I'm lookin' f'r...." But upon seeing Jesse, he grinned, "Jesse! Whoa. Now that's a black eye!" Mac chuckled, "I heard 'bout your *donnybrook* from Wit Schuyler. Y' little Jabberwock*!* You took your share of the snicker-snacks!"

Jesse half-smiled, and Mac pretend-punched him, "'One two! And through and through....'"

Jesse tried to rally, attempting the Jabberwocky finish, but all he had was: "'galumphing...back'"

Mac handed him a little brown paper bag, "Here's your key for Mr. Schuyler's shed. I put your wagon in for the night."

"Thanks, Mac," Jesse sighed again and rolled his one good eye up, "I know. I forgot my lessons."

"Well, Jesse. Here it is and here it goes: *bad* reminds you to find *good*. Every time you feel that blackeye, you'll remember to look for your grand *good.* Your good humming." He patted Jesse's knee, "It's yer magic, Jesse." His head bowed to Jesse's and he looked into the little boy's eyes. "Y' may believe in many things, Jesse. Always believe in your magic. It's all *good.*"

Another knock on the door, and there was Dearie. "Well, my *brillish* boy. You're the talk of the block!"

Jesse hopped down and hugged Dearie's legs.

"You're fine, Jesse," she quietly kissed the top of his head. "So fine. *All is well.*"

Jesse barely mumbled, "*And so it is.*" His hands went into his pockets. "This is for Conor. Grams gave it to me."

Dearie opened it. "Oh, what gemmy news. Conor will be so pleased. *The West Garden Theater* is offering an audition for their new musical."

Jesse sighed, "I'm ready to go home now." He hugged Mac, and turned to Grams. She startled as Jesse embraced her, saying, "Thanks, Grams. You're the best."

Grams stood in the kitchen, chewing her thumb. Mac was ready to leave, but she *murmeled*, "Never seen the likes of it...."

"Jesse?"

Slowly, her head nodded, "No blaming. No finding fault. With me. Or Billy." Her voice stuttered, "Just love. Jesse loves...me. And Billy. And...."

Mac *whistered*, "Jesse lives in love. That's what he's become: a little love."

A tear fell down Grams' cheek and Mac put his hand on her shoulder. Her lips disappeared as she pulled them together. She tilted her head. "Jesse...he's filled with loving *brí*."

Mac agreed knowing that *brî* was Gaelic for *energies*.

But Grams' face was a river of tears. "Oh Mac...I know I'm a wreck over Liam...but Jesse has me feeling...so ashamed of myself." She pulled the bloody handkerchief through her hand over and over again. "I know I'm just plain ornery. But I remember.... And I want it back.... That *brí*. Jesse's *brí*."

⁂

Silent. Jesse sat at the kitchen table. Dearie turned from the icebox and looked at him. They both began speaking at the same time.

"Dearie...."

"Jesse...."

They blurted a little laugh, though it hurt Jesse's face. He held his cheek and gestured for Dearie to go first.

She put her arm about him. Then she sat down opposite him.

"Sometimes, Jesse, when something like this happens, you think that the Light is outside of you; that you're separate from the Light and you're being put through some kind of dark test. Maybe between you and Billy. But it's really all about you, Jesse. You separated yourself from the Light. That's why you feel so bad. The Light always IS. Always here. Always shining inside you. Love-love-love. When you quiet yourself and drop the dark, bad feelings, you will naturally move back into that Light. It's waiting for you."

Jesse shook his head. "That's kinda what I told Grams."

Dearie smiled, "Of course you did." She reached for Jesse's hand, and he nodded, wincing a smile.

After supper Gypsy stood guard at Dearie's door. Billy was knocking. Jesse opened the door but said nothing.

Over her knitting needles, Dearie welcomed, "Come in, Billy."

The two boys kept their distance, until Billy said, "I'm not gonna clobber ya or nothin' Jess. I promise." He looked at Jesse's eye. "I feel so bad, Jesse. I've been feelin' so bad about Daddy. I...but Daddy wouldn't want me clobberin' you, Jesse, I know that for sure.... I wanted to talk to Siobhan. But she's been staying over, babysittin' her family all day and night. So I came up by myself." Billy breathed-in deep, "I just wanna tell ya, Jesse... I'm real sorry. I want you to still be my friend. And my partner. I hope you will."

Jesse *murmeled*, "Me too, Billy. I feel sorry." He tried to smile but it hurt and a little blood leaked into his eye. He dabbed it with his handkerchief and said, "I still want to be friends. And I still want to be partners. A lot."

With relief, Billy breathed, "Swell! I've got a plan." He took out his blue bandanas. "How 'bout, I give you a blue bandana, and you give me a red one. Then, when we sell the papers, we each wear the blue and red together. Like a team. Our team colors, red and blue. You and me, Jess."

Jesse's face opened into a big grin. He winced. It hurt again, and the blood dribbled, but he said, "That's a great idea! I'll go get my bandanas!"

Jesse and Billy put on their double bandanas at the long hall mirror. Even with his big black eye, Jesse brightened, "We look great!"

Billy slung his arm over Jesse's shoulder, beaming into the mirror, "You and me, Jess. The best team on the block!"

Jesse beamed, "Swell!"

Next afternoon, at the newspaper corner, Jesse and Billy helped each other roll the bandanas and tie them on.

This is great! Jesse thought and was surprised—but not surprised—when Billy said it out loud, "This is great!"

Jesse grinned to beat the band. But he heard something. Someone. Calling.

"Biiilllyyy!"

Jesse saw Billy's eyes rise up with his chin. He saw Billy's whole body shoot off the sidewalk! He saw Billy rocket down the street.

"Daddy!" Billy screamed. "Daddy!" He bolted, screeching down the street, "Daddy!"

Jesse watched Liam burst forward, running at Billy, the two meeting in a tangle of hugs and exclamations. Billy clung to Liam all the way back to the apartments, shouting, crying, laughing, "Daddy!"

Jesse stepped in front of the newspapers, expecting Liam's usual swirling hug. But suddenly Teresa was there, and Liam picked her up in the swirling hug. They hugged and kissed and *murmeled* and laughed. Then Siobhan was there. Then Grams.

Jesse was grinning with their happiness. But he stood aside. Alone. Watching this grand, wonderful, loving homecoming. He felt his heart billowing. And tightening. At the same time. Overflowing with longing.

Liam was draped in his circle of family as he explained, "The tug's wiring was knocked out; then the engine conked out. But I kept the crew signaling with flags, and finally a big ocean-going tug rescued us and towed us in."

Teresa's eyes danced and she laughed, "I just made your favorite fresh lemonade! Let's go up and hear all about it!"

They all turned in to the courtyard. Billy had Liam's arm, not looking back to the newspapers. The Maguire family was already climbing the stoop. Left behind, Jesse's chest tightened. He swished away a tear and took a deep breath. With his lips pulled into his teeth and his chin slowly rising, he pivoted on his foot. He turned to selling the papers, with his thoughts seesawing up-and-down.

Dearie would say I have to choose. Happy? Sad? He picked up a paper. *Oh, for gosh all sakes! Liam is back! Liam!* He sniffed a laugh, *Easy-please-y pivot!* He grinned. *Liam is back!*

He smiled at his customers and told them the happy news. Everyone was happy, so happy, for the Maguires. For Liam.

Jesse felt his heart fill like a balloon and he floated through his newspaper tasks, sold every paper, and put everything away, including his wagon. He started up the stairs, hearing laughter in the dust motes. Coming from the Maguire's apartment. A big smile covered Jesse's face. It felt so good to have Liam back!

Chapter Eighteen

Puzzle Out

Liam's tug was fixed up right quick, and he was out to sea again. Even so, Billy was remarkably fine. He was in a new place, a new attitude, and he wanted to talk to Jesse about it.

"I think I get it now, Jesse, what you were tryin' t' tell me about not worrying for Daddy. Daddy and Mommy explained it to me—that I can't love Daddy and worry about him, cuz one keeps out the other, and then only my worry follows Daddy out to sea. Not my love. And maybe my worryin' energies kept him out on the sea even longer." Billy shrugged, "I gotta keep my Light on. In my heart. I get it. And I'm sorry I didn't listen before."

Jesse looked at Billy and his eyes beamed their turquoise sparks. "Swell, Billy! Really swell!"

The Red and Blue Newspaper Team really was the best. Everyone thought their bandanas were just spiffy, and Jesse's wagon was the perfect transport for all the papers. The days went by swiftly, and one afternoon, Billy again invited Jesse to go to the pier to greet Liam's boat. They both put the wagon away, and Jesse ran into the *Lady Bird* to tell Dearie his plans, while Billy ran up to put away his tin coin box.

Tim Braedon was sitting in the kitchen with Grams, eating as fast as she put the food out. Everyone said Tim was a moocher. If he stayed long enough he'd eat you out of house and home. That's what they said.

Billy shook his coin box and yelled into Grams, "Gotta put my moola away. Jesse and I are going to meet Daddy at the docks."

Grams got up and stood by the open door till Billy returned. She put her hands on his face, "You two take good care of each other."

Surprised, Billy looked at her, "Yeah, we will."

Grams went back to the kitchen, but Tim was not there. She turned around to see him coming through the other door. "Had to use your bathroom, Maude. Now where were we?"

The boys bustled down Tugboat Street. At the pier, Billy didn't wait for the gang plank, but leapt over the gunwhales, landing on the deck.

Steve shook his head, setting up the gangplank for Jesse. Just then Liam appeared out of the pilothouse and when he saw Jesse he hooted, "There's m' boyo!" and he whisked Jesse into a whirling hug. Jesse's heart soared into the sky and Liam jolly-laughed, "Let's catch up in the Captain's Quarters."

Sitting on Liam's bunk, the boys babbled about the bandanas and the wagon and their new Red and Blue Bandana Team.

Then Jesse recognized the shape of Elizabethtown on the maritime chart on the wall. He popped off the bunk and stood on tiptoe, putting his finger on it.

"Elizabethtown," he said confidently.

"Look-at-choo, Jesse," Liam marveled, "You're gettin' taller everyday."

Jesse rolled his smile toward Liam, responding, "I am tall. I'm going to be one tall glass of water. That's what Conor and Dearie always say about my father, James."

Liam leaned his arms on the desk and winked, "You just do your own growing Jesse, no matter how tall your father was."

"Okay!" Jesse pointed to the maritime chart. "There it is—Elizabethtown!" *My quest,* he whispered to himself, *I still have my quest inside me.*

His fingers touched the thimble in his pocket. His kiss. *Hello Jane,* he smiled. And he smelled...*chocolate.*

Lighthearted, Jesse followed Liam and Billy up to their apartment, and he was surprised to find Dearie there, sitting with Grams. Jesse could see that Grams had been crying, and he backed away.

But Grams called to him, "Don'tcha be hiding yourself away, Jesse O'Neil. You're the reason I asked Dearie to come down here."

"Me?"

"Yep." She blurted a laugh. But not her shrieking laugh. Mocking herself, she said, "Strange. Yes, I am strange. I'm a stranger to myself." She harrumphed, "For long times by, I been feeling down-right sorry for myself when I have so much to be thankful for. Especially"—she looked at Liam—"having my boy back. But, *aegh,* you'd think I was trapped by the *daoine sidhe.*"

"The faerie folk!" Jesse blurted.

"Aye. Like I was under their spell. All I wanted"—she choked a little—"was to go home."

"Home? Where?" Jesse asked.

Grams looked a tad sorry when she said, "Port Haven."

"What?" Jesse almost shouted, "You lived in Port Haven?" He was so surprised, he looked at Dearie and proclaimed, "She's from Port Haven!"

"Yes, Jesse," Dearie smiled. "I've known that. Mac knew Willem Maguire from way back in Liverpool, when they helped build the ship *Titanic.* Then, Willem got himself to America—looking for a new life—a new light shining on all his dreams. And he found it. In Port Haven, as Captain of a tugboat."

"A tugboat captain! Just like Liam!"

Dearie nodded. "And when they came to New York City, Grams and Willem rented here in Mac and Bridget's apartments."

"Yep. All true," Grams admitted. "But, Jesse, nothing in my Port Haven life had anything to do with that grandmaw you're looking for. We lived way down at Queen's Harbor. Our big boarding house was across the street from the little beach there. My sister still lives there…an' I…I've been hankerin' to go back. That was my star wish. To go back. See the harbor, all the boats on the bay, the beach folk on a Sunday afternoon."

Jesse could see that Grams was smiling, but she had big tears in her eyes, and Jesse wondered, *Can you be happy and sad at the same time?*

Grams was still talking: "And, I wanted to go back to see the mansion I worked in. My first job. I got a real good taste of how the wealthy live, especially from the Missus. What a slave driver!" Grams shook her head. "But that's where I met the first love of my heart." She looked at Jesse, "With eyes like yourn. I tell you true, Jesse O'Neil, you and those turquoise eyes of yourn. It's all your fault. You set the spell. Makin' me remember so."

She wiped her eyes. "But you broke the spell, too. With your words. About my Billy. And now I don't need to go home. Cuz I'm already here. Just like you said. My dream did come true, and it all worked out just right. I am lucky, lucky, lucky."

Jesse and Dearie's eyes danced together. They both thought about how many times Dearie had laughed at luck.

Y' see, there's no such thing as luck. Or coincidence. There is only fusing yourself with the Light. The Well-Being that always is. People call it luck when they don't know their power, when they don't choose to weave with the glorious Light of Well-Being.

Dearie said nothing of luck, for in Grams' old familiar bossy way, she commanded, "Go ahead Dearie, tell that *Kints-gee* story you started to tell me about."

Everyone tucked in cozy for a Dearie story.

Dearie began, "This is a story from my childhood friend, Elliot, after he returned from a visit to Japan with his father.

"In the household of their Japanese host, young Elliot had broken a lovely porcelain dish. Elliot was sorry true, but their host was tranquil, telling him, 'It is a matter of *mushin*. That is, not being attached to anything. We, instead, exist in the now moment, allowing all, and we shall find serenity amidst the change. There will be no attempt to hide the damage. No. To the contrary, we shall illuminate the repair in the art of *kintsugi*.'

"Before they left Japan, the artful k*intsugi* dish was gifted to Elliot. He took it in his hands, amazed. It was the same dish, yet it was more beautiful than the original, for it had been repaired with shining gold set into every crack; indeed, illuminating all.

"Their host bid them good-bye with these words: 'All things, all peoples, encounter the fractures, the jolts of life. Love them all into illuminations. Golden illuminations.'"

Dearie said, "For this is the magic of how you come back to life: You break. You fill yourself with illuminations. You flow on. Humming with the illuminations."

She softly rolled her stone in her hand. The room was quiet.

Grams husked a 'thank you' to Dearie. Then, sniffling between her words, she spoke to Jesse.

"I've always said, Jesse—you and those turquoise eyes of yourn could charm a dog off a meat wagon." She snickered. "I wantcha to know, Jesse, you've worked some kind of magic *kintsugi* on me."

Grams, with all her puzzling, funny, crazy eccentricities, left off with her sharp nasties. It seemed her heart-cracks were indeed filled with gold, and she found laughter more to her liking. As did the rest of the apartment company.

When Jesse and Dearie returned to their apartment, Dearie put on a record Jesse had not heard in a while. It was the music of Edward Elgar: "Pomp and Circumstance". Jesse smiled at the majestic march, and dramatically paraded around the kitchen, helping Dearie rustle up their supper of cold ham salad. He laughed, "I could march all the way to Elizabethtown on this music!"

As they sat at the table together, the music changed to Elgar's "Nimrod".

Jesse inflated, "Ohhh, my *favorish.*"

The music was riveting. Full of *thrill-bumps*. They both sat quietly through the whole thing, especially the final power of the rolling, rolling drums. Jesse felt thunder. Beautiful thunder.

He was very still.

Unexpectedly, he asked, "Dearie, who is Rose? When I was at Mac and Bridget's I heard them talking—upset—about somebody named Rose."

"Rose is…she's like that music: Love. Mac and Bridget love Rose very much. When she was little she had a fever and everyone thought she was going to die. She didn't, but the fever left her deaf."

"Oh, like the lady Siobhan helps?"

"The very same."

"Siobhan likes them. She taught me sign language from them."

"Yes." Dearie hesitated. "Well. Now, it so happens that Rose has come down with polio. Mac and Bridget have been trying to help."

"Polio...." Jesse repeated. "Hunh." He paused. "Dearie, remember last winter? When I skated at Rockefeller Center? Remember Emma? She had polio and she got better."

"I remember Emma very well," Dearie smiled, "Especially when it turned out she was actually Tenley Emma Albright, Olympic silver medalist in figure skating. You and Emma wove together beautifully. And yes, she is a phenomenal example of succeeding with polio."

Dearie fiddled with her fork, "I believe Rose is, too. Her legs are paralyzed. But the strange-wonderful thing is, Rose is already making plans. For therapy. And a wheelchair. She's even got her husband, Hendrik, planning an elevator in their building. Still, it's important to remember, every case is different. Because every person is different."

"Well...I guess there's nothing we can do."

Dearie smiled an admonishment, "There is everything we can do. We can send her our Light. Just like you did for Grams." She sighed, "Jesse, you sent your Light to Grams. And she was filled up with *kintsugi* Lights.

"Remember your Lights," she continued, "You want them on for you. And you want to send Rose your Lights. That is a true quest. Light on."

"I can do that," Jesse smiled, and he seemed satisfied, gesturing with his fork, "And I'll send it to Mac and Bridget, too. Now I know why they've been gone so much. I get it."

⁂

Jesse was in the lobby the very next day, when the mailman, Mr. Paul, came in. He looked funny. He was growing a mustache, and it looked like a faded caterpillar stuck above his lip.

"Ah, Master Jesse," he said in his raspy voice, "a letter for the O'Neil family." He flourished it through the air, handing it to Jesse.

"This is from Elizabethtown!" Jesse hooted. "Thank you."

"Oh, I don't send them," Mr. Paul croaked, "I just deliver them. Fair thee well."

Jesse held the envelope with two hands and started up the stairs. But, something was wrong. He sat down.

"This is Dearie's writing," he said, feeling confused. Then he saw the red stamp on the back of the envelope: *Unable to Deliver - Return to Sender.* He felt like crying.

Dearie was coming down the steps. He showed her the envelope and she sat down with him.

Mac's door opened, and he and Bridget came out, not noticing Jesse and Dearie. Mac turned to Bridget and put his hand to her cheek. "Love," he said quietly, and kissed her forehead. She looked up at him through her glasses and Jesse saw her blue eyes filled with tears. But she didn't cry. She put her hands to Mac's face and smiled faintly, "You and I, Rose, and her little ones." They hugged for a precious moment and went out the front door.

Jesse felt his song swelling: *...the greatest thing you'll ever learn, is just to love and be loved in return.*

Dearie could tell that Jesse wanted to cry. But not for himself. Her heart knew his heart. Yes, he was disappointed in the letter. But it was a very small thing. He knew Mac and Bridget had much more than disappointment.

Dearie took Jesse's hand, and climbing the stairs she felt a rush of love. Jesse felt it too. He loved Dearie. For...everything. He kissed her hand. And felt her smile. Her blessing smile.

Chapter Nineteen

Shooting Star Days

"Dearie, are we broke?"

"Why, no, Jesse. I like to say we are as abundant as we think we are."

"But I heard Bobby Lewis talking about the fly-wires and..."

"Yes, they are more of an expense than I thought. But we are not going to starve. Money is just...a little tight."

"Sooo, no trip to Jessica."

"I...well...no...Elizabethtown...."

"Just so you know," he interrupted, "I can help. I didn't have to buy my wagon. So I still have my pennies. And I'll save more."

"How very, very generous of you." Dearie tried to smile, but she keenly felt Jesse's disappointment. The more he showed his sweet patience and fortitude, the more regretful she felt.

Jesse shrugged, taking the returned letter to the lumber room, "It's still my quest."

Absently pulling at her gold locket, Dearie watched him walk down the hall, and her heart rushed after him, yearning to fulfill his wishes. She was still fiddling with her locket when it clicked open. She looked at Galen. She felt his love. Holding her. She closed her eyes. But all at once, her eyes opened wide.

"Jesse," she called, "I'm going on an errand. I'll be back soon."

She scooted out the door and almost hopped down the steps. She was on a mission, and she didn't want anyone to stop her. Out to the avenue, past the *Lady Bird Theater*, past the Actor's Studio. She didn't see Conor wave to her from the alley.

Curious, he walked out to the avenue and watched her, thinking, *She's got a full head of steam! Where's she going?*

He saw her enter one of the small shops. Suspended above the door were the three gold balls of a Pawn Shop.

"Whaaat?" Conor exclaimed, and ran down to the shop.

Looking in the window, he saw Dearie take off her gold locket.

"No!" he gasped, "Nooo!" He flung open the door. "Dearie!"

She looked up in such surprise. "Conor!"

The man behind the gated counter put up his hands and turned away.

"Dearie...?"

"Oh Conor...I..." She tried to sound cheerful: "I'm conjuring gold for gold...money for train tickets and hotel...."

"Dearie, no...."

"Oh Conor, you know I carry Galen in my heart. Always. But it's time to go find Jessica."

"Dearie...."

"We are so close. We have her name, her address. Jesse is right. We just have to get up there and meet her." Her eyes were filling with tears, "My heart is...crinkling...watching Jesse. He's trying so...."

"No. This is so not you, Dearie. You know this isn't what Jesse would want."

Conor couldn't believe he was the one saying no. He shook his head and took the locket, fastening it around Dearie's neck. "You said yourself, we can't make it happen. We have to trust it's all working out." He turned her around, "Like you always say: believe." He softly smiled, "If you and I are fine, Jesse is fine."

Dearie stood a moment, looking into Conor's eyes. "Believe. Yes," she sighed. "Ohhh…Conor." It was her turn to shake her head, and she embraced him. "Oh my heart…you and Jesse. My heart…."

Jesse stood at the open desk in the lumber room. He looked at the returned letter. He thought of all the stories he had collected about Jane and Elizabethtown. He thought of shooting stars. Star wishes. His quest. Being determined. He came out of the lumber room as Dearie came through their apartment door.

"Dearie, I am going to write a letter to the Postman of Elizabethtown."

She smiled, "That's postmaster. I'll get you my stationery and stamps."

Jesse sat down and wrote:

Dear Mr. Postmaster,
My name is Jesse Seamus O'Neil. I am six years old, going on seven. I live in New York City.
My grandmother lives in Elizabethtown. Her name is Jessica Roberts.
She lives at 100 North Star Road.
She does not know anything about me.
I want her to get my letters. But they come back with a red stamp, Unable to Deliver.
Can you please tell me why?
Sincerely,
Jesse Seamus O'Neil

He showed it to Dearie and she breathed, knowing, *all is well. Truly, all is well.*

She helped him post his letter. Jesse felt his quest…going out…flying.

He crooked a little smile and unexpectedly blurted, "Dearie, I think I'm getting better at waggling my ears!"

"Really?" She smiled, marveling at Jesse. Loving him more than ever. His self-possession, his serenity, his fun. No matter what. She encouraged, "Let's see you waggle!"

Jesse held his head still and moved the muscles above his jaw.

"Oh Jesse!" Dearie clapped, laughing with delight, "You are doing it! Your ears moved! You're waggling to beat the band!"

⁂

The final days of summer flashed by like shooting stars. Every day, the courtyard filled with grownups, chatting and singing, and children, playing endless games of hide-and-seek, red light-green light, or red-rover. Jesse liked the way they picked sides with Joey Romano's version of eenie-meenie:

Eenie-meenie pepperini - Ooo-ahh-gumbalini - Itchee-Otchee-Goomerachee - I want Y - O - U!

The favorite game was Base-Pins, which was baseball, except, no pitcher and only one base, and played with a whittled-down clothespin. Mr. Bonheur taught them, after Jean—or was it Paul?—hit a baseball through Mac's window.

One very hot day, Danek and Andros's dad, Mr. Seph Gorecki, brought a huge, inner tube with a rubber liner, to create a swimming pool. Everyone took turns filling it up, using Mac's garden hose. Full blast, water shot out of the spigot! And Jesse could see every gleaming water bubble. His Lights!

Billy made a show of jumping in first, holding his nose and whooping-it-up in the freezing water! Everyone took turns splashing and frolicking. Then the Romanos brought watermelon and Joey showed everyone how to spit the seeds. Soon they lined up in front of Mac's garden in a delirious spitting contest.

The waning summer days swayed in like the new rope-swing that Mac hung from the oak tree, that even the grownups tried. When Conor flew across the courtyard on it, Dearie hooted, "Now *that's* an entrance!"

While waiting their turns, the children played hopscotch, set up new marble runs and yelled silly chicken riddles at each other.

Jean: *Why did the chicken cross the road, roll in the mud, and cross the road again? (He was a dirty-double-crosser.)*

Jesse: *How did the egg cross the road? (It scrambled across.)*

When Mr. Bonheur heard them, he cut in with a silly of his own: *What was the farmer doing on the other side of the road? (Catching all the chickens!)*

Time was blurring together in hazy, lazy days. One afternoon, Jesse saw a butterfly, flitting across the courtyard, and he bounced after it, thinking, *Maybe this is the caterpillar I saw in Mac's garden, way back last spring.* But as he hopped about, his thimble popped out of his pocket, skittering away. Jesse's heart bounced into his throat.... *I can't lose Jane's kiss,* he thought, rushing after it.

His fingers almost breathed a sigh of relief as he picked it up. *Golly-gee-willakers! I'd better put you away. Safe. In my nightstand drawer. Yes.* Thereafter, before climbing into bed at night, Jesse took out the thimble, put it on his finger, and kissed his mother goodnight.

The last days of summer fluttered away. And September fell –into their lives like the next best thing.

Part Five

Fall

You think much

on your past.

And even more

on your future.

But you'd be really surprised

at everything waiting for you

right here

in your present.

Chapter Twenty

The Dickens!

In the early morning, Jesse and Billy were in the courtyard waiting for the milk delivery. Jesse was filled with bubbling energies, waggling his ears without even touching them. But something caught his eye: a dandelion puff, nodding in the sun. Jesse picked it, blowing the soft, tiny parachutes into the air.

"Listen," he said to Billy, "I hear my song: *...travel very far, very far, over land and sea...*"

Billy watched Jesse with a warm heart, but he warned, "Best watch out, Jesse. If you leave and go to Elizabethtown, you might never come back. It might be an adventure, but it might be the end of you here in New York. Maybe you'll find new stuff on the island, or the farm. But you won't have Dearie's theater. Y' won't have all your friends in the apartments. Or school. Or the newspaper corner. The shops. The library, the parks. Everything and everyone here—well, it won't be there."

Jesse felt a tight squeeze on his heart. He quieted, blowing on the dandelion again, watching the last few seeds float into the air.

All at once, Time seemed to freeze. Jesse went tripping through his memories, feeling pictures in flashes of Light, bouncing from one to another.

The dandelion seeds were tiny snowflakes, wafting through the air on his birthday eve, and Jesse saw inner pictures of every tiny little thing since then—long streams of pictures, floating on his memories. He had a funny feeling. Like he just stopped time. And he traveled, just like the play *Harvey*: "go wherever he liked, and stay as long as he liked, with anyone he liked."

He blinked. "Billy...I'm gonna go." He smiled, "I will. But not yet."

He shrugged, "I'm fine. So fine."

The sun winked in Jesse's eyes, gleaming off something in the courtyard bricks. He bent down. "A dime!" he marveled. "Stuck in between the bricks!" He took out his knife and pried it out.

Billy laughed, "You have the best luck!" But he paused, "Oh, I forgot," he chuckled, "no luck. It was waiting for you."

"But look! Billy! Look at this! Here's another dime! Look!"

He pried it out and handed it to Billy. "One for each of us!"

He suddenly heard a whispering whistle, and he didn't have to turn his head. He knew it was Tim Braedon

Tim snapped his fingers, "Two dimes! What the luck! Maude tells me you're one lucky boy, Jesse. She says you found that there knife, too. Mighty slick looking blade. Looks expensive."

Jesse could tell…Tim Braedon had been drinking. He could smell it. He noticed, too, how disheveled Tim looked; like *Treasure Island* come to life: "a very dirty scoundrel…. Bad as his clothes were and coarsely as he spoke…"

Jesse quietly folded his knife and put it back in his pocket. Tim stared at Jesse, then walked up the stoop and fell through the door.

⁂

All summer long, Dearie and Bobby Lewis had prepared for *A Christmas Carol.* Ready or not, September arrived and Dearie began rehearsals in earnest.

On their first day, Jesse pulled the tower bell ropes, calling the cast to the *Lady Bird* lobby for their first meeting. Dearie smiled, saying:

"Bells play a very important part in our theater. Whenever you hear bells ringing, it is a time to stop and wonder. And breathe…energies in, energies out. The Irish believe that ringing bells call forth the faeries, who are a magical presence. So we ring the bells to invite in the magic."

Jesse smiled, and tugged extra hard on the bell ropes.

Once everyone was in the lobby, Dearie fiddled away, *Here We come A-Caroling,* and Bobby Lewis exclaimed, "Sing with us!"

The apartment cast sang heartily, cheered on by Mac. And Grams Maguire.

This was a new Grams, smirking, "Sometimes, I think I've lost my mind. Half of it just wandered off and the other half is out looking for it!" She shrieked her 'glar-ee-us' laughter, making them all smile and join in.

Conor and Dearie had talked about Grams' astonishing transformation, and Dearie had laughed, "Yes, you see, she does have a tender heart."

Conor had chuckled, "She can be downright ridiculous." But he shook his head, "Still, what a surprise. So this is what Jesse saw in her all along."

"Yes," Dearie had agreed, "Jesse saw Grams, shiny bright."

Dearie continued to fiddle away in the lobby, and she turned to lead half the cast into the theater, calling out, "Come along you *Christmas Carolers!* No *scally-laggers* here!"

Bobby laughed, watching Dearie strutting and playing like…like one who loves…simply loves. He turned and led the other half of the cast, holding poster words for all to see. Katelijne Schuyler added piano and Conor helped weave everyone through the theater.

For the many, many following verses, Bobby called out, "Now the young girls sing!" Or, "Boys turn!" "Let's hear the Misters!" "And the Missus!" (Of which Grams stole the show dancing and curtsy-ing throughout the verse.) Dearie moved them up to the stage for the last of it. And how they sang!

Dearie and Bobby felt *A Christmas Carol* coming to life!

Everyone loved the *Puddleducking*—wearing the light costumes that immersed them in their parts. Bridget took care of everything—costumes out—costumes in. The whole cast so looked forward to the rehearsals, and the apartments became a mirror of all the doings at the *Lady Bird Theater*.

Mr. Gorecki's deep, rich voice was perfect for the *Narrator*. His sons, Danek and Andros, repeated his lines incessantly with ridiculous squawky-deep voices:

Old Marley was as dead as a doornail. Andros, like a stiff cadaver, dropped into Danek's arms again and again…and again.

Dearie had rewritten familiar carols to help tell the story, and the Schuyler girls were up to their teacups in the songs, especially Annika, learning her part, and everyone else's. They loved the dastardly Scrooge song, set to "God Rest Ye Merry Gentlemen", with each child taking a line:

Scrooge!
He's squeezing, wrenching grasping! Hard and sharp as flint!
Scrooge!
He's secret – solitary – And he's worth a mint!
But what good does his money do him? He's a bleak, hard stint
ALL:
Only tidings of wintry weather chill – Never a frill
Scrooge is tidings of wintry weather chill!

To introduce the scene for the dreadly Scrooge (Mac), and his persistently cheerful nephew, Fred (Mr. Teppo Bonheur), Dearie arranged girls vs. boys singing back-and-forth, to the tune of "O Christmas Tree" beginning:

O Merry day! Bah! Hum-bug!
O Very gay! Hah! Glum-bug!

The music and words got inside everbody's ears and carried them away. In the apartment hallways, the boys and the Dutchies wailed away as they built marble runs along the stairwell. They loved the many 'Hum-Bugging' lines, even if others tired of their repetition. That would be Grams, as her old voice yelled from her door, "Quit-cher cat-er-wallin'!"

Bobby and Dearie took the time to talk to each actor, child, and grownup. Dearie told them, "You are acting even when you are not speaking. When you're listening. When you are singing. You are always acting. Your body is filled with instincts, feelings, passions. Let it show. Not just in your face. In your whole body. Light on. Make me believe you."

Jesse shook his head and whispered to Annika, "That's what Mac does."

"But how do *I* do that?" Annika asked forthrightly.

Bobby smiled, "I'm glad you asked." He looked at Dearie. "You all know how Dearie feels about beliefs. A belief is simply a thought that you keep thinking. You hear something, see something, and it makes you believe in it.

"So think the thoughts your character would think. You're a street urchin, cold and hungry, singing to Scrooge, begging for money. Or food. Or, you're at Fezziwig's party celebrating Christmas with plenty of food and drink, dancing and singing. Think about how you act when you're at a party, taking in all the fun. You look around a lot. Your voice gets loud and bouncy. You laugh and talk with the others.

"Believe in who you are up there," Bobby continued, tapping his brow. "When you do that, the audience will believe you. And you will transport them into a new world. I'll help you in those scenes. But for now, watch Mac. He's a master."

Bobby was right. Mac was a quintessential Ebeneezer Scrooge, transforming himself into a merciless, mean old miser. Right up his alley was the nightmarish scene with his old, very dead, business partner, Jacob Marley.

"Act One – Scene Two!" Bobby yelled, "*Da Capo!* From the top!"

The eager cast sat in the audience seats while Katelijne Schuyler played the eerie notes of "Things Are Seldom What They Seem" from Gilbert & Sullivan's *H.M.S Pinafore*. Over the notes, Mr. Gorecki's deep bass voice spoke Dickens' lines, which Dearie and Bobby had revised:

"Ebeneezer Scrooge cared not a button
for Marley's supposed face in the door-knocker.
Up he went, in the deep darkness...
for darkness...is cheap."

Along with the eerie music, clanging chains echoed through the theater.

But Bobby yelled, "Stop!" He ran to the back of the theater and murmured to Wit Schuyler who was playing Jacob Marley. The cast-audience could see Wit nodding his head. Then Bobby ran back and yelled again, "*Da Capo!*"

The audience shivered with Scrooge, as the Ghost of Jacob Marley crept down the aisle. Dragging his chains, his horrid specter poked at the audience, and they all cringed into their seats as he slinked up to the stage. Spine-chilling *shiverals* lurched through the audience, *b'jeekering* everyone, as Marley confronted Scrooge face-to-face. It took a moment before they applauded their appreciations.

At the break, Jesse was offering a stick of Marta Gorecki's dried apple-circles to the cast. But when he got to Dearie, she was brooding. "Scrooge and Marley. It needs something...some-thing unexpected."

Jesse popped off a circle of apple. "Like Roald Dahl."

Dearie's head came up. "Roald! That's it! Very unexpected!" A slow grin spread across her face. She went to find Bobby.

"Please rehearse Fezziwig, would you, Bobby? I'm going to the music room." She took Katelijne and Wit Schuylar with her. Bobby smirked. Something was cooking.

Bobby began rehearsing Fezziwig's party. But the cast was self-conscious and stiff, and Bobby was frustrated, trying to get them to authentically laugh. Jesse perked, "Bobby, I know how to get them laughing."

"Do you?"

"Dearie taught me."

Bobby smiled. "Okay everybody! I want you to follow Jesse. Whatever he says goes."

With his eyes sparking, Jesse began, "This is the Laughing Game. First, go be with your own family."

Starting at the back corner of the stage, Jesse had Mr. Bonheur lie down and Mrs. Bonheur, too, with her head on his stomach. The two of them started giggling instantly. And there was more laughing when Jean lay down with his head on his mother's belly, and then Paul's head on Jean's belly. They giggled and guffawed, hooting like kids at a carnival.

Mikey Romano pulled on Jesse's sleeve. "I want to do that!" Jesse was stunned. Not because of Mikey, but because he smelled chocolate. He breathed in. *Yes, chocolate.* He closed his eyes. *Jane,* he thought. *Jane.* But, curiously, he didn't feel her. He opened his eyes. Mikey was putting the remains of a chocolate bar into his pocket. Jesse let out his breath into a stage full of *giggle-snickens.*

The rest of the families were on the floor erupting in laughter. The more they laughed, the more they laughed. Bobby was laughing so, all he could do was give a thumb's up to Jesse.

After the Fezziwig shenanigans, the entire cast chattered about how much fun it was.

Marta Gorecki held her face. "I can't remember the last time I laughed so much!"

Jeneva Bonheur blurted, "It is an amazement! We *act* like we are having fun, and we end up truly having fun!"

"Who knew laughter is contagious!" Bernadetta Romano agreed.

Marijke was behind them, "Contagious? What's contagious?"

Katelijne took her hand, "Laughter, my little darling! Laughter!"

It was time for a redo of the Scrooge-Marley scene and the whole cast breezily plopped into the theater seats. A brand new musical piece began: the classic tango: "Por Una Cabeza", with Marley's metal-chains echoing from the back of the theater.

Mac leaned out of his enormous wingback stage chair and offered his trademark words, "Here it is, and here it goes."

Everyone laughed. And shivered. The Ghost of Jacob Marley appeared at the back of the theater in complete costume, covered in props of long chains hung with padlocks; he wore a scraggled hat, wig, and face bandages wrapping his head. And, he danced! A preposterous tango! Using his chains as a dance partner, Marley tangoed through the audience, kicking and flicking right up to Scrooge.

It was ridiculously hilarious, and Mac-Scrooge comically ad-libbed, "I'd give him a nasty look, but I see he already has one!"

The piano loudened and Marley tangoed behind Scrooge's chair, wagging a chain in front of his face. Mac riotously went cross-eyed, with his eyes tick-tacking back-and-forth following the chain.

Again Marley tangoed, outrageously dragging, flicking his chains. The cast-audience bawled in laughter, and Marley over-acted while he sang-croaked:

I am Jacob Marley - I have come to parley - You may not believe me -

But I hold the key…

to your liberty - from captivity - I'll send you three Spirits –
That your heart and soul must heed!

I am looking gnarly - See, my chains are snarly –
How they weigh me down for all eternity!
My wicked greedy ways - in all my wretched stingy days –
forged all these heavy links –
I drag in clanks and clinks!

[piano: DaDUM dumDUM]
Take Heed Ebeneeezer! You old money squeeezer!
If you follow my course - You shall die - in torturous remorse
Take Heed Ebeneeezer! You wretched old geezer!
You listen - take heed - Learn all that you will need
To transform your life-long deeds!

Wisky-dooly! The cast-audience clamored their applause. Marley stopped, made a little bow, and danced the last measures of his chain-link tango.

And, oh, the rollicking looks on Mac-Scrooge's face: appalling scorn, withering apprehension, and a lit-tle twitch at his shoulder, as if, maybe, he, too, would like to tango.

Scrooge & Marley took their bows, with the laughter and applause ratcheting to a frenzy. No one wanted it to end.

Billy MacGuire yelled out, "Do it again!"

That is when Marley took off the hat and wig…and bandages….

Jesse almost leapt out of his skin, "Dearie!!!"

The audience stopped in one big gasp. Everyone clapped and hooted. Bobby Lewis hollered, "Huzzah, Dearie! Huzzah!"

Most unexpected.

After Dearie's Marley episode, the frolicking in the apartments rose to a crescendo. The grown-ups tangoed. The children tangoed. Gypsy the cat tangoed. Up and down the hallways. Up and down the stairs. The tangos even went down the street.

Chapter Twenty-One

Flights of Surprise

Jesse and Billy swung down to the lobby, heading for the *Lady Bird Theater*. But Tim Braedon was standing in their way.

"Hey, boys," he opened the door, "Looks like you're up to somethin'." Abruptly, he let the door swing back, tumbling them into each other. When they untangled, Tim apologized, "Sorry, boys, I thought I had a grip on the door."

Jesse and Billy ran out, happy to get away.

In the *Lady Bird* costume shop, Jesse showed Billy the revolving clothes rack hung from the ceiling.

"Holy mackeral fanny, Jesse! You're right! It's just like the fly wires! All set up and waitin' for us!"

There were several harnesses on the table, and Billy fiddled with one for Jesse, talking to himself as he tied the knots, "Square knot here: right over left and under. Bowline there: rabbit up through the hole, around the tree...."

But he stopped. A *whispering-whistle* was buzzing out in the hallway. Billy and Jesse moved to the door, and smelled a trace of Tim Braedon hanging in the air. Yes. There he was. Trying to get into Dearie's office. But the door was locked. They stared at him.

"Oh, hi again," Tim oozed, "Just looking for Dearie."

"She's not here," Billy stated.

"Well," Tim replied, not looking at the boys, "I'll just have a look around."

Billy put on his Boss-of-the-Block voice and said, "You're not allowed in here."

Jesse was surprised—and relieved—when Tim backed down. "Oh. Well then...I'll be on my way."

Feeling nervously, victoriously, confident, the boys returned to the costume room. Billy took a big breath and fiddled a bit more with the harness. Then he hung it on the hooks and helped Jesse step in.

Jesse laughed, "It's like I'm hanging on a clothesline!"

Billy pushed the button on the wall. The gears started and Jesse squealed, "I'm going up!"

Billy laughed, "Jess! It's working!"

Jesse laughed, too," "This is *thrill-digging*!" But after a few spins, he cried out dizzily, "Okay, stop! Avast!"

Billy pushed the button to stop it. He pushed it again. "Oh g'ory! Jesse! It won't stop!"

Jesse's eyes rolled. "Push it again!"

Billy pushed, holding it down with all his might. But the motor kicked into HIGH gear. The costumes—and Jesse—went faster! Up-up-up, across-across-across, down-down-down!

"Oh-ohhh!" Jesse yelped, as he went faster and faster! Hysterically, he gasped, "Ssttooppp!"

"I'm tryin' Jess!" Billy pushed the wall-button again. "Oh no! It's goin' FASTER!"

Jesse was swinging like a flying trapeze. "Aaaaeeeeggghhh!" he squealed.

"I'll get help, Jess! Hang on!" Billy spun around and ran! Straight into Conor!

"What's goin' on in here?" Conor looked up and saw Jesse, "Jumbalayyya!" He ran to the control button.

"I've been tryin' t' stop 'im!" Billy yelled.

Conor punched his foot on the floor button under the table. The revolving slowed. He punched again. It slowed again. One more foot-punch. It stopped.

But Jesse was back at the top. "I'm up here!" he called.

"Okay, Okay, hang-on!" Conor pressed the wall button, and the rack moved slowly around, bringing Jesse down. Punching the floor button, it stopped.

"Whew!" Billy helped a wobbly Jesse out of the harness, "Sorry, Jess!"

Conor's voice rivaled his steeping, dark eyes, "I don't think I need to tell you. Stay out of here!"

"Yes, Conor," Jesse's *whistered*. "We were…daring the devil. Like Margaret Buck-Wheat. Trying to fly."

"Margaret Buck-Wheat? What?"

"You know. The photographer lady."

Conor tried not to laugh. "She's not one of *Spanky and Our Gang*! Her name is Margaret Bourke-White. And this was not daring the devil. This was a big mistake." He chuckled, "You know what they call a plane that's about to crash? An error plane. That's the two of you!"

Jesse didn't get it, but he vowed, "We won't fly in here anymore. I promise."

Billy put his hand up, "I promise, too, Conor. Thanks for saving Jesse."

Conor laughed, "Oh yeah, if I hadn't come along, Jesse'd be goin' round till kingdom come!"

That night, when Jesse prepared for bed, he reached into his pocket for his knife. But it wasn't there. "Huh?"

Jesse thought of the costume revolving rack. "Oh no. It must have fallen out when I went speeding around."

He opened his nightstand drawer. *Ahhh.* He sighed and picked up Jane's thimble, putting it on his finger. *My kiss. I've still got Jane's kiss.*

He got into his pajamas. "I'll go look for my knife tomorrow. Like Dearie says, it's not lost. It's somewhere."

Jesse looked everywhere, but he couldn't find his orange butterfly knife.

Dearie told him, "It'll turn up. Just when you least expect it. Carry on, and let it find you."

She gave him her nail clipper to cut the strings on the newspaper stacks. It was awkward, not like his trusty knife. But he carried on.

His days were full. And he felt full. When he visited Mac, there was so much to share: theater, songs, actors, characters, learning to fly on the fly wires; school, with his island quest notebook, and Dearie's dictionary; Billy's newspaper corner, selling all his papers and all the swell people who came by everyday.

"Well Jesse, which is it to be now? You talk or I read?"

"But...what about our new game? Chess?"

"Oh, I forgot," Mac laughed, "one more thing for you to choose."

They sat in the sunny window overlooking the street and Mac told him, "Chess is like a moving puzzle. You have to plan ahead for each piece, each move."

"Yes, I like the way each piece moves in its own special way." Jesse moved his queen to prepare to take Mac's rook.

Mac remarked, "The queen is the most special, cuz she can go in any direction. She's a Traveller true." Mac moved his knight to protect his rook.

Jesse smiled, "The queen is Dearie. Travelling around the board."

He grinned, "She's magic!" He picked up his queen, and streaked across the board to take Mac's bishop, triumphantly tossing it in the wooden box.

With that, Mac shook his head, "Well...." He moved his other knight toward Jesse's queen.

"Uh-oh," Jesse breathed. "Nooo!"

Mac handily captured Jesse's queen.

"Nooo!" Jesse wailed, "Not Dearie! I can't lose Dearie!"

Mac followed up with a pursed-lip grin and: "Checkmate."

"Great Lakes!" Jesse glowered at the board. "I lost." He deflated, "I am lost. Just like my quest. I can't get to Jessica."

Mac looked at Jesse's dispirited face. "Y' know Jesse, chess *is* like a quest. A journey. Yer never done. Y' got a lot of moving pieces." He smiled, "Y' learn with each move."

Jesse shook his head, "There are too many snags in this game."

"Right y' are, Jesse. But if a road doesn't have any snags, most likely it doesn't lead anywhere. Snags are a part of your journey. It's all in how you deal with the snags."

Jesse quietly helped put the pieces in the box, "I'll have to think about that." He closed the lid.

Mac looked him in the eye, "Light on, Jesse. Light on."

⁂

Most of Jesse's days were spent in school, and he really took to the new unit Missus K began about nocturnal animals. She had a little gold fox pin on her jacket and she showed it to the children.

"In the Netherlands, the fox is called a Vos. When I was a girl, we had a kit, a young fox, come through our farm at dusk. It was very cute. But it was also a sly thief, and often, the next day we were missing a chicken."

The fox was interesting, but Jesse remembered seeing the possum in

Belvedere Castle, and that was his favorite nocturnal animal. It was so clever, the way the mother possum carried her babies in a little pouch; and Jesse loved its 'prehensile' tail that could curl around branches. The best part was that a possum could play possum, and that meant, if it was in danger, it played like it was dead and the hunter animal would leave it alone and go away.

Missus K had the children play possum, and Jesse was exceedingly good at it. He'd breathe real quiet. Real calm. And stay limp as a dishrag… or a possum. His partner was Mikey Romano, pretending to be a fox. Mikey yelped, "Danger! I am the hunter. I am the fox. Danger!" And he crawled up to Jesse-Possum.

But Mikey could not get Jesse to return to the land of the living. He pawed at him. Nosed him. Sniffed all over him making the whole classroom giggle. Finally, Missus K rang her little bell and Jesse popped up in triumph.

⁂

With all the pre-costuming for *A Christmas Carol*, the children eagerly anticipated trick-or-treating for Halloween.

But Halloween arrived in a downpour of rain.

Dearie looked out the window and used a spoonerism: "It's *roaring with pain* out there." She waited for Jesse to translate, but he didn't. "Aren't you going to say, 'It's pouring with rain'?"

Jesse was sitting in the big stuffed chair staring out the window in a trance. He was thinking about *A Christmas Carol*. The Spirits. He wondered about James and Jane. *Were they Spirits? Might James and Jane visit on Halloween? Could they come through the rain? Could they take him to Elizabethtown? That's what the Spirit-of-Christmas-Past did, took Scrooge back to his childhood town.*

Dearie was talking. "Jesse, I know you wanted to go trick-or-treating in the neighborhood tonight, but"—she tapped his nose—"I happen to know there is another show in town: a Halloween rescue team."

And what a rescue it was!

Dearie hosted costumes and makeup with a fun house mirror that had the children hooting at themselves. In high spirits they began trick-or-treating door-to-door and floor-to-floor.

Secretly, Teppo Bonheur dressed up as a scarecrow with cornstalks sticking out of his collar and sleeves and pants. Then, with a real, hollowed out Jack-o-Lantern over his head, he propped himself in front of a hay bale at his apartment door. He sat perfectly still. Waiting.

Jesse met the Schuyler girls there. Unsuspecting, they thought it was a stuffed scarecrow. They knocked on the door, and stood by. Waiting.

Mr. Bonheur made them wait. And wait. Until: "AAARRREEE!!!" The scarecrow shrieked, lurching at them like a train jumping the tracks!

Screeching! Tossing! Baskets! Candy! Rocketing up! Kicking-squealing-gasping on the floor!

But there was more! The scarecrow began to remove his pumpkin-head. They squealed in terror, struggling to wriggle away. But the scarecrow laughed and laughed. The Halloween-sters opened their eyes. *Mr. Bon-HEUR!*

How they hullabalooed! Then they could hardly wait to watch the next victims. It was screaming-good Halloween fun!

Apple-spooning was next. Mrs. Bernadetta Romano was in charge with long spoons to capture the apples floating in Mac's big copper bin. Spoons flashed! Apples sloshed! The children went after the apples like swashbuckling pirates and water splashed like a tempest! All at once, Mrs. Romano got a full, head-to-toe soaking! She froze. The children froze. She *gaspered*. She shook herself. Like a wet dog! And she hooted! With laughter! Triggering another Halloween-ster *giggle-burst*. Nothing could stop the Halloween fun.

Decorum was restored in Mac's apartment, reading *A Christmas Carol,* and playing Twenty Questions, just like Dickens' jolly Christmas party game with Scrooge's nephew, Fred.

Back in Dearie's apartment, mothers and fathers appeared with cider and cookies, and Dearie popped popcorn. Seph Gorecki pulled out the fun house mirror again, and Elke laughed, "Look at the cat!"

Gypsy was in front of the fun house mirror hissing at her reflection like a real Halloween cat.

Teppo Bonheur picked her up, grinning, "Didja hear the one about the sick cat getting the diagnosis from the doctor? The Doc says, 'Sorry. Bad news. It's curiosity.'"

Amid the grown-up laughter, Marijke frowned, "I don't get it."

Annika explained, "You know! Curiosity killed the cat."

The grown-ups kept laughing, because Grams was trying out the mirror. She was captivated with herself: shrinking into round and fat, shorter than she ever was. Growing long and skinny, taller than she ever hoped to be.

"Hah! It's *glar-ee-us*!" she swaggered, "*Glar-ee-us*'!

Looping her arm through Dearie's, the two of them pranced back-and-forth, shrinking-growing, pointing-cackling, like two crows at a tea party; inviting more giddy laughter than anyone knew what to do with on this unforgettable Halloween.

Chapter Twenty-Two

Remembrance

After school, Jesse was heading up to their apartment, thinking of the jolly Halloween fun, when he heard that undercurrent of a low whistle, and noticed that funny smell. Sure enough, it was Tim Braedon, rough-whiskered and rumpled. Like *Treasure Island,* he looked drenched in "…drink and the devil…"

"Hi there, Jesse! I was visiting Maude—Grams Maguire—down at the fish market. She says you're a real magician. You can solve anything."

Jesse stepped back.

"So," Tim kept on, with his spidery fingers lacing the air under his cuffs, "have you figured out where your other grandmother is? On her farm in Elizabethtown?"

"You said you didn't know anything about Elizabethtown." Jesse said accusingly.

"Well…I been giving it some thought. I remember the farm my daddy worked on. The lady was named Miss Jessica. I swear! And her little girl was named Jane." He looked at Jesse knowingly.

Jesse thought, *Jane. Jessica. It had to be the very same farm.*

Tim continued, "The people in Elizabethtown said there was a treasure there. On the farm. Treasure." He watched Jesse's face, "Y'know, like *Treasure Island.* Grams says you're real good at making discoveries. Wouldn't it be the luck of the Irish to find the treasure on your grandmother's farm? Huh? Y'd be rich!"

Jesse wanted to know more about the farm, but he did not like talking with Tim Braedon. Still the scruffy voice went on.

"I could help ya. I know the lay of the land there. I could help ya find your grandmother and her farm and her treasure. She probably remembers my dad. Whaddaya think?"

Jesse looked at Tim Braedon and said, "I think…I think you need a bath." He sidestepped him, and ran up the stairs.

⁂

"What's Arm Stick Day?" Jesse queried.

"Arm-ih-stis Day. The end of World War I. November 11," Dearie began, "Remembrance Day. Galen and I were with the family of King George V of England, when he proclaimed it, in 1919:

At the 11th hour of the 11th day of the 11th month,
all work, all sound, all locomotion should cease,
so that in perfect stillness the thoughts of everyone
may be concentrated on
reverent remembrance of the glorious dead."

"Gosh," Jesse breathed.

Dearie added, "*Lady Bird* is hosting a tribute to veterans on their day: *Armistice Music and Remembrance."*

Conor looked at Dearie, "I hope you have the Dvorak music ballad, "Goin' Home" on the docket."

Dearie nodded, but corrected, "It is Dvorak's music, but it was one of his students here in America who wrote the words: William Arms Fisher."

"I like that song," Jesse heartened, spattering his turquoise lights, "but I really hope you sing the *Doughnut* song,"

Dearie queried, "The *Doughnut* song?"

"You know, he sang, "*Doughnut No Cheese Pasta'.*"

Dearie and Conor burst into laughter. But Jesse was puzzled, "It's not funny. It's peace-full."

Dearie dabbed at her eyes, "Yes."

Conor explained, "It's not 'doughnuts'. The three words are *'Dona Nobis Pacem'*. Latin words that mean 'give us peace'."

"Ohhh..." Jesse nodded.

Dearie smiled, "Peace-full. It's wonderful when a simple song can be so inspiring. Our remembrance will host Veterans, sharing songs and inspiring stories, for those who served in both wars."

Conor nodded, "Like Pa."

"Like Galen," Dearie agreed.

Strolling home from the Armistice celebrations, Dearie said, "Hmmm, past, present, and future all tumbled into one day: the old memories of loss and sacrifice, the relief of having the war over, the shining hope for tomorrow. I feel it now."

Jesse replied thoughtfully, "Ac-tu-al-ly, there is no such thing as now. 'Cause, as soon as you say now, it's gone. It's past."

Conor laughed in astonishment, "Now, that's a mind bender, Jesse! That brain of yours!"

Jesse slowly swished his small American flag back and forth, "It feels...a little...sad. All the people who died."

"Yes," Dearie murmured, "It is a tender sorrow." She pulled her cape close. "When we let the Light in, it shines on everything. And the happy celebrating can open up the sad missing."

She took a deep breath and let it out in her following thought, "With *A Christmas Carol,* I'm feeling the *Spirits* of the past. Connections with so many, from so long ago, who taught me the same lessons *A Christmas Carol* teaches."

Jesse owned, "Scrooge has lots of lessons to learn."

"Love lessons," Conor remarked and quoted,

'If you have Love, you don't need to have anything else.
And if you do not have Love, it doesn't matter what else you have.'

"Yes," Dearie declared, "James Barrie...."

Jesse hopped, "Peter Pan!"

"Yes, but those words of Barrie's are misquoted."

Conor was surprised, "Oh? What's it supposed to be?"

"It's from Barrie's comedy called *What Every Woman Knows*; the characters are talking about charm, not love."

"Well, I'll be," Conor retorted.

Jesse brightened, "Maybe love is more like my Dvorak song, *the greatest thing you'll ever learn is just to love and be loved in return....*"

Dearie touched Jesse's shoulder, "A perfect love song."

At the front of their apartment steps, Jesse tried to plant his flag, but the stick couldn't pierce the dirt. "Golly, I could shave a point if I had my knife." He exhaled, "I wish I could find it. This is where I found Mrs. Romano's bracelet."

Conor shrugged, "You know what Dearie says."

"Yes," Jesse shook his head, "Be easy and let my knife find me." He propped the flag inside the bannister and ran to pull open the front door.

Heading upstairs, Conor continued, "Remembrance Day. All day, I've been thinking about James and Jane and Pa. In a good way. Like I'm letting them find me. As you say, Dearie, Light on."

"Yes, it's not a wall, nor even a veil between us. They're right here."

"I'm feeling so good, I can feel them. Especially Pa," Conor murmured, "How Pa loved us. Loves us still. I think he's been with us. All day."

Jesse spoke up, "I've been feeling Jessica all day. Like she misses me...but then I remember, she doesn't know me."

Conor hugged Jesse from behind, "I am positive, we *will* visit Jessica. And she will get to know you, and love you to pieces!"

Dearie beamed, "Love. Like Dickens' spirits: past present and future."

⁂

In Jesse's bedroom the sunlight was clear, and the chair shadows were crisp on the wall and floor, like puzzle pieces trying to play with each other. Jesse stared at them as he changed his clothes, thinking, *Everything is like a puzzle, waiting to fit together.*

He left his puzzling thoughts in his room and ran off to find Billy. They were going down to the docks again. Liam had promised a ride around the harbor.

The boys grinned, seeing First Mate Steve. With a smile on his face, he was whistling. A song that Jesse recognized: "I'll be loving you... Always...With a love that's true...Always...."

Oddly, as Steve continued to whistle, Jesse felt...Jessica? Definitely. Jessica.

But instantly Steve stopped whistling and his smile jumped down his throat. He pointed behind the boys. "What's he doing here?"

Billy and Jesse turned around. There was Tim Braedon, following them. "Come on, boys," Steve prodded, "get on board. Quick." Once on the tug, Steve pulled in the gangplank and let out the lines at the bow and stern, saying, "We don't want the likes of him on board." He pointed at Tim, and glared him down, until Tim turned and walked away.

Liam came up on deck, and Steve thumbed over his shoulder. "That one—Braedon—he's a varmint if there ever was. He was following the cubs, so I secured the boat. Don't want the likes of him near our lads."

"Okay," Liam said. Watching Tim walk back down the street, he asked Steve, "Whadya know 'bout him?"

"He's a bad-un." Steve nodded his head slowly. "He's got light fingers like you wouldn't believe. Can steal your wallet, pull out what money he wants and put it back afore you know nothin'. Same with anything in any place. Steal it away, right under your nose. He's smooth. Clever. A thief, plain and simple."

"Hmpf. We all thought he was some kinda war hero." Liam remembered Grams' infatuation with Tim.

"War hero, my big toenail! He's a *blirtin'* liar. Never served a day in his life. Picked up that uniform at a second-hand shop."

Liam almost laughed, "To Grams, the guy's a movie idol. He reminded her of Cary Grant."

"That'll be the day. That guy's nothin' but a two-bit crook. Hangs out at the Shark House."

"The gambling den? That's a rough place. Wouldn't go near there with a ten foot pole." Liam looked at Steve, "So howd-ja get the skinny on him?"

"Braedon made the mistake of stealing my wallet. I went after him. Found him in the Shark House." Steve spat into the water. "Let's just say I got my money back."

Liam looked at the boys, who looked like they had seen a real pirate. Their eyes looked like two burnt holes in a blanket.

Liam cautioned, "You boys stay away from Tim Braedon, y'hear?"

"Yes, Daddy."

"Yes, Liam."

A brisk breeze, warm sun, and the tang of salt in the air filled the afternoon. As they chugged down river, they saw the Staten Island Ferry and Jesse thought, *Like the ferry to Elizabethtown. Jessica.*

Liam was pointing to the Statue of Liberty, saying dramatically, "There she is, the Lady of the Harbor, lifting her lamp beside the golden door."

"Where?" Billy's head swiveled, "What golden door?"

Jesse wanted to know, too, but Liam laughed, "It's the door in the poem, there on the Lady's stone base."

Jesse asked, "What's the poem?"

Liam raised his eyes to the green lady, "Don'know the whole poem. Alls I remember is that she's called the Mother of Exiles—exiles are the kinda people who leave their country—leave everything behind, an' they come to America with nothin' much but their name and their dreams. Part of what she says to them is: '*Give me your tired, your poor…I lift my lamp beside the golden door.*'"

Billy and Jesse stared in awe at the lofty green lady, holding her torchlight high into the sky.

"Like *God Bless America,*" Jesse nodded and sang, "*…and guide her, with the light through the night from a bulb.*"

Billy hooted, "Jesse, you make me laugh! It's not *a bulb*! It's *from above!*" He looked at Lady Liberty again. "I get it, she's lighting the way to the harbor for all the people, especially the ones who want a safe, new home." He leaned into Liam, "Like your daddy, Willem."

Liam put his arm around Billy and hugged him close. With a quiet smile, Billy hugged his daddy. And hung on. Tight.

It was late in the afternoon when the tugboat group got home to the apartments. At the side stoop they met Mac and Bridget, and Liam took a moment to talk with Mac. Jesse and Billy knew from Mac's face that Liam was telling him about Tim Braedon.

The next afternoon, Jesse was playing chess with Mac when they saw Tim Braedon climbing the steps. Mac got up and stalked out to him. Jesse could hear his every word.

"Tim Braedon," he began in a powerful voice that sounded like he was using a megaphone, "I know you. I know your kind from my Traveller days. Our leader, Old Barret, wouldn't let the likes of you into our camp. I tried to give y' an honest chance, but there's not an honest bone in your body. I've had enough of you! Borrowing money from everyone in these apartments, not making good on it; things have gone missing, even from young Billy's coinbox; and counterfeit *funny-money* is turning up in our shops."

Funny money. That reminded Jesse of a spoonerism, and he smiled to himself, saying it inside his mind, *Mad bunny. That means bad money*. He giggled nervously, as Mac finished.

"Your time is up here, Tim Braedon. You will take yourself off these premises by sundown. Move out!"

When Mac returned to the parlor, Jesse fiddled with the captured chess pieces in the box and asked, "Mac, do you think Tim Braedon took my butterfly knife? And maybe Grams' Claddagh charm? And Liam's gold watch?"

Mac sat and shook his head, "It wouldn't surprise me in the least. Probably sold 'em all at some pawn shop."

"Really?" Jesse looked hopeful. "Well, I'm going to tell Sergeant Hannity! I'm going to tell him every single thing that's missing. Maybe he can get it all back."

"That," Mac said, moving his rook down the board, "is a very good idea. Light on!"

Chapter Twenty-Three

Spirals

Jesse loved *A Christmas Carol,* and he loved every jot-and-tittle of being Dickens' *Spirit of Christmas Past.*

"I get to be a wise old man and a shining child. Both!"

When he was fitted for his costume, he kept looking at himself in the mirror, circling back to front. "I love my long white costume. And the silvery white hair wig. And I really, really love the glitter wreath for my head."

Like the *Lady Bird* Mirror Ball, his wreath was made of tiny mirror pieces that glittered when the stage light hit it. "I feel like a shooting star!"

Jesse also carried a large, pointed white cap: a symbol of a candle-snuffer. Dearie said, "It represents darkness trying to snuff out the eternal, glorious Light."

And Jesse *gaspered*, "Never!"

Most of all, Jesse LOVED *f-l-y-i-n-g!*

His harness took some getting used to. Dearie said it was like being in a baby swaddle, only it was made out of leather and canvas, with clamps and hooks and straps, back to front.

Dourly, Jesse remarked, "Not like a baby swaddle." But he boasted, "You can't see the harness at all under my costume." He lifted his white robe to show it off. "My costume has little openings for the fly-wires to attach. It's very clever."

He had to practice and practice. It was slow. Step by step. With the fly-wire man, Andy, managing the wire movement, and the stagehands holding him. He *quiver-quavered* the first time they let go and he was on his own. Hanging. But it wasn't at all like the costume rack. He was swinging. In mid air. Free. Like a bird. And then slowly Andy raised him up, up, up.

"Oh!" Jesse murmured, crying out, "This is, ohhh!"

He could see Bobby and Conor and Dearie and Mac. Their eyes were shining up at him. Jesse gleamed back at them and waved. This was better than he had ever expected.

And Jesse's fly-wire entrance was a stunner. The music was from the very ending of "Sleigh Ride", by Leroy Anderson. It had just the right notes, getting louder and louder, and ending with the crack of a sleigh whip. Then:

"I come in—*whizbang*!" Jesse told Billy. "I really rocket! Down—*whooosh*—to the stage! *Zhhhooosh!* And I land right in front of Mac!"

On top of that, Jesse had mastered waggling his ears, and as he waggled away, his wreath danced in its glittering lights. Bobby loved it, and told Jesse to waggle to his heart's content.

After that, Jesse-Spirit took Mac-Scrooge's hand, and they r-o-c-k-e-t-ed up together! Away! Into Scrooge's childhood. *Jigger-Whhhooosh!*

While the scene changed to the countryside, the orchestra quietly played "Lo How a Rose E'er Blooming", and the children's choir sang:

Lo, how your past is blooming – from tender mem'ries sprung
Glad childhood's lineage coming – fancies of loved ones,
old & young...

⁂

Mac-Scrooge turned giddy with memories, as next they flew off to everyone's favorite, Fezziwig's Christmas Party. The entire cast partied on stage, even Dearie, playing her fiddle as they danced in quick-stepping reels. It was led off by Mrs. Fezziwig, a lively, comical Grams, jigging with the best of them, to the tune of "Deck the Halls":

Feziwig's best Christmas party - Fa la la la la, la, la, la la
Clear the floor and let's be hearty - Fa la la la la, la, la, la la

Come the fiddler! Come the Dancing! - Fa la la la la la, la, la la
Come the happy guests advancing - Fa la la la la, la la, la la!

Then, just for *Dearie-fun*, the rhythm turned to a tango. Everyone tangoed. And Grams and Billy's tango took the cake!

In one more rocket with Jesse, Scrooge saw the love-of-his-life: beautiful, devoted Belle, played by Teresa Maguire. Jesse-Spirit tenderly warned Mac-Scrooge:

You must listen with your mind, see with your heart, feel with your soul, so that you may receive The Present.

Jesse noticed Dearie. Off-stage. Smiling. With tears shining in her eyes. *Just like Grams Maguire,* Jesse thought, *happy and sad at the same time.*

Then he wondered, *What would it be like to fly with Jane into her past? In Elizabethtown? Happy? Sad? Both?*

But at that moment, tetchy Scrooge tried to smother Jesse-Spirit with the pointed cap-snuffer, and Jesse had to escape down the trapdoor. He loved to *evaporish* down the trapdoor slide, calling back, "Scrooge, you'll never trap me!"

There was still more to come, for Jesse changed out of his Spirit costume and into the children's garb, so that he could be a part of the rest of the play and get to witness Conor and Dearie and Mac having the flying-time of their lives.

⁂

The Rockefeller Center Christmas tree lighting! It was such a dazzling kick-off to the holidays that Dearie put off rehearsals and invited the cast of *A Christmas Carol* to the Channel Gardens, where they were greeted by brand new, tweleve-foot-tall, wire Angels in snow-white gowns, each holding a trumpet, and each alight from the inside out.

A choir sang: "Angels We Have Heard on High," and the Christmas tree lit-up…

"…like a Christmas Tree!" Jesse giggled, catching Dearie's mittened hand. "Dearie, I love this! I love you!" He hugged her and looked up to her face, "You're an angel!"

"Oh no! I'm the Spirit of Christmas-Yet-to-Come," she joked.

"Your Spirit's an angel!"

Conor put his hands on the back of Dearie's shoulders, saying, "High praise, Dearie. High praise!"

Conor was the perfect Spirit-of-Christmas-Present, with just the right cheerfulness, swagger, and tenderness. And, a fantastic stage entrance.

Dearie had recalled Conor swinging on the rope in the courtyard; and now, in the theater, Conor had more fun than ever. A rope-swing dangled down, swaying back and forth, hypnotizing Mac-Scrooge, who was comically shifting his eyes back and forth with the rope. Then suddenly, the music played: "Christmas in Killarney"—Bing Crosby's hit song—and there was Conor! Swaying over Scrooge's head, shouting his jolly greetings. He showered Scrooge with brightly wrapped Christmas-candy-props that popped lightly all over the stage. They looked so real that the children ran on stage afterward collecting handfuls of them.

Conor looked superb, dressed in a green velvet coat trimmed with white fur and a holly wreath tilting precariously on his head. Back and forth Conor swung, performing effortlessly, when all at once, he grabbed Scrooge, taking him in tow, with both of them swinging from the rope!

On Scrooge's journey, Conor carried a flashlight shaped like a cornucopia. He told Scrooge, "My cornucopia is a Light revealing all Earth's Goodness, even in the darkest corners, especially the loving household of your impoverished clerk, Bob Cratchit."

Jesse kept thinking about Jessica. *Where would the cornucopia flashlight shine for Jessica?*

But the Schuyler girls distracted him. How they loved singing for Belinda Cratchit—Siobhan—to the "Carol of the Bells": It was the same melody, but new words. Dearie called it the "Carol of the Light".

"What?" Marijke burst, "Carol of the Lice? Dearie!"

"LighT," Dearie replied with a sigh, "LighT!"

The girls sang beautifully,

Hark! Bring a Light – Into this night – Hurry I say – Show them the way - Father is here – Bring him good cheer – Here's Tiny Tim – Ashen and thin

Yes! Light the lantern – One candle can turn – hopeless despairing – back to the Light.
This is the Light…Brighten this night…

Then did Scrooge feel the destitution of Bob Cratchit's family, who were still warm-hearted in spite of their meager life. Scrooge was actually tender-touched by the lame, sweet, Tiny Tim Cratchit—Mikey Romano. Real tears stung Mac-Scrooge's eyes at the thought of the child's imminent death.

Conversely, great merriment came to light when Conor-Spirit of Christmas Present showed Scrooge the entertaining Christmas party of his always-cheery nephew, Fred-Teppo. Everyone could hear the fun in Seph Gorecki's deep Narrator voice:

There is nothing in the world so irresistibly contagious
as laughter and good humor.

At that moment, like Jesse, Conor unexpectedly saw Dearie standing off-stage grinning, yet with tears sparkling in her eyes.

Dearie's Spirit-of-Christmas-Yet-to-Come had a sensational entrance from the balcony at the back of the theater, swooping low over the audience. The fly-wire engineers worked overtime, testing every facet, and she had a special harness to lift her legs as well as her torso. Finally, the test flight was ready.

Standing with Bobby Lewis, she admitted, "I feel…*skittley*."

"You mean you've never been up?" Bobby asked surprisedly.

She grinned, "Other than Andy's practice sessions on stage, no, never."

"Well," Bobby cheered, "get ready for the ride of your life."

Conor and Jesse went backstage to play the phonograph record for Dearie's entrance: Béla Bartók's "Music for Strings, Percussion, and Celesta: 3rd Movement".

Jesse *whistered*, "The spookiest music."

Conor agreed. "Bella Bartok was from Hungary, but he came to America in 1940 to get away from the war. I was only ten when Dearie took James and me up to Columbia University to hear his folksongs. We heard this piece too. After the concert, we got to visit back stage and Bartok told James and me that the rhythm is the Fibonacci Number Sequence: 0:1:2:3:5:8; then it reverses, 8:5:3:2:1:0. Weird, huh?"

Jesse blathered, "Whoever Fib-a-na-chee is."

Conor explained, "Fibonacci *was* an Italian math-ematician. He brought the ancient Arabic number system to Europe in the 1200's."

"*Oldy-the-hill*!"

"You said it. Here, look at this," Conor wrote the Fibonacci numbers.

0+1=1 - 1+1= 2 - 1+2 =?

"Three," Jesse answered.

"Okay, so, two plus three equals?"

"Five…?" Jesse looked at the numbers. "Oh, it's a pattern." He picked up Conor's pencil and wrote the next few sets.

3 + 5 = 8 - 5 + 8 =13 "I get it!"

Conor drew connected squares for each equation, from tiny to big to bigger, showing Jesse how they made a spiral. "See, it perfectly imitates the spirals in nature."

Jesse brightened, "Oh, just like Mac's nautilus shell."

Conor rolled his eyes, "Okay, you get it."

Just then, Andy, the fly-man yelled, "Here goes!" And Conor started the music.

"Ohhh!" Dearie wailed, "*Yikey-Dooodles*!" She emerged from the balcony. Flying. Soaring. High above them.

"Dearie!" Jesse clapped, "You're flying!"

She spiraled, spreading her arms, with her legs up behind her.

Conor cupped his hands, calling, "Dearie! You're a Lady Bird!"

Jesse clapped again, "A beautiful Fibonacci Lady Bird!"

Slowly Andy moved Dearie toward the stage, steadily dipping her over the audience seats.

"Ohhh," Dearie *giddy-ed*, "I can just imagine dragging my costume over the unsuspecting audience!"

She cork-screwed onto the stage, and Jesse ran to her open arms. Andy graciously lifted her, and Jesse, ever so slightly off the ground, in a soft spiral, with Jesse squealing, "Dearie! We're flying *Fibonaccis*!"

Chapter Twenty-Four

Lady Bird

Mac smiled at Dearie as she came down from the stage, "You are the Lady Bird, Dearie."

Bobby Lewis asked Mac, "You mean Dearie's theater?"

"No, I mean the ancient legend of the Lady Bird. You see, Galen was here in America during World War I, and when we met up I tried to explain Dearie. How dead-on she is.

Jesse blurted, "Dead-on means Dearie is so fine!"

Mac nodded, "I told Galen the story of the Lady Bird. And he knew why his love for Dearie was like flying in the Light."

"Well, now I gotta hear this story," Bobby enthused.

Mac sat down with the others perched on stage and in the seats beside him, waiting for the legend to begin. Mac said, "Here it is…"

And Bobby laughed, "…and here it goes."

The ancient people lived in a dark valley, inside a ring of steep, rocky mountains. The sun did not shine there. Except on one special day of each year.

On that magnificent day, the people awoke to the sound of beautiful bird song. They stood up, raising their heads and saw birds flying high above them. With the sun gleaming in their eyes, they smiled and laughed, sang and danced in celebration.

At the end of the marvelous day the sun went away again and the people quietly returned to their hobbled darkness.

One year, when the sun paid its visit, a young girl wanted to capture its Light. She ran to the mountains, sure that she could fly like the birds up to the sun if only she could climb to the very top of the mountains. The elders cried after her,

"No, little one! Come back!" - "It is too dark!" - "Too steep!" - "It is too dangerous!" - "There is nothing there for you!" - "You cannot fly!"

She ran to the mountains anyway. Others followed. But the elders were right. It was dark and steep and dangerous. One by one, the others gave up and turned back.

The girl climbed and climbed, until no one could see her any longer. She did not come back.

Another year moved slowly through the valley. When the special day of the sun returned. The people awoke to a beautiful new song. They stood and looked up.

It was the girl! Flying through the blue sky, singing in the glorious sunshine. They watched her in wonder and worry.

The girl flew lower. "Come!" she called out. "Come up the mountain while the sun shines! Come join me! It is magnificent!"

She heard, "No. Oh no!" from the elders.

Yet there were some who rushed to the mountains. The girl's voice made the rocks sing, and the ascending people were exhilarated, climbing eagerly all day.

But the sun began to leave them. It grew cold. The climbers slumped into the rocks, fretting with thirst and hunger. They could not hear the song. Some began to turn back.

The girl flew to the sun and lit a torch to guide them.

"Be easy. Climb up a little more! Follow the Light! You will find a place of abundance! Of rest and refreshment!"

With more Light, and true to her words, the climbers at last reached the high mountain meadow, and they were awestruck. A clear river ran along green fields, singing a new, more fabulous song. As far as they could see, there were boundless berry bushes and fruit trees. And the marvelous sun was shining warm and bright up here.

They felt a part of the sky itself, breathing in fresh, sparkling air. They laughed, singing and dancing in pure joy.

The girl flew above their heads laughing with them. "There is more!" she cried. "Now you are ready to fly! Come! Fly with me!"

Abruptly, they were struck with their old fears.

"Oh no! We can't!" - "This place is good enough." - "The sun is good ..." - "We are not meant to fly." - "We can't." - "No."

The girl encouraged again, "Yes! You are ready! Come! Make the leap!"

She swooped down among them, lovingly embracing them, murmuring her music in their ears. In a flash she had moved them to the wide, open meadow.

And in that moment they laughed once again and their hearts beat wildly with sudden anticipation. The girl sang a last, sweet note, and they felt themselves leap! Leap into the air!

They flew!

Mac's voice thrilled to the ending. "They. All. Flew!"

⁂

"Oh, Mac!" Jesse clapped his hands and everyone followed.

Bobby stood up, clapping and clapping.

Mac looked at Dearie and rustled, "Dearie…" He took her hands, "I can still say the same words I said to Galen all those years ago: You are that girl, Dearie. You are the bird song, the seeker of the sun, and the Light in the darkness. You take others into the sunlight. Into the sky. You are the *Girl Who Flew*. A true Lady Bird."

Jesse jumped down from the stage and went to Dearie. She was smiling with tears in her eyes, and she was holding Galen's gold locket between her fingers. Conor was smiling at her with a knowing nod. Jesse kissed her cheek, and turned the locket over, showing Bobby, "It's got words on the back: *To my Dearie Lady Bird.*"

Bobby said not a word. He couldn't. And Jesse saw that he, too, was smiling with tears in his eyes.

Chapter Twenty-Five

Spirits of Christmas

Stage makeup transformed everyone. Jesse was amazed at the ladies in their lipstick and eye shadow. He stared, gushing, "You look so *gahslahzerous*!" At which they hugged him, trying to kiss his cheeks. But the makeup artist yelled, "No kissing!"

As with the best-laid plans, a few snags cropped up. Uncharacteristically, Katelijne was late, and out of breath. "My little *Vos* is missing."

Jesse looked up, "Your little gold fox?"

Katelijne nodded, "It must have fallen off my jacket." She sat at the piano. "Well. Nothing for it." She struck a piano chord and said, "Time to warm up…"

Dearie stood at the door, exasperating to Bobby, "Oh, *bunky dinks*! It's our first formal dress rehearsal with a straight run-through, especially with the music ensemble. But Siobhan, Mac, and Bridget are absent."

Marijke leaned over and said to Joey, "I didn't know they have an abscess." She began to expound on the ickiness of an abscess, but Annika stopped her, listening to Dearie's words.

"Bridget has the costumes superbly organized, but she needs to oversee them all. Mac's part is crucial, and Siobhan simply enchants when she's on stage."

Through the buzz, Annika Schuyler stepped forward, "I can do it! I know all the parts!"

Bobby laughed to Dearie, "I am certain she does! Well! The show must…"

"...go on!" Dearie finished, "Hah!"

And didn't Annika make an adorable Scrooge.

But *sooner-later*, there was a commotion, from the three missing actors, with three new children in tow. Siobhan introduced, "David, Joshua, and little Rose Weiss."

Mac added, looking at Bridget, "Their mother, Rose, is in hospital. So we're helping out.

Dearie grinned, "I welcome you. But, I think Annika Schuyler does not! She is ready to scoop away your Scrooge character!"

Mac let Annika finish the scene, while he changed into costume and make up. Jesse had the most fun with the three Weiss children, explaining all the excitements on and off stage. "Wait till you see me *zwoosh* on stage! And when I leave, I go down the trapdoor."

Little Rose Weiss was horrified, "You go into a trap?"

Jesse explained, "The trapdoor is pure, *thrill-digging* fun!" David and Joshua caught on, but Rose was still worried, and Jesse conceded, "Just watch me on stage. It's like I come out of nowhere, and later, I go back into nowhere."

When Jesse made his fantastic stage entrance he heard Rose squeal in surprise. But when he popped into the trapdoor, he heard her gasp, "Ohhh! He's gone!"

Jesse triumphantly slid into the basement, heading to the costume room to change into the urchin clothes for the rest of the show. But he heard that familiar whistle. Tim Braedon. Prowling around the maze of hallways, trying to open the doors. Jesse saw his still scruffy face, looking...desperate. But Jesse had startled him, and Tim left by the backdoor.

Jesse also saw Aislinn in the theater. Conor greeted her, but Jesse was disappointed that he didn't get any chance to talk with her.

Bobby had their attentions and he kept after them all, "Watch every little thing. Stay focused. Stay in character. Every little nuance, every expression is important. Stay with me, here."

Everyone had eyes and ears glued to Bobby.

⁂

That night, in their apartment, Jesse tootled happily through Christmas songs, but he stopped playing to ask, "Tell me about the Weiss children."

Unexpectedly, Conor changed subjects: "Jesse! Tell us your Christmas wish!"

Jesse didn't hesitate. "I'd like an outing." He explained, "Go to Elizabethtown. For my quest."

Dearie thought, *This whole, long year, Jesse has patiently solved the puzzles to find Jessica: her island, her name, her address. It's time to go. Somehow....* She sighed and smiled to herself. *I have to practice what I tell Jesse: Dream. Believe. It is time to go. Let it come in.* Twinkling, she said, "Jesse, that is a wonderful wish. May I come, too?"

"Oh yes," Jesse laughed, "You, too, Conor. We can all go."

Conor beamed back, "Great. But...it'll depend. On whether I get my Christmas wish."

Jesse proclaimed, "Oh, you want Aislinn for Christmas!"

Conor smiled quietly, "No. No. Aislinn and I are not...well, we're not together anymore." He looked at Dearie, "It's fine." And he hummed, "All is well..."

Jesse brightly finished, "And so it is! But...Conor, what is your wish?"

"That's easy. A really great repertory theater, with a really great Director. A mentor, like Bobby Lewis. With as much fun as we're having in *A Christmas Carol.*" He leaned in, "Course, I have to graduate college...in

May. But what a dream! To graduate, and move on to just the right theater."

"That is a great wish," Jesse grinned, "How 'bout you, Dearie?"

Dearie laughed her beautiful silvery laugh and spoke in an exotic accent, "I want to: *Vive bene. Spesso l'amore. Di risata molto! Si! Si! Si!*"

Jesse's mouth wrinkled, "What's that?"

"It's Italian. Live well. Speak love. Laugh much! And say, Yes! Yes! Yes! To everything!"

Dearie was busier than ever, saying 'Yes, yes, yes!" to everything.

She shrugged, "That's what it takes to coordinate all the tasks and all the people that make our *Lady Bird* productions fly!"

Dearie counted on the volunteers and students who often needed extra attentions, from tickets to lighting, stagehands to riggers, set designers to set construction crew, costumers to makeup; runners to cue carders; playbill printers to ushers. People, people everywhere. It all had to come together. Every jot-and-tittle, ready for opening night.

And opening night arrived, as if the new Rockefeller Angels were trumpeting the way! A banner on the *Lady Bird* poster for *A Christmas Carol* read *SOLD OUT!*

The Dutchies were jumping up and down they were so excited. Annika almost shouted, "Look! We all have red pants!" Elke added, "Mama sewed on little bells! And we tinkle!"

Jesse laughed at that all the way to the tower. He rang the bells and the theater doors opened to their new magic. The small orchestra tuned up, and the music began, with the cast entering from the back of the theater singing, *Here We Come A Caroling*.

They could feel the excited anticipations from the audience, and they were richly rewarded: ovations, hoots, thrills, cringes, laughter, tears, and *gaspers* came at every *splendish* turn.

The audience was smitten with the children's chorus, singing and strolling the sets while they changed the scenes. You could feel the instant audience rapport with the deep bass voice of the Narrator, Seph Gorecki. They were as ready to boo-hiss Scrooge as they were wild about Marley's *fan-dango* tango—a real show stopper! They delighted in the r-o-c-k-e-t-ing Jesse-Spirit-of-Christmas-Past, and his ear-waggles brought bursts of laughter. They spontaneously applauded Scrooge rocketing up with Jesse.

The crowd got a kick out of Fezziwig's whooping dance party and another surprise tango, from the indomitable Grams Maguire. They relished Jesse's disappearance through the trapdoor as much as the swinging rope entrance of Conor-Spirit-of-Christmas-Present, though he got a bit carried away throwing his props of brightly wrapped cornucopia treats right into the audience; as well as Mac-Scrooge riding the rope-swing with Conor.

They doted on the dear Cratchit family, especially Tiny Tim—Mikey Romano; and the hilarious Mr. Teppo Bonheur as Scrooge's persistently merry, nephew, Fred. But they were besotted with the electrifying, swooping entrance of Dearie-Spirit-of-Christmas-Yet-to-Come! Spine-chilling!

As the play wound down, they savored Mac-Scrooge's farcical, mincey-toed transformation on Christmas Day; and were mad for Billy Maguire's cheeky tango as he dashed off to find a Christmas turkey for Scrooge. And they simply loved Mikey Romano's—Tiny Tim—finale of, "God Bless Us, Everyone!"

The shouts and applause had the cast and stars bowing over and over again. The curtain closed and opened with shouts of 'Bravo!' booming throughout the *Lady Bird Theater.*

Grams turned to Bobby and Dearie, "Glaree-us! Just glaree-us!"

Indeed, all the grown-up actors were flushed with appreciations. And the children were thunderstuck.

"They liked it!" Annika Schuyler uttered behind the curtain.

"They loved it!" laughed Marijke.

"They loved us!" little Elke smiled angelically.

Taking off the stage makeup and changing their clothes, Jesse and Billy were in a grinning daze.

"That was GRAND!" Jesse cock-a-doodle-doo-ed.

"THAT was a *never-forgetter*! F'r sure!" Billy proclaimed, "NEVER! EVER FORGETTER!"

They were not alone. Every one of the children, every one of the cast, every stagehand, every costumer, Dearie and Bobby Lewis, they all knew. It was magic.

⁂

Jesse couldn't sleep. He tried. He played his little music box over and over: "Twinkle, Twinkle Little Star". But he was still high up in the clouds of *A Christmas Carol*. With each blink he pictured something else to remember, to savor: every thrill of performing, singing, dancing, flying. He was living it all over again, and he never wanted it to end.

"Dearie?" he sat up, calling into the darkness. "Dearie?"

The door opened and a pie-shaped light appeared on the floor, with Dearie's head appearing round the door. "Yes, Jesse?"

"I can't sleep. I'm wide awake."

Dearie sat on his bed and sighed, "The rim of the world puts the sun to bed and wakes it in the morning. This is where children sleep and dream." She smiled with her eyes gleaming, "You've not quite found that rim, have you?"

"No Dearie," Jesse beamed back, "I'm still *thrill-digging*!"

She puffed a laugh. "I am so glad you enjoyed your first stage performance. You'll never forget it."

Jesse gushed, "I know! I feel like my fly-wires are connected to the stars and I'm flying through the Milky Way, and all at the same time I'm looking down on *A Christmas Carol* in the *Lady Bird*...and...Jessica on Elizabethtown. And everything's glittering like the stars."

"That's beautiful, Jesse. I am so glad," Dearie smiled. "You know, your quest is not over. And *A Christmas Carol* is most assuredly not over. We have the rest of this weekend and two more weekends after that."

"I can't wait!"

His grin was so big Dearie laughed. "Your mouth is ready to explode, Jesse!" She pulled the covers back, "I'll rub your back. See if you can relax."

Jesse rolled over and felt Dearie's hand on his back. It felt so good. So comforting. She talked quietly to him, "You know Jesse, Old Barret used to say, 'When you can't sleep at night it's because you're awake in someone else's dream'."

"That sounds tricky. How can I be in a dream inside somebody else?"

"Think of all the people you know, and they know you. And love you." She tickled him lightly. "I love you. And I dream of you often."

"You do? I like being in your dream. Maybe I'm in Jessica's dream, too, 'cause I've been thinking about Christmaspast in Elizabethtown...and...I wonder, about my Christmas-future in Elizabethtown. Just wondering...."

"Yes, just like *A Christmas Carol* is full of wonderments," Dearie reflected.

Jesse breathed a big deep yawn.

Dearie yawned, too. "Yawns are contagious," she chuckled quietly.

"Dearie? Will you lullaby me?"

"Again?"

Jesse's head went up and down on his pillow, and he *murmeled*,

"Conor sang me "Silent Night", but can you sing me one of your lullabies?"

"All right." She thought a moment. "This is the lullaby my Mam used to sing as I lolled under the stars."

♫ *Lullaby, Hush-a-bye, my darling sweet sleepy head.*
The sandman has sprinkled your eyes. Lullaby, Hush-a-bye,
now it's off to your trundle bed, Say goodnight to the stars in the sky.

Lullaby, Hush-a-bye, hear my soft gentle heart song - Rock you to sleep all night long. Lullaby, Hush-a-by, your dreamland is waiting…

… Bye and Bye, lullaby, Hush-a-bye.

"Good night, my *love-adore*. My *brillish* boy." Dearie kissed him again.

A slow, sleepy *murmel* replied, "G'night Dearie. I love you."

How could *A Christmas Carol* be even better? Oh, but it was! The next night, every song, every line, every act flowed in glorious fun.

Then came Dearie's entrance as the Spirit-of-Christmas-Future. Like shining clockwork, Bartók's eerie *Fibinocci* music began. At first, it was phantasma-fabulous, with the spotlight focused on Dearie and her sweeping costume: long, gauzy whites, wafting over the audience, spiraling toward the stage.

But, abruptly, Dearie stopped. In mid-air. Swaying on the wire. The audience gasped. Upturned faces, pointing fingers, whisperings were suspended in Bartók's strange, ticking rhythms.

Helpless, Dearie gurgled, "Perhaps…some uplifting music…?"

The audience tittered and she proposed: "How about 'Swinging on a Star'!"

Katelijne Schuyler *piano-ed*, while Dearie, and the audience, sang-out heartily. The whole song! Dearie ended with:

"So would you like to 'Swing on a Star'? -

Carry moonbeams home in a jar?

And be better off than you are! -

Then you would have to swing with me!"

With the last line, *Whirrr!* Dearie began moving again. Slowly. Forward. Stop. Backward. Forward -

"Whoaaa!" she giggle-shrieked.

Backward-forward, backward-forward. The audience whooped with her. Then suddenly: *Whir. Whirrr! WHIRRR!*

"Uh-Oh!" Dearie cautioned, "Wwwhoaaa!" Dearie was off to the races! Heading for the stage, looking like a surging octopus, the gauzy entrails of her costume flailing like mad. Mac-Scrooge guffawed loudly, and cringed.

Someone shouted, "She's comin' in for a landing!"

"*Who-o-o-a-aa...!*"

And there was Dearie! Bundle-heaped onto Mac's lap! The two of them burst into laughter. The audience burst into laughter. The Spirit-of-Christmas-Yet-to-Come. In a tizzy of raucous laughter.

Part Six

Circles & Spirals

When the world says
No,
love says
Yes.

Chapter Twenty-Six

Dear Life

"Where's Jesse?" Conor asked Dearie after the show. She was sitting alone in the dressing room.

"He's off with the boys and the Dutchies," she chuckled, "They want to learn how to waggle their ears!"

"Fun! And as for you, Dearie," Conor reveled, taking a backward seat on the wooden chair, "you had way too much fun on the fly-wires tonight!"

Dearie chuckled, "Oh Conor, it was more fun than you know!"

But surprisingly, Conor became quiet, "Mac and Bridget left right away. Rose is back in hospital. With pneumonia. It's serious."

"Oh dear," Dearie reflected, "sweet Rose...and Hendrik...and their three children. Such darlings. Amazing spirits."

Jesse's laughter preceded him through the door. "What spirits?" he asked.

Dearie smiled at him, "You, Jesse! You and your great, fun spirit!"

Jesse flopped sideways in the stuffed chair and snuggled in, closing his eyes while Dearie and Conor talked.

She ruminated, "Spirits. Odd. Tonight I was on the fly-wires, but, I was...somewhere...." She waved her hand nonchalantly. "It reminded me of the Dvořák/Fisher song "Goin' Home"

'*...It's not far, jes close by. Through an open door...*'

"There was an open door. I felt...I saw...like the night Jane died. That fairy-dust Light. Hundreds of thousands of *glintaling* Lights, hovering around Jane. Remember? Gorgeous. Tonight, I was in that Light. More! I *was* the Light.

The Great Illuminations."

Conor sucked in his breath.

Let me tell you. Dearie knew intimately of the Great Illuminations. There was a time, as a young woman, when she had more than her share of the darks, which, back then, she thought dwelt in death.

Servicing the hospitals of World War I, she faced the horrors of trench warfare, and the worldwide Spanish Flu. Death took her Da and Mam and dear friends, and untold tallies of men. Day after day, year after year. Gone. Till Dearie was left all alone. Trapped in a numbed emptiness where only the darks grew. Barely breathing. Dearie had stopped living.

But she found a tittle of Light. She couldn't miss it. And bit-by-bit, she found her way.

She had thought her loves were gone, lost in a dark divide of death. Yet every love-moment she had ever shared with them came back. Inside the Light. In love and laughter. Like a conversation with angels. In the endless circle of life. Heaven on earth. Dearie came back to life. And she returned to the glories of living more powerfully than ever.

She learned that death is simply more of life. We all move on. Eternal travelers. On our eternal path of coming and going. There is no wall that separates us. Not even a veil.

She heard her Da's tittering voice: *Do you remember when you fell into this world? Do you think you will remember falling out of it?*

She saw her Mam…smiling at her, saying, *Life is always in the Light, Dearie. Waiting for you…to stand in the Light, too.*

Dearie sat back and lightly *grimmled*, "I'm in it, Conor. Flying high in the Light. In the Great Illuminations. It's all right here. We're all in it."

She reached for his hand. "Just like being in this play. Coming and going on a stage. Coming and going in life and death. It's all the same. We are all in it, Conor.

"You already know. It's your dream, Conor. Bobby Lewis has been telling you, you're ready. Go. It's time to go. Follow your dream. Your own theater. You...the stuff of stars. Light on! Just go!"

She stared into the mirror. "And I'll tell you this, Conor: you follow your dreams...and there is no end. And, it is...glorious. Glorious!"

Conor stood up with a laugh, "Or as Grams would say, glar-ee-us! They both chuckled. It was late. *Go*...Dearie had said. *Time to go.*

Conor reached for Jesse, "Come on, little man. Wake up. Time to go."

Jesse soughed softly, "Mmm, I'm awake. I'm coming." He slowly got up and followed Conor, moving through the quiet theater in a trance, turning off lights, closing doors.

Dearie had not joined them. They heard her playing her violin, bowing music that Conor and Jesse had not heard before. A beautiful melody and harmony, like two beautiful voices...as Conor always thought of Galen and Dearie. Jesse felt the notes soar through his heart and he looked up at Conor. Beaming, he whispered, "Glorious."

⁂

Mozart played in the morning lights, as Dearie and Jesse enjoyed a late breakfast together, before heading to the *Lady Bird* for another practice run on the high fly-wire.

"Dearie, do you love flying?" Jesse asked curiously.

"I do. I love it," Dearie smiled broadly.

"Well, why did you stop? Last night? You always say that a glitch is uuu-sually 'cause you're blocking energy. Were you afraid or worried, like you tell me?"

"Ahhh," Dearie nodded, "Good question, Jesse. Hmmm. Why did the fly-wire really get into a knot?" She poured herself another cuppa. "Well. I was thinking about *A Christmas Carol*. Coming to an end. Maybe that stopped me." She laughed, "How I love this play. The music and dance and chorus. I love all the characters and all the people from our apartment. I love the lessons from the Spirits. I want to be in it, feel it all go on and on—like eternity. Never to stop."

Jesse agreed, "Forever. Like *Neverland*." He pulled off a corner of toast, chewing thoughtfully. "But Dearie, you always say everything lives on. In our heart energies."

"Yes. You are right, Jesse." She grinned, "Really, nothing is ever over and done with. Everything and everyone lives on, just as you say, in our heart energies." She reached across the table and squeezed his hand. "Just like you always live in my heart, Jesse."

"And Dearie, you always live in my heart."

She stood up, "Yes! Whenever I see a heart I know it's you, Jesse! Like a Valentine. Right there waiting for me!"

Jesse was all smiles, "Me, too!"

She looked at her clock and raised her eyebrows, "All righty then. Now, my Valentine, it's time to go."

Andy was waiting for Dearie. He wanted no more unexpected glitches. In the theater balcony, Conor helped Dearie into the harness. She waved down at Jesse and laughed, "Ready to fly with the Spirits!" She turned to Conor, "This is one Spirit who can use all the practice she can get." She dimpled, and lifted off into the cavernous spaces, opening her arms. "Aaahhh…! Light on!" She laughed her beautiful, silvery, lustrous laugh.

Conor joined Jesse down in the theater, both smiling up at her. Gypsy the cat was there, begging to be picked up, and Jesse lifted her, snuggling as he *murmeled*, "Conor, look at Dearie. She looks..."

"Yes..." Conor reflected, "She looks so...beautiful." He chuckled, "So joyful...radiant..." he chuckled, adding, "glorious!"

"Uh-huh...like an angel."

Gypsy purred loudly and Jesse stared at Dearie in a trance, surprised, but not surprised. His eyes saw her inside a glittering circle of Light. A radiating circle of spinning, sparkling Lights and colors. Inside those beautiful, glistening colors, Jesse felt himself floating. Floating with Dearie.

All the stagehands, who had been privy to her ridiculous performance the night before, hooted, "Higher, Dearie!" urging, "Let 'er rip!"

Up she flew! Almost to the rafters! "Oh!" she exclaimed, "Oh!" she laughed brightly, vibrantly.

Conor and Jesse laughed with Dearie, but Gypsy leapt from Jesse's arms, and teased at him to follow her.

"Gyp-seee!" Jesse chased her up the aisle, through the swinging doors, into the lobby. The little cat headed for the bell tower and Jesse exasperated, "You can't ring the bells, Gypsy!" But she pounced at the rope. "Oh, you cat!" Jesse laughed, "Okay, just one ring. Just for you, Gypsy."

He tugged and heard the bell ring out in one glorious peal, like Dearie's silvery laugh. Jesse felt it humming in his heart.

He bent down to pet Gypsy and she climbed into his arms, curling against his chest. "Okay, you silly cat. Is that all you wanted?" He stood up, "Let's go back and see Dearie."

But from the bell tower to the theater, everything had changed.

Dearie reveled, laughing, soaring under the rafters. The stagehands ballyhoo-ed and one of the lighting crew popped on the spotlight and followed her. Dearie was gliding in a bright beam of light.

Oddly, a bell had sounded. Pealing, humming through the *Lady Bird.*

"Ahhhh," they heard Dearie breathe in a silver sigh.

But, all at once, her voice stopped. Her hands clutched her heart. Her head dropped.

"Dearie?" Conor startled. "Dearie!" He ran to the stage, calling, "Get her down! Get her down!"

The fly-lines skimmed Dearie down, gliding her toward the stage, coasting her body onto the floorboards. There she rested and
Conor helplessly fell to his knees beside her.

Dearie. Quiet. Serene. He saw her hands: one holding her heart, the other clasping her gold locket. Conor's eyes moved to her face. *Dearie.* Her face. So beautiful. So pale. He touched her cheek.

"Dearie," he husked.

She opened her eyes. Conor lost his breath. Her brilliant eyes!

"Conor," she smiled delicately, breathing out: "I'm...fine...so fine.... G...l...orious...."

Jesse came through the lobby doors and Gypsy jumped down, leading him purposefully down the aisle. He saw Dearie lying on the stage. But he also saw a slow spiraling, glittering glow all about her. Hundreds of thousands of tiny, dazzling Lights, hovering about Dearie.

He silently moved into the glowing mist of Lights, kneeling at Dearie's side. Conor watched him, looking so small, bending to his Dearie. She cupped her hand at his little cheek.

"Mmmm," she breathed, "Jesse. My *brill...i...sh....*"

She stopped. Jesse felt the tiny Lights rising up. Spiraling. But he did not take his eyes from Dearie as a delicate gasp flurried through her body.

"Ahhh..." she *whistered,* "Mam, Da...you're here." A gulp of,

"James, Jane." A surprise opened her eyes, "Elliot…?" Then her eyes glowed with love: "Galen… G-a-l-e-n…." Her eyes rolled back. She smiled rapturously, murmuring one last word: "Yes."

Dearie closed her beautiful eyes.

Jesse was motionless. His eyes, filled with a beautiful Light. Golden. Sparkling. Shining. He stared. And stared. A beautiful expression filling his little face.

Gypsy pawed at his arm. Licked his hand.

Slowly, the Light within Jesse, slowly, slowly drifted away.

Jesse blinked. He looked. Looked. At his Dearie. His dear, darling, dearest Dearie. The moment lasted forever. And was gone in an instant.

All the color, all at once, drained from him. His heart choked. His heart stopped breathing. In the next instant, his heart was exploding. Erupting. And a deep, deep sound gushed up from inside him. Gushed up. Deep into his heart. Deep into his throat. Deep into his trembling body.

He flew into Conor's arms. Both of them, choking in sobs. Drowning in tears. Clutching. Holding on to each other for dear life. Lost in the blurrings.

Blurrings. Touchings. Hands. Pulling Jesse up. Pulling Conor up. Taking them home.

Blurrings. Wit Schuyler. Quiet. Steering them up the long stairs. Quiet. So quiet.

Blurrings. Billy falling up the stairs. The Maguire's door opening. Billy murmuring. Grams shrieking. Her sobs following them up the stairs, "Nooo…Dearie…."

Blurrings. Their apartment door swinging open. Conor, keeling onto the couch, weeping. Shaking in Wit Schuyler's arms.

Jesse. Alone. Trembling. Falling.

Billy. Catching him. Dragging him to the stuffed chair. Cradling him. Jesse whimpering. Sobbing. Billy holding him. Tight. So tight. Jesse. In Billy's embrace. So. Tight.

⁂

Dark. Deep. Darkness.

I can't see. Am I asleep? I can't see.

He felt Dearie's hand on his back.

He heard Dearie's voice.

"Jesse…there are things you cannot see. Yet you know they are here."

"Like what?"

"Like gravity," she laughed lightly, "like the wind" Her voice turned to silver. "Like love."

She hugged him. He felt the sweetness of her love wrap around him, like a warm blanket, all around his heart.

"*Ohhh, Dearie,*" Jesse slumped into her embrace.

⁂

Jesse's face was deep in his pillow, smothering his face. He couldn't breathe. He opened his eyes. Into a deep dark. A chill trickled over his shoulders. Jesse was alone.

"Dearie?" He called: "Dearie?"

He waited for his door to open. Dearie's Light to shine in. He waited.

"Dearie!" he cried. "Dearie!' Screaming. "DEAR-REEE!" His hand found Velvet. He clung to Velvet. Screaming. "Dearie! Don't leave me!" Screeching. "Please! Please!" Shrieking. "Come back!"

Screaming. "Dearie! *Dearie!!* D-E-A-R-I-E!!!"

Conor. Lifting him from his bed. "Jesse." he husked, "Jesse. I'm here

Jesse. I'm holding you. Jesse...."

But the screaming shrieked through Jesse.

Conor sobbed. "Jesse...." Conor choked on his tears. "Jesse...."

A long, drawn-out, graveling scream: "Dear-ie.... Dear-ie...."

Conor held Jesse close. Carried him out to the parlor. Stood before the window. Rocked him. Slowly rocked him, "Jesse..." he *whistered*.

The screaming stopped. But Jesse cried. His whole body. Crying. Trembling. Shuddering. His little fingers clutching his Velvet. Crying. Soaking Conor's shirt.

Conor tried to hum. A hoarse hum stuttered in his throat. He *scrinched* his eyes, with tears squirting into Jesse's hair. Conor opened his mouth. A grimace distorted his lips. He persisted. He sang:

Silent night, Holy night, All is calm, all is bright.
Round yon virgin, mother and child, Holy infant so tender and mild,
Sleep in Heavenly peace, Sleep in heavenly peace.

And Jesse slept.

Chapter Twenty-Seven

Mourning

Teresa and Grams commandeered the kitchen, with help from the other couples in the apartments. Endless trays of sandwiches and cookies, coffee and tea filled the dining table over and over again.

Grams was having a hard time of it. She was in the kitchen, alternately choking on a sob or talking to no one and everyone. "We all have a ticket out of this world, everyone of us," her voice wept, "but Dearie. Squenched out like a lightnin' bug. Dearie." Standing at the kitchen sink, she looked out the window, "I don't want to believe it. Dearie...." She was shaking. Crying.

Crying. All of the people came and went in tears. Crying. Their cheeks wet. Mouths, pulled together in pain. Jesse could feel the crying. Like it was burning. Strong. The crying wanted to come back into his face. Back into his heart. But Jesse didn't want to cry anymore. He didn't want to go back into the deep darks again.

He sat on the couch, his turquoise eyes, startle-bright in his pale face. So many people came and sat with Jesse, wanting to comfort him. He felt their love touches, but he felt their sadness, too. He didn't want to feel that.

Aislinn came. He leaned into her shoulder and felt her gentle hug. They had a quiet time together. But she tried to talk about Dearie,

"...her special Light, her radiance. Dearie, a floodlight of brilliance...that just went out. Like someone flicked a switch." Aislinn's voice thickened and she could barely speak. "It's too hard. To think she's gone." Jesse looked at Aislinn's hands. The tissue in her hand was all rumply. She hugged Jesse once more and stood up.

Aislinn was embracing Conor. Holding him. His head, turned into her neck, his face hidden by her dark hair. They stood together like that. Jesse saw Conor's shoulders shaking. Aislinn held him. Just held him. Then Conor quietly pulled away. She touched his cheek. Patted his heart. Took his hand. Their fingers whispered to each other. And he let her go.

The neighbors were all trying to help, but Conor took care of most everything. Greeting. Thanking. Talking. Directing. Good-bye-ing. He seemed to be clear-eyed when he was busy with all that.

Jesse moved to the stuffed chair. He was growing numb. Breathing slowly. Watching everyone. He felt arms around him, hands touching him. Lips moving. But he didn't want to hear anything. He let it all run together like very loud buzzing *murmels* all around him.

Annika, Marijke, and Elke Schuyler came, bringing a plate of cookies they had baked just for Jesse. He could smell the sweet aroma. He liked their love-hug, holding him in their little circle. But he could feel them crying. He quietly sat back on the chair, and Katelijne took the girls away.

Touching Jesse's shoulder, Billy hitched his head, saying, "Jesse, come on."

Jesse took Billy's hand and followed him. Up to the rooftop. The day was bright with cold gray clouds. Billy took off his jacket and hung it over Jesse's shoulders. He didn't say anything. He just stood with Jesse. Looking. Listening.

Jesse closed his eyes, looking for his Lights. But he was startled. The Lights did not come. Instead his eyes filled with dark tears and he felt his mouth pull at his face. His eyes flew open and he gulped his breath. That was that. This numb feeling was better than trying to find his Lights.

A strange thought flickered into his brain. At the dress rehearsal, he had been happily explaining the trapdoor to little Rose Weiss: "It's like, I come out of nowhere, and later, I go back into nowhere."

Jesse *scrinched* his eyelids together, and blinked away the tears. *Maybe nowhere is better than here.*

Billy seemed to read his thoughts and he put his arm around Jesse, pulling him close. They stood. Together. Silently looking out at the city that went on about its business, as if the world had not turned into a tangle of upside downs.

Gypsy appeared, winding between Jesse's legs. He picked her up and put his nose in her fur. She purred loudly and Jesse put his cheek to her body, feeling her heartbeat. He breathed. A real breath. He liked the quiet. Just…being.

⁂

Dearie's Memorial service was held in her *Lady Bird Theater*. Jesse and Billy rang the bells, and a never-ending stream of people came. Every seat was taken and others stood in the aisles and lobby, even going out the door.

From the bell tower Jesse watched as Bobby greeted the apartment families. Whatever he said to them, they looked surprised; but they nodded and went to find a seat.

The little orchestra in the stage pit was playing Dearie's favorite music. Jesse felt strange. He didn't feel Dearie. Not in his heart. Not even when they played her favorites, like Elgar's powerful "Nimrod", or Dvořák's soft "Goin' Home" song.

Bobby turned to Jesse, "May I talk with you privately?" Back in the tower room Bobby knelt down, eye-to-eye with Jesse. He started to speak. Stopped. Wrapped his arms around Jesse. Held him. Quiet and still. Jesse felt it and he took a breath. When Bobby pulled away his eyes were wet, but he spoke clearly.

"You know how I feel about you. Conor. Dearie.... So...dear."

Jesse nodded but he did not speak.

"Well...." Bobby's head wagged, "I've asked your neighbors to think about continuing *A Christmas Carol*. In honor of Dearie. For the love of Dearie. But your decision will count first, Jesse. You and Conor. If you are okay with it, then I'll ask the whole cast to decide. We'll meet tonight."

Jesse whispered, "Dearie said she wanted our *Christmas Carol* to never end."

"Yes." Bobby smiled. "Me, too." His tear-filled eyes met Jesse's again. "But what about you?"

"I like what Dearie said."

"All righty then."

"That's what Dearie always said."

"Yes. I think Dearie's here. For sure."

Beautiful flowers lined the stage. The most colorful ones were from Amanda. She was with her family in Georgia, facing the death of her father. She sent a Dearie favorite: a rainbow of flowers called Ranunculus. Jesse stared at the flowers and said the word over and over in his head. *Ranunculus.* A real flower. A real word.

The service began with a welcome from Conor. Jesse liked Conor's own words taken from a poem by James Whitcomb Riley:

She Is Not Dead.

I cannot say, and I will not say that she is dead.

She is just away.

With a cheery smile, and a wave of the hand,

she has left us dreaming,

while she wandered into an unknown land - - -

And how very fair it must be, since she lingers there.

But even you - oh you - who wildly yearn for her old-time step, and her glad return -

Think instead of her faring on, as dear in the love of There,

as the love of Here.

Think of her as still the same love.

I say, she is not dead—she is just away.

After that, people told stories about Dearie: how her words and laughter and music lit up their dreams, or helped them through a dark time. Some offered a tender prayer for Dearie and Conor and Jesse.

Most of it went over Jesse's head and missed his heart. It was like more of the very loud buzzing-*murmels.* Jesse didn't really hear it. Until Mac stood up. Slowly, with his voice shaking, Mac spoke:

"When someone dies, it feels like they have left us. But when you have loved a person, and that person has loved you, deeply, so deeply, then there are parts of her that death can't have, can't claim. That person, that lovely, loving person belongs to you now. That's our Dearie. Death can't have all of her. Dearie belongs to Conor. And Jesse. And all of us bless-ed ones, who have been touched by Dearie, and now, will always have a little piece of her. Inside each of us."

Jesse got a tiny *shiveral.* He put his hand on his heart. He waited a moment. But nothing came to him. No Dearie. He thought, *Dearie's heart must be broken. It's not working.*

Jesse's eyes stared at his hands. They seemed not to belong to him. He put them under his legs and sat still. Numb.

Afterward there was more food, and more coffee and tea, and more people. Weeping. Talking. Jesse was tired. Conor took him home.

The Schuylers walked with Jesse and Conor to the apartments. Elke tried to talk to Jesse, but nothing came out of him. He vaguely heard Marijke exclaim about something.

"Look what I found! Jesse! You walked right over it!" Surprised, she blurted, "A heart! Gosh, it's the heart locket for my Betsy McCall doll!" She stared at it. "How did it get down here?"

O' course, you know it didn't matter how the heart locket got there. It was Dearie, reaching out to Jesse from here in the Great Illuminations. But Jesse...well...he couldn't see or hear or feel Dearie.

Katelijne Schuyler smiled, "Marijke, I'm glad you found it."

Jesse paid them no mind. When they said goodbye to the Schuylers, Jesse looked up at Conor. "I haven't really seen Mac. Or Bridget. Since Dearie went...to the Great Illuminations."

Conor continued upstairs, answering, "That's because Rose is in the hospital. Pneumonia. Complicated by the polio. Rose was close to dying, and Mac and Bridget and Rose's husband, Hendrik, kept their vigil."

Jesse turned, "But she didn't...die...."

"No. Mac told me that it was Dearie who saved Rose. Sprinkling her grace—her sparkling Lights—on Rose. Bringing Rose back to life."

Jesse quieted, "Yes. I saw it," Jesse said. "Dearie's Lights." He tried to feel them again. But he didn't want to close his eyes. It was too dark.

Conor was talking, "Bridget is more cautious. She says Rose is not out of the woods. They want to stay by her side as much as they can."

"Golly. They must love her a lot."

Conor looked at Jesse. He closed his eyes. Finally he sighed and told. The long-hidden truth: "They do love Rose. Very much. You see…Rose is Mac and Bridget's daughter."

Jesse's eyebrows caterpillared, "Daughter?"

"Yes, but something happened in Rose's life, to make Bridget want to keep her a secret."

"A secret…." Jesse repeated. Jesse was done with secrets. He fell onto his bed and closed his eyes.

"I have to go back, Jesse." Conor kissed his cheek. "But Billy's here. He'll stay with you while you rest."

Jesse opened his eyes and saw Billy climbing up on the other bed, with his hand raised in a little wave, and he said, "I'll be right here, Jesse. Right here."

By the evening, the *Lady Bird Theater* cleared out from Dearie's Memorial Service, and filled up with *A Christmas Carol* cast & stage crew, all focused on Bobby Lewis. For Jesse, the words just ran together, until Bobby held up their playbill for *A Christmas Carol.*

"Every one of you has your name in this," he waved it in the air, "you are each an essential part of the production. So I leave it to you: do we 'fold up our tents...and silently steal away' like Longfellow's poem, *Day Is Done*? Or do we use the *Lady Bird Theater* stage to love and honor Dearie and everything she has gifted to us all? We still have two weekends to perform. That's six more productions. What do you say? All those in favor..."

The air waved with hands.

"All opposed?"

Not one hand. Bobby chuckled, "As Dearie liked to say, All righty then. The show must..."

The cast finished in a chorus: "Go on!"

Bobby laughed, "We'll have to rehearse ourselves back up to perfomance speed. I'll see you all back here tomorrow evening."

As chattering voices exited the theater, Bobby pulled aside the Schuyler family. "May I have a word with you? I have a proposal."

Chapter Twenty-Eight

The Show Goes On

Jesse went back to his school, lifelessly falling into the routines. Everyone was kind, yet their cheer—Christmas or otherwise—did not touch Jesse. When Missus K asked him if he'd like to continue Dearie's Dictionary, Jesse said, "No. I can't ask Dearie about any of the words anymore."

He sat quietly, staring out the window, rolling the clay back and forth on the board, wishing for his Dearie, wondering where she was. He did not notice the sun glimmering on a set of heart-shaped cookie cutters at the top of the table. When one heart slid down, landing on his clay, he heedlessly pushed it aside.

Jesse was not in receiving mode.

The weekend turned up all by itself, and it was time for *A Christmas Carol*. The *Lady Bird Theater* had another huge success, even though the cast was, at first, reserved. Bobby prodded them, "Let's make Dearie proud." He chuckled, "Dearie's out there in the audience. Put on your best performance ever!"

Jesse performed. In his Spirit-of-Christmas-Past, it was clear that the wise old man was in there, but the shining child was nowhere to be seen. And there were no waggles.

On the other hand, Annika was raring to go. Bobby had asked her, "Do you think you're up to taking over Dearie's role as the Spirit-Of-Christmas-Yet-To-Come?" He laughed, "I'd take it on myself, but my card…it's full."

Marijke exclaimed, "You have full Myocarditis? Heart

inflammation?"

"What?" Bobby was bewildered.

Annika jumped up and down like she was on a pogo stick, but Wit Schuyler first explained to Bobby, "Please excuse the interruption. Marijke is our future doctor, practicing every medical term she can get her mind on."

Annika couldn't contain herself a moment longer. Out she blurted, "Yes! Oh yes! I can do it. I know Dearie's *Spirit Of Christmas* doesn't get to say anything, but I know just what to do! I can do it!"

Bobby gave her his attention, "I trust you can, Annika. But I want you to understand, you will not be riding on any fly-wires. I have something else in mind."

It was another show-stopper.

When Bartók's eerie music began, there was an unearthly, warbling screech from the back of the theater. An exceedingly tall, wraith-like figure appeared in the spotlight. Flailing down the aisle, with a ghastly screech, was Annika, sitting atop her father's shoulders, dressed in floor length, filmy layers of white gauzes. The audience went crazy for her. And she shrieked all the more.

Wit Schuyler was fit enough to stalk to the stage with Annika, but she was too heavy to carry through the whole act. Consequently, Bobby had devised a funny solution that everyone applauded.

"It's like the *Wizard of Oz*," Bobby explained, "and you, Annika, will be like the Wicked Witch. Water will shrink you, but not to nothing. Just to your normal size."

"I get it!" Annika crowed, "Scrooge will be so terrified of me, he will throw his glass of water all over me!"

"Right! Then your father will release you on stage, and you'll be all set as the Spirit."

Annika thought it was so very clever. Wit was relieved to be free of her weight. Mac-Scrooge had a jolly time throwing the paper-confetti water all over her. And the audience was mad for the whole thing.

The second weekend performance of *A Christmas Carol* went off without a hitch, and they were on the way to the final weekend, like marbles racing down the curtain rods.

After the very last Friday night show, most everyone was feeling tuckered, including Jesse and Conor.

"I gotta hit the sack," Conor said.

Jesse agreed, "I feel like I'm sleepwalking."

As they walked up the stairs, Jesse yawned, "I'm so glad Liam got to see *A Christmas Carol* tonight.

"Yeah," Conor replied, "Liam's going out to sea tomorrow. Up the coast. He'll be gone for over a week. But that means he'll be home for Christmas."

"That's good he'll be home. When Liam's gone, I miss him, almost like Billy misses him."

"Yeah. Liam's pretty special."

The O'Neil boys fell into their beds like sugar cubes plopping into hot coffee, melting into their pillows of sleep.

In the morning, Jesse went down to the courtyard to help Mac close up his garden. The hay, which they spread over the dead plant stubs, was from the Bonheur's Halloween hay bale, and Jesse got a quirky little smile thinking of that screaming good trick-or-treating fun. But Mac was very quiet.

Just as they finished, Jesse saw the mailman, and he jumped up. "Maybe I'll get my postmaster letter from Elizabethtown."

He ran into the lobby.

"Ah," Mr. Paul rasped, "the US Mail conveys a letter to Master Jesse Seamus O'Neil." He smiled from under his long mustache. In his predictable manner, he gave it a flourish and handed it to Jesse.

"It *is* from Elizabethtown," Jesse gushed. "Thank you."

"I don't send," Mr. Paul croaked his worn old saying, "I just deliver. Fair thee well!"

Conor was excited to see Jesse's letter. "Gosh all fish hooks, Jesse, you did it! You got an answer. Let's see what it says."

Dear Master Jesse Seamus O'Neil,

Thank you for your letter of inquiry. It has taken some time to investigate your request, as I am the new Postmaster in Elizabethtown.

Your Grandmother, Mrs. Jessica Roberts, is alive and apparently well, living at Windy Hill Farm, 100 North Star Road, Elizabethtown.

Jesse looked at Conor. "Windy Hill Farm. Another clue! I know just where her farm is. There's a windmill across the road from that farm!"

"Jesse"—Conor smiled—"when it comes to Elizabethtown, you know more about it than anybody. But read on."

Mrs. Roberts' mail is returned to you stamped 'Unable to Deliver' because, years ago, she requested of the Postmaster that she wanted no one on her property. She removed her mailbox, and she receives no mail whatsoever, as is her prerogative.

Jesse frowned and looked at Conor.

"Prerogative means her right to say 'No, thank you, I don't want any mail delivered.'"

For your own information, Windy Hill Farm has no electricity, no telephone service, and no public water system.

In summary, it would seem, that if you wish to make contact with your grandmother, you would need to do so in person.

If so, perhaps we will meet one day. In the meanwhile, I wish you the best.

Sincerely,

Mr. S. Coleman, Postmaster, Elizabethtown - December 1953

"What a great letter, Jesse," Conor smiled.

"No it's not! There's no way we can write Jessica. It's impossible!"

Jesse stopped *I am possible* bounced into his brain. But he kicked it out and rasped, "I know we're never going to get up to Elizabethtown."

"Who told you that?"

Jesse didn't answer. He looked scornfully at Conor from under his eyebrows.

"Jesse, this doesn't mean never. It just means your quest is not done yet. Remember what Dearie always says, 'A bend in a road is never the end of the road, unless you don't make the turn.'"

Jesse said nothing, and Conor tried again, "Jesse, remember *Squirrel Nutkin*?"

"Beatrix Potter?" Jesse perked.

"Remember? Beatrix wrote: 'This looks like the end of the story; but it isn't.'"

"I wish it were the end."

"Do you? No more quest?"

"I don't mean that," Jesse huffed. "I just wish I could find Jessica. For real."

"And hasn't it been great solving Jessica's puzzles? Come on. You said it was *thrill-digging*! And isn't it wonderful still, to just think about all the possibilities in your wish coming true? We know for sure, Jessica is alive."

"Conor," Jesse sneered, "you're just trying to sound wonderful like Dearie. You know we're never going to go to find Jessica. Ever!"

Conor flinched. He was quiet for a moment. Then his voice came out, real mellow, "Come on Jess, remember what Dearie taught us: keep thinking and picturing the wonderful. It's waiting for you."

Jesse gave him that look again.

"Okay, okay, I admit"—Conor waggled his head—"I don't always practice that. But I wish I did. I know that when I get so furious at all these tangles, it just gets me more wrapped up in the tangles." He picked up the letter. "It was really great of the Postmaster to write you back with so much information. He didn't have to do that."

Jesse took the letter and put it back in the envelope, saying in his matter-of-fact voice, "I'll put this in the desk in the lumber room. Then I think Billy's coming up."

Conor was surprised and relieved. "Okay then. I'll be going over to the Actor's Studio. Bobby's waiting for me."

In the lumber room, Jesse grabbed the box with the red-black-white wooden stripes. Pushing roughly on the white slide, he noticed the window light shining on it. He thought of his Lights:

Where are they? He quickly closed his eyes. *No. Nothing. Gone. Like Dearie is gone.*

He felt the white stripe move smoothly under his fingers and he looked at the puzzle-piece key. There was no thrill. No *zippity-pip* going through him. He closed the slide, not bothering to finish opening it.

He put the box on the carpet and began collecting all the clues he had pulled together through this past year: the Jane-Jessica letters; his own

Elizabethtown Island booklet with all his notes and drawings; and the postcard of frozen Tanagasuq Bay; Jane's poem-map; her shells and sea glass; the ball of colorful yarns; the returned letters from Elizabethtown. He sat, staring at everything on the floor. *Dearie's gone. I have to go by myself. I have to go. Leave.*

Leave. Go.

Gypsy jumped to the windowsill, and Jesse stood up with her.

"I can go. Find Jessica," he said to Gypsy. "I can do it." *I-am-possible,* he thought. "Just like I found all the pieces of the desk puzzles. I have to go to Elizabethtown."

He looked out the window, down to the front stoop. Liam was there, talking to Grams.

"*Liam!*" Jesse's words wheeled excitedly: "Liam's going up the coast. I'll go to Liam's tugboat. I'll go! To Elizabethtown."

Jesse didn't actually know where Liam was going, and he felt a pang. Something telling him, *No, don't do this.* But he was already in motion.

He threw on his coat and went swiftly down the hallway and out the door, without saying a word to Conor.

Jesse's feet had wings as he swung around each landing, thinking determinedly, *I can do it.* Gypsy followed him, as he skimmed down to the last flight, riding the banister side-saddle to the lobby. He hopped off, and pushed out the side door.

Jesse ran smack into Grams and she startled, "Well! Hello, Jesse!" She looked down, "Hello there, Gypsy girl."

Gypsy didn't meow and Jesse didn't answer. They both ran to the sidewalk. Down in front of the drugstore, Mr. Schuyler was talking and laughing with Mr. Bonheur, Mr. Gorecki, and Mr. Romano.

But Jesse's eyes looked the other way. Looked for Liam.

There he is!

Jesse ran after him. He got to the end of the block and saw Liam's red head bobbing through the busy crowd on the avenue.

Liam's going the wrong way!

Jesse didn't know where Liam was headed, but he knew where he wanted to go.

I'll get to the tug, and be there when Liam gets there, he said to himself. *I know the way. All the way down Tugboat Street.* Jesse crossed the avenue and kept going.

But Gypsy stopped at the avenue. She turned back, and bolted, like black lightning, back to Mr. Schuyler's store. She leapt to Mr. Schuyler's coattails, but she tumbled off. Instantly she clawed her way up Mr. Romano's pant leg, and he danced like he was in a frying pan. "Help!" he cried, "Gypsy, I have no olives!" He kicked her off.

Blister-quick, Gypsy jumped on Mr. Bonhuer's leg, scratching up to his jacket. "What is going on?" He yelped, and threw her off.

Gypsy only turned again and leapt on Mr. Gorecki. He pulled her into his arms and purred to her in his deep voice, "What is it, Gypsy?"

The men turned away, shaking their heads. It was time to move on, to open their shops. But Wit Schuyler stopped in amazement. "Wait! Gypsy is telling us something! Look!" He pointed far down the avenue. There was a stream of holiday shoppers. And there was Jesse O'Neil. Bustling away. All by himself. They all saw Jesse. And someone else. Following Jesse. Tim Braedon.

Chapter Twenty-Nine

Trouble

Jesse's thoughts were bent on getting to Liam's tugboat. He moved past the crowd, listening to the rhythm of his feet. But he soon realized someone was behind him, keeping up the same rhythm. His heart wrinkled when he heard that odd whisper whistling. But it was too late. Jesse was grabbed from behind.

"Gotcha!"

Tim Braedon. Smelling as bad as ever. Maybe worse.

Jesse had no time to think, though he was aware that Tim had ducked up the next avenue. Jesse struggled, shouting, "Let me go!"

An older couple turned, pointing and staring. But Tim, smooth as ever, said loudly, "Now son, we have to get back to your mother. Come on now, don't make a fuss."

The older couple walked away.

"Help!" Jesse yelled after them. Help me!" But they kept walking. "Please!" Jesse yelled.

Like a sack of potatoes, Tim threw him over his shoulder, heading up the avenue.

"No! Let me go!" Jesse flailed, "I won't go with you! I won't!"

"You left me no choice, Jesse. Getting me kicked out of the apartments. You owe me. I'm down on my luck now, but there's a real treasure waiting for me. And you're gonna help me find it." Tim puffed, "You're my ticket outta here, and I'm gonna be on easy street. Now quitcher bellyachin'," Tim added, walking at a fast clip.

Jesse felt desperately confused. Tim shifted Jesse's weight on his shoulder. Jesse could feel his smell. His stink. He screamed. "Let me go!"

"Shad-up. I'm taking you on the train to Elizabethtown."

"What? Elizabethtown?"

Elizabethtown! Jesse's dream! But no. Jesse knew. He was in real trouble. Danger. He squeezed his eyes shut. Trying to find his Lights. His safe Lights. Just a speck. "Please," he *whistered*, and took in a quick breath. Oh! He saw a tittle of Light dart under his eyelids.

Jesse let out a gush of trapped air. *Think*, he told himself. *THINK*.

With a deep breath, he…choked. *Good glory, what a smell!* He scrunched his eyes trying to turn off his nose. He focused: *Danger*. His brain hopscotched from *danger* to another thought: Missus K's game of playing possum.

Jesse stopped struggling. He closed his eyes. Tried to breathe real low, quiet, calm. Real deep. He could feel the calm. On the inside.

Tim Braedon slung him forward and set him down, saying, "That's more like it, Jesse. Nice and quiet." He swiped his forehead with one hand, and Jesse saw a filmy sheen of mildew on his sleeve.

"Besides," Tim Braedon was saying with short breaths, "you're too big and too heavy to carry." He held Jesse's hand, "Relax. This your dream come true. Elizabethtown. Ya don't have Dearie anymore. Time to find your other Grandma. Don't worry, I'll take real good care of ya."

Jesse let his hand go possum limp. Then his body. Rolling his head, he melted to the sidewalk.

"Oh no. No. No y'don't!" Tim whined, and Jesse felt him trying to lift him. But those long thin fingers of his were useless. Jesse stayed as limp as a lumpy little possum. Like he had fainted. Tim bent over him, pushing and rolling, trying to grab him by the coat. But Jesse was too heavy and awkward.

Tim hovered, grousing over him, "Jesse. Get up." He bullied, "I'll have ta kick the livin' daylights outa ya if ya don't get up!"

Jesse's knees shot up to protect himself—and they slammed into Tim's jaw! Jesse saw him keel over onto the sidewalk.

Jumping up, Jesse's possum turned into a jackrabbit. He never ran so fast. Back down the avenue. A large street crowd was ahead of him. Jesse kept his eyes ahead and plowed into the crowd, disappearing from Tim Braedon. But when he peeked back over his shoulder, he saw Tim Braedon—like moving puzzle pieces. He was holding his face, looking, searching.

Jesse had one thought, pounding in his feet, humming in his ears: *Liam's tug. Get to Liam's tug.*

⁂

Conor couldn't find Jesse.

Grams told him, "Jesse ran off without so much as a how dee do. I was out saying good-bye to Liam, when we saw Tim Braedon across the street, like he was lookin' for someone. Next thing, Liam left and Jesse was tearin' out the door."

Conor didn't like the sound of it. He ran out of the building, right into Sergeant Hannity.

"Tim Braedon is wanted by the police," Sergeant Hannity told Conor. "And the station just got a call that Braedon was seen here, following Jesse."

Conor winced, "Tim Braedon? Following Jesse?"

"Tim Braedon's part of a counterfeit ring. Last night we raided the Shark House, arrestin' most everyone there; but Tim got away."

Conor jolted, "I've gotta find Jesse."

"No," Sergeant Hannity wagged his head, "the detectives are on this.

I'll phone in Braedon's whereabouts from the Cop-Box on the corner. You search the apartments. Jesse may still be here."

Soon, the rest of the apartments joined the search, and the families, one by one, discovered that the drugstore, the grocery, the laundry, the hardware were all closed. And their misters were nowhere to be found.

They congregated in the courtyard, even Mac and Bridget. The children were busy with hopscotch and jump ropes and marbles. But they could tell something was going on, as Marijka wondered out loud, "Where's Jesse?"

Billy hugged his mother. He knew—he just knew—Jesse was in trouble.

Most of the grownups were in a tight little group near the stoop. The word 'kidnap' was bandied about in desperate whispers. Conor was frantic to find Jesse.

But Bridget said, "Trust Sergeant Hannity. You need to be here when Jesse gets back."

Bobby Lewis came looking for Conor and got an earful.

"That Tim Braedon!" - "He's a criminal." - "He had us all fooled." - "Glad he's out of our lives." - "What a skunk he turned out to be."

Grams said nothing. She couldn't. Her throat was strangled with remorse. Eventually, she scraggled to Bridget, "I brought Tim Braedon here. My foolish foolishness. Now he's taken our Jesse away. Oh dear God in Heaven, please let Jesse be safe. Please God."

Bobby heard their mutterings, and he spoke above them all. "Now listen, we know better. Whatever is happening, Jesse needs our highest and best thoughts. Remember what Dearie would always say on stage. 'Our thoughts and words are real. Powerful. They are flowing electricity. That's how we plug-in with each other. So get into your best self. Light on!'"

The courtyard grew quiet. Teresa stroked Billy's hair, "Right," she breathed, "We can't worry about Jesse and love him at the same time."

Mac spoke, pulling his pipe from between his teeth, "Jesse knows. His heart-Light will be on, waiting for our good thoughts to help him, whatever happens."

Conor and Bobby weren't so sure of that. Jesse hadn't been Jesse lately.

Hidden in the avenue crowd, Jesse tried to catch his breath. He managed to be calm, breathing and thinking: *Swell. All is swell.*

He knew he had to get off the avenue. Get back onto Tugboat Street. Get to Liam. He would have to leave the crowd. He wasn't safe here.

He looked behind. Tim was coming after him, looking crazed. Like the pirates of *Treasure Island.* Jesse remembered N.C. Wyeth's picture and Mac reading: *We must go forward. For we can't go back.*

Jesse looked ahead. A woman in a white coat walked in front of him. A red leather purse hung over her shoulder. It was in the shape of a heart. Jesse stared at it. Not thinking, he bolted forward. Down the avenue. Running like blazes! His heart hammering. In a flash, he could see it, coming up: Tugboat Street! But, as he turned the corner, he was surprised: the familiar street rolled out before him, shining like a ribbon of Light. Shining!

Jesse ran. Ran on the Light. Ran for his life.

The pier. Liam's tug.

Tim Braedon followed, just a block behind. Jesse ran faster, feeling trickles of sweat wetting his cheeks, his breath burning in his chest, his heart bursting. He ran at a red target on the side of the big warehouse along the street. He'd never noticed the poster before. Closer. Closer. Looking down on him was a big red heart: *American Heart Association*

Jesse felt himself running, flowing, in a bubble of Light. Effortless. His feet hit the pier. Almost there. But Tim Braedon's footfalls pounded behind him. His own footfalls thumped in his ears, while in his eyes: Liam's shining tug.

But. No gangplank. Jesse couldn't think. His inner voice shouted at him: *Jump! Jump!* And he was flying through the air. Flying!

Landing on the metal deck, the shock shuddered through his legs. But he bounded up, pulled open the pilot house door and shot inside.

Right behind him, he heard Tim Braedon land on the deck.

Sliding open the door to the captain's quarters, Jesse jumped in, just as Tim opened the pilothouse door. Jesse's heart popped into his throat and sank to his toes, but in that instant he slammed the door shut, reached on tiptoe and pushed the lock. He watched the bar slide across, as if in slow motion, at last clicking into place. Jesse stood stock-still. Barely daring to breathe. He just stood still in the dusky dark and stared at the door.

He heard Tim Braedon pull on the door. It jiggled, but it held. Jesse heard Tim's footfalls walk back through the outer door.

Go away, Jesse's thoughts pleaded, *Get off this tug, Tim Braedon.*

Tim Braedon did not get off the tug. He walked around the pilothouse. Then all was silent. Until:

"I see you, Jesse!"

His stinking voice came through the porthole window.

Jesse shot off his feet. He looked to the little round window: Tim Braedon. Staring at Jesse.

Jesse climbed on Liam's bunk, stretching to close the brass window. Tim Braedon stared at him, as if he could somehow seize him right through the window. Jesse gasped. He struggled with the last turn of the porthole screw, trying not to look at Tim Braedon.

"I can wait," Tim threatened. "I'll be on board. Waiting."

Hearing Tim's feet move to the stern, Jesse wilted. He fell back onto the bunk and burst into tears.

He was crying full on. Tears. Burning through the chainlink knots in his head. Knots in his stomach. In his heart. He cried with fatigue. With worn out weariness. He cried with the stale, exhausting effort of not crying in all this time since Dearie....

Oh Dearie.

Jesse was done-in. His whole body cried. And finally, his body let go...let go of the numb, protective armor. His shield against the wasteland of his grief and heartache. Melting. Letting go.

In his free-flowing tears he unexpectedly felt the shreds and slivers of dark dazzlings. He saw glintaling shapes. He watched swirling, soaring, spiraling glitters. He shook himself. Knelt up. Looked. For the Light. His Light.

Out the window, the sun on the water...glittered like diamonds...filled his eyes. His eyes saw a shimmering circle of Light, like a gift, wrapped in tinsel. A radiating circle, of spinning, sparkling Lights. And colors. His eyes opened wide as he watched them gyrating in gold and silver, deep blue, purple, red. Inside those beautiful, glistening colors, Jesse felt Dearie.

"Dearie...."

Jesse's heart opened. Floated. With Dearie. On a streaming ribbon of Light. He thought of Tugboat Street. It had looked like a ribbon of Light. He thought of the red hearts his eyes had seen, waiting for his heart to open.

"Dearie...."

A bright laugh blurted out of him, "Oh, Dearie. Dearie!" He hung on the brass circle of the window and his face beamed into the bright water diamonds. Dearie was here. In Jesse's eyes. In Jesse's heart. Jesse's open heart.

And the glittering water reflections gave up even more. Jesse felt a surge, a cascade of love: Dearie... Jane and James. As if their photograph had come to life. And he smelled chocolate. He beamed. And then he felt...Jessica? The water diamonds glittered and Jesse felt more beings...star people.

A noise on the deck filtered into Jesse's ears, and he became aware of feet running on the deck. Many feet.

Then a roaring voice: "Whadar you doin' on this boat?"

It was First Mate Steve. Bellowing at Tim Braedon. Next thing, Steve boomed again, "Give me a hand fellas."

Tim Braedon's screamed, "Noooo!" followed by a big splash. And cheering.

Jesse felt his chest shake in *thrill-bumps* of rapturous relief. Of thankfulness. It was a quiet, sublime joy. Of deliverance. A sense of being free. With Dearie. Jesse put his hands over his heart, and closed his eyes. Spinning Lights winked brightly. Growing. Filling everything behind his eyes. Jesse felt more. Conor. And Mac. And Billy. And everyone. He felt their love. Their Lights. Bright. Sparkling.

"Oh!" Jesse laughed again, "Ohhh...."

He heard a heavy knock on the door. But Jesse stayed in the sparkles.

"Jesse."

More knocking on the door.

"Jesse. It's Steve here. Open the door."

The sparkles continued. Jesse didn't move.

"Jesse," Mr. Schuyler's voice gentled, "Mr. Romano, and Mr. Bonheur, and Mr. Gorecki are here, too. We're here to take you home, Jesse. Unlock the door."

In one scoot, Jesse was off the bunk, standing on tiptoe to slide the bolt back. The door skimmed open and he tumbled into the bright Light.

He blinked. There were stars. Everywhere. Star-people. Mr. Schuyler knelt at the door and Jesse fell into his arms, surrounded by a close circle of the others.... Star-men. Jesse cried and cried. Happy cries. Left over *feardy cat* cries. Relieved, grateful cries.

Jesse knew the vibration of Mr. Schuyler's voice, "We've got you, Jesse. We've got you,"

He felt other hands patting his back. Heard other voices murmuring.

Something poured through Jesse's body—poured into and out of his heart. He saw it, felt it, in the circle of Misters. And he surrendered into its embrace.

Breathing in, Jesse knew each one of them: the peppermint of Mr. Schuyler; the olives of Mr. Romano; paint and wood of Mr. Gorecki; laundry soap of Mr. Bonheur. He looked up at Steve, who had rolled up his shirtsleeve and was rubbing his arm. There was a tattoo there: a big red heart.

Dearie....

Time stood still. Jesse breathed. Closed his eyes. He knew now. He had closed off his heart and he had missed all the hearts Dearie had been offering him: his own heart when Mac spoke at Dearie's memorial service, Marijke's heart locket, the heart cookie cutters, the heart purse, the heart poster...and now, a tattoo heart. Dearie had been with him, showing him the way, back into his heart.

Dearie.... Jesse felt his heart pulsing her name.

Just then the pilothouse door opened. "What's goin' on?"

Liam.

Slowly Jesse pulled his head from Wit Schuyler's shoulder and swiped at his eyes. He hugged Mr. Schuyler and touched his cheek. "Thank you." He turned to Mr. Gorecki, who bent down and received the same touch, the same hug of "Thank you."

He hugged each man in the circle. He kept swiping at his own eyes, and was surprised to see them doing the same. Wiping away tears that glistened in their eyes. It felt like they were all winking.

Jesse felt something very powerful. Very gentle. Rising and falling in his chest. In his heart. And with each hug and each thank you, he felt himself coming back. Back to being Jesse. He even smiled—with tears in his eyes.

Liam saw Jesse smile. He knew it was not quite the full tilt, but he saw Jesse's eyes flicker in his old familiar turquoise sparks. Liam had no idea what had happened, but he breathed a sigh of relief watching Jesse.

Jesse, too, took a deep breath. And he knew. Jesse knew with all his heart. He was home.

The courtyard was filled. Everyone waiting. Two police cars pulled up. Eyes opened. Mouths opened. Car doors opened. And out poured Mr. Gorecki, Mr. Bonheur, Mr. Romano, Mr. Schuyler, Officer Hannity…and Jesse Seamus O'Neil. A hullabaloo echoed from one end of their block to the next!

Conor rushed to Jesse, picking him up, with Jesse's arms and legs wrapping around him like the ribbons of a gift. Billy and Mac moved to each side of them: unmatched bookends, holding them up while Gypsy purred in and out of Conor's legs.

Exclamations rang out, everyone talking at once. The other children were agog at Jesse, staring with their eyelashes stuck to their eyebrows. It was overwhelming. Finally, Mr. Gorecki, in his imposing voice, declared, "All right. All right now. Jesse has had enough excitement to fill an elephant's trunk. Let us each go home and explain from there. You, too, Jesse."

Conor let Jesse slip to the ground where he was enveloped first in Mac's embrace, and then Billy's. Mr. Gorecki moved the others up the stairs, but they all looked back at Jesse, uttering their well wishes. Gypsy winked at them all.

Still, Grams did not move. She stood to the side with her head in her hands, silently sobbing. Jesse let go of Conor's hand and stood before Grams. He wrapped his arms around her, and she burst a fresh gush of tears, leaning down, hugging him. Tight. So tight. Jesse felt her bobby pin click at the side of his head. She said nothing. Just hugged him. Conor reached to them both, and Grams stood up. She held Jesse's face and kissed his forehead. And with a tiny smile, she nudged him back to Conor.

Chapter Thirty

Circles

Jesse was exhausted. Though it was daylight, he snuggled into his bed pillow holding Velvet to his cheek. Gypsy curled up at his feet, and Conor sat in the chair, waiting for Jesse to settle.

"I have something for you, Jesse. I don't know why I didn't give this to you before. I want you to have it." He held out his hand, and in his palm was Dearie's smooth white stone.

Jesse gasped. "Oh, Conor...."

"I know. Dearie really is in this stone. I want you to carry her with you."

"But what about you? You need her, too."

"I have Dearie's *Lady Bird* Locket."

"Ohhh." Jesse held Dearie's stone and closed his eyes. "Conor, I...I...." His voice was small. "I'm sorry Conor. Real sorry. I was trying to start my quest. By myself. I knew I could do it." He quietly blathered, "I knew Liam could take me. To Elizabethtown.

"I just wanted to go find Jane." Jesse stopped. "I...I mean...Jessica." His eyes switched back and forth curiously. Slowly they came to a standstill and he said, "Jane and Jessica."

Conor cleared his throat and mopped his face.

Jesse closed his eyes for just a moment. "Tim Braedon wanted to take me to Elizabethtown. He's a bad-un. Steve and Mr. Schuyler and Mr. Romano and Mr. Gorecki and Mr. Bonheur threw Tim Braedon in the water. And Liam called the police on the ship-shore radio to come get him. And the police and Sergeant Hannity came real fast."

With a long, tired breath, Jesse said, "I…then, Dearie…was with me. In my heart. I knew she was really, really with me. She said she'd be in my heart. I was waiting and waiting. And now…she's here."

His head turned on his pillow. "And when all the Misters saved me. I knew Dearie was there, too. I liked the Misters all hugging me. They made a circle around me."

Conor blinked away his tears and said in a thick voice, "Jesse, you have so many circles of love around you. Starting inside of you. With Dearie and Pa…Galen; Jane, James; and Dearie's Da and Mam. All loving you." He gestured, "And you and I are another love circle. And Mac and Bridget. And Liam's family. Every family in these apartments. Each one, another circle."

Jesse looked at Conor, "I saw circles of Lights. And I knew it was Dearie. And I…I felt…Jessica. Shining. I think." Jesse nodded, "And all the Misters, and Liam, too, I saw them, like stars. Shining."

Conor *whistered*, "Yes, Jesse. I think you came back to us in your shining starlight. Love Lights. Like Dearie always says, spooling out and spooling in."

Jesse yawned long and deep, "Conor, will you lullaby me?"

Conor puffed a chuckle, and lovingly sang his come-what-may lullaby for Jesse: "*Silent Night, Holy Night, all is calm, all is bright…*"

He finished singing and kissed Jesse's cheek. "Rest now, you *brillish* boy," he copied Dearie, "you love-Light." But Jesse was already sleeping.

Sergeant Hannity was in their parlor. Jesse heard him say to Conor, "Let's surprise them!"

"Who?" Jesse asked.

The Sergeant saluted Jesse, "Glad to see you again, safe and sound."

Jesse sat on the floor at the low table.

"You know," Sergeant Hannity began, "it was you, Jesse, who

alerted us to Tim Braedon. Back in November, when you reported the missing items. It's only fair you get to see our results." Sergeant Hannity put his hand on a small metal box. "We connected the dots to Tim Braedon and a very disreputable Pawn Shop near the Shark House. We collected these items as stolen property, even before we made the connection to the counterfeit ring. Lucky they didn't sell, and we got 'em all back." He pushed the box toward Jesse. "Go ahead, take a look."

Jesse held his breath. This was downright *thrill-digging*. "My knife!" Jesse held it up, staring at the silver butterfly against the glowing orange side. "Conor! My knife came back to me!"

Conor laughed and they both looked at the other items. "Yes!" Conor hooted, "This belongs to Liam!" He held up the familiar gold pocket watch.

"And this is Missus K's Vos-fox!" Jesse surged with glee. "And here's Grams' Claddagh necklace!" His eyes danced, "Wait till they see!"

Sergeant Hannity couldn't stop grinning, and repeated in a scheming voice, "Let's surprise them!"

In the *Lady Bird Theater,* Jesse's heart felt like the new sponge on their kitchen sink; how it filled up, all swollen, dripping big drops of water. His heart was dripping big drops of love all over. In happy hugs and salutations from everyone in the basement of the theater. Some of the ladies treated him like a baby bird that needed to stay in its feathered nest. But Jesse didn't mind. He felt like hugging himself, he was so delirious. Dearie delirious.

Bobby called them together and everyone squeezed into the practice room, surprised to find Sergeant Hannity, holding a small metal box.

"I have a little present for some of you." He opened the box. "Our detectives were alerted by young Jesse here, so when we found these items, he identified 'em for certain."

One at a time, Sergeant Hannity held up: a gold fox pin—a gold pocket watch—and a gold Claddagh necklace. A grin filled his face, "Would the owners please step forward?"

Teresa, Katelijne, and Grams stepped up, hugged Jesse and claimed their long-lost property. Everyone clapped like crazy, slapping each other on the back and saying, "Dearie was right! They weren't lost! They were somewhere!"

It took a bit to settle everyone down again. Then Bobby said, "Let's bottle this happy energy and uncork it for the audience!"

Once the curtain opened on *A Christmas Carol*, Bobby went to the back of the theater, watching the delirious energies truly uncork scene after scene. When Jesse made his fly-wire entrance, Bobby nearly stood on his head. *Whhhoooshhh!* Jesse positively popped with new energy! It took Bobby's breath away. He could see Jesse's eyes sparkling to beat the band. And then! Jesse waggled his ears! The mirror-wreath on his head went up and down and the audience went wild applauding for him.

Jesse's new energies infected everyone, cast and audience alike. This performance was more fun, more surprising, more delightful, more poignant...more...than all of them put together.

⁂

That night, at home, Jesse put his butterfly jackknife on his bedside table. "Glad you're back," he spoke to it like an old friend. He kissed Jane's thimble and Dearie's stone, then got into bed with Velvet on his pillow.

Wide-awake. He thought of Dearie. How she had rubbed his back after their first *A Christmas Carol* performance. He felt a melancholy thump in his heart.

No, I don't want that, he thought determinedly. *Pivot.*

He got out of bed with Velvet and stood at the window, *whistering* to their reflections, "Gosh, isn't that a bright star up there?" He stared at it. "Dearie?"

He thought of Dearie's voice, talking to Conor, "*Fresh energies. Under the stars.*"

His bedroom door opened, "Still awake, Jesse?"

"Oh, Conor! Let's go get fresh energies! On the rooftop. Dearie's up there!"

Conor stood still. Then he, too, remembered Dearie's words about fresh energies. Jesse waggled his ears and Conor popped his eyebrows. "Let's go!"

A great laugh hooted out of them and they were off! Jesse laid Velvet on his pillow and pulled on his clothes, sliding his Dearie stone and his music box into his pocket. He ran out to Conor, helped grab some blankets and rushed to the rooftop.

Gypsy followed.

Up on the roof the *tinteling* air felt fresh and clear. Conor made a cocoon of heavy blankets, and he and Jesse lay, looking up at the night sky, with Gypsy tucked in, too.

"The stars are glittering," Jesse marveled through his frosty breath, "Maybe that's Dearie's star, blink-er-ing at me."

Gypsy looked up to where he was pointing, and Conor said, "That's the Dog Star. Sirius." Gypsy peered at Conor, as if the mention of a dog was forbidden. But Conor continued, "Sirius is in the constellation Canis Major—Big Dog. The brightest night star. Beating brightly in the heart of the dog."

"I would like a dog," Jesse blurted.

A startled Gypsy stared unbelievingly at Jesse, especially as he added, "Maybe I could have two dogs to play with each other."

Conor chuckled at that. "You have two dogs right up there: Major and Minor," he pointed at the fainter star of the Little Dog, Canis Minor."

Gypsy got up with her nose in the air and stalked to the door, silently withdrawing from such conversation.

Conor was saying, "Those two dogs belong to the great hunter, Orion." He pointed to the three stars in a row that made up Orion's belt. "And that other bright star is Orion's shoulder; a huge, red, super-giant star called Betelgeuse."

"Beetle-juice! What a funny name," Jesse laughed, then paused for a moment, "Conor, how do you know so much about the stars?"

"Dearie." Conor answered, as if Dearie was the only possible answer. Jesse remembered their summer night of shooting stars. Dearie, like the beautiful lady of the night sky, telling the star stories, describing, explaining.

Jesse hushed, "Dearie knew an awful lot."

"Yes, she did."

Jesse thought about that. Dearie had said that the universe is a lot—with no ending and no beginning. The universe just is. And every time we dream and wish, and laugh and love, the universe gets a little bigger.

Jesse sighed and smiled at Conor. "I like a lot of loving and laughing. It's a lot better than…well, I like it."

Conor rolled over and hugged Jesse.

And for no good reason, the *giggle-snickens* took over and ran right into the giggles! How they laughed! That barrel of monkeys, irrepressible laughter. The *brillish* stars seemed to laugh with them, and the two of them lay breathless, staring once again at the beautiful stars.

Conor pointed upward. "There's so much up there, Jesse. So many stories. Adventures. Connections."

Jesse was fascinated by the star pictures of Orion and his dogs. "I wish…I wish the dogs would leap down from the sky and play with me."

"Oh, then you have to make a special star wish, Jess."

"Special star wish? How?"

"Well, you think of your dearest wish," Conor said softly. "But you don't say it out loud. What you say out loud are the magic words."

"Do you know the magic words, Conor?" Jesse *whistered* quietly. Hopefully.

Conor rolled his head toward Jesse and saw the stars already smoldering in the turquoise sparks of his eyes.

"Oh yes. Old magic words..." Conor *whistered* back, immersed in Jesse's fervor. His believing.

Jesse clasped Dearie's smooth, white stone. "Say them, Conor. My dearest wish is in my heart." He scrunched his eyes closed. "Say the magic words."

Conor stopped. He looked again at the small body of his little nephew. Jesse was a little *love-adore*. Serene. Waiting.

"All right then, Jess, now, slowly open your eyes and find your star."

After a moment Conor looked up at the magical stars and began the simple verse in Celtic:

"*Realta solas, Realta geal, Cead realta mefeic anocht - - Is mian liom is mise fheadfadh, Is mian liom do theacht, Agam il mian, Is mian liam annocht.*"

As he spoke the words, Conor had a strange sensation. As if he had floated up above the roof. He saw himself and Jesse lying on the roof together, each so full of their wishes. Why, their bodies were humming with them.

Conor swallowed and said, "Now, close your eyes again and feel your wish. Like it's here right now. Feel it Jesse. As the secret treasure in your heart."

Jesse lay very still. In the silence he felt Dearie's stone in his hand. He felt her hand on his back. He heard her silver laugh. His head perked up. He smelled a faint whiff of chocolate.

Smiling, he played his music box. The delicate tinkling music danced into their wishes, and spiraled up to the brilliant stars.

Jesse stared at the stars, "Conor, when will we...go? To Elizabethtown? Really go?"

Conor rustled, "Well. After I graduate? Get my theater. May? June?"

"I can wait. I got my patience. And my fort..." He smiled, "My fortitude."

"You are so good at your wishes," Conor smiled, "It is going to happen."

Jesse nodded, "Yes. Just like my other wishes came true. But...I keep thinking about when I ran away. Why didn't it work out? I was sure, real sure, I could do it, Conor. I had this big feeling. Like I *can* go to Elizabethtown, and I *will* find Jessica. Determined. And. Mad. Like you get mad, Conor. I was mad, and I said, *Okay, I'm going.*"

Conor did not like to hear Jesse say, "mad, like you, Conor." He lay very still. Befuddled. He did not expect such a conversation with Jesse. *Dearie used to have these talks with Jesse.*

But Jesse explained, "So I began my quest in a mad mood." He shook his head. "Mad."

He sat up. "That's what I am puzzling. All my other dreams came true. And then, my quest to go to Elizabethtown did come true. But it was Tim Braedon taking me." Jesse *shiveraled* and his eyes puzzled, "Conor...I.... Did I cremate Tim Braedon?"

Conor snorted, "I hope you mean create." He poked Jesse and smiled. "So. You were humming angry. Upset. Then you ran away. And your angry threads went weaving together with Tim Braedon's bad threads." Conor pulled up the blanket around Jesse's shoulders.

"Yes," Jesse hugged the blanket. "Tim Braedon. Waiting for me. Like my puzzle pieces that didn't fit together. Tim would take me to my dream: Elizabethtown. But I didn't want my dream to come true with *him*."

Conor took a big breath, recalling a similar, long ago talk with Dearie. He almost felt her words in his mouth, rolling off his tongue.

"Well. Now you know, Jesse. The way you feel is everything. You felt angry and frustrated and you attracted the likes of Tim Braedon, plus all the trouble, fear and worry."

Jesse sat up. "Conor. It was my quest. Like *King Arthur*. But I think...well...I didn't have a pure heart...and my Light wasn't on."

"Right." Conor leaned up on his elbow, "It was you, Jesse. Dark inside."

Jesse's head tilted. "Dearie used to say I stepped out of the Light. I needed to pivot. Back. Into the Light."

Conor smiled again. "And you did just that. When you decided to let go. Breathing real quiet, like the possum. You pulled yourself back into your shining place..."

"Yes. Everything was shining!" Jesse beamed. "And, even though I was scared and I had to run really, really fast, I was okay. I felt Dearie with me. Then, you and Mac, and everyone. And all the Misters were really there. And they saved me."

"I think you saved yourself, Jesse." Conor beamed back, "Still, it is so good to know you had such wonderful people there with you."

"So. I really, really know. It's me. What I think and what I hum. I want to be pure like *King Arthur*. I don't want stinky Tim Braedon."

"Yes, now you know, Jesse." Conor leaned over and kissed his forehead.

Laying back, Jesse smiled and stared at the stars. He was pretty sure they smiled back at him.

⁂

Jesse walked lightly through the theater. He felt Light. He thought of the theater lights, foot lights, spot lights, mirror lights. Lights inside him. Lights in his eyes. In his heart. Forever Lights. Forever.

He looked at the clock in the basement hallway. It was time: the final, two o'clock matinee performance of *A Christmas Carol.*

The Dutchies were outside the costume room. Annika was crying.

"What happened?" Jesse asked. "Are you okay?"

"It's over," she sobbed. "Today." She snorted a little piggy *sniggle*, "The end."

Elke agreed, "It feels rotten."

Marijke looked sanguinely at Annika. "*Rotanny Fever*. It's a child's fever. Maybe you have a fever, Annika."

Annika snorted even louder. "Noooo! I just don't want it to end!"

Jesse touched her shouder and smiled, "Annika, Hiss and Leer. He joked with Dearie's old spoonerism and added another, "it's an *Eyeball*...."

"*Hiss and leer!*" Marijke crowed, "that's *Listen here!*"

"And I remember *Eyeball!*" Elke waved *bye all!*

"Whaaat? Eyeball...? Ohhh..." a laugh blurted into her snort, "Bye, all!"

Bobby Lewis came up behind them smiling kindly. "Annika...? Don't you know it's never over? *A Christmas Carol* is more than a hundred years old. And it just goes on and on, and it gets better and better. And you know why?"

Elke, Marijka, and Annika gushed, "Whhhyyy?"

"Because of you!" He tapped their noses. "You keep it alive. This play is just like Dearie. It lives forever. And the best part is, it lives inside us."

Jesse nodded. He looked at Bobby, "Forever."

⁂

Their last performance of *A Christmas Carol* went too fast. All of a sudden it was "God Bless Us, Everyone", and the audience was on its feet.

Jesse saw the audience. Their hearts. Spilling over. Like they, too, never wanted it to end. So. Everything moves on. But, love stays. In your heart. For sure. Jesse could feel it.

Jesse saw everyone on stage with their happy smiles connected to their shining, wet eyes. Happy and sad. Especially when the curtain closed.

Mr. Gorecki said in his deep voice. "Well. It's over."

Mac added with a misty smile, "Done and done."

The grownups turned to the wings to begin peeling away costumes and makeup. Jesse knew Bridget would be waiting for them down in the basement, ready to hang up their outfits for the last time. He saw the grownup feet walking across the stage, over the trapdoor.

The trapdoor. Jesse smiled, tapping Billy's shoulder, gesturing to the trapdoor. Billy grinned. He turned to the Romano boys and towed them right to the middle of the stage. The rest of the children followed, watching him pull open the door and make a show of holding his nose. Down the slide he bounded, down to the mattress at the bottom. He jumped up and gleefully yelled, "Come on down!"

Joey stood aside and let Annika go down, and she screeched like a true *thrill-digger*. One after the other, the children jumped in, and down they went. The mattress at the bottom was soon a pig-pile of blissful shrieks, squeals and rolling laughter, splitting their sides.

Jesse saw everyone lapping up the fun. This theater, this play, this fun! It felt like how Dearie had described his quest: 'It's about life's energies coming in to play with you. The energy dancing inside you. That is what your quest is all about. It's not finishing your quest. It's about the thrill of being on your quest.'

Billy let out a gush of air, "Well! That was a *never-forgetter*! For sure!"

Bobby Lewis stuck his head in, "What are you kids doing in here?"

The children's beaming faces turned and answered in unison, "*A NEVER-FORGETTER*!"

⁂

The street was hung in twilight purples as Jesse and Conor left the *Lady Bird Theater*. Walking to the apartments, Jesse held Conor's hand. Just because.

Noticing the light on at Bridget and Mac's apartment, Jesse murmured, "I miss Mac and Bridget."

"Me, too, Jesse. Me, too."

They let themselves in to the dusky lobby, and much to their surprise, they found Mac. Standing at his door. Mac. Filled with a golden Light.

Jesse stared. Transfixed. He smiled, gushing a quiet breath, "Dearie."

He flew to Mac, hugging his legs, looking up into Mac's face, beaming, "Oh, Mac. Dearie's here!"

Mac's eyes hushed, and a tender smile erased the sorrowful furrow there. He wordlessly embraced Jesse. And Conor joined them, feeling Mac holding them. The way Pa used to do. Strong and gentle. Conor wanted to stay in his embrace. Just be. Stay. Just a little longer. He felt a trembling rush. As if he was back on the empty stage with Dearie. That moment when Dearie had died....

Like Jesse, Conor could feel her. Here. With them. Now. *Dearie,* he thought, *Dearie.* And he felt a strain of music. It was "Goin' Home" filtering through his heart.

It's not far, jes' close by, Through an open door...

there's no break, there's no end, Jes' a livin' on;

Bit by bit, Mac gently pulled away. Bridget appeared, putting her arm through Conor's, pulling him inside, and inviting, "You'll stay for a little supper with us, won't you?"

Conor let Jesse take Mac for himself, to Mac's big old chair, where they nestled together.

"So you've done it, Jesse," Mac quietly smiled at him. "You got clear. And you brought Dearie into your heart. And here she be. You and Dearie and the universe, playing together. Blue ribbon, you."

Jesse *hmphed* another little smile and hugged his heart. His heart, filled with Dearie. There he sat, in the quiet, Dearie-love-hug of Mac's embrace.

"Mac," he said eventually, "I've missed you. A lot. Since Dearie...went...to the Great Illuminations."

"Right. I've been at the hospital. With my own little girl," Mac breathed, "my own darling Rose."

"I know that now. I found out that Rose is your daughter. I never knew that."

Mac's head went up and down.

Jesse murmured, "I know that Dearie sent her Great Illumination sparkles to Rose. I didn't know it was Rose. But I saw it. I saw the sparkles."

Mac looked down at Jesse, "Didja now?" He took out his handkerchief and swiped at his nose. "That Dearie. She's still the Lady Bird. The Light in the darkness. She takes others into the sunlight. Into the sky. She's a true Lady Bird."

Jesse liked hearing Mac talk like that. His liked his words. They sounded like music. He sat back, his brain ticking with his heart. Dearie was here, and everything felt just right. Yet, that didn't mean Jesse wouldn't find a puzzle somewhere in his thoughts. And there was a puzzle in there.

Rose was a puzzle. Jesse's brain sorted through what Conor had told him. All at once, Jesse knew something he had not put together before: "Rose is Rose Weiss. David and Aleksander and little Rose Weiss. They're…not just the family Siobhan takes care of, they're…your grandchildren…" He looked at Mac's face. "Oh…" Jesse tapped his forehead, "I get it. Now I get it."

Mac nodded his head.

Jesse *quizzled*, "But…why…?"

"Oh, it's a long, layered story. The only thing worth telling is…I love her. My Rose. And her three darling little ones. And I love her husband, Hendrik. He loves Rose, too. And that is all that matters."

Jesse slowly shook his head. "Mmm," he sighed. "Love." He hushed for a moment. "It really is the greatest thing…the greatest thing you'll ever learn."

Mac looked at Jesse. "It's your song, Jesse. It always will be."

Jesse breathed in. He felt his Light on. He thought of Dearie. Her very last word. And Jesse breathed out, "Yes."

The stars are glittering. Aye.

You. Your wishes. Making them all glitter. You. Shining back at the stars.

Wishing.

Oh, the world cannot do without the glittering stars. Just as the world cannot do without you.

Together you are the brightest, the shiniest of everything in the universe.

Light on.

Dearie's Dictionary

* = *an actual world, though sometimes archaic or literary*

Baby Grand – proper n. *Dearie has two children and only one Baby Grand:* grandchild – the music of our lives

Blabber-gab - v. *Marijke blabbergabbed on and on, not making much sense at all:* jabber - blather

Blether – v. *Elke blethered on and on with her sister, neither making much sense at all:* (Scottish) blather – babble - jabber

B'jeekers – exclamation. *B'jeekers, Jesse! You scared me:* expression of surprise or fear

Bliss-t – n. *Jesse had a bliss-t expression and laughed with joy:* (bliss-ed) – elation – blessedness

Blisterquick – adj. *Blisterquick, Jesse ran after the ball:* speedy – quick – swift - (gasper- quick)

Blue ribbon, you! - Expression. *How clever! Blue ribbon you! :* good for you – praise – salute

Brain-Bonkers – n. *You are one clever brain-bonker:* smart

***Brî** – n. *Rose glowed with a light-filled brî in her eyes:* inner energies (Gaelic – pronounced breee)

***Brillish** – adj. (from Lewis Carrol "The Jabberwocky") – *The day was brillish with sunshine*: brilliant; *He perked up with a brillish idea:* clever

Bunky-Dinks! – exclamation. *Oh bunky-dinks! We'll never find our way! :* Oh no!

Chatter-babble – v. *"You know," Jesse chatter-babbled, tripping over his words….* : speak in a quick stream of words

Chiggle – n. *He chiggled with laughter:* chuckle – giggle - laugh

Chitter-chat - n. *They shared a quick chitter-chat of conversation:* heart-to-heart - confab

Coolifying – adj. *The morning breeze felt coolifying:* refreshing – crisp - invigorating

***Cracker pet -** adj. *Oh, we had a cracker pet day:* Cracker = spectacular / pet = unseasonably warm

***Daoine sidhe** – N. (Deenee shee): faerie folk (Celtic)

Deaf as a doorstop – expression. *Grams was hard of hearing… deaf as a doorstop:*

Diggety-boo – exclamation. *Diggety-boo! Let's go:* Cool! – Fun!

Dim-Witles - expression. *Oh dimwittles! I never thought of that happening!* – silly me!

Dreadly - adj. *The August day was dreadly hot and steamy:* terrible – disagreeable (frizzled)

Easy-pleasey – *He tied his shoelaces easy-pleasey*: cinchy – a sure thing – for certain

Eye-bonker – adj. *He was eye-bonkered with astonishment:* surprised

Evaporish – v. *He evaporished through the trapdoor:* disappear

Fab-you-lush – *You created a fab-you-lush adventure!* : fabulous – phenomenal

***Fairlight** – n. *Dearie is a true fairlight in the glow of her being:* glory lights – enchanted lights

Favorish - adj. Out of all my dolls, she is my favorish: favorite – best loved - dearest

Feisty-dregs – n. *Billy felt miserable and took his feisty-dregs out on Jesse*: wretched - determinedly touchy

Feisty –goggle - v. *He feisty-goggled the other newsboys:* glare

***Fiddly** – adj. *Tim Braedon jiggled the fiddly lock:* tricky – complex

Fool-rashy – adv. *He shoved the bully in a fool-rashy tantrum:* impulsive - reckless
Fussy-fit – n. *She stomped her foot in a determined fussy-fit* : temper tantrum - snit

***Gander** – v. *Teresa Maguire gandered the sky looking for fair weather:* look – glance

Gasper – v. *Mac gaspered in utter surprise:* gulp – exclaim – choke

Gasper-quick – adj. – *Jesse ran gasper-quick, fighting to find his breath:* very fast

Gem-my – adj. *What a grand, gem-my idea!* : marvelous – charming

Giggle-burst – n. *Jesse's smile erupted into a spontaneous giggle-burst:* surprised laughter

Giggle-snickens - n. *The children burst into hilarious giggle-snickens:* fun laughter

Glintaling – adj. *The glintaling light looked like diamonds on the water:* gleaming - glittering

Gossywims – n. *Her costume was a fanciful gathering of gossywims*: whimsical – inventive – dreamy – faerie-flecks

***Grandee** – adj. *She put on a grandee performance:* impressive - classy

Grasp-grabble – v. *He desperately grasp-grabbled for her hand:* snatch – grip – clasp

Great Illuminations - expression for Heaven, Nirvana, Paradise (many words, same Light)

Grimmel – n. *Her lips corkscrewed into a grimmel of satisfaction:* a closed mouth, playful grin, sometimes of surprise or disbelief

Gusher – v. *A silence gushered into the room:* flow with a quiet shushing noise

Hearwaxers – n. *Grams acts like she's deaf – like she's got real hearwaxers*: hard of hearing

Help-handy – adv. *Conor was help-handy with any task:* useful – practical – co-operative

Hitherlands – n. *I dreamed you right out of the hitherlands*: ethereals
How- the less – expression. *How-the-less she accomplished that we will never know:* how-on-earth

***Humdinger** – n. *What a fast humdinger that sled-ride was!* : dandy – doozy – whopper

Imaginator – N. *He was a true Imaginator - creating everything in his magical shoppe:* an out-of-the-box thinker

Jemimas! – expression of surprise

Jigger-jolly – n. *He jumped up in delighted jigger-jollies:* fun surprise

Jim-Jams – n. *Billy felt the jim-jams shivering up his spine:* chills – frights – thrills

Kafluffle - v. *Jesse quickly kafluffled into his clothes and tore out the door:* act in a quick – somewhat – disheveled manner

Kidlins – n. *The kidlins played hopscotch and marbles and jumping ropes*: children - youngsters

Kintsugi - Japanese word (kint-s-gee): when a porcelain dish is broken, it is repaited with the art of *Kinsugi:* more beautiful than the original, for the breaks are filled with shining gold set into every crack, illuminating all.

Lip-smackey – adv. *That tapioca is the best lip-smackey dessert ever:* delicious

Love-adore - v. *Dearie love-adores her Jesse:* hold dear – cherish – treasure; n. *Jesse is a little love-adore:* darling - dear-one

Lucht Siúil – n. (look – see-ul) 'the walking people' – the Irish gypsy travelers

Lushkey – adv. *She danced through her lushkey life:* lucky – fortunate – providential

Lush-us – adj. *Her stew was yummy lush-us:* delicious

Marvelush – adj. *This birthday was simply marvelush:* amazing – splendid;
v. She gushed and marvelushed over the new toy*: murmur happily*

Memory-fizz – n. *She gazed into the clouds in a far off memory-fizz:* remembrance

Memory-smile - v. *Dearie memory-smiled and told of her Travelling gypsy days*: smile with eyes gazing at remembrances

Merri-cheers – n. *He raised his glass in a toast of merri-cheers:* happy, joyful acclaim

Mincey-toe – v. *He mincey-toed silently down the hall*: tiptoe surreptitiously (secretly)

Moogle – v. *His eyes closed as he quietly moogled an answer:* speak hesitantly; confused

Murmel – v. *His voice murmeled quieter and quieter*: murmur (sometimes confusedly)

Mushin – Japanese word (moo-shin): not being attached to anything physical

Mystery-us – adj. *My disappeared grandmother is mystery-us*: puzzling

***Nimbly** – adj. *Her nimbly fingers set the knitting needles clacking*: flexible – quick

Nippity-zip – adv. adj. *Nippity-zip, he slid down the sliding board:* speedy – quick – swift

Nixer – n. *She stopped abruptly, doing a nixer:* ending - stoppage

Nothingly – adv. He waited quietly, feeling nothingly: empty – not occupied

Oldy-the-hill – adj. *She is ancient – really oldy-the-hill*: old – over the hill

Pilfer-loot – v. *The young pirates pilfer-looted the treasure from the Sergeant:* steal;

Pilfer-looter - n. *The children were called pilfer-looters after they ate all the ice cream:* thieves

Pip-Singer – n. *Bravo my chorus of pip-singers:* young children song-singers

Play-jollies – n. *The little pirates swashed-and-buckled through their play-jollies*: fun times

Pooka – N. Harvey is a six-foot tall invisible rabbit! A *pooka*!: a mischievous faerie-folk, from Celtic mythology

Puddleducking – v. *The cast was puddleducking, wearing the light costumes that immersed them in their parts*: lightly dressing-up – costuming – gussy-up

Puzzley-do - puzzle-out - v. *He did a puzzley-do with the jigsaw pieces; He puzzled-out the clues:* discover – realize – work-out

***Quatchkopf** – German word (kwach – kopf) – just plain silly

Quiver-Quavers – n. *She shook uncontrollably in a fit of quiver-quavers*: shivers

Quizzle – v. *Jesse's eyebrows knit together as he quizzeled Sergeant Hannity:* ask curiously

Rest-pit - n. *Jesse told Conor that Dearie was on a rest-pit for a few minutes*: rest – respite

Rough-n-gruff – adj. *Billy had a rough-n-gruff side to him that felt bad-tempered*: abrupt – brusque - cross

***Ruckus – n.** *The children raised a noisey ruckus up and down the hallway:* disturbance – disruption

Rule of Tongue – expression – *"Rule of Tongue!" Dearie declared, "No name-calling!"* : use only highest and best words

Scally-laggers – n. *Be on time, for we'll have no scally-laggers:* late-comers

Schmoodle – v. *Jesse sat in a daze letting his mind schmoodle*: loll – idle – do nothing much

Scootle – He *scootled down the sidewalk like a bat on wheels*: move erratically

Screel – n./v. *Annika screeled hysterically as the Pirate, Lady Commander*: long screech-scream

Scrinch – v. *Jesse scrinched his eyelids together, and blinked away the tears:* close tightly

Shiveral – n. *Jesse's shoulders twitched in a little shiveral:* chills – frights – fun thrills

Shugah beet – expression of endearment (using sugar) – *Take a seat Shugah Beet!* –

Skep – v. *Conor skepped doubtfully at Dearie's reply:* disbelieve

Skittley – *His voice was skittley, cracking in his throat:* nervous

Slidder – v. *He shimmied and sliddered out of his clothes*: move snake-like

Sniggle – n. *She snorted a little piggu sniggle*: small reverberating snort

***Snuggery** – n. *Dearie fell asleep on the bed in her cozy snuggery:* an archaic term for a warm, cozy place

Sooner-later – adv. *Sooner-later she found the missing key:* eventually – ultimately

Splendish – adj. *She bowed the fiddle in a splendish finale:* superb – majestic – lavish

***Squench** – v. *The light was squenched by the deep darkness*: extinguish - smother

Squintle – v. *He squintled into the darkness, looking for the lamp:* peer

Swelting-smelting – adj. *The day was swelting-smelting hot:* humidly hot

Swiggle – v. *He swiggled down the cod liver oil in one go:* swallow

***Taradiddle** – v. *Don't taradiddle me with your wild exaggerations!* : lie – pretentious nonsense

Tattle-lips – n. *You are stretching the truth, you little tattle-lips:* exaggerator – liar

Techy – adv. *He is on edge today, very techy indeed*: irritable - testy – touchy

Thrill-digging – adj. *He leapt up with a thrill-digging whoop:* enthusiastic – reveling – exciting

Thrummy – adv. *It was a long, exhausting day and he felt utterly thrummy:* worn-out; also, *'**thrums'** = yarns hanging off of a woven fabric

Tiddly-wink – v. *His eyes smiled and he tiddly-winked at the little boy*: encourage – cheer

Tinteling adv. *He shivered in the tinteling cold*: frosty-breath-cold

Tittle-winkler – n. *They sat, barely breathing, still as little tittle-winklers:* still as a mouse

Trapture v. *There's no way out! We're traptured!* : trapped and captured

Tribble-trap - adj. *Don't talk tribble-trap:* crazy: nutty

***Triquetra** – N. *She traced the Triquetra on the metal mug*: trinity knot pattern of three intertwining circles.

Tummy-hollow – adv. *Billy missed breakfast and now felt tummy-hollow:* hungry

Twiddle – v. *He quietly sighed as if twiddling a yarn about his finger:* think – muse – mull over

Twiddly – adj. *Jesse took out every twiddly little thing from her jewelry box:* trivial – trifling

Twiddley-Dee! – expression of surprise

Twirly-purr – v. *Gypsy the cat twirly-purred around Jesse's legs:* winding oneself about while resonating contentedly

Weep-sobbing – v. *Her eyes gushed in weep-sobbing bawls:* cry wetly – tear-streaming, crying

Whirly-Wander - v. *He whirly-wandered from one continent to another*: travel

Widdly-skiddly – adv. *Widdly-skiddly, he roller-skated down the sidewalk:* hurtling –carreen - whiz

Wiffle – v. *He waffled a crackling laugh:* erratically puff a breath

Wimsy-wish – v. *He wimsy-wished through his day, not knowing where it led him:* daydream;

n. *His wimsy-wishes felt more real than anything that was real*: daydreams

Winkwhile – adv. *In the winkwhile, we'll wait for you at the restaurant:* meanwhile – for now

Wish-wallow - v. *He sat in the chair for endless hours, wish-wallowing the day away*: loll about, hoping for a dream-come-true

Wisky-dooley – expression of unexpected, sometimes wild, quickness

Wispy-slips – n. *He fell sound asleep into his dreamland of deep wispy-slips:* sleep - the land of Nod; also: eternity

Walloper – n. *This is a wallopper of a surprise!:* a whopper – big – huge - amazing

Wonder-gaze – v. *Conor wonder-gazed at Jesse. Hmmpf, he thought, six-year old wisdom:* marvel – be amazed

Wonder-lush v. *Jesse wonder-lushed over the castle rising above the quarry*: marvel – gape - goggle

Wonderly – adj. *He raised his eyes to the wonderly stars*: amazing - awesome

***Yonks** - adj. *That is ancient history, from yonks and yonks ago:* a long time ago

Zippity-pip – adv. *He ran zippity-pip, all the way up the stairs:* very fast

Patsie McCandless

About the Author

Patsie McCandless grew up on Conanicut Island in Jamestown, Rhode Island, where she learned to swim and sail and took a ferry to high school. After graduating from Rosemont College in Pennsylvania, she returned to the island, married, raised two children, and worked as a primary school teacher for thirty years.

Self-taught in the fine arts, Patsie is an award-winning watercolorist and paper artist. Her work has been exhibited in galleries, art centers, and museums throughout the United States and in Mexico. She led the island art association, sang in the community chorus, and took up flute to help create the community band.

In Florida, Patsie served on the board of the Dunedin Fine Arts Center; the Board of Consultants for The Florida Orchestra; and is in the permanent art collection of the Saint Petersburg Opera Company. Her artwork is also displayed at the gallery shop in the Museum of Fine Arts, Saint Petersburg.

A special gift led Patsie to a monastery on the Hudson River in upstate New York for a writing retreat with Madeleine L'Engle, and she has not stopped writing since. She also delivered a TEDx Talk on "Saving the Magic of Childhood." A woman of multifaceted talents, Patsie continues to create as she enjoys the magic of childhood all over again in the everyday delights of her Baby Grands—her grandchildren. She and her husband live near Philadelphia, PA and enjoy the cultural delights of the city.

To learn more about Patsie and her writing, art, music and TEDx talk, please visit PatsieMcCandless.com.

Made in the USA
Middletown, DE
25 September 2018